I wandered up to the bar and sat down on a stool as I ordered a Diet Coke. The closest thing to liquid courage I could consume and still be able to make the drive safely back to Pacific Beach. As the bartender filled my glass I scanned the club, a sinking reality settling in my stomach. There was no way I could do this. No way I could just walk up to a guy and say—

"Can I squeeze in here?"

I jumped at the feel of a warm hand on my bare shoulder, a husky voice in my ear. Whirling around, I found myself face to face with—

Oh. My. God . . .

He was tall. Broad shoulders that narrowed to a tapered waist. Athletic looking, but with long, lean muscles that would have made my yoga teacher weep with joy. His hair was the color of wheat, cropped short, and his eyes were a brilliant blue—the color of the sky on a cloudless day. He wore slouchy jeans, hung low on his narrow hips and a tight black T-shirt stretched across his chest in a way that practically begged me to stick my hands underneath and run my fingers down his obviously perfect six-pack.

Oh, and his hand? Still resting on my shoulder. At this point radiating so much heat I was seriously wondering if it would leave me branded for life. I also wondered if I would mind all that much if it did.

Just This Night

MARI MADISON

BERKLEY SENSATION, NEW YORK

BERKLEY SENSATION

An imprint of Penguin Random House LLC
375 Hudson Street, New York, New York 10014

JUST THIS NIGHT

ISBN: 978-0-425-28313-4

PUBLISHING HISTORY
Berkley Sensation mass-market edition / March 2016

PRINTED IN THE UNITED STATES OF AMERICA

10 9 8 7 6 5 4 3 2 1

Penguin
Random
House

To Jacob—
the most amazing husband and father.

Full disclosure:
I might have stolen some of you and Avalon's
daddy/daughter moments
for this book . . .

I'd like to thank my awesome editor Kate Seaver who once recognized something in me and bought my very first book over eleven years ago. Ten books later and we're still going strong! And thanks to the rest of the Penguin Random House team—you've always been so great to work with and have put my stories into readers' hands around the globe.

Thank you to agent Kristin Nelson for shepherding my career, even when I've gone off on crazy tangents. We've had quite a journey together and I'm lucky to know you.

And thanks to all my TV newsroom pals from over the years. Especially my very first mentor, Hank Phillippi Ryan, who took a scared little girl wearing Hello Kitty barrettes and turned her into an Emmy award winning investigative producer. You are the real deal! (Sorry, couldn't resist.) And Mary Schwager, my favorite producer cohort who almost got me killed in an effort to expose bad backyard breeders in an undercover sting. Your passion for your job—and animals—is continually inspiring. And to all my awesome former TV news bosses—Nancy Lynch, Susan Krivelow, Charlene Bert, Desiree Miller, Mark Berryhill, Tracy Langer-Chevrier, Rebecca Millman, Marjorie Bekaert Thomas, Betty Bon Fleur, Cynthia Sucher, Wendy MacNeill and so many more.

And, of course, I must thank all the amazing photographers I've worked with in TV news over the years. You were my partners in crime and I miss our long car talks and leftover lunch radio jams. Chris Fadale, Errol Henry, Anne Marie Spaulding, Kurt Hartwell, Charles Janey, Marty Glembotzky, Mike Monroe, Rusty Reed—just to name a few.

There are so many more people I want to mention that I worked with in my TV news years that were inspirational to this book. So stay tuned for book 2 for a continued list. (See what I did there?)

one

JAKE "MAC" MACDONALD

Mommy! Mommy! *Mommy!*"

I jerked up in bed, swinging around, my feet hitting the floorboards before my mind had a chance to process the movement. For a split second, fighting the fog of deep sleep, I didn't know where I was. What time it was. Why I was here.

"Mommy? Where are you, Mommy?"

But I knew that voice. And the rest didn't matter.

"I'm coming, Ashley!"

Bolting from the bedroom, I dashed down the hall, bursting into her room like some kind of superman on steroids. Ashley was sitting up in bed, hugging her grubby stuffed lion—the one I'd bought her from the hospital gift shop the day she was born, four years ago last month. Tears streamed down her chubby little cheeks and her thumb was firmly lodged in her mouth.

Dropping to my knees I pulled her into a fierce hug, forcing myself to be gentle and not squeeze too hard as my heart thumped wildly in my chest, working overtime to rid my body of the excess adrenaline her cries had unleashed.

She was fine. She was safe. She was okay.

"Shh," I whispered. "Daddy's here, baby. Are you all right? Did you have a bad dream?" I could feel the sweat dripping down her back, soaking through her thin princess nightgown as she snuggled closer, pushing her head against my chest as if she was literally trying to crawl inside of me and hide. My heart squeezed. Poor little thing. Was she actually shaking?

"I was scared," she whimpered. "I woke up and I didn't know where Mommy was."

I could feel her head lift off my chest and realized she was looking around the darkened bedroom. As if her mother might magically appear out of thin air at any moment.

Sorry, kid. No magic in the world was that strong.

"We talked about this, sweetheart," I reminded her gently, the bile churning in my stomach now. "Mommy has an important job to do far, far away. She can't be with us right now."

"I don't want her to do her important job," Ashley sobbed, dropping her head to my chest again. "I want her here, with us."

Closing my eyes, I forced myself to draw in a heavy breath. "I know, baby, I know. You and me both." I stroked her hair, leaning in to kiss the top of her head. "Now why don't you lie down and I'll use the magic pixie dust on you, okay? So you can fall back asleep."

Ashley whimpered. "What if I have another dream?"

"If you do, it'll be a good one," I assured her with a confidence I didn't feel. "That's the great thing about pixie dust." I reached for the tub of glitter-infused baby powder sitting on her nightstand. "It only allows for happy dreams about princesses and puppy dogs and hungry little caterpillars . . ." I turned the tub upside down and squeezed, releasing a puff of powder. The glitter dusted her skin and she smiled, snuggling against her stuffed lion again and looking up at me with wide brown eyes. Her mother's eyes. Which was so unfair.

"I love you, Daddy."

"I love you, too, baby girl," I managed to say, my emotions swelling. I leaned down to kiss her cheek. "More than anything ever."

"Anything ever . . ." she repeated sleepily, her eyes

fluttering closed. "Hey! I think the magic pixie dust is . . ." She trailed off, drifting back into sleep.

For a few moments, I didn't move. I just sat there, watching her. She looked so tiny in the giant king-sized bed that took up most of my sister's guest room. So sweet and fragile and precious. How could anyone willingly walk away from this little girl? Hell, I would rather die a thousand times over than leave her for just one night. But her mother. Her own goddamned mother . . .

I realized I was clenching the sheets with white-knuckled fists. Forcing myself to release them, I rose to my feet, the churning anger making me sick to my stomach. I stormed from the room, shutting the door behind me a little too hard and I paused for a moment, listening, making sure I hadn't woken her. But the magic pixie dust had done its job and the room remained silent. My princess was asleep.

"Is she okay?"

I looked up. Lost in my tortured thoughts I hadn't seen my sister, Sadie, hovering at the landing, dressed in an oversized Padres jersey and boxer shorts. Her long brown hair hung down her back in a tangle of curls and her face was washed clean of all makeup.

I sighed. "She's fine. She just had a bad dream."

Sadie gave me a sympathetic look. "Poor kid. Moving can be tough. And then being in a strange house . . . I'm sure she's going to feel a lot more adjusted once you guys get all unpacked and settled in your new place."

"Yeah," I stared down at my feet. "Probably so."

I could feel her peering closely at me. "What about you? Are you okay?"

"I'm fine," I said quickly. Probably too quickly.

Sure enough, Sadie raised an eyebrow. "No offense, bro. But you don't look so fine from here."

I sighed. She was always too perceptive, my sister. "I'm just . . . frustrated, I guess," I admitted. "I mean, I want to be a good dad, you know. But no matter what I do I can't give her what she really wants. And it makes me feel so fucking helpless."

My voice broke and Sadie moved to wrap her arms around me. But I shrugged her off. I didn't need her pity. It was already bad enough I was practically a charity case, moving cross-country to San Diego to take advantage of her offer of free babysitting while I was at work. I'd offered to pay her, of course, but she had argued that she was already staying home with two kids—how hard could one more be? And like the pathetic broke bastard I was, I allowed myself to believe it to be true.

Sadie, to her credit, didn't try to press me. Instead, she smiled. "I'm going to go make myself a sandwich. You want one?"

"Sure," I reluctantly agreed. It wasn't as if I was going to get back to sleep anytime soon anyway. Then I looked down at my current getup. I'd been in such a rush to reach Ashley's side I'd forgotten I was bare-chested, only wearing a pair of ratty boxer shorts. Not exactly good houseguest attire. "Let me grab a shirt and some pants and I'll meet you down there."

By the time I reached the kitchen a few minutes later, Sadie had already gotten out all the sandwich supplies and was currently spreading a thick layer of mayo on my ham and cheese. I sat down at the breakfast bar, scrubbing my face with my hands, trying to banish the memory of Ashley's frightened eyes from my mind. Her cries for "Mommy" that would never be answered.

God, I hated lying to her. But what else could I say? The truth?

The bitch left us, baby girl. She's not coming back. But trust me—we're much better off without her.

"Is this some kind of brother and sister secret powwow or does a poor, hungry husband stand a chance at scoring a sandwich, too?"

I looked up, stifling a groan as Sadie's husband, Joe, stepped into the kitchen wearing a black Batman bathrobe and bare feet. Great. Ashley must have woken the whole house with her screams.

"What, are your hands broken? You can't make your own?" Sadie shot back with mock grumpiness. But I caught the adoring looks they exchanged when they thought I wasn't looking.

"Hey! I'm just saving my strength for that extra-long back massage I plan to give you once we're back in bed," Joe said with a sly wink. My sister laughed.

"Oh, fine. Just this once. But it better be a damned good massage." She grabbed two more slices of bread from the bag and tossed them on the counter. Then she caught my look and her smile faded. "Are you sure you're okay, Mac?" she asked worriedly.

Joe turned to look at me for the first time. "Yeah, man. You look like hell. No offense."

I groaned. "Why thank you. I'll be here all week."

To my annoyance, he continued to study me. "You know what this guy needs?" he asked, turning to Sadie. "To get out of the house. A night on the town. That would fix him right up."

"Uh, no," I interjected before my sister could answer. "I'm good. Really."

Joe turned back to me. "When's the last time you went out?" he demanded. Before I could reply he added, "And, no, Chuck E. Cheese does not count."

"Joe . . ." Sadie said warningly.

"What?" Joe asked, holding up his hands in mock innocence. "I'm just saying. A man needs a night out with grown-ups every once in a while." He grinned wickedly. "Think about it, Mac. Endless lines of tequila shots, pretty girls, maybe some sexy, sexy times?"

"Joe!" Sadie's voice rose.

"Okay, okay! Jesus." Joe snorted. Then he turned back to me, lowering his voice. "You know I'm right though. Right?"

I sighed. I had to admit, the idea did sound pretty awesome. I hadn't had a night away from Ashley since *that* night. And that night was pretty much a lifetime ago at this point. Just the idea of sitting at a bar, having an adult beverage as I people watched. It sounded like a little slice of heaven.

It was also impossible. I wasn't that guy anymore. I mean,

I probably was, deep down, but I had other priorities now. My life was not my own.

"Dude!" Joe cried, slamming his fist against the counter, as if something had just occurred to him. Though I had a pretty good idea he'd been working up to this from the moment he'd started in on me. "I've got a great idea!"

I could see my sister shooting him another disapproving look, but he ignored her, rushing in before she could interrupt. "I'm supposed to check out this new club for my company's Christmas party tomorrow night. You could totally come with me. They say it's a hot spot for reporters—News 9 is right down the street. So it'd be perfect." Joe nodded enthusiastically, as if he'd already gotten me to agree. "We'll have some drinks, take in the sights . . ." He waggled his eyebrows. "Maybe even find you a little hotness for the ride home."

I rolled my eyes, waiting for my sister to jump in and save me again. Instead, to my surprise, I found her nodding slowly. "You know, that's not a terrible idea," she said. "I could watch Ashley while you were out."

"No, thank you." I shook my head firmly. "No way am I just going to go and take off and leave Ashley to go clubbing."

Sadie frowned. "Uh, Mac, you do realize you're going to be forced to quote 'take off' on her every day once you start your new job, right? Consider this a trial run—not to mention a good lesson for the both of you. Like, you learn it's still possible to have a life in addition to being a good father and Ashley learns that when Daddy goes away, he always comes back. It's kind of perfect, actually."

"It's completely perfect," Joe agreed. "In fact, you'd be a terrible father to stay home and deny your daughter this all-important life lesson. And I know you don't want *that*."

I sighed, looking from one expectant face to the other. They weren't going to drop this, I realized. And I was sick of arguing.

"Fine," I said. "I'll go. But," I added before they could break into celebration, "don't expect me to bring home anything but a hangover." I'd go to their club, I'd have some drinks, but when it came to picking up women? That was off the table.

Joe snorted. "No problem. I'm sure Sadie can hold off picking out china patterns a few more days." He paused, his playful face fading. "But seriously, bro, keep your options open. I mean, no pressure or anything—just see what's out there. After all, it's not fair to write off the entire female race just because of what happened with Victoria."

I cringed. And there it was. The name that, spoken aloud, still had the power to send a cannonball of hurt straight through my gut. Hell, they might as well have put my balls in a vise and started cranking the handle.

"Look, I said I'd do this nightclub thing," I ground out, forcing the lump back down my throat. "But we have to make a rule right now. From this point on no one ever, ever mentions that bitch's name in my presence again." I paused, then added, "*Ever.*"

I pushed back on my stool as I rose from my seat, the force of the movement causing it to crash to the floor. As I turned to pick it up I could feel my sister and Joe's pitying stares burning into my back. Which, if I was being honest, was worse than their teasing.

I wanted to turn around and tell them I was just fine. That Ashley and I did awesome on our own and I didn't need some stupid female to complete me. But I knew if I even started down that rabbit hole, I'd look like I was protesting too much. And in the end, it was better to just drop the whole thing all together.

The bitch was gone. I was still here. And evidently I was going clubbing.

It's just one night, I told myself. *What could happen in just one night?*

two

ELIZABETH "BETH" WHITE

Don't even think I don't know what you're doing under those covers."

I guiltily peeked my head out from under my comforter. My roommate, Stephanie, stood in my bedroom doorway, looking at me disapprovingly, arms crossed over her chest. She must have just gotten off work because she was still wearing a red pencil skirt and silky white blouse, paired with sensible black pumps. Very reporter chic. Her midnight black hair, however, had been freed from its day job constraints and fell in cascades of curls down her back. As if to say "ready to party" which Stephanie assumedly was.

She always was.

I looked down at my ratty University of Illinois sweatshirt and threadbare black yoga pants and wondered what they, along with my bedhead hair, said about me. Besides "should have done laundry five days ago," that is.

"I'm not doing anything," I muttered, involuntarily glancing down at my phone as yet another Facebook alert chimed. The wedding posts had been popping up approximately every five seconds, it seemed like, for the last hour or so. So many that I half-felt like I was attending the event myself at this point, instead of being a thousand miles away.

The ceremony was amazing!

The cake is beautiful!

The bride is stunning!

And I was about to throw up.

"That's it. I'm calling for an intervention." Stephanie dashed across the room. In one swift motion she swooped in, grabbed my phone and pulled it out of reach. I cried in protest, but she only shook her head, holding the phone behind her back. "This is for your own good," she scolded. "I can't believe you're even looking to begin with."

I groaned. She was right. It was the stupidest thing I could possibly be doing. But still, I was only human. And it was my own family who was posting the photos. I couldn't just block them all, right?

"Come on, Beth. You knew this day was coming. And you knew when it did it would suck balls. But now, it's over, right? It's done," my roommate pointed out. "The two of them are man and wife and you're finally, finally free. Now all that's left to do is brush your hair, lose the sweatpants, and move on with your life." Her eyes twinkled merrily. "I mean, really. Don't let that bastard keep you from being the sexy, sexy slut you know you can be."

I sighed. I knew she was trying her best to cheer me up, but she just didn't understand. After all, her relationships had an average lifespan of three weeks—so of course she'd bounce back after a few pints of Ben and Jerry's and a new pair of Louboutins. But Ryan was different. Ryan was supposed to be the One. He was supposed to move out to San Diego. He was supposed to propose to me. We were supposed to get married and have babies and a freaking house with a freaking white picket fence for God's sake.

He was the One. The only one. The only one I'd dated since freshman year in high school. The only guy I'd ever loved. And I'd thought he'd loved me too. Sure, it'd been rough when I scored the reporter job in San Diego and he had had to stay behind in Illinois until his dad could hire a replacement at the lumber store. But he'd promised it was only temporary. That he'd be here before I knew it and we'd be together forever.

He promised. And he kept promising. Until a month ago when, out of the blue, he called and told me he was getting married.

Not to me. Not to some random girl he met at a bar either. That would have been ugly but somewhat understandable.

But no. He was getting married to my younger sister.

Got married, I reminded myself, my stomach twisting painfully as my phone binged another alert from behind Stephanie's back. *As of one hour thirty-three minutes ago they are officially man and wife.*

I let out a small moan.

"Stop thinking about it!" Stephanie scolded, catching my face. "He doesn't deserve even a microsecond of your thoughts. He's an asshole. You're a sexy, sexy bitch. You need to get out of bed and out of the house and show him you don't give a fuck." Her eyes locked on me. "Face it, Beth. You need to get laid."

"Eww," I protested, boxing my ears with my hands. "Seriously, do you have to put it like that?"

"Oh, I'm sorry," she said, her mouth quirking as she glanced over at the tower of well-worn historical romance novels stacked on my nightstand. "Let me rephrase. You, Miss Elizabeth White, must go forth and find a strikingly handsome fellow to thrust his throbbing love lance into your delicate—yet also throbbing—silken love cave." She smirked. "Is that better?"

I grabbed a nearby pillow and flung it in her direction.

"So I'll take that as a yes?" she returned, without missing a beat.

I glanced longingly at my cell phone, which she'd set on the dresser. She gave me a scolding look.

"Look, you have tomorrow morning off, correct? Why don't you come out with me tonight? We'll grab dinner at that awesome new tapas place downtown and then hit Club Rain afterward. That place is crawling with hot men."

"And even hotter STDs."

She groaned. "Come *on*, Beth! You're twenty-six years old. Who knows how many hot years you have left? Are you going to waste them all in bed? *Alone* in bed?" She shook her head. "Look. It'll be fun. I promise. And if you don't want to hook up, you don't have to. But I'm telling you, the best cure for a doomed romance is a good old one-night bonk fest. No strings attached."

I opened my mouth to argue. But at that moment my phone dinged again. From where I was sitting I could just make out Ryan and my sister having their first dance as man and wife. I couldn't see the expressions on their faces, but my imagination did a pretty good job at filling in the fuzzy parts. The two of them looking into each other's eyes. . . . Whispering naughty innuendos about their wedding night to come. . . .

So much hell.

I squared my shoulders, firming my resolve. Stephanie was right. By holing up in my bedroom like this, I was only punishing myself. Not him. It was clear he couldn't care less where I was or what I was doing.

It was time for me to do the same.

"Okay," I agreed. "I'll do it. I'll go to the bar and hook up with the first throbbing love lance I see. And maybe I'll even take a selfie and sext it to the bastard mid dirty deed."

"Whoo-hoo!" Stephanie cheered. "That's my bitch!" Her eyes flashed with excitement. "Ooh and I've got the perfect outfit for getting your slut on, too. You're going to love it! Be right back."

She turned and ran to her room, all victorious and glee-ful. I shook my head, wondering what I'd just gotten myself into.

Just one night, I reminded myself. *What could happen in just one night?*

three

BETH

God, this had to be the worst club ever. The poor excuse for a DJ had the iTunes collection of a fourteen-year-old girl (no offense to fourteen-year-old girls) and the air conditioner couldn't be belting out more than 5,000 BTUs. And if one more nasty meathead wiped his stank on me as he pushed past (without even saying excuse me, of course), I was seriously going to hurl. What had I been thinking, agreeing to come here in the first place? I could be home, binge watching *Doctor Who*. Or an engrossing series on the history of toilet paper for that matter. Even that would have been more enjoyable than this place.

But no. I was here, gross and sweaty and waiting for Stephanie to show her face again. After all, she was the one who had forced me to come to this hell on earth in the first place. Girls' night out my ass. Three seconds after we'd arrived, she'd taken off, with the first 'roid head who'd smiled in her direction. So much for sister solidarity.

In any other circumstance I would have gone home, but I couldn't ditch her, in the remote possibility she failed to find a stranger's bed to crash in and needed a ride home.

Yes, in addition to being talked into going out in the first place, I'd volunteered to be the DD.

Yes, I really was that lame.

Okay, to be honest, the night *had* started out kind of fun. We got to walk past the ridiculously long line and go through the VIP entrance while everyone still waiting outside seethed with jealousy. Also, I had actually gotten to utter the words *I'm on the list* like you always hear people do in the movies. Of course, technically I was on *Stephanie's* list. As star TV newsgirl and practically professional partyer, Steph was probably VIP at every club in town.

Me, on the other hand? The girl who did the morning newscast that even the earliest commuters slept through? I was not on any lists.

I looked around with a sigh. When I had first come to San Diego, two years ago, places like this had seemed magical. The glitz, the glamour, the silicone. About as far away as you could get from my hometown in Illinois where the night-life started and ended with Pete's Pub and the local Denny's. In fact, ever since graduating from college, journalism degree in hand, I'd been dying to pick up and move away and come to a place like this. Where opportunity lay around every corner. Where I could actually make something of myself.

Of course all I'd managed to make so far was really strong middle-of-the-night coffee.

Okay stop it, Beth. This pity party was not helping matters. I was at a hot club, I reminded myself. I needed to at least try to have a good time. After all, how else was I supposed to find that throbbing love lance I was supposedly looking for? That *was* the whole reason I'd agreed to come to this hellhole in the first place, right? To find a guy willing to help me get over the fact that my ex-boyfriend was now my brother-in-law? And the sooner I found him, the sooner I could leave.

Of course that was easier said than done. In fact, what had seemed like a semi-logical plan back in the comfort of my bedroom now seemed a completely ridiculous indecent proposal here at the packed club. I mean, seriously, how did one even go about getting a strange man to agree to take one home and plow one into forgetting one's ex? I'd only slept with one guy in my entire life and we'd dated for a year before we had the sex discussion. How was I supposed to condense all that precoital courting into just one conversation? If only Stephanie were here. She had one-night stands down to a science.

Frustrated, I wandered up to the bar and sat down on a stool as I ordered a Diet Coke. The closest thing to liquid courage I could consume and still be able to make the drive safely back to Pacific Beach. As the bartender filled my glass I scanned the club, a sinking reality settling in my stomach. There was no way I could do this. No way I could just walk up to a guy and say—

"Can I squeeze in here?"

I jumped at the feel of a warm hand on my bare shoulder, a husky voice in my ear. Whirling around, I found myself face to face with—

Oh. My. God.

Okay, okay, so I know everyone's always like, "hottest guy ever" when they see someone good-looking and obviously not every one of these "hottest guys ever" can actually *be* the hottest because, you know, there can be only one and all that. But seriously, if you looked up *Beth's perfect dream guy* in the dictionary, *guaranteed* this dude would have a full two-page spread.

He was tall. Broad shoulders that narrowed to a tapered waist. Athletic looking, but with long, lean muscles that would have made my yoga teacher weep with joy. His hair was the color of wheat, cropped short, and his eyes were a brilliant blue—the color of the sky on a cloudless day. He wore slouchy jeans, hung low on his narrow hips and a tight black T-shirt stretched across his chest in a way that practically begged me to stick my hands underneath and run my fingers down his obviously perfect six pack.

Oh and his hand? Still resting on my shoulder. At this point radiating so much heat I was seriously wondering if it would leave me branded for life. I also wondered if I would mind all that much if it did.

"Sorry," he said, quickly pulling his hand away. His mouth quirked at the corners, causing my pulse to race like it had just entered the Kentucky Derby. "I didn't mean to startle you."

Yeah, well, I didn't mean to continue to gawk at you speechlessly as I imagined you fathering my children. We all have our problems.

He had a strong face, Roman nose, square jaw. High cheekbones cut of glass. And his lips—oh God. Full, firm. The kind of lips a girl could kiss for days and days and never get tired of.

Suddenly I found myself wondering about his love lance.

"No, I'm sorry," I managed to stammer at last, scooting over my stool to give him room. "It's all yours."

And so am I.

He smiled, dipping his head in thanks before moving in, his thigh inadvertently brushing against mine as he sidled up to the bar, sending a fiery torch of heat straight to my belly . . . and other places. Holy crap. It didn't help that I could smell him now—his clean, soapy scent—so masculine and so unlike the cloying body sprays the rest of the male population here must have bathed in before going out tonight.

I bit my lower lip, suddenly scanning the room for some random female type waiting for a drink from her man. Because this guy had to have come here with someone, right? Guys that looked like him—that smelled as good as him—should not be allowed out of the house without a properly possessive chaperone of the opposite sex.

But there was no one else. Just him. And me.

Oh sweet baby Jesus, hold me now in my time of need.

I watched, as if in a dream, as the bartender floated over and I knew I was running out of time. The bartender would take his drink order. Then he'd leave to make the drink. Which gave me about thirty seconds to one minute—depending on the complexity of the drink in question—to make my move before this guy wandered back into the techno soup and I remained a one-guy girl for the rest of my sad and pathetic—and probably cat-infested—life.

I forced myself to lean in slightly, hoping to catch the exchange between him and the bartender over the din of the club. Maybe that would give me an opening.

Bartender: "What kind of tequila?"

Mr. Potential Love Lance: "I don't know, what d'ya got?"

Uh, oh.

Now you gotta understand, in any other bar in any other city, this would be a normal question, right? After all, outside SoCal and Texas everyone just assumes tequila is simply another alcoholic beverage for frat boys to do shots of and puke up the next morning. Here, however, it was a freaking lifestyle, with restaurants holding tastings and, according to my Yelp research, this particular tequila bar even offering a free paid trip to Cabo if you were able to complete a punch card by sampling all their brands. (Thankfully not in one sitting or see: Puking up the next morning, above.)

In other words, they took their tequila seriously. And could smell a tourist a mile away.

Sure enough, the bartender huffed loudly, rolling his eyes in the way hipster bartenders have down to a science when dealing with someone "too mainstream." As if to make absolutely certain the person knew just how much they were bothering them by having the nerve to ask them to do their freaking job.

"We have seventy-five different types, sir," the bartender replied, motioning to the rows of fancy bottles displayed in a gold-trimmed cabinet about him. "Would you like me to list them alphabetically? Or by region? Or . . ." His gaze roved over his customer's casual attire. "Perhaps . . . *price*?"

He was practically salivating now, waiting for this guy to say something unimaginative like Patron or, even worse, something plebeian like Cuervo so he could have the opportunity to give a derisive snort and bathe in his tequila-tasting superiority when he went home to jerk off tonight.

Yeah. Sorry, asshole. Not this time.

"Ask for the Chinaco Anejo," I whispered out of the corner of my mouth. During a rare dayside shift a few weeks back, I'd covered a charity event that included a tasting of the stuff. According to the experts I'd interviewed, it was a smooth, complex tequila. Had won some major awards last year and was fast gaining popularity with aficionados, yet remained esoteric enough to sound cool to lame hipster bartenders like this one.

Also, I'd read on Yelp they didn't stock it here, a fact that had knocked a few stars off their overall rating by tequila tasters.

So, you know, the perfect request.

The guy leveled his gaze on the bartender. "I don't suppose you serve Chinaco Anejo here," he said smoothly, with just the right hint of skepticism. I could have hugged him I was so proud.

Sure enough the bartender's smug smile faded at the edges. "Um, no, sorry," he stammered. "We don't actually carry that here."

"Oh really? That's such a shame," my new best friend/ throbbing love lance replied, shaking his head as if he felt sorry for anyone who would be forced to work in a place that didn't stock an ample supply of the best stuff on earth. "How about . . ."

"Don Fulano," I whispered.

"Don Fulano," he finished without missing a beat.

Now the bartender's face was turning a peculiar shade of purple. "Yeah, sorry. I don't think we stock that one, either."

"Really?" The guy looked up, meeting the bartender's eyes with clear disbelief. Beside him, I stifled a giggle. "Wow. And here I had heard such good things about this place." He gave an overexaggerated shrug. "Okay, well then how about . . ." He glanced over at me with a raised eyebrow.

Shit. Those were the two I'd read about.

I had nothing.

But I couldn't leave him hanging.

"Anejo . . . Banjo Tolito," I blurted out. That sounded like a tequila brand, right?

The guy gave me a *duh* look before turning back to the bartender. "Well, yes, of *course* they *must* have Anejo Banjo Tolito," he assured me.

The bartender couldn't have looked more upset if the guy had punched him in the throat. I could practically see smoke coming from his ears as he attempted to spin a lie to save his bar's reputation. "Uh, I . . . think we're fresh out of that," he stammered. "I mean, it's a really popular brand, of course. Hell, I order it all the time when I'm out . . ."

Now it was me who was probably turning purple as I attempted not to burst out laughing.

"Okay, well, why don't you surprise me, then," the guy said, offering up the same condescending smile that had been given to him mere minutes before. "With whatever swill you *do* have left lying around the bar." He waved his hand, effectively dismissing him, and the bartender scurried off like a scolded child to go make his drink.

Once he was gone, I burst out laughing. My new partner in crime regarded me with an amused look. "Anejo Banjo Tolito?" he repeated, his eyes dancing.

"What?" I asked, holding up my hands in mock innocence. "It's supposedly very popular!" I cracked up again, not able to help myself.

He laughed. A warm, rich laugh that had my stomach doing flip-flops. Then he nodded respectfully. "Well played," he said. "Very well played."

I beamed. God, he was cute. Those eyes. The slight hint of stubble whispering across his cheeks. And was that some kind of tattoo snaking just beneath his T-shirt sleeve?

I sucked in a breath. *Come on, Beth. This is your big chance. Your one and only opportunity to say something witty and smart that will make him want to continue the conversation instead of riding off into the tequila sunrise once the bartender returned.*

Frustrated, I combed my fingers through my hair, a vain attempt to disentangle blond curls as I searched my suddenly empty mind for even a semi-engaging follow-up. Out of the corner of my eyes I watched the bartender finishing up the drink. Which left me little time.

"So where are you from?" I blurted out. Which was admittedly slightly better than "What's your sign?" or "Come here often?" though not by much.

He chuckled. "That obvious huh?"

"Sorry," I said, feeling my face heat. "I didn't mean to—"

But he shook his head. "Boston," he said. "Just moved out here last week."

"Oh, nice. I love Boston. I'm actually from Illinois myself," I told him. "I've been here two years working over at—"

"Here you go," the bartender interrupted, handing the guy his drink. He looked at him eagerly, as if waiting for him to take a sip. "I hope you like what I picked out. It's another anejo, maybe not quite to the caliber of the Anejo Banjo but . . ."

Oh my God. I was dying. So freaking dying.

"Thank you," the guy said, not taking his eyes off me. The bartender stood there, awkwardly for a moment, then eventually slunk away.

I smiled. My new friend smiled back. Then he grabbed his glass and held it up in a toast. "To my own little Tila Tequila," he teased.

I snorted. "I'm not sure that's a compliment."

"Please, if it weren't for you, I'd be drinking dog piss right now."

"Don't be too sure you aren't. I mean, did you actually watch what he put in your drink?"

"No," he said simply. "I was too busy watching you."

Oh God. Oh God, oh God, oh God.

And now it was my turn to watch as he pulled the glass to his mouth, his perfect lips parting to accept the liquid gold inside. Suddenly I found myself wondering if it were possible to come back as a highball glass in another life. His highball glass.

He set the glass down on the bar. "So how did you become such a tequila expert?" he asked.

"I'm not really," I confessed. "I just like to research places online before I go. Figure out the good, the bad, the ugly." I shrugged. "Though I did used to be a waitress back in the day, and suffered more than my share of guys like that behind the bar."

In fact, I had waitressed for years at Pete's during college and then later while attempting to make it in TV news. My first job at the local cable news station paid a whopping nine dollars an hour and waitressing had become a necessary evil to make rent. It had been more than a bit embarrassing though, to have customers recognize me from the TV. No one ever understood why a "celebrity" would be forced to sling drinks on her day off. But a girl did what she had to do to achieve her dreams.

Not that I'd been very successful at unlocking the whole dream-achievement badge so far, but at the very least I no longer had to moonlight.

"Well, that explains it then." He downed the rest of his drink, his lips once again caressing the glass in a way that made me want to scream. "Another please," he declared, addressing the bartender. Then he turned to me, "Can I get you something, too?"

I fiddled with my straw. "I'm still working on my Diet Coke. But thanks for asking."

"No problem," he replied, more to the bartender than me. "I totally understand. I mean, maybe if they had Anejo Banjo to offer . . ."

The bartender sighed mournfully as he went off to make his drink. I stifled a giggle. This guy was funny. Sexy, funny, and nice, too. Which made me wonder, why the hell was he still talking to me? Did he feel like he owed me one, after the last minute tequila save? Was he itching to slide off the bar stool and resume his hunt for Stephanie-esque prey? She was the one guys always talked to, after all. Sure, sometimes they turned to me. But usually only to inform me that my "room-mate's super hot" and was she DTF? (That's Down To . . . well, you know. And the answer, by the way, was always a resounding yes.)

"Thanks, but I'm the designated driver," I explained, feeling lame all over again.

"Really? Cool," he said, surprising me. Then he turned back to our bartender friend. 'You know what? Make that a Diet Coke."

"You don't have to do that," I stammered. "I mean, you're not driving, right?"

The corners of his mouth quirked. "No," he admitted. But he didn't change his drink order. Instead, he slid his long fingers up and down his empty glass in a way that shouldn't have been as sexy as it was as he scanned the club. "So, they tell me this is the place to see and be seen. Any idea what I'm supposed to be looking at?"

I shrugged. "You'd have to ask my roommate that one. She's the regular here. Though," I added with a long sigh, "I have no idea where she is at the moment."

"Sounds about right. I came here with my brother-in-law," he explained. "But evidently he got an emergency call and took off on me. Didn't even find me to see if I wanted to leave, just called halfway from the office and told me to take an Uber home. Nice, huh?" He leaned in, the sudden close proximity making the air crackle between us. "I gotta tell you though," he confessed, "I feel a little old for this whole club scene."

"Me, too and I'm only twenty-six," I admitted, relieved he wasn't a club guy. As a morning show reporter who was forced to wake up at three A.M. to get ready for work, I couldn't imagine going out with a night owl.

Um, okay, where had that thought come from? I wasn't going out with anyone, remember? This whole thing was solely a means to get my groove back, not get caught up in another romantic entanglement. After a thirteen-year relationship gone to hell, I needed time to reconnect with myself, find my inner diva, all that self-help shit.

I needed a love lance. Not a boyfriend.

It was just a damn shame this particular potential love lance happened to be so funny, nice, and not the least bit stuck up. And those piercing eyes of his? They should be freaking illegal for what they were doing to my insides.

You can enjoy them all you want tonight, Beth, I reminded myself. *Drown yourself in them if you must. But tomorrow it'll be time to say good-bye.*

He laughed and put out his hand. "Sorry," he said. "I have no manners. I'm Mac. What's your name?"

Mac. What a cool name. Very manly. Very him. "I'm Elizabeth," I told him, suddenly wishing my parents had been more creative when naming me. "Elizabeth White. Though most people call me Beth."

"It's nice to meet you, *Elizabeth*," he said, emphasizing my full name, as if wanting to differentiate himself from "most people." (Which, let's be honest, he'd done from hello.) It rolled off his tongue, as if it were a dessert he was savoring and suddenly I'd never loved my name so much.

I realized he was still holding out his hand. I reached out, hoping the slight tremor in mine didn't give away how damn nervous I was feeling all of a sudden. And when his large fingers closed over mine, his grip sent a chill straight down my spine. For a moment, we just held on, hands clasped, eyes locked on one another. The club spinning and screaming all around us, yet everything feeling perfectly quiet and still.

"Here's your Diet Cokes," the bartender announced, snapping us back to reality. Our hands jerked apart and we dropped our gazes, flustered by the invasion of reality. I grabbed my beverage, running my hand up and down over the condensation of my glass in a vain attempt to cool my steaming palm.

Mac raised his glass. "To friends who don't ditch you at boring nightclubs," he toasted.

I raised my own glass. "And to Anejo Banjo tequila!"

We both laughed and then drank, Mac downing his soda in one long gulp, then setting the glass down on the counter. "So what now?" he asked, a twinkle in his eyes.

Come home with me! Let me borrow your love lance!

But the words stuck in my throat. And instead I just gave him a lame shrug. Stephanie was going to be so disappointed in me. "I don't know . . ." I started to say.

Then I clamped my mouth shut. No. I was not going to screw this up. I was not going to let this once-in-a-lifetime opportunity slip by. One way or another, I was going to get this guy to come home with me.

I looked up, meeting his intoxicating eyes with my own. Then I put out my hand. "We are at a nightclub," I declared. "Perhaps it's time we get our dance on."

four

MAC

Okay, Mac, what the hell do you think you're doing?

I mean seriously. It was one thing to joke around with a girl sitting beside you at the bar. Quite another to wrap your arms around her tiny waist and twirl her around the dance floor. I hadn't been lying when I'd told Sadie I was done with women for good. So how come I'd jumped like a fucking frat boy at the first one who'd made me laugh?

Maybe I should blame the music. The DJ's driving techno beat. It brought out the primitive and suddenly it was as if I were some caveman, unable to focus on past hurts and future consequences—just this hot little body pressing up against mine.

Or maybe it was just being out of the house in the first place. It'd been way too long since I'd been out on my own, not a care in the world. Even longer still since I'd held a girl in my arms, unabashed interest sparkling in her wide, brown eyes. In all my years with the Bitch I was pretty sure she'd never given me such a look. The kind of look that was able to stoke me in a way that should have required hands and fingers.

Slow down, Mac. You're getting carried away.

I forced myself to squeeze an inch of space between us. But her electrical pull soon drew me back in. As if she were some kind of industrial strength magnet and I was helpless as metal file shavings.

And who could blame me? It wasn't just that she was hot, though she definitely was. Long blond hair tumbling down her bare back in waves, curves in all the right places, and skin kissed golden by the San Diego sunshine. She had long eyelashes and full lips—and dark beguiling eyes that had danced with mischief as she had effortlessly brought that bartender to his knees.

Yes, she was definitely hot. But what I liked even better was the natural dorkiness she was obviously trying to hide beneath her goddess-like exterior. Like, for example how she was wearing this green scrap of fabric that could barely qualify as a dress, but kept yanking down on it self-consciously every five minutes as if she wasn't used to wearing something so short. Fifty bucks it belonged to that roommate she mentioned.

And when we were walking to the dance floor, she'd almost ate it as she teetered awkwardly in her high heels— even though she hadn't had a drop to drink. (Eat your heart out, J. Law.) She'd also stepped on my feet at least three times during our brief dance, which should have been annoying, but was actually kind of adorable. The Bitch, who had effortlessly managed to wear six-inch Jimmy Choos until the day she gave birth, would have rolled her eyes. Which was probably why I found it even more endearing.

Oh, and the way she'd jumped in to save me from that asshole bartender? That was straight up superhero shit, no question.

"So you lived in Boston? What was that like?" she asked, forced to shout in my ear to be heard over the music. Her fingers grazed my hip as she leaned in, causing a jolt of electricity to shoot straight to my groin. Did she have any idea what she was doing to me? The fact that I was pretty sure she didn't made it all the more enticing.

"Boston?" I managed to choke out. "It's nice. But, uh, it can get pretty cold."

Jesus. Did I just say that? Seriously I couldn't possibly have less game if I came here with a Parcheesi board.

"Oh yeah?" she said. "Well, San Diego can get pretty hot."

"I think I'm learning that," I said, not able to help a small smile. Damn she was adorable. I found myself reaching up to brush a lock of honey-colored hair from her eyes, managing to reveal, then promptly lose myself in, her huge, dilated pupils. For a moment, she looked back at me, wide-eyed and fucking beautiful, then her long lashes swept down, her cheeks taking on a rosy glow.

So she was shy. Shy in the way that made me believe she didn't do stuff like this all the time. That she didn't go to clubs and dance with strangers. That she'd made an exception for me.

Like I was making an exception for her.

Something stirred deep within me. *Just don't kiss her, Mac. It's okay to dance. Just don't you dare kiss her.*

Don't kiss her? Hell, it was all I could do at this point not to slam her against the wall, grab that tight ass in both hands and let her wrap her legs around my waist as I took her right here and now in this club before God and everyone. Not that someone as sweet as her would likely appreciate such a gesture. She was a good girl. The kind who deserved candles and roses and all that romantic stuff.

The kind of girl who deserved better than someone like me.

The music slowed and I thought about breaking apart, thanking her for the dance and walking away before it was too late. Grabbing that cab, heading home, checking on Ashley and letting her know everything was okay. Her daddy was home safe and sound.

But Ashley was asleep. I'd texted Sadie half a dozen times before she told me she was turning off her phone. *Don't call me. I'll call you if I need you. But I won't need you, because she's* fine. *And she'll still be fine, even if you somehow manage to fall ass-backward into having a good time for once in your life.*

You deserve it, Mac, she'd told me. And I knew if she could see me now she'd tell me I deserved her, too.

And so I pushed past the guilt. I didn't break apart. Didn't walk away. Instead, I allowed my hands to circle her waist, pulling her ever closer. She was small—I could probably crush her with little effort—but at the same time her body was firm, tight, with the exception of her soft breasts, now pillowed against my chest. I could feel my jeans tightening and hoped she couldn't tell how turned on I was getting. Or at least wouldn't mind if she could. Hell, I couldn't even remember the last time I had a hard-on for anything but my own hand. And for a moment, I forced myself to forget everything, except the dance—and her.

"So, um, Boston. You didn't like the cold?" she murmured, her mouth brushing against my chest as she spoke.

"Cold? No." I swallowed hard. "In fact, I think I could get pretty used to the heat."

five

Holy. Crap.
   I forced myself to swallow down the relentless butterflies that had evidently decided to throw an impromptu
full-on rave in my stomach. I couldn't believe I was actually
doing this. Not only doing this—but doing this with the
hottest guy I'd ever seen. And it was working, too! I was
turning him on. I was making him hard. I was doing all the
things I'd never been able to do before now and I was loving
the hell out of it. I mean, what would Ryan say if he could
see his sweet little Beth now? He wouldn't even recognize me.

   But screw Ryan. Screw Ryan and his tiny little life with
my tiny little sister. They could have their five kids, their
white picket fence, while I, for the first time in my life, was
actually free. Free to reach for the stars. To be anything and
anyone I wanted to be—with no one holding me back. I could
give up all my hang-ups, all my inhibitions. I could be the
sexy nightclub nymph Ryan would never let me be.

   This guy? He didn't know me. He didn't know anything

about me. And yet here I was turning him on by sheer force of will. The power of the idea was exhilarating. The possibilities endless. I hadn't drunk a drop of alcohol tonight, yet I felt completely intoxicated.

"Damn, you smell good," he whispered. He brushed my hair off my shoulder, leaning in closer so his mouth was mere inches from my ear. "It's driving me crazy." His whisper tickled my earlobe, sending my pulse skyrocketing all over again, and I was pretty sure the lacy thong Stephanie had made me wear "just in case" was completely soaked at this point.

I drew in a shaky breath, wondering what would come next. Was he going to kiss me? Or maybe I should kiss him? Was that too forward? Then again, I was playing the part of the sexy stranger tonight. The girl who wasn't above going after what she wanted.

And, oh, man did I want him.

Drawing up my courage, I reached up, daring to trace his rugged jaw with my fingers, delighting in the friction of his five o'clock shadow. I loved that he hadn't shaved to come here. Hadn't gelled up his hair like the rest of the Euro trash. He was all man.

And at this moment, he was all mine.

He groaned and I couldn't help but smile as I realized the effect I was having on him. Usually when I'd try to make the first move with Ryan he'd turn away to watch the football game. Our lovemaking had been scheduled, penciled in, during times he wasn't too tired or too busy. But this guy, he didn't seem to be checking his Daytimer as he checked me out.

And so I decided to go for it.

Standing on my tiptoes, I closed my eyes, leaning toward him. Ready to press my lips against his and—

"There you are, slut!"

I jerked—reality crashing over me like a tidal wave as a finger poked me in the back. Whirling around, I found my missing roommate, sans her bodybuilder friend, standing behind me, arms crossed over her chest, a sly smirk on her face.

"Well, well, well," she drawled, her voice slurring as she spoke. "Looks like someone found their throbbing love lance after all."

six

ELIZABETH

was beginning to think you took off," I frowned, reluctantly stepping out of Mac's embrace as real life crashed the party of my fantasies.

"I did. I've been to three other bars tonight." Stephanie tossed her long black hair behind her shoulder, shuffling from one kitten-heeled sandal to the other. She looked wasted. Okay, let's not kid ourselves, she *was* wasted.

"Oh, of course. Thanks for letting me know," I muttered. I could feel Mac's gaze on me, tempting me back to fantasyland. And though I'd been looking for my roommate all night, suddenly I wished she'd just go away.

But no such luck. Instead Stephanie caught my arm and started dragging me toward the bathroom. "Steph!" I hissed, trying to subtly nod my head back to Mac who was now standing alone in the middle of the dance floor.

"Oh. Sorry." Stephanie released my arm and sauntered back up to Mac. She laid a hand on his shoulder and dragged her nails down his arm, stopping to trace his tattoo in the way I would have liked to have done had I dared. I bit back a surge of sudden jealousy. Stephanie could have anyone here. If she even dared to go after my one guy . . .

"Don't go anywhere, hot stuff," she drawled. "We'll be right back. Girl talk, you know?" Then, before waiting for his reply, she returned to me, seizing me by the elbow. "Bathroom. Now."

I reluctantly allowed myself to be dragged into the ladies' room. Once inside, Stephanie fished for a compact from her purse and began to powder her dewy face. "So who's the hotness?" she asked, not looking over at me.

I bit my lower lip, suddenly not wanting to tell her anything. I wanted Mac to be mine. My guy. My experience. My fantasy come to life. Not something to be dissected and over-analyzed by a meddling roommate. But when Stephanie turned to give me an expectant, yet impatient look, I gave in. "His name's Mac."

"He's smokin'." Stephanie stashed her compact and stared in the mirror with a critical eye before reaching for her lip gloss.

"I did notice that before you dragged me away." I crossed my arms over my chest, feeling annoyed and sweaty again. What if Mac got bored and took off? Or thought that the bathroom thing was just a girl ploy to let the guy down gently without having to say the words? After all, I'd seen Stephanie play that game numerous nights—with "Be right back" loosely translating into "Sayonara, sucker."

"Don't worry," Stephanie interjected, as if reading my thoughts. "He won't go anywhere. I saw that look in his eyes. He's definitely into you."

"Do you think?" I couldn't help but ask, hating myself for sounding so needy the second the words left my lips.

"Totally." My roommate tossed the lip gloss back into her purse. "That's one throbbing love lance ready to go."

I moaned, leaning against the bathroom stall, staring up at the ceiling. "I was seriously hoping you'd forget about that."

"Are you kidding? I would never prematurely evacuate on Operation: Get Beth Laid!" Stephanie protested. "I mean, seriously, what kind of friend do you think I am?"

I decided it was best not to answer that.

"Look, you've already done all the legwork on this one. Trust me, the hookup vibes are radiating across the club. All you have to do now is seal the deal."

"And I do that, how?"

"Come on, Beth. This isn't rocket science. Hell, this isn't even third grade math. Tell him you're leaving. Ask him if he wants to leave with you. I think he'll get the hint."

I let out a frustrated breath. "I feel stupid," I replied. "What if he says no?"

"He's a guy, isn't he? And you're a hot, hot slut, ready for some between the sheets bingo. What red-blooded man could say no to you?"

I could think of a few. Like Ryan, for example. But I decided not to go there.

"Fine," I said, giving up. "Give me five minutes. I'll see what I can do."

Stephanie jumped up and down and cheered. "That's my bitch!" she crowed. "Boo-yah!"

Rolling my eyes, I headed out of the bathroom, making my way over to where Mac was leaning against the wall, looking unhappy. When he saw me his expression lifted.

"You're back," he observed, a smile hovering at the corners of his lips. So he *had* assumed I was going to just ditch him. Stupid Stephanie.

"Yeah, I'm sorry," I said. "My roommate. She's a piece of work."

He gave me a knowing look. "I've had roommates like that."

"Yeah." I shuffled from foot to foot, suddenly feeling nervous as hell. I tried to remind myself that this was the same guy I'd almost been locking lips with mere minutes before. Nothing had changed. "Well, she's pretty drunk. I think I need to get her home."

"Yeah?" For a split second his eyes flashed with what looked to me like disappointment. At least I wanted it to be disappointment. Then he nodded. "I should probably call a cab, too," he said. "It's getting late."

"A cab?" I sucked in a breath. Okay, there was my opening. My chance. I could not blow this. From across the room I could see Stephanie giving me two overenthusiastic thumbs up, grinning like a loon, which almost made me want to walk away. But this wasn't about her. This was about me. About Mac.

About Mac and me.

And I wanted this, I suddenly realized. Not as some kind of sex intervention. Not as a way to get my groove back. I just wanted to spend more time with him. Even if it was only for conversation. I liked him. I didn't want to say good-bye just yet.

And so I went for it. "Or, you know, you could catch a ride with us. If you wanted to . . ."

He looked at me with a piercing gaze. "I actually live pretty far up north," he said. "It'd probably be way out of your way."

"Um. Right." I bit my lower lip. Was he not getting my hint? "Well, you could just . . . I don't know . . . crash on our couch or something? And I could give you a ride home in the morning?"

There, I said it. I actually said it. Though now I was pretty sure I wanted to take it all back, as I observed the weirdest look on his face. The hesitation before giving an answer. Had I read him completely wrong? Was he just not that into me after all? Suddenly all my Ryan-induced insecurities came raging back with a vengeance.

But before I could take it all back, to tell him I was totally just kidding, he smiled. "That'd be great," he said. "And I can get my brother-in-law to pick me up in the morning. So you don't have to drive all that way. He owes me, after all, for ditching me here tonight."

And I owed him—big time.

"Perfect," I said, relief washing over me in waves. "Then if you're ready, let's go."

It was done. Except, actually, it was just beginning.

seven

BETH

Fifteen minutes later and we were pulling into the driveway of the small Pacific Beach bungalow Stephanie and I shared. To her credit, my roommate disappeared into her bedroom almost immediately after we walked through the front door, leaving me alone in the living room. Alone with Mac, that was. Suddenly the nervous butterflies swarmed through my stomach all over again and I had to lean against the wall for support.

What had I done? Only invited a practical stranger into my house in the middle of the night, that's all. With some kind of vague promise of letting him "crash on the couch." And now I wasn't exactly sure how to proceed. Had he effectively translated "crashing on the couch" to "having your way with me all night long"? Or did he really expect a quiet night's sleep alone?

"Nice place," he commented, taking a seat on the couch in question, stretching out his long legs and revealing a pair of scuffed black boots. I stole a glance, my heart racing, as I pondered my next move. Under the crazy club lights he'd been hot. Under the soft glow of the living room lamp? He was downright scorching.

I forced myself to turn away, walking across the room to pull the picture window's vertical blinds, revealing the distant ocean view. "I love this house," I admitted, trying to focus on the ebb and flow of the tides and get my raging hormones back to a non-heart attack level. "Growing up in the Midwest I always dreamed of living near the beach." In fact that had been one of the reasons I'd agreed to move in with Stephanie in the first place. She'd needed a roommate to pay half the rent, I needed a room with a view.

I felt hot breath searing my shoulder and I nearly jumped out of my skin. I hadn't heard him rise from the relative safety of the couch. Now he was standing behind me, so close I could feel the brush of his jeans against the back of my bare thighs, causing me to shiver.

"Beautiful," he murmured in a husky voice that gave me the distinct suspicion he wasn't talking about the view.

I wanted to ramble on, to break the spell he'd somehow put over me, but it appeared I'd been rendered speechless. And so I stood there, mute, as his hands found my shoulders and began kneading the muscles, massaging slowly, deeply. I drew in a breath and closed my eyes, trying desperately to quell my nerves and enjoy the sensation of his calloused hands on my sensitive skin. *This is what I wanted*, I tried to remind myself. Why I'd invited him here to begin with. I couldn't wimp out now.

And besides, if we were being honest here, it was nice to be touched. To feel appreciated, cherished even. I'd spent far too long waiting for Ryan to keep his promise and move to San Diego. Far too many lonely afternoons, sitting by the phone after work, waiting for him to call. I had missed the touch of another human being. The warmth prickling across my skin.

I might not know Mac all that well. But I liked him. I liked what he was doing to me, too. And deep down I realized I wanted him to do more.

As if he could read my thoughts, he brushed aside the

barrier of my hair to better access my neck. Goosebumps rose as his hands reached around to stroke my collarbone and I found myself leaning backward, into him, melting into his tall, strong frame and allowing him to support my weight. I could feel his desire pressing against my backside, but it didn't scare me as much as it probably should have. Instead, it filled me with that same intoxicating sense of power I'd felt back at the club. He wanted me. This beautiful stranger desired me. The girl whose own boyfriend ditched her for her sister.

He lowered his hands, drawing his arms around me, skimming my midriff through the thin silk of the dress Stephanie had let me borrow. At the time I'd argued that there wasn't enough fabric to call it a dress. Now it felt bulky, cumbersome, a barrier to the skin-on-skin contact I was dying to feel. Heat burned low in my belly as he traced my hipbones with lazy fingers, and it was all I could do not to turn around and jump his bones right then and there.

Eventually I did turn around, still pressing against him, looking up at him with heavily lidded eyes. I wanted to say something though I wasn't sure of the appropriate Emily Post manners for a situation like this. Or if my tongue would even cooperate if I tried. But it didn't matter. He cupped my face in his hands and smiled slowly at me, meeting my eyes with his own deep, dark blue ones. Then he leaned in, pressing his lips to mine.

He tasted like mints. Fresh, sweet, delicious. A gourmet dessert I never wanted to stop tasting. But at the same time, I recognized something darker, fiercer, just beneath the surface of the gentle kiss. A pressure, an urgency, a need. And when he pulled away from the kiss, I found myself licking my lips, desperate for more.

"Yum," I said shyly, smiling up at him. It was ridiculous, but at that moment I couldn't think of another single thing to say.

He chuckled softly, brushing a strand of stray hair from my face, then studied me with a concerned look in his eyes that both scared me and excited me more than anything had up until this very moment. Then I watched, concerned, as a shadow of doubt flickered across his face. "Are you sure about this?" he asked in a gravelly voice. "Because I really don't mind sleeping on the couch."

His consideration—the fact that he cared, the fact that he'd asked—made me want him even more. Not as a one-night love lance, I realized suddenly. Not as a cure for my sexual slump. But as a guy I wanted to stick around the morning after so I could make him breakfast and grill him about his life. Sure, there were a million reasons I wasn't ready for a new boyfriend. But if Mr. Perfect shows up at your front door, are you really going to slam it in his face?

"Couch?" I murmured. "Well, sure. But it's not very comfortable to tell you the truth."

He raised an eyebrow. "Oh?" Lowering his hands to my bottom, he pulled me tight against him, the hard planes of his body molding perfectly to my soft curves. His erection was stiff against my belly and I was soaked with desire. "Well then, where do you suggest I sleep?"

He leaned in, not waiting for an answer, his tongue darting out to tease my lips open and then plunge into my mouth. I moaned in delight, scissoring his thigh and pressing against him to relieve some of the pressure. "There's . . . always . . . the bed . . . room," I managed to gasp between kisses.

He pulled away, giving me a look that was both skeptical and amused. "I don't know," he drawled. "Is your *bed* comfortable?"

I swallowed hard. "You'd have to try it to know for sure."

He grabbed me in his arms, scooping me up like a baby, and I squealed in delight as he carried me to my room, his strong arms cradling me as if I weighed nothing at all. Once we were inside, he kicked the door closed, then lowered me tenderly onto the bed, pulling a pillow from the pile to cradle my head on. The sweetness, the thoughtfulness of such a simple gesture almost made tears spring to my eyes. And, after shucking off his jacket and throwing it on a nearby chair, he surprised me by pulling me into his arms, continuing to kiss me over and over again until I lost track of kisses and time.

And suddenly I realized *this* was what I had really needed all along. *This* was what had been missing from my life. Not some wild sexual romp. But to be touched, to be kissed, to be treasured. The way Mac was looking at me now—with fascination mixed with adoration and maybe a little fear, too—that was what I needed tonight. That was what had the power to make me whole.

I knew if I asked him to stop—or to not go any further, he would have agreed with no questions asked. He would have taken me in his arms and cuddled me all night long without a single complaint. But I was feeling so warm by this point, so safe, my nervousness completely abandoning me. Instead I found myself reaching up, grabbing the hem of his shirt with both hands and pulling it over his head, revealing the smooth, chiseled chest I'd been dying to touch since he'd first walked up to the bar. And let's just say I was not disappointed.

He was lean, all muscle and sinew. Carved in stone from an honest day's work, not honed in a gym. I wondered, suddenly, what he did for a living, but it seemed silly to ask him now. Maybe tomorrow morning when I served him that breakfast and we lingered over coffee I could get to know the 411.

Right now all I wanted was the foreplay.

As I ran my fingers over his abs, enjoying the sensation of silky skin laid over hard muscle, I could feel his chest heave in and out, mirroring his labored breathing. He was as turned on as I was and I loved that. Loved that he wanted me, that he desired me, that he was having a hard time taking his time with me—but did so anyway. I reached up to trace the tattoo I'd first seen peeking from his sleeve, realizing it was a letter A written in Celtic-like script. I wondered what it stood for.

Amazing?

Astounding?

Awesome?

He grabbed my hand, pulling it away and pinning it above my head. Then he leaned down and kissed me hard on the mouth, his other hand dragging down the inside of my arm, skimming my breast and belly before landing between my legs. I groaned, squirming against him as he explored the inside of my thigh, the heat and ache pooling to the point of combustion. Desperate, I reached down with my other hand, guiding him to where I needed him to be and he cupped me in his palm for a moment before deftly sliding his fingers underneath my panties and finding my core.

"Oh God," I whispered. "Don't stop."

He smiled wickedly against my mouth. "Believe me, I'm just getting started."

As he stroked me with long, even strokes, he lowered his head, planting hot kisses on my shoulder before reaching down to pull the spaghetti straps of my dress away, followed by my bra. Before now I'd only been naked in front of one other guy but at this point I had long since stopped caring about being so exposed. Instead I only whimpered as Mac nipped, then licked my right breast, his fingers ever stroking my nub. The combination of his deft fingers, combined with his velvet tongue rolling across my nipple made me burn like wildfire and soon I was arching my back and grabbing handfuls of sheets as I bit down on my lower lip to keep from screaming and waking my roommate.

With Ryan I'd hardly ever been able to climax. In fact, I'd assumed I was one of those girls who just didn't have it in her to come, except by her own hand. But Mac—Mac evidently had the power to bring me to the precipice without any effort whatsoever. And soon I found myself shattering into a thousand stars of light as I came hard against his hand.

"Wow," I managed to say after the aftershocks of orgasm finally shuddered through me. It was all I could say.

But it wasn't all I could do. And before I knew it I was grabbing at his belt, somehow managing to unbuckle it with my shaky fingers, ripping it from its loops before working on his fly. I could see his erection straining under his jeans as if it couldn't wait to be freed from its constraints.

And then it was. *There* it was. The throbbing—

No. This wasn't some fantasy romance purple prose.

This was a cock. Mac's cock. And it was magnificent.

I reached out, closing my hand around his length, rejoicing in the feeling of silky soft skin over hard erection. I stroked the crown with my thumb and he jerked in my hands.

"Fuck," he whispered in a hoarse voice. "Don't stop."

A smile crept to my lips. "I'm just getting started."

As I ran my hand up and down his shaft, I placed my other hand on his chest, feeling his erratic heartbeat against my flat palm. He groaned, his face tormented with pleasure. I could see his hard swallow. He wasn't going to be able to take much more. And so I lay back in bed, still holding him in my hand, and began guiding him into me.

"Wait," he said suddenly, his voice struggling for composure. I cocked my head in question.

"What?" I asked, a little worried.

His face flushed. "I don't have any protection," he confessed. "I wasn't planning—"

"Oh." I sucked in a breath, relieved. Then I smiled. "Don't worry, I've got it covered." I leaned over to my nightstand and pulled open the top drawer, now thankful for the night when Stephanie had pranced in, right after Ryan had dumped me, filling the drawer with an obscene amount of condoms. Now that I was "free," she had declared at the time.

I drew one from the nightstand, angling so he couldn't see how overflowing the drawer was—I didn't want him to get the wrong idea. Then I shyly handed it over to him.

The relief on his face was palpable. He leaned down and kissed me again, his hands working to remove my panties in one deft movement, leaving me bare beneath him. Once properly sheathed, he climbed on top of me, his hands gripping my hips as he lowered himself onto me. Into me. It wasn't difficult—I was soaking wet by this point. Ryan had never been big on foreplay and we'd always had to supplement with lube. Not today.

His first thrust was slow, tentative. Almost exploratory. Filling me, stretching me, finding his place inside me. The second thrust had more power behind it, causing a gasp to escape me as he pushed deeper inside. I wrapped my legs around the small of his back, breathing in deeply, trying to match his movements with my own as chills racked through me at an almost alarming rate. God, he felt even better than I'd imagined—and I'd been imagining quite a bit. As he pushed deeper inside of me, his mouth grazed my earlobe, sending shivers straight to my core while my body burned with wildfire.

"God, Elizabeth, you are so fucking beautiful," he breathed as he lifted his hips, then brought them down again. Over and over, harder and harder, higher and higher until finally we both crashed over the threshold together and this time I couldn't hold back a loud cry. Stephanie was going to have a field day tomorrow—but I didn't care. At that moment nothing else mattered but the waves of ecstasy cascading over me. Mac's hot body against my own.

He collapsed on top of me, his ragged breath in my ears, his hands still wrapped around me. Then, after discarding the condom, he pulled me close, spooning me against him, his hands on my belly, his head nestled in my hair.

I sighed contentedly, wondering if I should be feeling guilty. After all, I'd slept with a man I'd only just met. But truth be told, at that very moment, nestled in his arms, it felt as if I'd known Mac forever. And I couldn't bring myself to regret a thing.

eight

MAC

Ugh. I rolled over, burying my head in my pillow, trying to ignore the persistent beams of sunlight boring through my blinds in a way-too-enthusiastic announcement of morning. I just wanted a few more minutes of sleep—was that so wrong? Then I'd get up and be the dad, get Ashley ready for preschool as I did every morning. That was what you did when you had kids. Sleeping in became nothing more than a dream. ·

But when I stretched out, trying to find a more comfortable position for my last five minutes of peace, my fingers brushed against something soft. Smooth. Something like a . . .

Breast?

I jolted up in bed, suddenly realizing where I was.

What I'd done.

Who I'd done.

Fuuuuuuuuuck.

I sucked in a breath before daring to look over to my side, dropping my eyes to the sleeping beauty beside me. My gaze involuntarily raked up the entire length of her, completely naked save for a rumpled bed sheet bunched at her waist. My eyes took in the smooth, tanned skin, the rise and fall of her flawless breasts as she peacefully slumbered, as if she hadn't a care in the world. It was all I could do not to lean down and see if I could kiss her into consciousness, like the princes always did in the movies.

But I wasn't a prince. I was a weak-willed bastard. And I'd already done way too much.

What had I been thinking? Hadn't I just said to my sister not twenty-four hours ago that I was through with women forever? And now I just jump into bed with the first one I come across? Seriously what was wrong with me?

And what about Ashley? I glanced at the nightstand clock. I had to get home before she woke up. Before she wondered where Daddy was and if he'd left her. Left her like Mommy had.

The night the Bitch had walked out on the two of us, I'd made a vow. A vow that I would never, ever let my baby girl wake up alone and scared. And I wasn't about to break that promise now—especially for my own selfish pleasure. Ashley needed me. I was all she had in the world. Which meant any type of a personal life needed to take a backseat . . . at least for now.

I would not let her down.

I would not be her mother.

Quietly, I slipped out of bed, grabbing my jeans off the floor and sliding them over my hips. Then I grabbed my shirt and shoes and headed toward the door. Just before exiting, I found myself turning around for one last look.

God, she was beautiful. Her golden hair now splayed out on her pillow, her long lashes curtaining her beguiling dark eyes. Her mouth was so sweet and sensual and I couldn't help but replay all those hot, wet kisses from the night before in my mind. Hell, it was all I could do to restrain myself from jumping back into bed and continuing where we left off, consequences be damned.

I forced myself back to the door. Goddamn it, what was wrong with me? I had to get out of there. Fast. Before she

woke up and wanted things like phone numbers and future
dates and relationship status changes on Facebook. Things
a girl like her totally deserved. Things a guy like me couldn't
give.

Guilt knotted in my stomach as I sank down onto the
couch to slip on my shoes. The couch I was supposed to have
slept on last night. If only I had stayed strong, never agreed
to come here in the first place. I wasn't an idiot. I knew what
she'd been asking. I knew what would happen if I agreed to
come home with her. But I had been like a crack addict being
offered the perfect fix. I couldn't say no.

Hell, I hadn't wanted to say no.

Drawing in a breath, I looked around, searching for pen
and paper. I needed to at least leave her my phone number.
So we could talk about what had happened. Talk about why
it could never happen again. I could tell her that it wasn't her,
that it was me, and that in this case the cliché line was actually true. She was so sweet. So nice. She deserved for me to
let her down gently. To understand that she was perfect—
completely perfect. And I was the damaged goods.

"Well, well, well. If it isn't Mr. Throbbing Love Lance
himself, making a beeline for the door."

I looked up startled. Beth's roommate—Stephanie?—was
leaning in the doorframe, dressed in a scanty pink negligee
that barely covered the important parts. She was voluptuous,
with full lips and big eyes and even bigger boobs. The kind
of girl most guys would fall over backward to get with. But
to me, she had nothing on her friend.

"Excuse me?" I said, glancing longingly at my watch and
then the front door. It was getting later and later and I didn't
have time for conversation. But I didn't want to be rude. The
two of them were going to hate me enough after this—I
didn't need to give them additional ammunition.

She chuckled meanly. I noticed her eyes were black from
smudged mascara and her lips still stained with the remnants
of blood red lipstick. "Don't worry," she purred. "I wasn't
planning on cooking you breakfast. I just wanted to thank
you before you took off."

I cocked my head. "Thank me?" I repeated.

"For doing the deed. Getting Lizzie laid. Trust me, she'll be so much better off, now that she's got the first one down."

I stared at her, uncomprehending.

"I'm sorry," Stephanie said, looking anything but. "Did she not tell you? That was the whole reason she went to the club last night in the first place."

"What?" I asked, sudden unease creeping into my stomach. "What are you talking about?"

She smirked. "Come on, does Beth seem like a club kid to you? She hates those kinds of places. But she needed a quick screw to get back at her stupid ex-boyfriend. And where better than Club Rain to hunt for easy prey? Well, obviously *you* know."

She winked at me and I scowled at the implication. I wanted to argue—that Beth wasn't that type of girl. That she and I had connected. That what we'd done hadn't been some empty screw. That *I* was the bastard making what could have been a wonderful friendship into a one-night stand—not her.

But was that really true? While I didn't trust her roommate as far as I could throw her, thinking back on it now, I realized the whole night was a little odd. Meeting a girl like Beth in such a skanky bar—a silk purse surrounded by sow's ears. She claimed she was waiting for her roommate—fine. But why had she agreed to come in the first place? Had she just been humoring Stephanie? Or had she had another plan in mind from the start? Had I truly stumbled on her by chance? Or had she been parked at the bar all night, fishing for someone—anyone—willing to get her off.

No. I frowned. She wasn't like that. She wasn't that type of girl.

Though . . . She *had* been the one to ask me to dance. The one who had tried to kiss me on the dance floor. Talked me into coming home with her. Told me the couch was not as comfortable as her bed.

Had a drawer full of condoms at the ready.

Jesus. I raked a hand through my hair. And here I'd been all worried about breaking *her* heart.

It was ironic, really. I'd been feeling like a bastard for sneaking out on her first thing in the morning and now I realized she was probably hiding in her bedroom, at this very moment, praying I'd leave without a fuss. To make a quick exit and avoid all that morning after awkward and all the fake promises that came with it.

And if that was true, well, that was the perfect scenario, really—for both of us. We'd had a great time, gotten what we'd needed from one another, and now we could both move on.

No hurt feelings.

No big deal.

Except . . . I grimaced, finding myself glancing over at her bedroom door again, almost against my will, an unexpected swell of disappointment sweeping through my stomach. It kind of felt like a big deal. And my feelings? Well, they kind of fucking hurt.

Come on, Mac. Grow a pair. This is for the best and you know it. You got a pass, you lucky bastard. Take it and be grateful.

I finished the note, signed my name. Debated on leaving my phone number and then decided against it. What good would it do? If she did call, it would only prolong the inevitable. Double down on my mistake. Sure, she'd probably think I was a bit of an asshole. Or a coward, maybe. In truth, she wouldn't be wrong.

She doesn't want this any more than you do, I reminded myself. *It's for the best.*

I shook my head. *And this is why you need to stay clear of women,* I reminded myself as I set the note on the counter and headed for the door. I could feel Stephanie's eyes still on me, a small smirk playing at the corners of her lips.

I sighed. "See you later," I said.

She snorted. "I doubt it."

Yeah. Me, too.

nine

BETH

I opened one eye, then the other, squinting for a moment at the bright sunshine peering curiously through my bedroom window. Scarcely able to breathe, I rolled over quietly, not wanting to wake the sleeping man in my bed.

The sleeping man in my bed!

A delicious tingle of adrenaline wiggled through my stomach as my mind replayed scenes from the night before. Mac taking me into his arms. Mac peeling off my dress. Mac touching me in all the right places. Mac making me come like I'd never come before.

Mac . . . who was not, it turned out, still sleeping in my bed.

For a crazy split second I entertained the idea that I had dreamt it all. The mind-blowing sex, the postcoital cuddling. Drifting off into dreamland, cradled in warm, solid arms. Had that really all happened? I stuffed my face into the pillow beside me and breathed in deep. It smelled just like him and suddenly I knew it had all happened—just like I remembered it. And it had all been amazing.

I lifted my head, scanning the room. My eyes fell upon an unfamiliar jacket, tossed over my desk chair. I let out a sigh of relief. For a moment I thought maybe he'd taken off early, without even saying good-bye. But he was still here. I smiled to myself. Maybe he was out in the living room, checking sports scores on his phone. Or taking an early jog on the beach. Maybe he was even in my kitchen, right this very second, fixing me a big breakfast in bed.

I hugged myself, grinning at the idea. Imagining him returning to the room clad only in his boxers, carrying a tray piled high. He'd straddle my legs and dip a fork into fluffy scrambled eggs (knowing somehow that they were my favorite), feeding me between tender little kisses. Then, once we were done eating, he'd put the tray aside and continue where we'd left off. In the end, we'd accidentally spend the entire day in bed, forgetting the world outside until Monday morning called.

And maybe then I'd call in sick to work.

I flopped back onto my pillow, staring up at the ceiling, unable to stop smiling. It had been far too long since I'd felt like this. Far too long that I'd put up with Ryan and his empty promises. If only I'd known what else was out there. *Who* else was out there. Maybe I wouldn't have dealt with disappointment for so long.

Seriously, I owed Stephanie a major thank-you.

At last I shrugged off my sheet and swung my legs from the bed to the floor. Stretching my arms over my head, I let out a long yawn, then slipped my feet into my fuzzy slippers. I glanced over at my closet, debating getting dressed, then determined a robe was a better bet, to save Mac the trouble of tearing off my clothes again after breakfast. The thought made me giggle—and I felt my face flush. Seriously, it was like I'd been transformed into an entirely different person overnight. Ryan wouldn't even recognize me.

Opening my bedroom door, I headed down the hall, trying to muster up an appropriate greeting. What would Emily Post say about addressing a sex god the morning after? I bit my lower lip, suddenly feeling a little nervous. Was this going to be awkward? Would the light of day make things weird between us? But no, Mac had been so cool. So nice.

He'd made me feel so comfortable. With him, it wouldn't be awkward. It would just be . . .

. . . nonexistent.

I looked around, confused. The living room was empty. The TV was off. There was no clattering of pots and pans, no smell of frying bacon wafting from the kitchen. My heart sank a little. Did he really leave? Maybe he had to go to work or something—I never did get a chance to ask him what he did for a living—maybe it involved weekend hours. Heart fluttering nervously, I walked into the kitchen. My eyes fell upon a piece of paper on the counter.

Hey Beth,

Had a great time last night. Sorry I had to bail early—got a ton of unpacking to do before I start my new job. Thanks again for letting me crash. You were right, the bed was MUCH more comfortable than the couch.

Thanks again,
Mac

I stared down at the note, my stomach swimming with nausea. Then I turned it over, thinking that couldn't be it—that there had to be more. A phone number, an email at the very least . . .

But there was nothing.

Nothing. Nothing. Nothing.

Blood began to pound behind my temples and a gnawing fear ground at my stomach. I didn't want to believe what my mind was telling me, but what other explanation could there be? Mac had woken up, bright and early, to exit my life as abruptly as he had entered it, leaving the most cursory note behind. Which could only mean one thing.

A one-night stand.

My heart wrenched, realization hitting me over the head with the force of a ten-ton truck. I, Beth White, had just had a one-night stand. A one-night stand with a stranger. A stranger I would probably never see again.

Okay, okay, sure, that *was* the original idea of going to the club and finding a guy to begin with. But wasn't *I* supposed to be the one to call the terms of the arrangement? Wasn't *I* supposed to be the one to say thank you for a wonderful night and then walk away?

Okay, that sounded totally selfish, didn't it? And it wasn't like I was going to actually have done that. Not to Mac anyway. Mac who was cool and funny and sweet and had held me all night long.

Held me like I meant something.

Had I meant anything at all?

I wandered back to my room, half in a daze, my stomach knotted as if I were hungover, even though I hadn't drunk a drop the night before. As I sank down onto my bed—my oh-so-empty bed—I tried to tell myself that it was no big deal. That this was how it was supposed to work from the very beginning. That I should be grateful he saved me the awkwardness of a morning after good-bye.

But all the rationalities in the world couldn't stanch the ache in my heart. Because no matter what I had intended, the reality was, I liked him. I really, really liked him. And I never would have gone through with any of this—despite Stephanie's urging—if I'd realized it would end like this.

Did he not feel any of what I had felt? Had it all been an act—just to get in my pants? Or had I said something at some point to make him change his mind about me? Did I talk in my sleep? Snore really loudly? Something—anything—to make him bolt for the door?

Disappointment, mixed with hurt, welled inside of me as my mind tried to comb through everything that had happened the night before. Had he planned this from the start? Had I completely missed the signs? But no. He'd been a total gentleman. He'd asked me repeatedly if I was sure I wanted this, clearly ready to back down—to sleep on the couch—if I'd shown any hesitation. Not to mention afterward, we had cuddled all night long. Why would he bother, if he was just after the sex?

And if it wasn't just about sex, why not a second date? Why wouldn't this smart, interesting, cool guy want to see me again? Or hell, at least give me the courtesy of a lie, a promise of a phone call that would never come. Wasn't I at least deserving of that?

At least now I knew what the *A* stood for on his arm. *Asshole*.

I sucked in a breath, trying to regain my sanity. The night had happened, I tried to rationalize. The deed was done. No tears or crazy revenge plots were going to change anything now. In fact, it would probably be best just to chalk the whole thing up to a learning experience and move on. After, of course, vowing to never listen to Stephanie again.

I glanced over at the phone, charging on my nightstand, having the sudden urge to call Ryan and then hating myself for even thinking it. After all, what would he say to me if I told him how stupid I'd been? That I deserved what I got? That I was an idiot? A slut? That my sister would never do this kind of thing?

I shook my head, feeling a pang of loneliness deep in my gut. I considered waking Stephanie and telling her what had happened, but I already knew she wouldn't understand. In fact, she'd probably see this as a perfect opportunity for me to now hunt down guy number two.

I sighed, my eyes falling once again to the black jacket, hanging on the back of the chair. *His* jacket. In his rush to leave, he'd left his jacket behind. I stared at it for a moment, wondering if throwing it on the fire pit in the back yard and having a little bonfire would make me feel better.

But no. I wasn't the kind of girl who did that, even if the man in question deserved it. I would rise above. Return the jacket, assuming he'd left some kind of ID inside to help me locate him. (Bet he was wishing he left his phone number now!)

I slid off the bed and began digging through the pockets,

seeing if Mr. One-Night Stand left the dude equivalent of a glass slipper behind.

It didn't take long for me to find the wallet, cradled in the inside pocket. With shaking fingers, I pulled it out and flipped it open. Inside I found a few singles, credit cards, a Massachusetts driver's license belonging to a Jake MacDonald, twenty-eight years old. I sighed. So much for that plan. Even if I wanted to return this to him, I didn't have any idea where he currently lived.

Sliding the license back into the wallet, I pulled out the final piece of paper from the billfold, unfolded it and started to read . . .

. . . and almost dropped the letter.

Oh. My. God.

I stared down at the letter, my eyes filled with horror.

No.

This could not be happening.

This could *so* not be happening.

I stared at the letter again, as if reading it over for the tenth time would make the words change on the page. But they remained stubbornly in place. Black and white. And impossible to argue.

It was a letter of employment.

A letter of employment from Mac's new employer.

A letter of employment from Mac's new employer, News 9 San Diego.

A letter of employment from Mac's new employer, News 9 San Diego, where I currently was employed, too.

Yes, it seemed the very man who had waltzed in and out of my life in just one night had already signed on for a much more permanent gig—as my TV station's newest videographer.

This was so not good.

ten

BETH

"Morning, sunshine," I remarked wryly as Stephanie half-walked/half-stumbled into our kitchen two hours later, wrapped in an overly fluffy pink terrycloth bathrobe. Her normally sexily tousled hair was now mussed and snarled and black smudges ringed her blue eyes, giving her the look of a rabid raccoon. I glanced at my phone. "Or should I say afternoon?"

"You should say nothing," she grunted. "Unless it's 'Do you want coffee?' I could handle 'Do you want coffee?' Maybe."

"*Do* you want coffee?"

"You're really asking me that?" Stephanie slumped into the chair across from me, her head plopping down onto the table. I rose to my feet, walking over to the counter and grabbing two News 9 mugs, pouring freshly brewed java (my second pot of the day) into each. Looking at my room-mate now I was pretty glad I'd agreed to be designated driver last night. Otherwise I'd be enjoying this humiliation sundae with a hangover on top.

After adding a generous dollop of pumpkin spice creamer

to each cup, I walked over to the table and handed one to Stephanie before sitting back down across from her with my own mug.

"Oh my God, you seriously win roommate of the year," she muttered, taking a long slug, then setting the mug precariously on the edge of the table. I dove to save it from crashing to the floor, setting it back in front of her. She sighed heavily. "Like first place. Like, you should have an actual trophy and stuff."

I snorted. "Great. I'll clear a spot next to all my imaginary Emmys."

Stephanie nodded absently, staring into her coffee with a blank expression on her face. "I am never, ever drinking again. Ever."

I'd heard this one before. "Whatever you say."

"No. Seriously, I mean it this time." She sighed. "Well, besides next Tuesday. I have a date with Rob next Tuesday—the bartender from Tito's? Guy makes a killer Mexican martini. Extra olives, just how I like it." She took another sip of coffee, this time miraculously managing not to spill any on her robe. Then she set down her cup and studied me with a cockeyed look. "But enough about me and my pathetic spiral into alcoholism and misery. I want to hear about your night. Did you have fun? I seem to recall a few fun-sounding noises, coming suspiciously from the vicinity of your bedroom . . ."

My face prickled with heat. I grabbed my own coffee cup in both hands, bringing it to my lips, as if it were a shield to protect me from the impending inquisition. But sadly, I knew in my heart, even the power of pumpkin spice couldn't stop a rabid reporter like Stephanie from getting the scoop. I could stall, but eventually resistance would prove futile.

"It started out fine," I admitted at last. "Great, actually." I bit my lower lip, setting my coffee down. "Until this morning, that is."

"Oh?" Stephanie tilted her head in question, the oh-so-innocent way I'd seen her do countless times when trying to get her interviewees to relax and spill the beans. "What happened? Did he take off quick or something?"

"Let's just say the Road Runner's got nothing on this guy."
Elbows propped on the table, I cupped my chin in my hands
and sighed deeply. "I woke up and he was gone. He left a note,
but no phone number. No email. Hell, I'm half-convinced he
wiped away his fingerprints before making his exit, just to
make sure I wouldn't be able to track him down."

Though he did forget his jacket, I reminded myself quietly. But I wasn't ready to go there just yet.

I chewed on my lower lip, frustration washing over me
once again. I'd gone over the entire night in my mind, countless times throughout the morning, and I still didn't have a
clue as to what had gone wrong. Everything had been so
perfect. We'd clicked, we'd connected, we'd freaking spooned
all night long like we were in love. How could a night that
felt so special to me mean absolutely nothing to him? Was
this just a *Men Are From Mars* or *He's Just Not That Into You*
kind of thing? Or was there some piece to this puzzle I was
missing? Like . . . A horrifying thought niggled at the back
of my brain. What if he was married? I cringed. I so did not
want to go there.

"Dude! What's with the long face?" Stephanie demanded,
interrupting my worried thoughts. "Don't you see? This is
perfect! Absolutely perfect."

I raised an eyebrow. "Are you still drunk?"

She rolled her eyes. "Seriously, Beth, this is what you
wanted, remember? This is why you went to the club with
me in the first place! One night of hot sex, no strings attached.
And now, bonus! It's not even awkward. You don't have to
give the throbbing love lance the boot. You don't have to deal
with some stage five clinger, texting you desperate love
poetry 24-7 until you're forced to block him on Facebook."
She shuddered. "Instead, you can just chalk this up to a night
of awesome and move on with your life." She reached across
the table, holding up her hand for a high five. "Forget the
roommate trophy. I'm getting you a dirty slut one. Which, I
might add, is way cooler than some silly Emmy."

I groaned, leaning back in my chair and staring up at the

ceiling. "You don't understand," I protested. "I mean, trust me, I wish it were that simple. But it's not. I can't just move on and forget about him. Even if I wanted to."

Stephanie lowered her hand and narrowed her eyes. "Elizabeth White. Do not *even* tell me you've somehow managed to develop feelings for this dude after just one night."

I closed my eyes. My mind flashed back to Mac, wrapping me into his arms. His hot breath searing my shoulder as he cuddled me close, taking care to pull the blanket up over me so I wouldn't be cold. Then I shook my head. *Don't even go there, Beth.*

I turned back to my roommate. "No. I mean I literally can't. Look." I rummaged through my pocket and pulled out the employment letter I'd discovered in Mac's jacket, presenting it to her. She took it from me and scanned it quickly, then looked up, confused.

"I don't understand. Who's Jake MacDonald?"

"MacDonald," I emphasized. "As in *Mac*Donald. As in, 'You can call me Mac' Donald."

Stephanie's jaw dropped. "Hold on a second. You're telling me that your one-night throbbing love lance is going to be working permanently at News 9?" She narrowed her eyes suspiciously. "Did you know that before you hooked up?"

"Of course I didn't know that!" I cried, exasperated. "Do you think I'm a moron? He left his jacket behind. I found it in his wallet."

Stephanie pursed her full lips. "Wow. Well, this changes everything."

"No kidding. I mean, how can I even go to work now—knowing he'll be there? What if he goes and tells everyone what we did? What if they all think I'm some horrible slut? God, I have half a mind to quit. 'Sorry Richard,'" I quipped, making up my resignation speech to my boss on the fly, "'I know I have six months left on my contract, but I didn't take into account you hiring a guy I hooked up with. As you can guess, I couldn't possibly stay.'"

Stephanie rolled her eyes again. "And they call *me* a drama queen." She shook her head, her black hair swishing from side to side. "Come on, Beth. Let's not overreact. I mean, God, if I quit every job where I hooked up with a fellow employee or four? I'd be perpetually unemployed."

I stared down into my empty coffee mug, deciding not to comment on that. While sex with strangers might be Stephanie's typical MO, it certainly wasn't mine. Besides, what was that ugly analogy about not crapping where you eat?

But it was too late now.

Uninvited tears pricked at the corners of my eyes. This was so unfair.

"Oh, sweetie." My roommate's expression softened. She leaned across the table, placing her hands on my shoulders and giving me a comforting squeeze. "Do not even. You're awesome. He's an asshole. He doesn't deserve even a single one of your precious tears."

"I know," I sniffled, feeling like an idiot. "I know, I know. It just . . . sucks, you know? Of all the newsrooms in all the world . . ."

Stephanie pursed her lips, seeming to ponder this. Then her face brightened. "Well, think of it this way," she declared. "You know he's not working the morning shift. Your photog Javier would have totally given you a heads-up if he was changing shifts. Which means Mac Daddy must be on days or evenings." She nodded her head enthusiastically. "Which means you'll probably never even see the guy, save for the News 9 holiday party. And at that point, I'll make it my personal mission to get you too drunk to care."

I laughed, despite myself. "Maybe they'll end up assigning him to you."

"I hope so." My roommate's eyes gleamed wickedly. "'Cause payback is a bitch, Mac Daddy. No one hurts my little love muffin. Not on my watch!" She held up her hand again in a high five. This time I didn't leave her hanging.

She was right, I told myself as I brought my mug to the sink. Plenty of people worked at News 9 that I barely ever saw. It would be no big deal. I never had to talk to him. Except to return the jacket, of course. Though maybe I should just leave it at the front desk. Even better.

And that was the one satisfying thought in all of this mess. At least I wouldn't be surprised to bump into Mac Monday morning. I had time to mentally prepare.

He, on the other hand, was in for quite a shock.

eleven

MAC

It was Monday morning and I was pulling my SUV into the News 9 parking lot for my first day of work. The day was beautiful. Perfect temperature with a warm sun beaming down on my pale-ass New England skin. Back home it was probably snowing. My sister was always bragging that San Diego had the best weather in the world. I was beginning to believe it.

Ashley and I had spent most of yesterday on the beach, making sandcastles and dodging warm water waves. She'd laughed so much that she'd given herself a stomachache by the time we headed back to the car. Though, in hindsight, perhaps it was the mountains of ice cream she'd consumed that were partially to blame. Either way, I couldn't remember the last time she'd looked so happy and content—and, bonus, she hadn't asked about her mother once the entire afternoon. For the first time since we'd arrived, I found myself thinking that maybe this had been the right move after all.

If only I didn't have this smothering black cloud hanging over my head. Regret worse than any hangover, eating away at me without mercy. I tried to push the whole thing from my mind, chalk it up to a huge mistake and move on. But try as I might, the night kept replaying itself over and over on endless loop and I didn't know how to make it stop.

I should have never let my sister and Joe talk me into going out in the first place. I should have stuck to my guns. Seriously, this was why I had determined not to get involved in all this dating shit to begin with. From now on, there would be no more bars, no clubs, no temptations.

God, she had been such a temptation.

And that was the worst part. Even with all the rationalizations in the world, I still couldn't manage to get her out of my head all weekend long. No matter what I tried to focus on, my traitorous mind kept wandering back to her long, smooth legs, wrapping around my waist, her soft breasts pillowing against my chest. Her hands, running up and down my stomach—and other places. Her wet, pink mouth, pressing against my own.

Goddamn it.

I rammed the vehicle in park, then opened the door and stepped out of the SUV. My new workplace loomed in front of me, tall, gray, intimidating, and I wondered, not for the first time, what it was going to be like to work there. Would it be challenging? Interesting? Would my new coworkers be cool? Or would I find only more backstabbing snakes like the ones I'd left behind in Beantown?

Sadly, that seemed more likely. It was still TV news, after all.

Before I had reluctantly accepted the job offer at News 9 I had considered getting out of the biz altogether. To leave it all behind. To start fresh with something less vile. Unfortunately, after talking to various recruiters and conducting a slew of Internet job searches, I couldn't find a single opportunity outside my field. I knew TV. And only TV.

Not that I didn't like being a videographer. Even after six years in the business I still got a thrill out of the whole thing. The adrenaline rush of shooting and editing a breaking news story, the coolness of seeing your work broadcasted on every TV—you couldn't get that anywhere else.

No, it wasn't the craft I didn't enjoy. It was the slime. The scum. The people of the TV news world. People like my ex-wife.

I grabbed my backpack and slammed the SUV door shut behind me. Taking a deep breath I readied myself to face whatever the new job might throw my way. But just as I'd almost convinced myself that things could be different here, I was blindsided by an all-too familiar face crossing the parking lot. I stared, unable to breathe. It couldn't be.

But it was. It was her. It couldn't be anyone but her.

Sheer panic warred with sudden, complete arousal as I watched her approach, my knees threatening to buckle out from under me. What the hell was she doing here?

I assessed her quickly. Her once flowing blond curls were now restrained in a severe knot at the back of her head and the scrap of a dress she'd worn to the club had been replaced by a smart, baby blue suit jacket. The skirt she wore, however, was still too short, in my opinion, to be legal and soon I found my eyes involuntarily running up and down the length of her bare legs, just as my hands had done only two nights before. Oh God. I felt my jeans tighten as I remembered all too well the satin smoothness of those thighs. Against my hands. Against my mouth. The mewing sound she'd made as I moved across her core. The sweetness she left on my tongue.

Down, boy.

I shook my head, trying to clear my thoughts and focus on what was unfolding in front of me. She was getting closer. She was definitely heading my way. And for some reason she didn't look half as surprised to see me as I was to see her.

Then I remembered: the wallet.

I had realized I'd left my jacket with my wallet behind just as I'd gotten back to my sister's house and attempted to pay the cabbie. But I'd decided it'd be easier just to cancel my credit cards and apply for a new California license than go back and grovel for its return. I'd figured since my license had my old Boston address on it she wouldn't be able to track me down. I'd conveniently forgotten about the letter of employment.

I swallowed hard. She was close now. And I was a deer in the headlights, not sure what to do. Half of me wanted to run. To turn around and dive back into the SUV and speed away. But of course that was stupid. Not to mention fucking cowardly.

Come on, Mac. Grow a pair. Take the jacket, make up some lame apology, and you'll never have to see her again.

"Hey, Mac!" she called in greeting, giving me a small smile as she stepped into my bubble. A calm, friendly smile. Almost too calm, too friendly. Was she planning on confronting me for taking off like I had? Or would she pretend it hadn't happened, just to avoid the awkwardness? After all, this wasn't all me, I reminded myself. She'd wanted to keep it casual, too. To get back at her ex or whatever. She probably didn't want to see me as much as I didn't want to see her.

Except . . . I *did* want to see her, I suddenly realized. In fact, against everything sensible inside of me, I was pretty damn happy to set eyes on her again. Which was completely stupid, but evidently par for the course when it came to this girl. There was just something about her. Something . . . nice.

She doesn't want you, Mac, I scolded myself. *And you certainly don't have room in your life for her.*

"Um, hey," I said, forcing my voice to stay casual. As if it was all no big deal. "I didn't expect to see you here."

I watched as, sure enough, she reached into her bag and pulled out my jacket. "You left this at my house," she said. Her voice was still calm and friendly, but from this closer proximity I could see her hands were shaking a little. Not so calm as she wanted me to think, I realized. For some reason the thought made me feel a little better.

I reached out to accept the jacket, our fingers accidentally connecting as they made the exchange. A zap of electricity shot through me and I involuntarily jerked my hand away then glanced over at her, wondering if she had felt it, too. From the startled look on her face, I decided she had and I had to hide a smile. Hey, at least it wasn't just me.

"Thanks," I said with forced bravado. "But seriously, you didn't have to come all the way down here."

She gave me an odd look I couldn't quite decipher. Then she followed it with a small embarrassed smile. "Oh. Well, I was . . . in the neighborhood. No big deal."

I tucked the jacket under my arm. "Well, I appreciate it," I said lamely.

She didn't reply, just looked at me and the silence stretched out between us, long and suffocating. Shuffling from foot to foot, I wondered if I should say something else. Like apologize or something, for leaving like I had. But no. That had been what she'd wanted. I'd done her a favor. And now it was best to get the hell out of there before she managed to unnerve me further. This was my first day on the job. I didn't need to be filling out HR paperwork with a raging hard-on and a gut full of regret.

"I've got to get inside," I told her. "But thanks for the jacket. And, uh, maybe I'll see you around."

Her expression stayed neutral, but I caught a flicker of something unhappy in her eyes and it sent a pang of guilt rocketing through me all over again. But no. I wasn't the asshole here, I reminded myself. We were both adults and we'd both gotten what we'd wanted. Now it was time to cut the cord and walk away.

I extended my hand, meeting her eyes with my own, as if daring her to take it. She looked taken aback for a second, then went for it, closing her hand over mine. I gave her a firm shake, trying not to think about what she looked like with no clothes on as we clung together a second too long— skin to skin.

She yanked her hand away. "So yeah. Anyway. Uh, see you later," she stammered, her cheeks now flaming red. Before I could respond, she turned, her heels clicking on the pavement as she crossed the parking lot with rapid steps, putting distance between us. I watched her go, feeling the inexplicable desire for her to turn around and give me one last look. Like you always see people do in the movies. But, of course, she didn't. And why should she? This wasn't the beginning of a beautiful friendship. This was good-bye forever.

Which should have made me happy. Relieved. So why

was there suddenly a pang of loneliness stabbing me in the gut instead? Why was it taking all my willpower not to call her back and ask her if we could have another chance?

"Are you Jake MacDonald?"

I whirled around at the sound of the gruff voice behind me. A bearded Latino man wearing jeans and a plaid button-down was approaching, a coffee in each hand.

"Yeah," I said, forcing a hard swallow as I turned my attention back to the job. "You can call me Mac."

He smiled with crooked teeth. "I'm Javier," he informed me. "Morning show photog. I'm supposed to show you around." He pushed a coffee into my hands. "And, of course, give you your first welcome cup of News 9 joe. Tastes like shit, but it's loaded with caffeine—something you'll need around here."

"Thanks. Nice to meet you." I took the coffee, then held out my free hand. Javier grabbed it with a firm grip. After we shook, I took a long slug. He was right. Not that tasty but damn strong—just the way I liked it. I started to relax. She was gone. And now I could turn my focus to what was really important. My new job. My new, clean, uncomplicated life.

"Well," Javier said. "I'd hoped by coming out here I'd be the first to greet you. But it looks like Beth has beat me to it."

I choked as my coffee went down the wrong pipe.

"Jesus." Javier laughed. "I know it ain't Starbucks, but it's not that bad, is it?"

"Beth?" I managed to choke out, my entire world sliding out from under me with one single name.

So much for focusing on my new job.

"Oh, sorry, I meant Elizabeth White." The photographer waved a hand in the direction of the parking lot where Beth was getting into her car. "I just assumed she'd introduced herself."

"She . . . works here? Here at News 9?" I found myself blurting out, all Captain Obvious. My mind flashed back to Beth's weird smile. The way she'd said she'd been in the neighborhood. The way I'd completely not put two and two together.

"Sure. She's a reporter. She and I do mornings together."

Frustration shot through me like a bullet and I raked a hand through my hair as my mind tried to comprehend his words. Beth worked here. The girl I'd slept with and taken off on worked here. Here at my new job.

And . . . so much for that whole new, clean, uncomplicated life thing.

I screwed up my face. All this time I'd been deluding myself, thinking my new job—clear across the country—would serve as an escape hatch from all the drama I'd dealt with back in Boston. And yet, now, somehow, I'd brought it all upon myself all over again—in just one night. That had to be a record, even for me. Would she tell everyone what happened? Did I already have a reputation with my new colleagues before ever stepping through the front door?

I realized Javier was laughing. "Yeah, that was my reaction when I first met her, too," he teased, mistaking my look. "Hell, man, if I wasn't twice her age and happily married . . ." He shook his head, taking a sip of coffee. "Anyway, enough about her. You ready to go inside? Get the lay of the land?"

I closed my eyes for a moment, forcing myself to reset. Then I opened them again. "Sure," I said, through clenched teeth. What else could I say? I needed this job. For Ashley's sake if nothing else. And I wasn't about to let some one-night fuckup ruin my little girl's second chance. "Lead the way."

twelve

BETH

I slipped into my car, my face aflame and my stomach twisting into knots. I knew it'd be hard to see Mac again, but I had no idea just how hard it would actually be. To take in his long, lean frame, his broad shoulders, his piercing blue eyes. To force myself to stay cool, calm, collected and not throw myself at him all over again. But that would be beyond stupid. After all, he'd made it pretty damn clear he wasn't interested. And I needed to retain what scraps of dignity I had left if I was going to be able to find a way to be coworkers from here on out.

I frowned, thinking back on the encounter. I guess I'd thought at the very least he'd offer up some kind of lame apology. Or maybe an excuse or something. Didn't I deserve *that* at the very least? Even a "Thank you for letting me crash at your place" would have been something.

But no. All I got was a "See you around" and a lame-ass handshake.

I closed my eyes, my mind falling back to the handshake in question. From the very same hand that had explored every inch of my naked body just two nights before, the very same fingers that had made me scream—now they might as well have belonged to a stranger.

They *did* belong to a stranger, I scolded myself. As Stephanie kept reminding me, that had been the whole idea.

But now they also belonged to my new coworker.

With a heavy sigh, I reached down to insert my key into the ignition. I'd been at work since four A.M. and was very ready to go home and crawl into bed for my regularly scheduled midmorning nap. But before I could pull out of my parking lot space, my phone vibrated on my lap. A blocked number, which meant it was probably work.

I put the phone to my ear. "Elizabeth White speaking."

"Elizabeth!" my news director, Richard, barked into the phone. "Are you still in the building? I wanted to catch you before you left for the day."

I bit my lower lip, looking around the parking lot. I could tell him I'd already pulled out—he'd never know. But no. Then I'd just wonder all day what he'd wanted from me.

"Yeah, I'm still here."

"Great. Come swing by my office. I want to talk to you for a minute."

"Why? What's up?" I asked, before I could check myself. When the big boss tells you to come to his office, you didn't ask why. You just went.

"It'll only take a minute," he added, then hung up without explaining.

I stuffed the phone in my purse, my hands shaking a little as my nerves tensed. What did he want from me? Had I done something wrong? My mind raced over the stories I'd covered the past week, trying to think of anything that might have warranted a meeting with the news director, but I couldn't think of a single thing. In fact, if anything, I'd been feeling pretty good about my performance of late. Even when covering inane feature stories like the Lemon Grove craft fair, I'd managed to keep a positive attitude and I hadn't missed any of my live hits. Hell, I'd even gotten a few viewer fan emails over the last week.

So what could Richard want from me?

I waited until Mac and Javier entered the building before getting out of the car. Didn't need to run into him twice in one day. As I headed across the parking lot, I wondered what he would think when he discovered that I worked here. I knew I probably should have broken the news myself when I'd returned the jacket—that had been my plan originally, anyway.

But seeing him again had disconcerted me so much, the words had stuck in my throat and I had walked away without playing my hand. And who could blame me, really? No matter what Stephanie said, I knew this was going to be so damn awkward. And a lot harder than I cared to admit. How was I going to work in the same building with him day in and day out? A walking, talking reminder of my big mistake.

I shook my head, trying to swap my focus. There would be time for me to stew over my love life—or lack of it—later. Right now I needed to stay professional and find Richard. Find out what I did wrong and grovel appropriately to appease him. So as I pushed through the newsroom door, I fought also to push Mac from my mind.

The inside of News 9 looked like something out of Tomorrowland at Disney World. A sci-fi nightmare dressed in neon lights and littered with TVs strategically placed on every available surface. I guess the idea was to create something that appeared bustling and busy, but in truth, it usually looked more like an epileptic seizure waiting to happen.

As I crossed the newsroom, passing producers and writers preparing for the noon broadcast, I spotted Joy Justice back at her desk. Our station's main anchor had been "on vacation" for the last three months and must have just returned. And while she had announced her destination as Cabo San Lucas for a little "fun in the sun," rumor had it was really for a little nip and a tuck. Sure enough, even from here I could tell something was different about her face. I shuddered a little, trying to imagine going under the knife. I think I'd rather deal with wrinkles—even if they did mean possible death to my on-camera career.

Shaking the thought from my head, I made my way to

Richard's office and knocked tentatively on the door. The news director glanced up from the call he was on, and motioned for me to come in. I sat down in the chair opposite his oversized, over-cluttered desk and tried not to squirm. Looking down at my hands, I realized they were shaking and shoved them under my legs before he noticed

"I don't give a shit what that PR hack told you," Richard was yelling into the phone, raking a hand through his thick brown hair. His dark brown eyes suggested that the fifty-something-year-old news director might have been quite handsome back in the day. But years of job-related stress had left him with a haggard, worn look. "You get in there and you get that interview and you get it in time for the five o'clock newscast or your ass is out the door!"

He slammed down the receiver. Then looked up at me. "Sorry about that."

"Uh, yeah, no problem," I squeaked, now more nervous than ever.

"Damn Stephanie," Richard growled, shuffling through some papers on his desk. "San Diego is the twenty-eighth largest television market in the country. And I have interns who could do a better job."

I gnawed on my lower lip, wondering if I should speak up for my poor roommate. I was probably already in trouble for something and arguing her good points would likely only serve to aggravate him further. But still . . .

"Stephanie's a good reporter," I tried. "She's just . . ."

I trailed off. Just what? Hungover? Still drunk? Despite her promises of never drinking again, my roommate hadn't gotten home from the bars until after three A.M. last night, just as I was heading out the door to work.

"That's sweet." Richard waved me off, pulling a piece of paper from the stack and filing it away in a manila envelope. "But do you know how many live shots she missed last week?" He gave me a smug look. "Three."

Wait, what? I raised my eyebrows in surprise. Missing live shots—your time slot to report during the local newscast— was pretty much a mortal sin around here. And Stephanie had missed three? That didn't sound like my roommate. I mean, sure, she could be a flake, but she was usually very serious about her career. I needed to talk to her when I got home—make sure everything was okay.

I realized Richard was looking at me intently. I squirmed under his gaze. "Uh, yeah?" I stammered. "Sorry. You wanted to see me?"

He nodded. "How long have you been with us, Elizabeth?"

"Uh, just over two years."

"And you've been on the morning show the entire time?"

I bit back a frown. He knew that. He had to have known that. What was he getting at here? "Yes, sir."

He leaned forward, meeting my eyes with his own steely ones. "Do you *like* the morning shift, Elizabeth?"

I swallowed hard, my mind racing with what he expected me to say. *Why yes, Richard, I love the morning shift. Especially the part where I get to wake up at three A.M. every day to go to work. And my social life has simply been off the hook since I started going to bed at seven thirty each night, just to get enough sleep. And as for doing live shots in the pitch dark that even the earliest commuters sleep through? Dream come true, boss. Dream. Come. True.*

"It's been a great experience," I declared with as much bravado as I could muster. "The morning show crew is wonderful and I consider myself very blessed to be part of the team."

Richard rolled his eyes. "In other words it totally sucks and you want off, ASAP, correct?"

"Uh." I stared at him. "I mean . . ."

"It's okay," he said with a smirk. "I know the morning shift isn't exactly Glamour City. I worked overnights for ten years back when I first started producing and I'm pretty sure I was a zombie the entire decade." He shook his head, as if remembering. Then he looked up. "How would you like a change?"

My mouth dropped open. "A change," I repeated. "You mean, like a shift change?" And here I thought he was going to yell at me. Instead he was promoting me?

"I'm taking your little roommate off air for a while," Richard explained. "She can write copy for the newscasts until she gets her act together." He leaned forward again, a smile on his face. "And I'd like you to take her spot reporting for the evening news."

I stared at him, speechless. This was the moment I'd been waiting for since I first walked through the station's front door. A chance to report during the day, when people were actually awake and watching. A chance to live a normal life with a normal schedule. This was a huge career boost. This was a dream come true. This was—

A huge, huge blow for my roommate.

"What about Stephanie?" I found myself asking.

His smile faded. "Look, Elizabeth, I'm running a top market newsroom here, not a little league team. Not everyone gets a trophy. If you don't want your big break because of some misplaced loyalty you have to a girl who doesn't even care enough to show up to work on time, that's fine. Trust me, I have plenty of other opportunists clawing at my door. Stephanie's off the shift, whether you replace her or I get someone else."

"Right." I swallowed hard, my heart pounding a mile a minute. "I'm sorry. I get it. And yes, I'll take it. Of course I'll take it. Thank you."

Richard nodded knowingly, as if he'd predicted my answer all along. And of course he had, I realized, feeling a little sick to my stomach. I tried to tell myself that Stephanie would have done the same thing in my position. That I would *want* her to do the same thing. But, in truth, it didn't make me feel much better.

"Excellent," he declared. "You start tomorrow." He paused, then, "Make sure you show up on time," he added. "You have one month to prove to me you can do this before I make the job permanent. Screw this up and you'll not only lose this shift, but your entire position here at News 9. There's no going back."

"What?" I cried before I could stop myself. The idea of losing my job was terrifying. As much as I hated the morning show, it had always been somewhat safe and secure. If I got let go now, what would I do? It wasn't as if reporter jobs were easy to come by, especially in good markets like San Diego.

"Having second thoughts?" Richard asked, raising an eyebrow. "If you think you aren't ready, it's better you let me know now."

"No!" I blurted, horrified he might change his mind. "I can do it. I swear. It'll be great. I won't let you down."

Richard's expression softened. "I know you won't," he assured me. "Or I wouldn't have made you the offer. You're a good reporter, Elizabeth. And I'm looking forward to seeing great things from you."

"Yes, sir. Thank you, sir," I babbled as I rose from my seat, attempting a graceful exit on legs made of Jell-O.

"Oh, and one other thing," he added, just as I reached the door. I froze.

"Yes?" I squeaked out, turning back to him, my heart in my throat all over again. What now? Did he want me to sign the new contract in blood or something?

He laughed. "You can wipe that look of terror off your face. It's nothing bad. It's just, I don't know if you heard, but I hired a new photographer. Jake MacDonald out of Boston. Supposedly he's really good—won a ton of Emmys. Today's his first day."

I stared at him, my pulse thrumming madly. "Oh, yeah?" I managed to squeak out. Why was he telling me this? Why did I need to know this? Warning bells began to go off inside my head.

New position . . . New photographer . . .

Surely fate wasn't *that* cruel.

"I'm assigning you two to work together," Richard announced cheerfully, sending any faith I ever had in karmic justice crashing and burning into the ether.

I stumbled backward, only managing to knock a spider plant off its stand by the door. It crashed to the floor, dirt flying everywhere. Face flaming now, I dropped to my knees to pick it up. I could feel Richard's stare burning into me as I set it back on its table.

"Are you okay?" he asked, sounding a little suspicious. "Is there some problem with you working with Jake?"

"No problem," I managed to squeak out somehow. "I mean, how could there be? I don't even . . . know the guy."

"Right. Of course." Richard laughed. "Sorry. For a moment there, I thought you were going to say he was your ex-boyfriend or something. The look on your face!" He shook his head. "Leave the plant. I'll get maintenance in here. You go home, get some sleep, kiddo. You've got a big day tomorrow."

I nodded, making my way to the door, careful not to knock anything else from its place with my hasty exit. "Thank you, sir. You won't regret it."

Once I'd exited the office, I leaned against the hallway wall, sucking in a deep breath. Then I forced my wooden legs to walk me back to my car.

After all, as Richard said, I had a big day tomorrow.

And he didn't know the half of it.

thirteen

BETH

*O*h Beth, you feel so good. . . ."
    Strong hands circled my waist from behind, slipping beneath the hem of my shirt and skimming my belly with deft strokes. Closing my eyes, I leaned back, moaning as soft curves melted against solid steel. I could feel his desire, pressing hard into my back, unapologetic, unrelenting, strong.

    "You don't feel so bad yourself," I managed to mutter as his hands continued their exploration, traveling upward, cupping my breasts, calloused fingers circling the tips until they hardened to sharp peaks. I bit my lower lip, squirming as the ache pooled in stomach. My legs clenched together, begging for release.

    His amused laughter rang in my ears. "Hang on now, princess, that's my job," he scolded. Then he lowered one hand, his touch searing across my stomach before slipping between my thighs.

    Oh God.

    I moaned, involuntarily rocking against his hand, desperate to relieve the exquisite torture his touch had invoked.

It'd been so long since I'd felt this way. Too damn long.
Maybe I'd never felt this way before at all.

Now his thrusts matched mine. Harder and harder,
higher and higher. My vision spinning, my fingertips numb.
My back arching, my head thrown back. My hands grabbing
fistfuls of—

Sand?

I jerked awake, the sharp piercing ring of a cell phone
rudely breaking through my dreamland. Mind still foggy, I
struggled to sit up, blinking my bleary eyes to clear them.
It was then that I realized where I was. Where I'd fallen
asleep. Where I'd been having the most erotic dream ever—
right out in the open in front of God and everyone.

And not quietly, either, judging from the disturbed faces
of my fellow beachcombers. My face flushed. Oh dear.

I'd originally swung by the beach on my way home after
my conversation with Richard, hoping a quick swim would
alleviate some of the tension headache brought on by today's
events. But I hadn't even made it to the water. After spreading
my towel out on the sand, my heavy eyes had simply closed.
And now, glancing at my still ringing cell phone, I realized
the two minutes of shut-eye I'd promised myself had stretched
to two hours.

I pressed the accept button. "Hello?" I asked, still groggy,
after bringing the phone to my ear. "Elizabeth White
speaking."

"Beth." The assignment editor's voice barked on the other
end. "We have breaking news. Can you work this afternoon?"

I clutched the phone, suddenly wide-awake. Breaking news?
They wanted me, Beth White, to work breaking news?

Of course they do, you idiot. You're a dayside reporter now,
remember?

My heart fluttered excitedly in my chest. My hands gripped
the phone tightly between my fingers. When Richard had first
offered me the promotion it had seemed so unreal. And I was
half-convinced on the way home that I was going to wake up
and find out it was all some crazy dream. But no. This was
really happening. Right here. Right now.

There was breaking news. And they wanted me to cover it.

"Of course," I said, trying to sound as professional as possible, nervous adrenaline spiking through my veins. "Where do you need me?"

"There's a fire in East County. At least one home involved. We don't know much else," the assignment editor informed me. "We'll have you head down there and check it out. If there's anything good, Richard wants a package and a live shot for the six o'clock news."

"No problem," I declared with a grin. This was awesome. So awesome. "You want me to head to the station now?"

"No. There's no time. We'll have the new guy—Jake MacDonald—swing by your house and pick you up in the live truck. He's maybe five minutes out."

My smile faded. Right. Jake MacDonald. Jake MacDonald, swinging by my house. The very same house that he'd ravaged my naked body in only two nights before. The very same house he'd vacated without a trace first thing the next morning.

Hell, at least he wouldn't need GPS . . .

I swallowed hard, the thrill of breaking news suddenly blanketed by sheer dread. Sure, I'd already known they'd be pairing me with Mac. But I guess I'd hoped to have twenty-four hours to get used to the idea. Maybe even find a way to meet up with him for coffee before our first official shift tomorrow morning to discuss the whole thing. We could have talked it out, made jokes about karma, and promised not to let the awkwardness affect our work.

But that, evidently, wasn't in the cards. The news waited for no one. And I knew asking for another photog during a breaking news situation was only going to make me sound like a diva. I had one month to prove to Richard that I deserved this promotion. And no one—not even Morning After MacDonald—was going to mess that up for me.

"Beth? Are you still there?" the assignment editor asked, sounding impatient.

"Yeah, yeah, sorry," I sputtered. "Tell Mac to head on over. I'll be waiting."

"Mac?"

My face flamed. "Sorry. Jake MacDonald. I . . . I . . . Anyway . . . Yeah."

I hung up the phone, cheeks still burning as I tossed it into my beach bag. As I pulled my arm away, I accidentally brushed it against the canvas and let out a yelp as pain seared through me. I looked down, my eyes widening as I realized the aftereffects of my accidental sunbathing: my skin reduced to a crimson colored mess. I cringed. This was going to feel awesome up close and personal to a raging fire. Not to mention the boiled lobster look was sure to be a real hit with the viewers back home.

Seriously, I could not catch a break if one was lobbed directly at my freaking head.

But there was nothing I could do about it now and I was running out of time, so I gathered up my things and started the five-minute walk back to the house. Stephanie wouldn't be back for a few hours, which was another bummer since I'd wanted to discuss the whole shift change thing with her—hoping to soften the blow a little. I could have called her, I supposed, but she was probably busy getting ready for the nightly newscast. And this was definitely something that would be better discussed face-to-face anyway.

I wasn't stupid: I knew there was no way she wasn't going to be pissed—I mean, who wouldn't be? But, at the same time, I had to make her understand somehow that it wasn't my fault. That my promotion had nothing to do with her demotion. That if it wasn't me, Richard would have assigned someone else to take her shift. It was just an unlucky coincidence that I was first on his list.

Yeah, maybe it was better I had time to work on this little pep talk.

Beeeeep!

A loud honk startled me back to the present. I looked up, surprised to see a News 9 live truck pulled up in front of my driveway, Mac in the driver's seat. He was here already? I'd hoped to at least have time to change out of my bikini.

My breath hitched as I caught sight of his face behind

the windshield. Seriously, why did he have to be so freaking hot? I mean, that rugged jawline, those piercing eyes, that hint of stubble whispering across his cheeks—what that stubble felt like whispering across my thighs. Suddenly my erotic beach dream came raging back to me and I swallowed heavily.

Get your mind out of the gutter, girl. And back on the job.

"I'll just be a minute," I yelled across the lawn, turning my key to open the front door. Once inside, I dropped my cover-up and worked to swap bathing suit for business suit with the speed of Superman in a phone booth, gritting my teeth to ignore the excruciating pain of wool rubbing against raw, sunburned skin.

Beeeeeep!

I looked up, annoyed. Was he honking again? Geez. I'd just gotten the call five minutes ago. What did he expect? At the very least I had to glop foundation over my lobster skin. Was that so much to ask?

Beeeeeeeeeep!

I scowled. Okay fine, I'd apply my makeup in the car. Grabbing my phone and purse I ran out the door, across the front yard, and into the truck, just in time for him to lay on the horn again.

Beeeeeeeeeeeeeeep!

"I'm here, okay?" I cried, slamming the door behind me. "I mean, I know it's breaking news and all, but it's not like I could report live from my bikini."

He turned, giving me a puzzled look. "What?"

"The beeping, of course!" I gestured angrily to his steering wheel, still a little out of breath from running to the vehicle. "It's rude and unnecessary. I was going as fast as I could. I don't know how you do things in Boston, but here we try to show our coworkers a little respect."

"Respect," he mumbled under his breath. "That's a good one."

I stared at him, incredulous. "Excuse me?"

"Look, a cat crawled under the truck when I first pulled up," he said flatly. "I didn't want to run it over when I pulled out." He paused, then muttered, "I guess that's just how we do things in Boston."

A . . . cat? Oh God. I stared at him, speechless. He sighed, shook his head, then laid on the horn one more time. Sure enough, a moment later, a black and white tabby shot from under the vehicle, crossing my neighbor's yard and leaping over the fence.

Mac gave me an expectant look, his blue eyes flashing something unreadable. "Now. If you need more time to get ready . . ."

I swallowed hard, pretty sure my already sunburned skin was now a disturbing shade of purple. "No," I stammered. "I'm fine. Let's go."

Mac nodded, putting the truck in gear without another word, guiding it back onto the narrow beach road that led out of my neighborhood and onto the freeway. As he drove, I stared out the front windshield, feeling hot and stupid. Not to mention humiliated beyond belief. Why had I snapped at him like that? I was supposed to be trying to make things less awkward. Instead, I'd somehow managed to create a hostile work environment our first five minutes on the job. What if he went back and said something to Richard? What if he asked for another partner? What if Richard took that as a sign I wasn't ready for the new gig after all?

What if I let my hurt feelings over a stupid one-night stand end my entire career?

"I'm sorry," I said, turning back to Mac. He was staring out the front window, gripping the steering wheel with white knuckled fingers. "I'm a bit . . . flustered right now. I just got promoted and this is my first breaking news assignment. I didn't mean to take it out on you."

He gave a small nod, so slight I could scarcely recognize it. I waited for him to say something, but he remained silent. I squirmed in my seat. I had to make this right somehow. Or we'd be living through hell each and every workday.

"Look, can we somehow start over?" I blurted out. "I mean, I know the situation is beyond awkward. Trust me, if I had any idea who you were in that club, I would have never,

ever . . . well, you know." I wrung my hands in my lap. "But it happened. It happened and there's no way to take it back. And now we're stuck together, whether we like it or not."

Mac grunted, giving me the distinct impression he was in the "not" camp.

I sighed. "As far as I can see it, we have two choices. We can continue to fight and make each other miserable for the foreseeable future. Or we can suck it up and move forward and do our jobs like professionals. I don't know about you, but this job is a really big deal to me. And I'm not about to let something this stupid screw up everything I've worked for my entire life."

I paused, the silence stretching out between us. For a moment I thought he wouldn't answer. But finally, he cleared his throat. "I need this job, too," he said, his voice gruff.

Relief flooded my insides. "Great," I said. "Okay. Then we're in agreement. We're moving on. From this point forward, this car will be a magically awkward-free zone!" I forced a grin, waving my hands in the air in emphasis, as if casting a spell. Out of the corner of my eye I thought I saw his mouth twitch, but I couldn't be sure.

I sighed. Spell or not, this was going to take some work.

I reached toward the dashboard, turning up the police scanner. Then I grabbed my reporter notepad and started to take notes. We wouldn't have a ton of time once we got to the fire and I wanted to have some questions ready for the potential interviewees. As a bonus, I hoped it would serve as a distraction from Mac's flashing blue eyes.

But *that*, I soon realized, was going to take a *lot* more magic.

Though most tourists probably considered San Diego a tropical oasis, to the east of the city stretched miles and miles of desert. Each year the lack of rain would turn the area into a powder keg for brushfires. And when the winds picked up, those fires could decimate entire towns.

I peered out the window as we pulled up alongside the

blaze, pinpointing the displaced family, standing a little ways away, watching the ravenous flames make a quick meal of their home. A toddler, wearing sooty-footed pajamas, sat on the curb, innocently playing with a stuffed bear. A young mother held a baby close to her chest, tears streaming down her face, splashing on the child's bare head. A heavyset man put a meaty arm around her shoulder and she laid her head against his.

My heart panged; my first world problems suddenly seeming so trivial and ridiculous in the face of what they must be suffering. Here I was, all stressed out by a one-night stand gone wrong and an uncomfortable work environment while this family had literally just lost everything they owned.

Mac put the truck in park, then turned to me. "I'll go get some good flame shots while you scout out who's in charge and have them make an official statement. I assume you want to interview the family as well, so go see if they'll talk. I'll be back in about ten to do the interviews which will give us plenty of time to edit and feed our video back to the station."

I agreed and opened the door to jump out of the truck. After smoothing my skirt, I went to seek out the fire marshal, giving the danger zone a wide birth. The firefighters were doing their best, but this was clearly a losing battle. They might be able to contain the fire and keep it from spreading to other areas, but this house was a total loss.

A weight fell over my shoulders, effectively smothering my previous adrenaline rush. It was strange: This was exactly the type of breaking news I'd been looking forward to reporting since I'd first arrived in San Diego. But now, somehow, being here, feeling the intense heat of the flames and smelling the horrid stench of destruction . . . It was more disturbing than exciting. Not to mention just plain sad.

I found the fire marshal and he agreed to do the interview. As I gathered the preliminary facts that I hadn't already gleaned from the scanner, I watched as, out of the corner of my eye, Mac shot video of the burning house. He was all over the place: hand held, crouching on his knees to get a close-up, then holding the camera high above his head to get a wider shot of the scene. I worried, for a moment, that his eagerness was going to put him in danger of being burned, but he seemed to have some kind of inborn sense of exactly where was too close, allowing him to skirt the line without crossing it.

After gathering the necessary video, he approached the fire marshal and me, as planned, and I held out the microphone to conduct the quick interview. The story was pretty simple. The fire had been contained. Only two homes destroyed—one which had already been vacant. Nothing suspicious. Just an unfortunate gas leak at the wrong place and the wrong time.

"Thank you," I said to the official, once we were finished. I turned to Mac. "Let's get the family now."

He nodded and we approached the husband and wife, who were still standing on the opposite side of the road, watching the scene. Did they have any place to go to tonight? I wondered. Did they have relatives to stay with? Friends? Money for a hotel? They lived out in the middle of nowhere; would someone take them in? They wouldn't have to spend the night in a shelter, would they?

I motioned for Mac to lower his camera as we got closer. Didn't want to scare them off by coming in, guns blazing. Over the years on the job I found there were two types of people in this world. The first, overeager to get their fifteen seconds of fame in any way possible and the second, who would run screaming in the other direction at the first sight of photography equipment.

"Hi," I said, stepping up to them. "I'm Beth White, a reporter with News 9." I gave them a sympathetic look. "I'm so sorry about your house."

"Yeah, well, it's not your fault," the man grumbled, yanking his wife a little closer to his side. "Or your business for that matter."

His sudden movement woke the baby, who let out a piercing wail of protest. I cringed, my heart flooding now. I tried to imagine what it'd be like—to just stand there, utterly helpless, watching everything you loved go up in flames.

And not just material stuff either—the stuff insurance would take care of. But the personal things. Family photos, mementos of trips, memories you could never replace.

I motioned for Mac to lift his camera, then held out the microphone to the man. "Can you tell me what happened?" I asked gently.

He stiffened. "I think that's pretty obvious."

I sighed. Yes. Yes, it was. But that wasn't going to give me anything I could use in my story.

"How does it make you feel?" I tried again, then winced, realizing how stupid the question sounded the second it left my mouth. How did it make them feel? *Seriously, Beth, you get three guesses and the first two don't count.*

"Look, miss," the woman interjected. "I know you're just doing your job and all, but this is our life here." She gave me a pleading look. "We don't want it splashed all over the TV."

I swallowed hard, guilt tearing into my insides. The family had been through so much—and, of course, they wouldn't want their personal tragedy to be playing out live in everyone's living room. Who would? But at the same time, like she said, this was my job. The station expected victim interviews. The story was almost worthless without them. If I walked away now, without even trying to eke out at least one useable soundbite, I'd basically be proving I wasn't ready for this gig. Not cut out for dayside reporting.

Sure, right now, Mac and I were the only ones on the scene, so maybe I could get away with saying the family wasn't present. But other stations could be on the way. And it would just take one obnoxious reporter to wear them down and force them to talk. And then, everyone would know I had failed.

But still, these were people, not a means to my professional success. And I wasn't about to forget that. I wasn't that girl.

I turned to Mac. "Why don't you start uploading the video you shot and put together a few sequences? I'll be right there."

He frowned and I knew exactly what he was thinking. That I was giving up too easily. That I should have shoved that mic right back in their faces and forced them to talk regardless. That it wasn't even worth putting together a story if we couldn't get victim interviews. That we might as well just pack up and go home now and forget the whole thing if I couldn't make it work.

But to his credit, he didn't argue. Instead he turned on his heel and headed to the truck. I watched him go for a moment, then turned my attention back to the family.

"Do you have somewhere to go tonight?" I asked the woman. "Do you need a ride somewhere? Or something to eat in the meantime?"

She shook her head. "No, we're okay. My sister lives up in Ramona. She's on her way down to pick us up." She paused, giving me a reluctant smile. "Thanks for asking. But we'll be fine."

Her husband snorted. "My wife, the eternal optimist." He waved a hand angrily in the direction of the burning house. "How is this going to be fine? We've lost everything. And for what? 'Cause those assholes are too lazy to do their damn jobs?"

"Rick . . ." She shot him a warning look. "This isn't helping anything. And you're upsetting the kids."

"Wait," I interrupted. "What do you mean? Who was too lazy? They told me the fire was because of a gas leak in the house next door."

"Exactly," Rick said, turning back to me. "Place was abandoned six months ago and I've been begging the city to do something about it ever since. It had this weird smell. Every time I walked by—I just knew there was something wrong in there. I tried to check it out myself, though I'm no expert. When I walked in I almost passed out from the smell."

"So, you reported the leak and they never fixed it?" I asked, incredulous.

"Nope. They'd promise, of course, every time I called. I even went down there once to fill out a report in person. But no one ever actually followed through. Guess we're not high on the priority list out here in the sticks." He grimaced. "And, hey, no skin off their backs, right? They'll be sleeping all snug in their beds tonight, counting their tax dollars, while we shack up ten to a trailer at her sister's place."

I bit my lower lip, my mind racing. "Look," I said at last, looking up at him and meeting his eyes with my own. "I know you don't want to talk about what happened to your family on TV. And that's totally fine, I get it. But this—you can't just keep this quiet. What if there are other people out there in a similar situation? What if there are other gas leaks the city isn't checking out properly? What if they cause more fires and hurt other families?" I gave them a pleading look. "By going on TV you could expose these people who ignored you. And you could conceivably save other houses—maybe even other lives in the process."

Rick and his wife exchanged glances, and I could practically see the cogs whirring in their heads as they considered what I was saying. I hoped they didn't take this as me trying to press my advantage. Because honestly, I would have been perfectly fine to walk away without the interview—if it was just them talking about their feelings of losing their home.

But this was clearly bigger than that. And it could have longer legs than just a quick piece on the local news. We could air the basic story tonight and then I could go down and request the call records from the city. Find Rick's original report he'd filed. Prove he had tried to warn them but was ignored. Not to mention I could look at other calls of a similar nature and see if they had been answered. After all, this could be an isolated incident, or it could be something much bigger. Something rotten at the city's core.

I turned back to Rick. "What do you think?" I asked with bated breath.

He paused for a moment. Then, "I think you've got yourself an interview."

fourteen

MAC

As I rolled up the cables, packing up to head back to the station after our live shot and re-interview of the fire marshal (who was much less friendly, I might add, when it came to Beth's not-so-softball new questions), I glanced over at Beth, who was on her cell, still arguing with some poor city hall employee who had clearly drawn the short straw today when picking up the phone. I smiled a little at the fierceness I saw on her face. She was like a pit bull with a bone and she wasn't going to let go until she got what she wanted.

And why should she? She might have actually uncovered something really good here. Really newsworthy. Turning a simple day-of fire spot news piece into a long-term, law-changing investigation. As I set my camera into its bracket in the back of the truck, I felt a stirring of grudging admiration. She could have just as easily chosen to bully the family into a simple soundbite. Or she could have wimped out and walked away. But she had done neither. Because she had treated them as human beings, not just items on her nightly news checklist. And because of that, she'd gotten a scoop most reporters would have totally missed out on.

She hung up the phone, swinging her long legs out of the truck to head toward me, a look of determination clear in her eyes. Strands of gold had escaped her ponytail, framing her heart-shaped face. Even with her brutal sunburn, she was drop-dead gorgeous, and I felt something involuntarily stir inside of me as my mind chose this inopportune moment to remember what was hiding under that severe black suit of hers.

But, in truth, her body wasn't what was turning me on now. Not really. After all, there were plenty of beautiful women in the world. Victoria had been beautiful, too, at least on the outside. Beth's attractiveness, on the other hand, was clearly more than skin deep.

She'd stood up for me at the bar. Now she was standing up for these poor people at the fire. It was the kind of thing you didn't see much in the modern world of TV news.

And it was totally hot.

"So?" I asked.

Her eyes danced mischievously. "Let's just say they weren't exactly thrilled by the request. But I reminded them it was a public record. They could let me look at it now, or I could just send a FOIA—a Freedom of Information Act request through the mail and force them to send it to me eventually."

"And . . ."

"And . . ." She glanced down at her phone, then up at me. 'We've got a date with city hall tomorrow, first thing."

"Nice!" I cried, lifting my hand in a high five. She smacked it with her own, a huge grin spreading across her face. "Way to stick it to the man."

She laughed. "I can't wait to see the look on Richard's face when we tell him what we have. He's going to be so psyched! Maybe he'll even take me off probation, since I clearly rock this new job." She snorted, then turned to me, her eyes sobering. "Thank you," she said. "I mean, for going along with it all. I know you probably just wanted to get home tonight. I appreciate you staying late to work the new angle.

Especially since . . ." She trailed off, looking embarrassed, staring down at her feet, her former enthusiasm deflating like an old balloon.

"Hey, hey!" I cried. On impulse, I reached out, cupping her chin with my hand and guiding it upward, forcing her brown eyes to meet my own. Then I gave her a crooked smile. "Come on now, I thought we were supposed to be in an awkward-free zone," I teased. "Does the spell need recharging already? 'Cause I can do that, if necessary. You might not know this, but I've got mad skills with pixie dust."

"Oh, yeah?" She raised an eyebrow.

I patted my chest with my free hand. "Please. Hogwarts graduate. With honors. I even have the wand."

"Wow. I had no idea!" She giggled.

I swiped my thumb across her cheek, rejoicing in the feel of her impossibly soft skin against mine, then reluctantly released her.

"Look, Beth, no matter what happened in the past between us, from now on we're a team," I reminded her. "I've got your back. And I hope you have mine, too. That's the only way this will work." I paused, then added, "Deal?"

A shy smile spread across her face. "Deal."

"Then let's get the hell out of here," I said. "I think we both deserve a shot of tequila after today."

"Only if it's Anejo Banjo Tolito."

"But of course! I wouldn't dream of drinking anything else."

fifteen

We finished packing up our gear and soon were headed back into town. I told Mac I'd have to take a rain check on the all-too-tempting tequila offer, since, with the exception of my brief beach nap, I'd been up since three A.M. and all I wanted to do was fall into my bed and pass out until morning. We had a big day tomorrow, after all, following up on the fire story. He told me he understood, and offered to drive me home.

On the ride back, we chatted about News 9, the weather, and other inconsequential things while listening to music on the radio. Nothing too deep, nothing too personal. Just two new coworkers, making small talk, no big thing. By the time Mac pulled off the freeway to drop me home I'd almost convinced myself that this could actually work. That the awkward-free spell could hold and we could actually find a way to work together as a team after all.

I sighed, glancing over at him now. If only we hadn't met at the bar like we had. If only I hadn't let Stephanie talk me into taking him home. We could have met under completely different circumstances, had our relationship develop naturally, instead of fast-forwarding to stranger sex. Who knows what could have happened then?

I turned away, glancing out the window again as Mac pulled onto my street. What was done was done; we couldn't change anything. All we could do now was move forward and make the best out of what fate had dealt us. Still, at least now I wasn't quite so upset about having a new partner.

In fact, I was kind of excited about it.

"Is this the place?"

Mac's hesitant question shot me back to reality. I looked out the window, my eyes scrunching in confusion. It looked like my street. It looked like my house. Except . . .

The front lawn was strewn with brightly colored clothing and scraps of wood that might have once been furniture. Toiletries and other cosmetics had been dumped out onto the grass amidst corpses of no-longer-stuffed animals. It was as if a tornado had swept in and gutted the place. My heart leapt to my throat. What the . . . ?

"Can you hang on a second?" I asked, opening the door to the truck with shaky hands. "I think I might have been robbed." I hopped out of the vehicle, my pulse skittering erratically as I took in the scene. Even in the dim twilight I started recognizing some of the items as mine. My clothing. My furniture. My childhood teddy bear. Ripped to shreds or chopped up almost beyond recognition. What the hell was going on here?

"Do you want me to call the police?" Mac called from the truck, sounding, to his credit, quite concerned. But I shook my head, biting my lower lip to stop the sobs from escaping. I stormed up the front steps, whipping open the front door, ready to face whoever was terrorizing my house.

As I did, I smacked right into someone heading outside. Someone carrying my bedroom TV. I stumbled, almost losing my balance, as the girl shoved past me, taking the television and slamming it down onto the pavement with force. I let out a cry of horror as it exploded in a crash of breaking glass.

The person throwing the deranged yard sale was not a thief at all.

It was my roommate.

sixteen

BETH

"What are you doing?" I cried, staring at Stephanie in disbelief.

"What am *I* doing?" she repeated, her voice thick with contempt. Her normally sparkling blue eyes had frozen to icy daggers, aimed directly at me. "I should ask you the same question. How dare you just come back here, like nothing's happened? You think I'm going to let you live in *my* house after what you did to me?"

I shrank backward, suddenly all the puzzle pieces sliding into a sick sort of place. Oh God. Richard must have told her about her demotion . . . and, worse, my promotion.

"Look, Stephanie—"

She held up a hand, cutting me off. "Don't even," she cried, her voice cracking at the edges. "Nothing you can possibly say is going to make this any better." Angry tears spilled down her cheeks as she squared her shoulders and crossed her arms over her chest. "I thought you were my friend! I let you move in with me. And yet, here you were, all along, scheming to take my job!"

"It wasn't my fault!" I protested, my own eyes blurring with tears. "I didn't ask to be moved up."

"You didn't exactly refuse, either," Stephanie reminded me. "You know, if I was in that situation I would have stuck up for you. Fought for you."

I wasn't exactly sure this was true, but that fact didn't help assuage the guilt from stabbing through my stomach as I stood there now. I should have at least warned her. Or discussed it with her before giving my okay. That way I could have tried to make her understand that this wasn't my fault. That the demotion and promotion were essentially unrelated. Or, at the very least, stopped her from throwing a deranged yard sale at the expense of my belongings.

Was it too late to call Richard and tell him I'd changed my mind? But no, I remembered the news director's warning all too well. If I screwed this up, I wouldn't be going back to the morning shift. I'd be gone for good. And the position would just go to someone else. Any grand gestures I might choose to make wouldn't help Stephanie in the end. And they could destroy me.

I sighed. "I'm really sorry, Steph."

"Please. You don't even know the word sorry," she growled. "But you will. I am going to make sure you will."

She ripped my purse from my arms, fishing inside until she withdrew a set of keys. After removing my house key from the chain, she sent the remaining keys, along with the bag itself, sailing through the air. It landed in the yard with the rest of my stuff.

"Consider this your eviction notice."

And with that, she turned, storming back into the house, slamming the door behind her. A moment later I heard the deadbolt slide defiantly into place.

I sunk to the front steps covering my face with my hands, not bothering to rein in my sobs. What was I going to do? Where was I going to go? I'd have to find a new apartment. Buy new furniture. How was I going to afford either? I barely made enough to cover my shared rent with Stephanie. And with only a handshake agreement and no official lease, I had no legal grounds to even ask for my security deposit back.

"Are you okay?"

I looked up, horrified to see Mac standing over me. Oh God. He was still here? Why hadn't he driven off? Had he just witnessed this entire thing? My face burned with humiliation as he plopped down next to me on the front stoop.

"I'm fine. You can go," I managed to say.

He raised an eyebrow. "And leave you here like this? I don't think so."

"I'll be fine. Really."

"Sure you will. I'm still not leaving."

I sighed, hating the fact that this made me feel a little better. "Fine, I guess I can't force you."

"Goddamn," he swore, looking out over the yard. "You told me your roommate was a piece of work. But I had no idea the extent of her craftsmanship." He turned back to me. "What the hell happened?"

"She's pissed 'cause I got a promotion," I explained flatly. "And she was demoted."

He scowled. "Typical fucking reporter," he muttered under his breath.

"What?"

"Nothing," he corrected quickly. "Anyway, you need to call the police. She can't just kick you out like that. Get them to come over and mediate the situation."

I let out a frustrated breath. "I wish I could."

"What's stopping you?"

"If I call the police, this'll end up in the newspaper. The gossip columns will have a field day. Richard will be furious—he's very protective of News 9's public image. He'd probably fire both of us."

"But it's not your fault."

"No. But it won't matter.'

Mac closed his eyes for a moment, frustration washing over his handsome face. "Well, then, do you want me to talk to her?"

"No!" I looked up, horrified at the idea of him getting involved. As if he was my boyfriend or something.

Okay, fine, admittedly the idea of him storming in there and defending my honor was the slightest bit appealing. But I couldn't allow for it. This was my battle. I had to fight it alone. Or, perhaps more accurately, shrink away in shame alone.

"I'm good, really," I assured him.

He gave me a pitying look, but thankfully didn't argue. "At least let me help you gather your things."

Oh, right. I bit my lower lip. I'd have to do that, wouldn't I? I looked around the yard, sudden exhaustion blanketing me. I'd been up since three A.M., worked two shifts, and only had a short nap on the beach. My sunburn was itching like crazy and all I wanted to do was crawl into my warm bed and go into a coma for the next twelve hours.

But my bed was still inside the house. Which meant it might as well have been on Mars.

"Do you have someplace to go tonight?" Mac asked as he walked over to the truck and pulled out a couple of large garbage bags. He handed one to me.

"Of course I do," I retorted before I could help myself. What did he think, I was some kind of social reject with only one friend?

Okay, so that was kind of true. Having worked the morning shift, I hadn't exactly gotten out much to make friends and influence people. In fact, for the last two years, I'd pretty much put my personal life on hold for my career—not to mention my long-distance boyfriend. Which was pretty pathetic, I realized, looking back on it now.

But Mac didn't need to know any of that.

I could feel his eyes on me, but I ignored them, forcing myself to rise from the steps and slowly begin to grab articles of clothing and shove them into my bag.

"Where?"

I looked up, annoyed. "Where what?"

"Where do you have to go?"

"Why do you care?"

He sighed, placing a ripped black silk dress—my favorite silk dress—into his bag.

"I just thought you might like a ride."

"I have a car." I motioned to my Prius, parked in the driveway. The one with the four newly shredded tires. *Thank you, Stephanie.* I had to admit, she may have been a lousy reporter, but she was an expert in enacting revenge.

"I don't think you'll be going anywhere in that," Mac remarked causally, grabbing my Kindle Fire, which, I noted, now sported a cracked screen. Seriously, why were we even bothering to pack up this stuff at all?

I dropped my bag, giving up the game. "Fine," I said. "You got me. I don't have a place to go. I don't have any money. I guess I don't even have a car. I'm the ultimate loser. Happy?"

"Why would that make me happy?" he asked in a quiet voice. His intense blue eyes zeroed in on me. I turned away, unable to face the concern I saw in his face. *This guy walked out on you*, I tried to remind myself. *He used you and then tossed you away much like all of this garbage.*

"Look, I'll be fine, okay?" I blurted out angrily. "I'll just sleep on the beach or whatever. Figure it out in the morning."

His mouth dipped to a frown. "You are not sleeping on the beach."

"It's not that cold out."

"But it is that dangerous." He raked a hand through his hair. "I wouldn't be able to sleep myself, knowing you were out here." He sighed. "Look, this may sound crazy, but why don't you come to my house? Just for the night."

I stared at him, incredulous. "No. No way."

"Why not? It's a perfectly practical solution. You need a place to stay. I have a guest bedroom."

Guest bedroom. I scowled. Just like I had a really comfortable couch.

"Look, Beth, this isn't some sleazy proposition," he added, catching the look on my face. "Just a nice, friendly, platonic coworker offer." His mouth quirked and held up two fingers. "Scout's honor."

I sighed. I wasn't sure just how much honor a guy who

had just walked off after a one-night stand without leaving his number had, but I knew beggars couldn't be choosers. I had few options at this point and the exhaustion was starting to overwhelm any decision-making capability I might have had left.

Not to mention, I really, really didn't want him to just drive off now and leave me here alone.

"Okay," I relented. "Take me home."

seventeen

MAC

Okay, Mac, what the hell were you thinking?

I hoisted the heavy trash bag into the back of the truck, careful to wedge it in between two others, in case there was still anything left unbroken inside. Once it was secured, I turned questioningly back to Beth. She gave me a weary looking half smile, then shook her head. That was it. All she had left in the world, packed up into one small corner of a TV news live truck.

My eyes narrowed as they shifted to the locked front door of her now former residence, anger surging through me all over again, my nails biting into my palms as I squeezed my hands into fists. It was all I could to restrain myself from charging that door, from breaking it down with my bare hands. From giving that bitch a taste of her own medicine.

Instead, I bit my lower lip, forcing my fury at bay. This wasn't my fight. She didn't want me to get involved. Not to mention, I couldn't do things like that anymore. I was a father. I had responsibilities. Getting myself arrested for some stupid knight-in-shining-armor bullshit that wouldn't even make a difference in the long run—I couldn't do that to my baby girl.

But still . . . I scowled, glancing over at Beth, my heart wrenching in my chest. She looked so lost, so goddamned sad. The invitation to stay at my place had flown from my lips before I could help it.

I groaned. Here I was supposed to be keeping her at arms' length, remaining professional and uninvolved. Instead, I'd somehow essentially invited her to a sleepover at my house. Which was pretty much as unprofessional and involved as one could possibly get.

But what choice did I have? I couldn't have just left her here, sitting on the stoop, all alone in the world. She probably would have slept in her car, as she'd threatened to do. Or worse—I shuddered—the beach itself, which was beyond crazy. I supposed I could have rented her a hotel room for the night, but she just looked so upset—I didn't have the heart to drop her off to an empty room. There'd been too many nights in my own past, recently, where I'd lain in one of those cold, hard beds, staring up at the ceiling, unable to sleep. Unable to do anything but rehash over and over again what Victoria had done to us. At least I had Ashley on those nights; I could crawl out of my nightmare and soothe myself by listening to her rhythmic breathing in the next bed. But Beth would have no such comfort.

She needed a friend. And it appeared I was the only candidate.

I slammed the truck door closed. It wasn't a big deal, I scolded myself. It was just one night. And Ashley wouldn't even be there; she was at my sister's house, thanks to my original plan to stay up all night unpacking. The house would be empty. No complications, no big deal.

At least I hoped.

Hopping into the truck, I turned the key in the ignition. Beth joined me in the passenger seat and I pulled out onto her street. The station had instructed me to keep the truck for the night and bring it home the next morning for my shift. And so I pulled out onto the freeway and headed north to the small Escondido subdivision I now called home.

The house belonged to my sister and Joe. They had

recently moved to a bigger place to accommodate their growing family, but had decided to keep it as a rental until the market went back up. It was the kind of house Victoria would have loved: a mini-McMansion with little lot line and even less personality. Sure it had all the granite and the stainless and the upgraded comforts of home, but in truth I preferred something a little more unique and rough around the edges. Yet beggars couldn't be choosers and Sadie and Joe were letting us live there for almost nothing. And so, for now, it was home sweet home.

"Here we are," I announced as I pulled into the driveway, hitting the garage door button to open it. It was packed floor to ceiling with boxes still, as was most of the house itself. Which, I decided, was probably for the best; the way it looked now, it could be a hotel. No photos or memorabilia on display to give Beth a peek into my personal life.

We headed through the mudroom and into the house proper. Beth, playing the part of the perfect houseguest, remarked admiringly on various details: pretty granite, great fireplace, love those hardwood floors.

"Not exactly the hip, happening bachelor pad you expected?" I couldn't help but tease as I made my way to Ashley's bedroom door, shutting it discreetly. I felt a little shameful for doing it—like I was trying to hide her, or something, which I would never do. But, at the same time, it felt too soon—too personal. Beth was my coworker, not my new girlfriend, I reminded myself. And the less she knew about my personal life, the better.

She snorted. "Not a leopard-sheeted bed nor a ceiling mirror to be found. I'm truly disappointed."

"I could put some Barry White on the stereo . . ."

"Yeah, I think I'm good." She gave a strained laugh, plopping down on the couch. My heart squeezed again. She was putting on a brave face, I realized, but she was still hurting inside. Poor thing.

"Are you hungry?" I asked. "I haven't done a big grocery shop yet, but I could whip up some mac and cheese or something."

She looked up. "I don't want you to go to any trouble."

"It's opening a box and boiling water. I think I can handle that. Besides, I'm starving myself."

"Okay." She gave me a small smile. "Then that sounds good." I watched as she kicked off her shoes and pulled her feet onto the couch, tucking them under her. Good, she was relaxing. Making herself at home.

"Can I pour you a glass of something?"

She raised an eyebrow. "Anejo Banjo?"

"Fresh out of that," I said, filling my voice with mock sorrow. "But I think I can rustle up a decent cab."

She sighed dramatically, flopping down on the couch. "I suppose that will have to do."

I laughed, reaching into the cupboard to pull out one of the bottles of local wines from nearby Temecula that my sister had given me as a housewarming present. After opening it, I split the contents between two red plastic cups, bringing one over to her.

"I know, I know," I said as I caught her looking at the "stemware." "I run a classy joint here."

She looked up at me and smiled. "It's perfect," she assured me.

I nodded, turning away quickly and taking a big slug of my wine as I went to make the mac and cheese. It was kind of perfect actually. And not just the wine either.

Which was a problem.

A potentially really big problem.

eighteen

"Are you sure you don't need any help?" I called over to Mac as he bustled around the kitchen, busily preparing our gourmet dinner of mac and cheese from the bright blue box. And not just any mac and cheese, I noted with a smile, but a *How to Tame Your Dragon*–themed variety. How adorable was that? Beneath the trappings of a rather grown-up looking house, Mac was evidently still a kid at heart. Or at least the consummate bachelor. Kraft Mac and Cheese, red Solo frat cups. Ten bucks said his pantry was stocked with Top Ramen as well.

Not that I was one to talk. Hell, I'd probably be dining on quite a few Ramen noodles myself in the foreseeable future. If I could afford them.

I let out a frustrated breath, reality rushing back with a vengeance. It was funny; for a few blissful moments, I'd actually allowed myself to forget what I was really doing here. To imagine that I was out on a date or visiting a good friend. But no: Mac had only invited me here because he felt sorry for me. Because I literally had no other place to go.

Pathetic, Beth. Truly pathetic.

Pathetic and . . . well, a little scary, too. What was I going to do? Where was I going to go? I mean, sure, I was safe here for the night and totally grateful for his generosity. But what about tomorrow? I'd have to go out and buy all new furniture. All new clothes. And not just any old clothes, either, but expensive clothes, suitable to wear on air. I also needed new tires for my car. A new apartment. First, last month's rent. Maybe a security deposit, too. My head started pounding as the bills racked up in my brain at a startling speed, compounded by the memory of my savings account, hovering near zero balance.

And the worst part? I couldn't even ask my parents for help this time. Not after I'd pretty much disowned them for supporting my sister in her campaign to marry my boyfriend. They'd made it clear from the start that they hadn't wanted me to move out to San Diego. And when the news had surfaced about Ryan and my sister—well, my mom had all but declared, "I told you so." As if it were my fault. As if by prioritizing my career, I didn't deserve a man.

If I crawled back now, they would probably help. But I would rather die of starvation and poverty than face their gloating. Their smug faces as they affirmed their belief that they had been right all along.

Grabbing my cup, I downed the rest of the wine in one large gulp.

"Need a refill?"

I almost jumped out of my skin as Mac sat down beside me on the couch, holding out the bottle. I'd been so lost in my misery, I'd almost forgotten he was still in the room— that I was still a guest at his house. My body, however, quickly reminded me, practically vibrating from his sudden close proximity and I wondered, wildly, if there was any good way to scoot over and put distance between us, without it being obvious that I was doing it.

Instead, I tried to be a grown-up, holding out my cup, willing my hands not to shake as he filled it. Then, I concentrated on taking another sip—a small one this time— before setting it down on the coffee table in front of me and staring at it, as if it were a crystal ball that held all of life's answers. In turn, I could feel Mac staring at me and my skin flushed in response, my stomach flip-flopping madly.

Suddenly, I was no longer hungry. Not for mac and cheese anyway.

Come on, Beth, get a grip!

I closed my eyes trying to reset my libido, not to mention my sanity. I mean, seriously, all the guy had done was sit down and offer me a drink. He hadn't even touched me. And here I was, practically orgasming on his sofa.

I so should have slept on the beach.

I started to rise from my seat, needing to get away, to put some sort of temporary distance between us until I could get my emotions in check.

"I need to use the—ow!"

I cried out as I managed to scrape my already raw skin against the rough material of the couch. Glancing over my shoulder, I winced at what I saw. My sunburn had looked bad earlier. It looked even worse now.

"Are you okay?" Mac cocked his head in concern.

"Yeah." I reached up and ran my hand along my shoulder. It was hot to the touch. "It's just . . . this stupid burn. I fell asleep on the beach earlier, like an idiot. And now it's killing me."

"Hang on." He rose to his feet and headed over to his refrigerator, opening the door and sticking his head inside. I watched as a moment later he resurfaced, holding up a bottle of aloe vera. "My sister swears by this stuff," he said.

"Thank you," I replied, relieved. I took it from him and squeezed a generous dollop into my hands. Then I pulled aside the strap of my camisole and pushed my shoulder forward, while struggling to reach the sore spot with my other hand.

"Here, allow me."

Mac took the bottle from me, then gestured for me to turn around. I swallowed hard, realizing what he was offering to do. Oh God.

I opened my mouth to argue, then somehow managed to

close it again. After all, how could I properly explain how much I didn't want him to do this—and yet, how much I *did* want him to do it—all at the same time? Finally, I gave up, reluctantly repositioning myself to give him full access to my back. As his hands slid under my camisole, I sucked in a shaky breath, trying to mentally prepare myself. But no preparation in the world could prevent the gasp that escaped me as his fingers—wet and slippery from the aloe—connected with my bare skin.

"Sorry," he said with a laugh. "It's cold, I know."

It *was* cold. But it was also scorching at the same time and the juxtaposition of ice and fire was making my head spin. As was the sensation of his rough yet tender fingers, gently massaging the aloe into my thirsty skin with firm, deft strokes. It didn't take long for another quiver to surge through me, my nipples tightening and straining against the thin fabric of my bra.

He's just soothing your sunburn, Beth. Not trying to turn you on.

But I couldn't help it. My body tingled with every stroke, my breath catching in my throat, a hot ache pooling between my legs. It was too much, too fast. And too soon it was all I could do to remain still. To stop myself from whipping around and tackling him on the couch. To straddle his thighs and grind myself against him in an attempt to relieve the exquisite torture his touch had stirred deep inside. To take this where we'd gone before. And maybe even further.

Instead, I remained perfectly still, sucking in a breath as his hands shifted direction, moving forward, skimming my hipbones, then brushing across my stomach, my sunburn evidently forgotten. My earlier beach dream came raging back to me with a vengeance and suddenly all I could think of—all I could pray for—was for those hands to keep traveling upward. Easing my bra aside, cupping my aching breasts, tracing the rock hard peaks.

I found myself edging backward, involuntarily curling my body into him, pressing myself against him, rejoicing as I was rewarded by the feeling of his erection against my back. Thank God—I wasn't alone.

I started to turn, wanting desperately to see his face. Wanting to read the same things on it that I knew were written on my own. Attraction, desire, a willingness to see where this could go—tomorrow and its consequences be damned.

Just one night. Just one more night.

But before I could meet his eyes, a sudden blaring noise interrupted the scene. Startled, I leapt back, wondering wildly what it could be. It took me a moment to recognize it as a smoke alarm. Was our passion really that hot? That it set off actual bells?

It was then that I remembered the mac and cheese on the stove.

"Goddamn it," Mac growled, scrambling to his feet and running to the kitchen. Sure enough, the forgotten pot and its pasta were smoking madly. He yanked it off the stove, throwing it in the sink and turning on the tap. Then he switched off the burner and pulled open a nearby window. A few moments later the smoke alarm fell silent.

I giggled. I couldn't help it. Could this day get any stranger? "Guess those cheesy dragons are just too hot to handle, huh?" I joked.

But, I realized, Mac wasn't laughing. Instead, he raked a hand through his hair, looking flustered and upset. I tried to meet his eyes with my own, to better glean what was going through his head. But he turned away, choosing instead to stare down into the sink. My smile faded and my heart flip-flopped nervously. This couldn't be good.

"Sorry," he muttered, turning back to me, an uncomfortable look on his face. "I should have set a timer." He paused, then added, "Do you want me to order pizza or something?"

I stared at him. Everything inside me wanted to get off the couch. To storm over to him and take him into my arms. To insist the only thing I was hungry for right now was him.

But the look on his face forced me to stay in my seat. "It's okay," I said sadly. "I'm not really that hungry anyway."

He closed his eyes for a moment, then opened them. "Are you sure?" he asked.

I frowned. I wasn't. At that moment, I wasn't sure of

anything. Except, maybe, for the fact that if I tried to make another move, I'd be turned down flat. The moment was over. The opportunity lost.

But maybe that was for the best.

"I should probably go to bed," I said, rising from the couch, feeling stupid and more hot and flustered than I'd been before the aloe. I glanced over at the front door, wishing there was somewhere else I could go—anywhere else in the world would be less awkward right now. But I knew in my heart that would only make things worse in the end. I could run away screaming tonight, but tomorrow we'd still have to work together.

And no anti-awkward spell in the world would be powerful enough to make that okay.

nineteen

MAC

BUZZZ!!
I groaned as the morning alarm blared in my ear, dragging me back to consciousness with the delicacy of a sledgehammer. Rolling over in bed, I reached out, slamming my fist against the snooze button, then pulling the comforter back over my head. I couldn't believe it was morning already. I felt like I'd just closed my eyes a second earlier. Which probably wasn't far from the truth.

I'd tossed and turned for hours the night before, unable to chase sleep. Unable to stop my heart from pounding in my chest or my balls from aching in my groin. I'd considered relieving myself of the pressure about a hundred times, but always ended up staying my hand. It just felt . . . weird. Disrespectful, maybe, knowing the subject of my hard-on was sleeping innocently in the next room.

Which led me to the other thing that had kept me awake. The idea that I was so close. That it would be so easy to simply crawl out of bed, cross the hall, and slip into her room. What would she do if I just slid in behind her in bed? If my hand wrapped around her, slipping between her thighs. Finding and parting her panties—which were lacy, bare scraps of silk in this fantasy scenario, by the way—my fingers slipping between her soft folds. Would she moan in pleasure, half-asleep, but fully turned on? Would she rock against my hand and murmur my name as she rode the wave to orgasm? Would she, once sated, want to roll over and return the favor?

I groaned. *God, Mac, what is wrong with you?*

My mind flashed back to the evening before. How things could have ended up, had the macaroni not burned. Talk about being saved by the bell! Here I'd promised the poor girl a safe, platonic place to stay, no strings attached. Then, before I know it, my hands are up her shirt, my cock pressed against her back, my mouth mere inches from devouring her whole. If I had a gentleman card, I would certainly have been forced to turn it in. No passing Go; no collecting any two hundred dollars.

And that wasn't the worst part either. The worst part had been the look I'd caught in her eyes as I'd turned back from dumping the pasta in the sink. The hurt and confusion radiating from her dark pupils when I refused to rejoin her on the couch.

She didn't understand and I couldn't explain.

I tried to tell myself that turnaround was fair play. That she was the one who had used me to begin with—and that payback was a bitch. But, try as I might, instead of justified, I felt nothing but a mixture of guilt and remorse.

But it couldn't be helped. I'd made a promise and I was determined to keep it. And while there was no way to take back that first night, I sure as hell wasn't going to double down on a second. I had vowed to stay away from romantic entanglements. To always put my daughter first. And from now on I planned to do whatever it took to keep that promise.

Once Beth walked out my front door this morning, she wouldn't be back. We could be coworkers; we could someday maybe be friends. But that was as far as it could go. I refused to put myself in such a compromising position again.

But, oh, what a position. I closed my eyes, thinking back to the feel of her skin. Hot and slick under my aloe-drenched hands. And her scent! How was it possible for her to smell so sweet after spending all afternoon by a smoky fire? At the time it was all I could do not to rip off her shirt and lick every inch of her and then go back for seconds.

I groaned, rolling over in bed. My morning wood pressed against my boxers, begging for release. This was getting ridiculous. I closed my eyes. If could just manage to tune out for even a few more minutes of sleep . . .

Unfortunately a few more minutes turned into a few more and the third time I must have accidentally shut off the alarm instead of hitting snooze. When I finally did manage to claw my way to consciousness the clock on my bedside table read quarter to eight.

Shit. I jerked up in bed, all sleepiness forgotten. Sadie was supposed to bring Ashley home in fifteen minutes so I could get her ready for school. And Beth was presumably still in the guest room.

Muttering a curse, I bolted out of bed, then proceeded to unceremoniously slip on the pair of jeans I'd left on the floor the night before, nearly causing me to fall flat on my face. Cursing again, I managed to grab the pants and slide them over my hips, then make my way out the bedroom door, still shirtless. I had to get Beth up and out of here before Ashley showed up.

I stopped short, just before the kitchen, sniffing in confusion. Was that bacon I smelled? Did I even have bacon in my fridge? Scrunching my eyebrows, I turned the corner, my eyes widening as I entered the kitchen. Not only was Beth awake, but evidently she'd been up for some time, judging from the amount of food piled on the kitchen counter. Mountains of scrambled eggs, stacks of fluffy pancakes, slices of thick toast, dripping with butter. And, of course, the bacon. Cooked extra crispy, from what I could tell, just the way I liked it.

For a second, I considered the idea that I was still dreaming. After all, I couldn't remember the last time I'd woken to such a feast. As the mac and cheese last night could attest, I wasn't exactly a master chef and Victoria couldn't boil water.

"I was about to wake you," Beth said, pushing a plate of food into my hands. Her sunburn looked better this morning and she was fresh-faced and makeup free. Her hair was piled in a messy bun on the top of her head, a few strands left free to frame her face. My stomach wrenched—and not only with hunger. "I didn't want it to get cold."

"Where did it come from?" I stammered, still feeling a little dumbstruck.

She grinned, looking proud of herself. "Not from your cabinets," she teased. "But I'd noticed the convenience store down the road as we drove in last night. I figured I'd just walk down this morning and grab a few things."

A few things. She must have cleaned out half the store. "That's . . . awesome," I managed to say. "So sweet of you."

But it was more than sweet. It was goddamned heroic and way more than I deserved.

My eyes traveled back to the clock, guilt knotting in my stomach. I was running out of time. And yet—how could I just kick her out? After she'd clearly gone through so much effort . . .

"Aren't you going to eat?" she asked, her smile slipping a little. "I cooked a little bit of everything. I wasn't sure what you liked . . ."

"Thank you," I said, my heart pounding in my chest. "You really didn't have to . . ."

"I wanted to," she declared firmly. "In case you didn't notice, you kind of saved my life last night. I wanted you to know that I was appreciative."

"It was nothing," I declared. "But thank you all the same." I forced myself to take a large bite of eggs. They were delicious. And suddenly all I wanted to do was sit down with her for a leisurely meal and good conversation—forgetting reality for the rest of the day.

But reality was going to arrive on my doorstep any second now, whether I liked it or not. I had to get Beth out . . . and fast. I made a show of glancing at my wrist, realizing too late that, of course, I wasn't wearing a watch.

"Did you need to get to work?" I asked.

She gave me a puzzled look. "I don't have to go in until eleven," she told me. "Just like you."

Oh, right. Of course. "Well, did you . . . want to go look for a new apartment in the meantime?" I tried again, desperation making my skin itch.

She frowned. "Are you trying to get rid of me or something?"

"No! I mean, of course not." I cried, trying my best to look surprised. Insulted even. My pulse skittering erratically as I tried and failed not to look at the door.

She walked around the breakfast bar, scanning my face with worried eyes. "Mac, you're scaring me," she said. "What's going on? Did I do something wrong?"

I glanced at the door again; I couldn't help it. And when I looked back at Beth her face had turned white as a ghost's.

"Oh my God, you're married," she whispered. "You're totally married, aren't you?"

"No!" I protested, horrified. "I mean . . . I was. Not anymore. I'm single. I swear to God, I'm single. I would never . . ." I trailed off, giving her a tortured look.

She bit her lower lip. "Okay then," she said in a slow voice. "If you're not waiting for your wife to walk through that door, do you want to tell me who you're expecting instead?"

I drew in a breath. Guess it was time to come clean. "My daughter," I said.

twenty

BETH

I stared at Mac, my heart thudding in my chest. "You have a daughter?" I demanded. "Since when do you have a daughter?"

He gave me a sheepish look. "Since four years ago? When she was born?"

Right. Of course. My mind raced trying to make sense of this sudden development. Mac had a daughter? A four-year-old daughter? A four-year-old daughter that in all the time we'd spent together he'd never got around to mentioning?

A strange feeling of hurt trickled up my throat and I frowned, trying to push it back down. I mean, really. The guy was just my coworker, after all. He didn't owe me an in-depth look into his personal life. I had no right to be offended at what he decided to keep private.

But still! A daughter. A four-year-old baby girl. And he hadn't brought her up once!

"Okay . . ." I said, scratching my head. "So . . . you have a daughter. I assume she lives with her mother?"

His face flashed something I couldn't identify. "She lives with me," he replied in a curt voice, evidently not ready to offer a more detailed explanation. "She was at my sister's last night," he added, catching my look.

My mind spun, trying to make sense of it all. Why wouldn't he have told me about her? Was he afraid a kid would cramp his style or something? But no, he didn't seem the type to care about things like that.

I realized he had moved to the window and was pulling back the curtains to peer outside. A minivan had pulled into the driveway and parked.

"Shit," he muttered under his breath. Then he turned to me, his eyes wide and anxious. "Look, I'm sorry, but I can't have her see you here. She might not understand. She's had a tough time with the . . . divorce. And seeing a stranger here is just going to confuse her."

"Right." That, at least, made sense. Even if it did sting a little more than I wanted to admit. "What do you want me to do?"

He grabbed a set of keys off the counter and tossed them in my direction. "The live truck is just down the street," he told me. "Go ahead and take it to the station and I'll meet you there once I drop Ashley off to school."

Ashley. I stared at his arm. At the *A* snaking up his bicep. "So *that's* what it stands for," I realized aloud, before I could stop myself.

His cheeks colored. "Yes," he said. He glanced out the window again, then back at me, his eyes pleading.

"Okay, okay!" I held up my hands in surrender. "I'm out of here." I started toward the back door.

"Beth?" he called out, stopping me.

"Yeah?"

"I'm . . . sorry," he stammered. "I mean, I don't mean to—"

I flashed him a sympathetic smile. "You do what you need to do, daddy," I said. "I'll see you at work."

The relief on his face was palpable. "Thank you," he said. "I appreciate you understanding."

I nodded. Because, suddenly, I did understand. In fact, everything up until now made so much more sense. All his strange behavior, his running out first thing—all the hot and cold. It was as if I'd suddenly found a missing puzzle piece and now everything was sliding into place.

And it was kind of sweet, too. To realize he wasn't some asshole who screwed and ran. Just a dad, worried about the well-being of his little girl.

Of course he could have at least told me the truth; he wasn't off the hook for that. But it was likely an awkward conversation to have with someone you'd just hooked up with. And, I decided, I could probably find it within myself to give him a pass, just this once. As long as he promised no more secrets from this point on.

I found the live truck where we'd left it and I turned the key to open it up and step into the driver's seat. Once inside, I dared take a look back at Mac's house. There, I watched a pretty, young redheaded woman climb out of the driver's seat—Mac's sister, I presumed. She walked to the side of the minivan and pulled open the sliding door. A small blond girl popped out of the van, making a beeline for the house. Mac, who I hadn't realized had come outside, intercepted her halfway, swinging her into a huge hug and twirling her around.

I smiled at the scene, something tugging at my heart as I watched him set her back down and kiss the top of her head. She was clearly trying to tell him something, her arms gesticulating earnestly while her legs bounced her up and down like Tigger from the Winnie the Pooh tales. I looked back up at Mac, taking in his face as he dropped to give his daughter a bow, before going over to hug his sister. No longer haggard, no longer stressed or worried. But relaxed, happy, smiling.

As Ashley and his sister walked into the house, Mac remained outside for a moment. I watched as he scanned the neighborhood, his eyes zeroing in on the live truck. I blushed, realizing I'd been caught spying. I gave a sheepish wave. He nodded slowly, then lifted up his hand in a salute before turning and walking back inside.

twenty-one

MAC

"Daddy! Daddy! We're back, Daddy!"

"Hey, baby girl!" I cried, intercepting my daughter as she jumped out of the minivan and ran down the driveway to meet me. Scooping her up in my arms, I swung her around, planting a giant kiss on her cheek before returning her to earth, my heart swelling as I gazed down at her shining face. She'd only been away one night, but damn if I hadn't missed the little munchkin like crazy. "And how's my favorite princess this fine morning?"

"I'm not a *princess*, Daddy," Ashley declared in a voice that would make any teenager proud. "*I'm* a queen."

I snorted. "Of course you are, your majesty." I gave her a mock bow, then turned to give my sister a hug and a kiss on each cheek. "Let me guess," I said wryly. "*Frozen* marathon."

Sadie held up her hands in mock innocence. "I swear she only watched it twice." At my skeptical look, she added, "Okay, maybe two and a half times. But she went to bed like a good girl and besides one teensy, eensy chocolate cupcake sharing incident, she was a model citizen the entire visit."

I shook my head. Princesses movies, chocolate cupcakes—going to Sadie's house was like a trip to Disney World. Ashley was going to be sorry to be back home.

I smiled at my sister. "Thanks again for taking her overnight. I really appreciate it."

"Anytime. Did you get a lot of unpacking done?"

I grimaced. With all that had happened, I'd almost forgotten that was the reason she'd taken Ashley to begin with. I'd hoped to have half the boxes gone by now. But instead, I hadn't cracked a single one.

"Not exactly," I confessed. When she raised her eyebrows in question, I glanced down at my daughter. "Go inside and get your uniform on," I told her. "We leave for school in five minutes."

"Aw," Ashley moaned, stamping her foot. "Queens don't have to go to school."

"They do if they want pizza for dinner . . ."

Her brown eyes widened. "Pizza?" she cried. "Pizza for dinner? Really?"

"Only if you're a good queen who does what her daddy tells her to."

"I'm a good queen!" she cried. She turned and dashed to the front door, hopefully to prove this fact by following my instructions. Laughing, Sadie followed her inside.

I started to join them, then stopped, scanning the neighborhood to see if Beth had made it to the truck okay. I felt like such an ass, sending her away like that. But at the same time, what choice had I had? I hadn't been exaggerating when I told her it would confuse Ashley to find another woman in the house. A woman who was not her mom.

And yet, at the same time, I wished Beth could have stayed.

My eyes locked on the live truck and I saw Beth was inside. Watching us, I guess. Probably desperate with curiosity about the whole situation. I'd have time to come clean later—and to apologize for my sins of omission. I watched as she waved at me and I gave her a small salute back. To thank her, best I could, for being a good sport even if the situation was totally unfair to her.

Sighing, I walked into the house to find my sister. She turned to look at me, then gestured questioningly to where Beth's homemade breakfast was still laid out on the table. I'd eaten a few bites, then put the plate down, feeling too guilty to properly enjoy any of it. She'd worked so hard to make it all. And in my haste to get her out, I'd acted like an ungrateful bastard.

This is why I needed to stay away from women.

Sadie surveyed the kitchen. "Well, I'm beginning to get a sense of why you didn't unpack," she said with a slow smile.

"Got time for a long story?"

She grabbed a piece of toast. "Any excuse to get out of CrossFit."

And so I told her everything. About meeting Beth at the club and going home with her. About our one night of passion and the not-so-good morning after. About finding out she was not only my new coworker, but also my new partner. And about what had possessed me to take her home last night after our shift was done.

As I paused for breath, my sister gave a low whistle. "That's some crazy story."

"And you wondered why I didn't want to take Joe up on the whole clubbing thing."

"Please." Sadie shook her head. "You can so not put this on Joe. This is straight up 'I did something horrible in a previous life and am now being punished for it' shit."

I groaned. "Unfortunately, I'm not sure you're wrong."

"Still, you did the right thing," she added. "The poor girl. I can't imagine what that must have been like, having all her stuff thrown out on the front lawn like that. She was lucky you were there to save the day."

"I don't know if *she* thinks that. At least not after this morning." I continued the story, explaining the whole breakfast thing. "I pushed her out the back door like she was some dirty secret I needed to get rid of."

Sadie waved me off. "Don't beat yourself up over it. I'm sure she understands you were only looking out for Ashley."

"If I was truly looking out for Ashley, I would have never invited her here in the first place. Or hooked up with her that first night." I sighed. "Seriously, sis, when did I become such a weak-willed bastard?"

"When you came out of the womb with a Y chromosome," she teased. "Come on, Mac. You're making a bigger deal out of this than it needs to be. So you met a girl. A pretty girl, from what I've seen on TV. You liked her, you did what nature intended guys who like girls to do. What's the big deal?"

"I'm a father," I protested. "I don't have time to do what nature intended anymore. I have responsibilities. I mean, what if things end badly between us and she goes and tries to get me fired? Do you know how hard it was to get a TV job here in San Diego near you guys?" I scowled. "I made a promise. To always put Ashley first. And I'll be damned if I break that promise over a pretty face."

Sadie gave me a sympathetic look. "Putting Ashley first is a good thing," she agreed. "But putting yourself last isn't doing her any favors. You keep saying you want her to be happy. But trust me, she'll never be truly happy unless Daddy's happy, too."

I sighed, hating that she was making sense. I slung an arm around her. "Oh Sadie, when did you get so wise?"

"When I came out of the womb with two X chromosomes," she replied with a grin. "Now come on, bro. Let's not let this kick-ass breakfast go to waste."

twenty-two

BETH

Three hours later and I was back at News 9, ready to start my shift, after what would henceforth be known as the apartment hunt from hell. I'd trudged all over America's finest city all morning long, only to discover that every place up for rent was either too far, too expensive, or too roach-infested to call my own and desperation was starting to set in.

San Diego was one of the most expensive cities in the country and I was beginning to realize the only way I would be able to swing a new place on my salary was to find someone who needed a roommate. Which wasn't going to be easy on such short notice. I had found one potential on Craigslist, but they hadn't been able to meet up until tomorrow. Which meant I'd need to find another place to crash tonight, at the very least.

A place that was definitely *not* Mac's house.

"Well, well, there she is. The woman of the hour."

I startled, crashing back to the present at the sound of a familiar voice behind me.

Whirling around, my eyes widened as they fell upon none

other than News 9's main anchor herself. Joy Justice was leaning against a nearby desk, giving me an elegant looking slow clap.

"Excuse me?" I stammered, cocking my head in question, my pulse kicking up a notch. What was she talking about?

A smile creased the anchor's otherwise smooth face. She gestured for me to approach, then held out a perfectly manicured hand. I took it, still a little uncertain.

"I understand congratulations are in order," she exclaimed. When I looked at her blankly, she added, "Your recent promotion? Sounds like you're the one to watch here at News 9," she added, then laughed softly. "No pun intended, of course."

"Oh. Right!" I cried, my face flushing. Of course. So much had happened, I'd almost forgotten the whole promotion thing. But I guess the news had spread around the station since yesterday.

A warmth crept through my stomach. Up until now I hadn't been sure Joy Justice had even been aware of my existence on the planet, never mind her newsroom, even though she'd been my personal idol since I'd first arrived at the station two years ago. But now, here she was, congratulating me and shaking my hand. Literally calling me "one to watch." How freaking cool was that? It was as if, after all this time, I had finally arrived.

"Thank you," I said. "It's a really big honor."

"One that I'm sure is well deserved," she said, giving me a long-lashed wink. "Who knows, maybe you'll end up taking over for me someday."

I laughed before I could stop myself. "Yeah, right. That'll be the day." After all, it was one thing to get a promotion to dayside. Quite another to be admitted to the ranks of someone like Joy Justice. The woman had at least twenty-five Emmys to her name and a long-standing reputation as being the face "San Diego Trusted Most" to bring them the important news. While the majority of San Diego's population wouldn't be able to pick me out in a lineup if their lives depended on it,

Joy had her own official fan club and about a million followers on Twitter.

Joy gave me a motherly smile. "Reach for the stars, kid. You'll never know unless you try."

And with that, she turned, sauntering back to her private office at the far end of the newsroom, her hips swaying with each step. For someone clocking in closer to sixty than fifty these days, she still had the presence of a supermodel and the body to boot. If I could look half as hot as Joy when I approached her age, I'd be pretty happy, to say the least.

I turned back to my own desk, pretty sure my face was glowing at this point. But any warmth quickly vanished as I suddenly felt an icy stare bite into my back. I glanced over, only to find Stephanie standing at the back of the newsroom surrounded by her new news-writer coworkers, who were all currently glaring at me with narrow eyes. I sighed, attempting to give my former roommate an apologetic smile—a vain attempt to thaw the hatred I saw on her face. But it only made her frown deepen. And I watched, uneasily, as she leaned over and whispered something to Jessica, the five o'clock producer. And from the look on Jessica's face, I could tell that *something* wasn't all that complimentary.

Ignore them, I scolded myself as I switched on my computer. *They're just jealous.* The fact that Joy Justice herself had come over to talk to me probably didn't help things either. That said, I couldn't help feeling just a bit of immature satisfaction that the anchor had chosen a time Stephanie was watching to single me out.

I'm not going to let you ruin this for me, I thought, giving Stephanie one last look before returning to my desk. I had one month to prove myself and I wasn't about to let some high school mean girl drama detract me from realizing my dreams. What was it Joy had just said? *Reach for the stars.* No one was going to stop me from doing my best.

I squared my shoulders. Screw them anyway. I had more important things to worry about. Like going down to the Lemon Grove city hall this afternoon to go through those call records and reports—to prove the city had failed to respond to the family's repeated requests to investigate the abandoned house. And to see if any other gas leaks had been reported and ignored.

Grabbing my notes, I headed down the hall to Richard's office. When I reached the door, I sucked in a breath, trying to mask my nervousness with a confident smile. After all, what did I have to be afraid about? I'd rocked my first assignment and parlayed it into a major investigation. Not bad for a first day on the job.

"Hi, Richard," I said, sauntering into his office. "How's it going?"

He looked up from his papers and grinned. "There she is," he cried. "My burgeoning star."

He motioned for me to sit down and I complied, barely able to control the urge to beam from ear to ear. *Burgeoning star.* I liked the sound of that. And surely a burgeoning star would be pretty secure in her new position, right? No one would want to see a burgeoning star sent packing, after all.

"So how does it feel, kid?" Richard asked. At my questioning look, he added, "You single-handedly won the newscast last night. None of the other stations had anything like it. They were too busy trying to get that family to boo-hoo on camera to look at the bigger picture."

"Thanks," I said, allowing myself to grin widely now. "And that's just the beginning of the story—I'm sure. I'm planning to head down to Lemon Grove city hall today and comb through all the records. Maybe we can find a pattern— other instances. I think it could be a big deal."

"Oh, yeah, it's a great story," he agreed. "But don't worry, we're on it."

"Wait, what?" I stared at him, confusion clawing at my gut.

"I sent Jodi down first thing this morning," he added, referring to one of News 9's investigative producers. "She's going to take things from here."

"But I was the one who discovered this!" I protested, horrified. "It's my story."

He gave me a patronizing smile. "No offense, sweetie, but stumbling upon a tip is not the same as conducting a full investigation. That's why we have an I-Team—to take these stories and run with them."

My heart sank in my chest. They weren't going to let me do the story? *My* story? The one I had uncovered. That wasn't fair!

"Besides," Richard added. "We need you on the dayside rotation. I'm sure Jessica's already got you slotted for something in her show. We can't just pull you and leave her with no one to cover breaking news."

"Right," I said, staring down at my hands, trying to stanch the disappointment in my stomach. "Of course not."

"Look," Richard's voice softened. "You did good, okay? In fact, you did great. But we're a team here. We work together. You hand over your notes to Jodi and she will do you proud, I promise. And hey, maybe we can even give you a little producer credit or something when the piece finally airs."

"Thank you. That'd be great," I said flatly. I rose from my seat. "Now if you'll excuse me, I better go get my assignment."

Richard nodded, looking relieved. "You do that," he said. "I'm expecting nothing less than another home run today." He grinned. "Congrats again, Beth. I'm proud of you."

I walked out of the office, shutting the door behind me, before heading back to the newsroom.

It's no big deal, I scolded myself as I made my way over to the assignment desk. *You got the credit. He knows you did good. What more do you want? Heck, you just got promoted yesterday—do you suddenly expect to be running the station twenty-four hours later? Besides, they need you for breaking news. That's just as important—maybe even more so. Maybe you'll cover a hostage crisis. Or a high-speed chase. A political scandal, perhaps. Or maybe a—*

"Water safety demo."

Wait, what?

I cocked my head, staring at the producer who had just stepped into my path, shoving a packet of papers into my hands. It was Jessica, I realized in dismay. The same producer who had been talking to Stephanie earlier.

"I'm sorry, what did you say?"

Jessica gave me a smug smile. She spoke slowly, deliberately, as if addressing a young child. "Down at Fiesta Island. They're doing a water safety demo for underprivileged kids. I want a package at five."

"You want me to spend the day at the beach?" I asked incredulously, the words spilling from my lips before I had a chance to check myself. Fiesta Island was a small piece of land in the Mission Bay area of San Diego. People would go there on weekends to race Jet Skis and practice water skiing tricks. Kids could splash in wave-free waters and parents could barbecue in designated fire pits. It was a fun place to hang out, but not exactly what breaking news stories were made of.

"Isn't there something . . ." I searched for the right words. "More . . . important to cover?" Being taken off my story for breaking news was one thing. But wasting my time on something like this? That was so not cool.

"Sure, there are plenty of *important* stories," Jessica sneered. "And I've already assigned them to *important* reporters." She shrugged her shoulders. "Looks like you're beach bound, Beth. Unless you want me to go talk to Richard on your behalf . . ."

"No!" I blurted, fear slamming through me at the mere suggestion. Richard already thought I was trying to step beyond my station. I had to prove to him that I could handle anything they threw at me, whether death defying breaking news or pointless fluff.

Still . . . I couldn't help stealing a glance over at Stephanie, who was still hanging out at the assignment desk, giggling with one of desk editors—way too "cat that ate the canary" for my liking. Could *she* have had something to do with this particular assignment? It seemed so grade school. But, at the same time, I wouldn't put it past her. She had a vested interest, after all, in having me fail. If my spot were to open up, she might be able to convince Richard to put her back in it.

I frowned. *Sorry, bitch. That's not going to happen. You just watch: I'm going to rock this silly story till it's worthy of an Emmy.*

"I'm on it," I told Jessica, giving her a curt nod before heading back to my desk. But I stopped halfway, as I spotted Mac sitting in my chair. My heart fluttered in my chest as I took in his slouchy jeans and the tight gray T-shirt that hugged his chest. He'd shaved, I noted, and his strong, clean jaw looked etched out of granite. He had grabbed a bottle of hairspray from my desk and was casually tossing it into the air, catching it with his other hand.

"Hey," I said, walking up behind him. "You made it."

He looked up, his expression more than a little sheepish. "Just barely," he said with a laugh. Then he frowned as he caught my face. "Everything okay?" he asked.

I tried to swallow back the lump that had formed in my throat. "Sure," I ground out. "Everything is awesome."

His frown deepened and I could tell he didn't believe me. But to his credit, he didn't press for an answer. "Are you ready to head out to Lemon Grove?" he asked instead. "I've got the car all loaded up."

I shook my head. "Actually, we're on a different beat today," I told him with as much false enthusiasm as I could muster. "Water safety demo!"

"What?" He frowned. "We're not following up on the gas leak?"

"Nope! The I-Team has that covered evidently."

His face fell. "Oh, Beth . . ."

The sympathy in his eyes was almost too much and I could feel the traitorous tears spring to my own. The fact that he understood—that he was the only one who really understood here—it was almost too much. And suddenly all I wanted to do was throw myself into his arms and let him smooth away my tears.

But then I caught Stephanie looking at me again. And so instead I swiped the tears away with my sleeve. There was no crying in TV news, after all. And I wasn't about to let those bitches see me fall apart. Instead, I grabbed my cell phone off my desk and the hairspray in Mac's hand and stuffed them both in my tote bag.

"Let's go," I said.

He looked at me for a heartbreaking moment, then gave me a pitying nod. Unable to look at him for a second longer, I turned on my heel and headed toward the back door where his truck would be parked.

This was going to be a very long day. But at least I got to spend it with him.

twenty-three

BETH

We arrived at Fiesta Island ten minutes later. The sun sparkling off the water momentarily blinded me as I stepped out of the truck, and I quickly reached for my sunglasses. It was your typical perfect San Diego weather day. Seventy-five degrees with a light breeze. In December. Back home they were probably going through yet another snowpocalypse, digging themselves out of freezing snow.

Instead, I was here. Outside. On the perfect beach day. Children's laughter and screeches echoing through my ears while the salty seaweed smell tickled my nose. Suddenly it didn't seem like the worst assignment in the world after all. I mean, let's face it, there weren't a lot of jobs that paid you to spend the day on the beach. Sure, it wasn't going to be a boon for my career, but it wasn't exactly torture on the rack either.

Plus, maybe it'd give me some time to talk things over with Mac. Find out the real scoop on the mysterious daughter and the evidently absentee mom.

We hadn't talked much on the way over. He'd driven, I'd scarfed down the breakfast he'd brought me from home. The breakfast I had cooked, but hadn't had a chance to eat. The breakfast he'd carefully packaged up and brought to work, in case I was still hungry. What a guy—I bet he cut the crusts off his daughter's PB&J every morning, too.

After Mac parked the truck, I jumped out, walking around to the back to help with the gear. I grabbed the tripod while he swung the camera strap over his shoulder. Then together we walked down to the shore where the swim lessons were taking place. I smiled as a lifeguard came up to us and introduced herself as Darcy.

"The children are so excited you're here!" she informed us, her own eyes twinkling with a matching enthusiasm. "We've never met a real life TV celebrity like yourself, Ms. White."

I could feel my cheeks heat. "Oh no. I'm hardly a—"

"'Scuse me?"

I felt a tugging at my skirt and looked down. A little girl with thick black braids gazed up at me with wide eyes.

"Yes, sweetie?" I asked, dropping down to her level to greet her.

"Are you the reporter lady?"

"Um, yes. I'm Beth White. I work for News 9."

The girl's mouth stretched into a huge grin. "Can I have your autograph?"

I wanted to laugh. Me, give an autograph? That was a first.

But the girl was so sincere—so earnest in her request— how could I turn her down? Instead I found myself scrambling for a pen and notepad and scribbling my name onto it, feeling more than a little self-conscious as I did so. I wondered if Mac thought I was putting on airs. I finished with a smiley face and then ripped the paper from the pad, handing it to her.

She stared down at my scrawl, as if I had written my name in pure gold. "What do you say to the nice lady?" Darcy prompted, looking amused.

"Thank you," she whispered shyly. Then she bolted, back to her friends. From behind Darcy I could see her showing off her paper. "I got the TV lady's autograph!" she informed them proudly. And a moment later I found myself surrounded.

"Kids, kids!" Darcy exclaimed. "Ms. White doesn't have time to sign all your autographs. She's very busy!" The lifeguard turned to me apologetically. "I'm sorry. As I said before, they're just excited."

"Oh, I don't mind," I assured her, feeling a warmth rise within me. And to think I'd almost turned down this assignment! "Mac's got to set up and get some B-roll anyway. I can sign until he's ready for me." I glanced over at Mac for confirmation and he nodded, looking a little amused.

And so I got down on my knees and began signing. Notebooks, napkins, a volleyball—one kid even requested I sign his forehead. I drew the line on that, of course, not wanting his parents to freak when he got home. Still, it made me laugh. And soon we were all laughing together and my personal troubles seemed far, far away.

Maybe this assignment was meant to be a punishment. But it was turning out to be a real pleasure.

At that point Mac was ready and so I grabbed the microphone and proceeded to interview the children. I took care to give face time to every child brave enough to speak, even though I knew I wouldn't be able to use every soundbite in the actual piece. Still, they were so excited, I didn't want to leave anyone out. And they were smart, too, spouting off facts about the importance of water safety and wearing life jackets. By the time I was done I was more than a little impressed.

After I finished the interviews, Darcy stepped back in, continuing her water safety lessons. Mac shot video of an overly dramatic drowning dramatization and the kids' grossed-out reactions to the idea of mouth-to-mouth resuscitation.

I stood back, watching him work the scene, just as thoroughly as he had for the breaking news fire. He could have taken it easy—phoned it in this time. It wasn't an important story. But he shot it as if it could be Emmy worthy. And I had to admire him for that.

Well, that and the way his jeans showcased his perfect

backside every time he crouched down on the sand. Oh Lordie. My face heated and I forced myself to turn away.

After he finished shooting, we walked back to the truck to write and edit the story. As I scribbled down my script, the wind picked up and I brushed my hair from my face for what felt like the thousandth time. At this point I probably resembled a beach bum Medusa and would definitely have to spend a few minutes to brush my hair back and secure it with mega hairspray before my live shot.

When I had finished writing and voicing my story, I popped out of the truck so Mac could begin his work piecing the story together. Kicking off my shoes, I stared out over the water, once again allowing myself to enjoy the beautiful day.

Take that, Stephanie. I'm having a good time, despite your best efforts.

"I gotta admit, this beats the hell out of a dirty, smoky fire."

I looked up to see Mac emerge from the truck and my heart flip-flopped in my chest, despite my best efforts. God, why did he have to look so damn delicious all the time? It would be a hell of a lot easier to play professional if he were some ugly troll. Why did he have to be so tall, so broad-shouldered, so self-possessed as he walked toward me? Why did he have to lock those mesmerizing blue eyes on me or flash those perfectly straight, white teeth? It wasn't fair.

"Yeah," I said, exchanging my view of him for that of the ocean, praying the ebbs and flow of the tide would serve to calm my raging hormones. "Not bad at all."

I could feel him watching me, his eyes roving over my body, and I stifled the urge to squirm under his gaze. *You have no power over me,* I scolded him silently in my head, only wishing I had the courage to say it out loud.

Or, you know, really believe it to be true.

"You were really good with those kids, by the way," he observed. His voice was casual, but I thought I could hear the thread of something else underneath. Something admiring? "After all, you know what they say about working with kids and dogs . . ."

"I'm sure you'd know better than me," I muttered.

He blushed and I immediately felt bad for bringing it up. But before I could speak, the radio in the live truck crackled to life. "Unit Five, are you ready?" Saved by the live shot.

Mac's eyes flickered to me. "You good to go?" he asked.

I started to nod—then remembered my unruly hair. "Give me one minute. I've got to fix this," I said, gesturing to the locks in question. Richard expected his reporters to always look perfectly coiffed, despite the weather. And I wasn't about to give him any reason to doubt my ability to do this job. Whether it was by uncovering scandal or just ensuring a good hair day.

Mac glanced at his watch. "Okay, but hurry," he said. "We have four minutes before we're live."

I nodded, dashing to the truck and grabbing the bottle of hairspray he had been toying with at my desk earlier in the day, then ran back to the beach. I'd forgotten my mirror, so I had to brush and spray by feel. *It should be fine, though*, I considered. After all, we were on a beach. I should look a little windblown.

Suddenly laughter and squeals of delight broke out amongst the children. I glanced over, wondering what was suddenly so funny. I realized, uncomfortably, they were all laughing and pointing at me.

"What is it?" I asked.

"Your hair!" cried Marla, the brown braided girl who'd originally asked for my autograph.

I frowned. "What's wrong with my hair?" I asked. It couldn't be *that* windswept, could it? I mean, not enough that little kids would find it funny. I glanced worriedly over at Mac, who was just now looking up from his viewfinder.

"Two minutes to . . ." He trailed off, a horrified look washing over his face.

"What?" I demanded, adrenaline now spiking through my veins. We had two minutes. We didn't have time for a problem. Confused, I reached up to try to pat my hair down—maybe some of it was sticking out in a weird direction? But everything felt in place. Everything, except . . .

I pulled my hands away and looked down at them. My eyes widened. My breath caught in my throat.

My palms were stained a bright blue color.

Which could only mean . . .

"How in the hell . . . ?" I whispered, horror rushing through me.

I reached down, grabbing the seemingly innocent bottle of hairspray. With trembling hands, I pumped a small stream onto the sand. Sure enough, the mist stained the crystals blue.

Suddenly, Stephanie's words came raging back to me. *You don't even know the word sorry*, she'd said. *But you will.*

Now I was beginning to believe her.

twenty-four

MAC

I watched, for a moment frozen in place, as Beth reached for her hair, batting it madly with her hands, as if she would be able to brush out the blue by sheer force of will. But obviously that wasn't going to work—at least not in the next sixty seconds, before she was due to be live on TV.

"Forty-five seconds," the producer barked in my earpiece, back at the station. "Talk to me, Jake. I don't see Beth. Is she ready? Are you guys going to make your slot?"

I glanced over at Beth, who was so, so not ready. I opened my mouth to inform the producer, but before I could speak, she caught my eye, shaking her head desperately from side to side.

Shit. We couldn't miss our live shot. That was certain death in TV news. But at the same time, she couldn't exactly go on air like this—looking like a deranged Smurf. That would equally spell career doom. But what alternative did we have? My mind raced madly, trying to come up with a solution on the fly. There was no time to go down to the water to try to rinse the blue out. And no time to retrieve my baseball cap from the truck . . .

Think, Mac. There's got to be a way.

Then, suddenly it hit me—with all the force of a ten-ton truck. Something Ashley used to do to me all the time on rainy days when we were bored and stuck inside. She'd dubbed it the Bald Game, and it was actually pretty funny the first fifty-three thousand times we'd played it.

Now it might just save Beth's career.

"We'll be ready," I barked at the producer, then stuffed the lens cap over my camera so the folks back at the station couldn't watch what I was about to try to pull. I turned to Beth. "Get in position and kneel down," I instructed. "Kids, gather around Beth, okay? As close as you can."

"Mac, I can't go on like—" Beth cried. But I waved a hand to cut her off; I had no time to explain. Instead, I met her wide, fearful eyes with my own and gave her my best reassuring look.

"Do you trust me?" I asked softly.

It was admittedly kind of a loaded question, given our recent history, and I wouldn't have been at all surprised if she'd shaken her head no. But instead, she squared her shoulders and nodded. Whether to my credit, or because there was no alternative, I had no idea.

But I'd take what I could get.

"Twenty seconds," the producer shouted in my ear. "Mac, what's wrong with your shot? We can't see anything."

"We'll make it," I told them, with an assurance I didn't quite feel. Running up to the kids, I hoisted little Marla up onto Beth's shoulders, then dropped down to face her. "You're going to be the superhero, okay?" I told her. "But there's something I need you to do."

She nodded solemnly, staring back at me with ultra-serious eyes.

"Now put your hands right here," I instructed, placing them over the bright blue stain on Beth's head. "Cover up the blue spot."

Marla did what she was told, now beaming with excitement at being singled out. Below, Beth's eyes widened, as she started to realize what I was trying to do.

"Whatever you do," I told Marla. "Don't let go." I turned to the rest of the kids. "Are you guys ready?"

The group cheered. Okay, that would have to be good enough. I raced back to my camera.

"Five seconds," the producer said.

I yanked off the lens cap and pointed to Beth.

"Go!"

"Good afternoon. I'm down at Fiesta Island," she began with a slight tremble in her voice. But as she continued, I could hear her confidence growing stronger. "Where, I have to say, I'm having a great old time hanging with these guys." She gestured to the kids. "We're all here as part of a city-wide water safety initiative that was introduced this year by . . ."

I watched through the lens of my camera, pretty much holding my breath, while praying the little girl would keep her hold on Beth's hair.

Ten more seconds. Just ten more seconds . . .

"And you're clear," the producer proclaimed into my earpiece. "Thanks, guys."

I let out a breath of relief. Looking up from the camera, I gave Beth a thumbs-up. She let out a shriek of excitement and the kids all cheered, hugging her, hugging each other, jumping up and down. Beth reached up to help little Marla from her shoulders and gave her a big hug. "Thank you," she said, her voice cracking a little. "You just saved the day."

Marla grinned like the Cheshire cat itself, puffing out her chest with pride. "He said I was a superhero," she said, pointing to me.

Beth laughed. "I think he might be right," she agreed, planting a kiss on the top of the girl's head. "Now go on, Supergirl. Go finish your lesson."

As Marla danced over to the others, Beth rose to her feet and turned to me, giving me a shaky smile. I beamed back at her, feeling a little like a superhero myself.

"Thank you," she murmured. "I thought I was totally dead there."

"Please," I scoffed. "They're going to have to try a lot harder than that if they want to take us down."

The smile slipped from her lips. She sighed and dropped down onto the sand, absently picking up the hairspray bottle. "That's what I'm afraid of."

I gave her a rueful look. 'Do you think *she* did it?" I asked, realizing there was no need to speak the name aloud. It was pretty obvious who would be behind such a mean trick.

Beth shrugged. "She promised to make me sorry. Gotta say, she's off to a terrific start."

I scowled, the situation all too familiar for comfort. Another day, another station. God, sometimes I hated TV news. I mean, here I was, on the opposite end of the country, reliving the same old drama I'd tried to escape from back home. I was beginning to realize that no matter where I went, the story was always going to be the same. For every reporter like Beth—who truly seemed to want to right wrongs and make a difference—there were dozens of grown men and women, reenacting their own version of the TV News Hunger Games, vying for just a few more precious minutes of airtime.

I'd seen reporters like Stephanie too many times before. Addicted to the stress, the fast pace, the glory and the prestige. Falling victim to the idea that you weren't anyone—if you weren't on TV. And then, when that on-air identity was stripped for one reason or another, they crashed like drug addicts in detox, losing sight of themselves, chasing after the fleeting public persona like that was all that kept them glued together.

If Stephanie was like the others—and I had no doubt she was—blue hair would only be the beginning. I just hoped Beth would be strong enough to handle it. Maybe if I was there to help . . .

Then again . . . My thoughts drifted to another reporter who I'd once tried to protect. Victoria herself. But I hadn't been able to save her from the rotten business. And, in the end, I was the one who became the true victim. Well, Ashley and I, that was. And I had no interest in repeating that little slice of history, thank you very much.

No, it was better to stay professional. Stay aloof. After

all, the last thing I needed was to get dragged down into more drama. Mixed up in another scandal. The whole Boston fiasco had nearly ruined me—and Ashley was still suffering from the shrapnel. I needed to put her first this time. Keep my head down. Not cause a scene. Stay on the sidelines and let Beth fight her own battles and remain uninvolved.

It was for the best.

But it was also going to be hard as hell.

I realized Beth had risen to her feet and was pacing across the sand like a caged tiger, her hands still clutching the bottle of hairspray. "She wants to play?" I heard her mutter under her breath. "Well, I can play. I can—"

"Take the high road?" I suggested.

She whirled around, looking at me with scorn. "Why should I? She doesn't deserve that!"

"No. She doesn't," I agreed. "She deserves all you could throw at her and then some. But Beth, you'll just be playing into her hands. Don't you see? She wants you to be pissed. So pissed that you'll do something stupid that will get you fired." I shook my head. "You don't need to stoop to her level. You're better than that."

Beth winced and I could tell my words were hitting home. She looked up at me, her eyes pleading. "It's just not fair. And I'm so mad."

"It's okay to be mad," I assured her. "You can bitch about it to me all night long if you want to. Just don't let her win." I gave her a sorry look. "Trust me, I say this from experience."

She raised an eyebrow. "What do you mean?" she asked, sounding curious despite herself.

But I only waved her off. It was the last thing I wanted to get into right about now. "Just . . . try to rise above and not let her get to you."

"What if she tries something else?"

"I have no doubt she will. But we'll get through it. Whatever it is."

She bit her lower lip. "We?" she repeated doubtfully.

Shit. Did I say we? So much for all my good intentions

of staying aloof. *Mac, the idiot knight in shining armor, charging in, once more with feeling.* I sighed.

"Yes," I assured her. "Like I told you yesterday, we're a team. And I've got your back—no matter what."

She let out a choking sob and against my better judgment I found myself pulling her into my arms. She felt so small, so fragile cradled in my embrace, and I felt a fierce protectiveness wash over me, despite my best efforts. Mostly because she was right—this wasn't fair. She had done nothing to deserve this and it killed me to just stand there and comfort her without promising to go forth and defend her honor, even though I knew it was the last thing in the world I needed to be doing.

I'd tried that long ago. And look where it had gotten me.

Okay fine, I couldn't fight her war. But I could pull her closer to me, until her body was flush to mine. I could let her head rest against my chest. Could stroke her hair, rejoicing in the silkiness of each strand—and assure her that, in her case, blue was still beautiful.

She pulled away then, looking up at me with large tortured eyes. My heart wrenched in my chest and I reached up, swiping away the tear that had slipped down her cheek. Her skin was so smooth—so impossibly soft.

Her lips parted, as if she was about to speak. But suddenly I found I didn't want her to. I didn't want her to say all the sensible things I knew she was about to say. I didn't want her to break the spell. I didn't want to be forced to let her go.

And so instead I did the dumbest thing I could have possibly done in a situation like this.

I leaned down. And I kissed her.

twenty-five

BETH

I startled as Mac's lips came crashing down on mine, so swift, so unexpected that, in an instant, my brain seemed to short-circuit and I forgot everything I was about to say. Like a hard drive, erased by a heavy-duty magnet, I suddenly found myself a blank slate as his mouth covered my own. I couldn't think. I couldn't speak. I couldn't focus on anything at all except the heat that coursed through my body like a wildfire.

His kiss was firm, yet soft. Demanding, yet inviting. And when I let out a shuddering breath, his tongue took advantage, plunging into my mouth as if in search of an even deeper connection between us. Soon my heart was hammering against my ribcage and I was forced to cling to him as my knees threatened to buckle out from under me. He smiled against my mouth and seemed to pull me tighter, one hand secured at the curve of my lower back, the other tangling in my hair. My breasts tingled, now squashed against his solid chest and my skin erupted into goosebumps.

For one blissful moment there was no Stephanie. No News 9. No job in jeopardy.

But it didn't last.

It couldn't.

And sure enough, a moment later, he pulled away, stumbling backward. The break in our connection caused a sudden pang of emptiness deep inside—like the phantom pain one feels after losing a limb. But I ignored it as best I could—what else could I do?—focusing instead on trying to still my racing heart and steady my breath.

"I'm sorry, I can't do this," he said, pacing the beach with marked agitation.

"Um, I didn't ask you to," I mentioned, feeling annoyance creep in amongst my unhappiness. This hot and cold thing he had going on needed to stop if I was going to retain any sense of sanity. "You kissed *me*, remember?"

He raked a hand through his hair and groaned. "I know," he said quietly. "And I'm sorry for that. You just looked so goddamned beautiful, I couldn't help myself."

"Oh yeah, I'm truly stunning," I declared sarcastically. "A truly stunning Smurfette!" Flipping my blue stained hair, I broke into a little Smurf dance. "How did their song go again? La, la, la la la, la. La, la, la, la, la."

He groaned and sank down onto the sand, scrubbing his face with his hands. "Oh God," he said. "That should *so* not be as sexy as it is."

I rolled my eyes and plopped down next to him on the sand. Then I cocked my head so I could peer into his eyes. "Mac," I said, getting serious, "I think it's time you tell me what's really going on here."

He nodded slowly, giving me a tortured look. His eyes were red, I noticed. And he looked tired. As if he hadn't slept a wink the night before. As if he hadn't slept well all year.

"Look, Beth," he began. "You gotta understand. I never meant to drag you into my screwed-up life. When I went to that club, I had no intentions of hooking up—I had sworn off women for good and was just there to get my brother-in-law off my back." He sighed. "But then you walked in, stunningly gorgeous and clever as all hell, tricking that bartender with the tequila thing. And then when we started dancing?" He groaned. "I was like a drug addict fresh out of rehab and you were my perfect vice." He gave me a rueful grin and I wrinkled my nose, trying not to feel pleased at the backhanded compliment.

I drew in a breath. "No offense," I said, trying to gather my courage. After all, we had to be honest with one another if this was going to work somehow. "But it's not like you're married, right? I mean, what's stopping you from pursuing a relationship?"

"Just the fucked-up mess I made of my last one," he replied without missing a beat. "With Ashley's mother."

"Oh." I fell silent, my heart thrumming in my chest. "Right."

He kicked at the sand with his shoe. "Trust me, I don't need to go into the gory details. Let's just say it almost ruined me. And it pretty much tore my baby girl apart." He sank his head into hands. "I can't risk putting her through something like that again." He lifted his head, his eyes fierce. "I won't," he clarified. "She's my priority now. To pursue anything beyond her—that would just be selfish." He glanced over at me. "I'm sorry."

I gave him a sad smile, my heart aching at the pain I saw on his face. "I understand," I said. "And it's not something to apologize for. If anything, it's admirable. Like father-of-the-year level admirable."

He snorted. "Uh, yeah. It may be a while before I win any trophies," he said. "But I'm trying." He paused. "In any case, I'm sorry again for dragging you into all of this. I wanted to tell you everything that first night—but I was actually kind of enjoying the fantasy of it all. The idea that I was, for once, totally free to do what I wanted to do—not what I was supposed to do." He gave me a shy look. "It was a great night, Beth. Probably the best in recent memory."

I felt a blush creep to my cheeks. "I enjoyed it, too," I admitted. "It was . . . special. Way more special, I guess, than a one-night stand has any right to be."

"Yeah, well, hopefully you got what you needed, too," he said with a shrug. "Showed your ex or whatever."

"Wait, what?" I stared at him, my heart suddenly pounding in my chest. "Where did you hear about my ex?"

He looked sheepish. "Your roommate said something about it as I was leaving. That you were trying to get back at him or whatever. That's why you hooked up with me."

My cheeks burned and I turned away, too embarrassed to even look at him. "Oh my God. I am going to kill her," I muttered. "I am literally going to kill her."

Mac put a hand on my shoulder. "It's okay," he assured me. "It's just . . . I think we both needed something that night. And I'm glad we were there to give it to each other."

"Yeah," I said thoughtfully. "Me, too, actually."

He opened his arm and I crawled to him, cuddling my head against his shoulder. For a moment, we just sat there, staring out into the ocean, focusing on the ebb and flow of the tides. The sounds of the children had faded in the distance and all we could hear was the crash of the waves against the shore. It should have been awkward. But it wasn't. In fact, it was strangely peaceful. It felt right.

Suddenly Mac blurted out, "Do you want to meet her?"

I raised my head, turning to him in question, my adrenaline spiking in my veins. "Who? Ashley?"

I could see his hard swallow. "Yeah," he said. "I mean, if you wanted to, anyway. You could come over. I could order pizza."

"Are you sure you want me to?" I asked. "I mean, I don't have to."

He closed his eyes for a moment. Then he opened them, locking them on me. "Yes," he said. "I'm sure."

The look on his face told me this was a big deal. A really big step for him—maybe one he hadn't ever taken before. He was letting me in. For real, this time.

"I would be honored," I said.

twenty-six

MAC

We arrived back at my place around 6 P.M. I showed Beth the shower so she could attempt to wash the blue dye from her hair, then called Sadie, letting her know she was free to drop Ashley off at any time. I could almost hear the evil grin in my sister's voice as I added that she should let Ash know Daddy was having a friend over for dinner and she'd get to play with her. Thankfully, my sister didn't tease me too much.

I still didn't know what the hell I was doing. Or if this was even a good idea. All I did know was that I'd been a real jerk—and it was time to man up. Beth had enough shit going on in her life right now, without having me complicate things further. If we were going to be coworkers—and maybe even friends—we had to sit down and talk like two adults. Figure out what was going on between us and figure out a way to stop it before it got any more complicated.

Which means no more making out, I reminded myself. *We're talking pure friend zone from this point on.*

I groaned as my mind flashed back to the kiss on the beach. To the feel of her soft, sweet lips sweeping hungrily against my own. To the way she had clung to me, as if I really was some kind of superhero with the power to save the day. Instead of a burned-out photog with a kid in tow.

In another life, in another world . . .

I heard the shower turn off and sighed in relief. It'd been hard work, concentrating on not thinking about Beth in my shower. Not thinking about her running my bar of soap up and down her slick, wet, naked body. God, that soap was a lucky bastard.

The old me might have taken advantage, slipped into the bathroom, dropped trou, and made sure she didn't miss any of her 2000 parts. First with soap, then with water.

Then, if all went well, with my tongue.

The new me? Well, he would evidently content himself with breaking out in a cold sweat, while simultaneously breaking the cork in the bottle of wine he was trying to open.

Oh yeah. I was hot stuff, that was for sure.

This isn't a date, I reminded myself for the thousandth time. *She's about to meet your daughter, for God's sake. Not exactly time to get your shower sex on.*

Besides, Beth had a lot more to deal with without having to worry about being licked head to toe by her horny coworker. She had been cruelly sabotaged. Her job almost put in jeopardy. Not to mention she still didn't have a place to live. Right now, she needed a friend. And I was determined to fill that role.

Even if it ended up killing me.

I gave the corkscrew a tug. The cork gave way and the wine burst out with it, succeeding in splashing all over my shirt. Awesome. By the end of the night I was sure to be leading contender for Bachelor of the Year. Sighing, I set down the wine and headed back to my bedroom to grab a new shirt, only to smack into Beth in the hallway.

Beth, who was clad only in a towel.

"Oh!" she cried, startled, losing her grip on the towel in question. Only for a split second, mind you, but it was enough. Enough for me to glimpse the swell of her perfect breasts, the rounded flare of her full hips, the dark thatch between her legs. And just like that I was thrown back to the one night we'd shared. When my hands had wrapped around those hips, pulling her tight against me. When my mouth had suckled those breasts, my tongue swirling around the tips. I could almost hear the soft mewing cries that had escaped her lips as I thoroughly ravaged her without apology.

And . . . so much for friend zoning.

"Sorry!" I cried, trying to garner up all my strength to turn away and pretend to be a gentleman. "I was just . . . I didn't know you were . . ."

"I forgot to bring my clothes into the bathroom," she stammered, her face bright red as she clutched the towel tight to her body with white-knuckled fingers. It was then that I realized I was still standing in her way.

"Sorry," I said again, angling so she could move past me. I could feel my erection pressing hard against my jeans and prayed she didn't look down. Thankfully, she kept her eyes averted as she pushed past me to enter the spare bedroom, closing the door and clicking the lock behind her. I let out a heavy groan, then retreated to my own bedroom to change.

Had this been a really, really bad idea?

After donning a new shirt, I headed back to the kitchen, grabbing the bottle of scotch from the counter and treating myself to a decent pour. Liquid courage and all that. The rate that things were going, I was going to need it.

A moment later Beth emerged from the bedroom. The towel was gone, but what had replaced it did little to calm my libido. From the emerald green tank top that clung to her breasts and accented her flat stomach, to a free-flowing skirt made out of some kind of filmy material that swished against her hips as she walked. God, it wasn't fair. Though, truth be told, I was pretty sure she could have stepped out wearing a garbage bag and I would have found myself just as aroused.

"You clean up nice," I teased her, desperate to lighten the mood.

Her cheeks took on a rosy glow. "Thank you. I got a few things at the mall this morning before my shift. Most of my regular clothes are pretty trashed thanks to you know who."

I gave her a rueful look. "Well, you did good," I assured her. "The green really brings out your eyes."

"More than the blue?" she snarked. Then she sighed. "I guess I should be grateful she didn't decide to use something more permanent." Reaching down, she grabbed the glass of wine I'd poured her and took a long slug, then plopped down onto the couch.

For a moment, silence fell over the room. But strangely, it wasn't an uncomfortable one. In fact, it felt weirdly peaceful, just sitting side by side, not saying a word. Victoria had been such a talker, always bitching about how someone had done something that she found offensive; I ended up tuning her out half the time. And now I had Ashley, who I loved more than life itself, but seriously never shut up.

The doorbell rang. Speak of the devil.

I gave Beth a small smile, then rose from my seat to head to the door. I could feel my heart pick up the pace the closer I got, and I realized I was more nervous than I thought I'd be. I tried to tell myself it was no big deal. Ashley would understand that Daddy could have friends, just like she did. And she was far too young to understand that these "friends" could be anything more.

"Daddy!" she chirped as I opened the door. Without pause, she threw her arms around my legs in a big preschooler embrace. In turn, I swooped down, scooping her up into a proper daddy bear hug.

"How's my little queen?" I greeted, kissing her on the nose.

"I'm not a *queen*," Ashley interjected. "I'm a pony, Daddy. I'm Rainbow Dash." She tossed her hair as if it were a horse's mane and gave me her best *duh* look.

"Of course you are. Silly Daddy."

I ruffled her hair and set her back down on the ground. Then I waved to my sister, who was getting back into her minivan. Sadie pointed to the house, cocking her head in a questioning look. I sighed and nodded. She grinned, giving me a way-too-enthusiastic two thumbs-up, then climbed into the driver's seat. Thankfully she had the other kids in the back—or I would have probably been forced to make introductions, which I was so not ready to do.

Instead, I turned back to my daughter. "So how was school?"

The grin fell from her face. "Not good."

"What do you mean? I thought it was a very nice school."

"It's not a nice school. I don't like that school."

"You said you loved it. You said they had the best playground ever." My brow creased. "What happened?"

"Nothing."

Frustration began to build inside of me. "Sweetie, I can't help you if you don't tell me what's wrong."

Ashley shrugged her little shoulders, her Windbreaker sliding off her arms and onto the floor. The normally well-trained child made no move to pick it up. "They laughed at me," she said at last. "They said I talk funny. And they wouldn't play with me."

I winced at the hurt look I saw on her face and my heart panged in my chest. I knew moving here was going to be an adjustment for all of us, but I had been holding out hope that Ashley's outgoing personality and self-confidence would win her new friends immediately. But evidently her slight lisp was making her stand out in the crowd.

Suddenly all I wanted to do was march down to that school and punch the shit out of a bunch of four-year-olds. No one could blame me for that, right?

Instead, I raked a frustrated hand through my hair, trying to channel my inner grown-up. It was funny, as a kid I'd always assumed parents had all the answers. But these days, more often than not, I was left clueless.

"Don't listen to them, sweetie," I said, trying to pull her into my arms for another hug. But she held back this time, stiff and unyielding. "I think you talk just fine."

"You don't want to talk like those *California* kids anyway."

I whirled around at the sudden voice, surprised to see Beth standing in the doorway, a sly grin on her face. "You know,"

she added, mimicking an overly exaggerated Valley Girl
speech straight out of an eighties movie. "Like totally grody
to the max, dude!"

Ashley giggled, a little shyly, pressing her head against
my shoulder. I took this as my cue and donned my best surfer
voice. "Yeah, Ash, dude! I gotta, like, totally catch this tubu-
lar wave, bruh."

The giggles increased. "They don't talk like that!" she
protested.

"Oh right. Gag me with a spoon fer shure," Beth replied,
throwing in a toss of her hair for good measure.

"Like totally," I agreed with mock seriousness. I kissed
Ashley's freckled nose. "Babe."

She squealed. "Like, totally, dude, spoon, shure!" she
cried, jumping up and down. Then her eyes focused on Beth.
"Who are you?"

I drew in a breath. Here went nothing. "Ashley, this is
my friend Beth. Beth, this is Ashley."

"Are you and my dad having a playdate?" she asked.

A smile crept to Beth's lips. "Something like that."

Ashley seemed to consider this for a moment. Then she
nodded her head. "Can you play the car game?" she asked.

I groaned. My daughter's level of respect for any adult,
these days, seemed to hinge directly on their skills on Mario
Kart. "Honey, I don't—"

"I love the car game," Beth broke in before I could finish.
"And I'm really good at them, too." She grinned. "So you'd
better watch out!"

"Yeah, well, *you* better watch out for my daddy!" Ashley
proclaimed proudly. "He's the best ever!" She grabbed Beth's
hand and started tugging her in the direction of the living
room. "Come on!"

I watched for a moment, something strange stirring inside
me as the two girls headed for the game console. Here I had
worried about Ashley finding a stranger in the house. I should
have known my daughter better than that. To her, a stranger
was just a potential friend. And Beth—the way she'd deflected
the school crisis was just pure unadulterated magic. I mean,

here I was, the actual dad, totally stumped and she'd waltzed in there like it was the world's simplest parenting problem. And she didn't even have kids!

I headed into the kitchen and grabbed the phone. I'd already programmed the pizza guy into my contacts. After placing the order, I peeked into the living room. Beth and Ashley were on the floor, Wii steering wheels in hand, locked in a mad game of Mario versus Princess Peach. It was enough to do me in.

I tried to imagine Ashley's mother playing a videogame. Hell, playing anything with her daughter. She worked crazy hours and when she came home, she'd go straight to the liquor cabinet, saying she needed to "unwind." And so it would be up to me to act out scenes with the Disney Barbies or My Little Ponys, while she sat on the couch, busily conversing with her Facebook fans instead of her family.

I wondered how Beth had become so good with children. Was she a natural or had she had some experience—maybe with nephews or nieces or young siblings? It was strange; I'd spent so much time with her over the last few days, but I knew very little about her. For all of her accusations that I had been less than forthcoming about my own personal life, she was even tighter lipped. I knew she'd come from the Midwest. I knew she'd once worked as a waitress. I knew she had some kind of ex-boyfriend . . .

But what really made her tick? Why had she come out to San Diego? What were her goals and dreams? Did she take one sugar in her coffee or two? Did she even drink coffee at all? Suddenly I wanted to know it all.

But first, it was time for a throw down.

"I get next game," I announced from the doorway. "So get ready to get your butt kicked big time."

twenty-seven

BETH

I whirled around at the sound of the voice, simultaneously
succeeding in wrapping my race car around a virtual pole.
Lost in the game, I'd almost forgotten Mac was still in the
house. But there he was. Standing there, all tall and broad-
shouldered and hot as hell. The sexiest single dad in all of
SoCal—and maybe the world.

"Guess what, Daddy? Guess what?" Ashley dropped her
controller and ran over to her father. "Me and Beth are going
to go find snow in California!"

Uh . . . I could feel Mac shoot me a look and I felt my face
heat at the little girl's misinterpretation of my words. All I'd
really said was that there *was* snow in Southern California—
after Ashley told me she missed the snow back home—not
that we'd go out and actually find it together. Mac was so
protective of his daughter. The last thing I needed was for
him to think I was already overstepping my bounds, a mere
ten minutes into the big meet and greet.

"Ashley I didn't actually say—"

"It's in the mountains," Ashley broke in over me, using
her most authoritative voice. "Up high where it's still cold."

She looked up at her father with pleading big brown eyes. "Can we go, Daddy? Please can we go? I want to see the California snow!"

I glanced up at Mac who was looking down at his daughter with eyes filled with affection. She had him wrapped around her little finger—I could tell.

Maybe I needed to be hitting her up for advice.

"Please Daddy? Pleeeeease?"

He ruffled her hair. "We'll see," he told her. "If you're a good little pony all week long and eat all your vegetables, then maybe this weekend—"

"I'm not a *pony*, Daddy!" Ashley declared. "*I'm* a reporter. Just like Beth!" She pointed a finger in my direction. Mac raised an eyebrow and I shrugged helplessly, positive my face had now gone from red to a disturbing shade of purple.

Mac shook his head, turning back to his daughter. "Well, reporter Ashley, *I'm* a big bad monster," he declared. "And you know what big, bad monsters do to reporters, don't you?" he teased, grabbing her and putting her in a headlock.

She shrieked, wriggling like a worm to free herself, to no avail. Mac lifted her upside down and twirled her around the room and she alternated giggling and screeching. Mac was laughing, too. A sincere, unguarded laugh that made his face light up brighter than any Christmas tree. Watching the two of them I felt my heart warm. What a sweet little family. What an awesome dad.

Which made me wonder, all over again, about Ashley's mysterious mother. Mac had implied that it had ended badly between the two of them, but where did that leave Ashley? It was unusual for the father to have sole custody unless there was a serious issue with the mom. Had she gone to jail? Rehab? Had she just walked out on her family without looking back? It seemed insane to me that anyone could just turn around and abandon this unbearably cute father/daughter pair. Why, if I were Ashley's mother. . . .

I shook my head. *Don't even go there, Beth. Don't trick yourself into seeing this as more than it is.*

After they had finished wrestling, Mac sat down beside

me, grabbing the Wii steering wheel. "Are you ready for this?" he asked.

I laughed. "Bring it."

He chose his character and loaded the game and we started playing. Turned out we were pretty evenly matched and I was actually ahead by one race by the time the door-bell chimed.

"Saved by the pizza guy," Mac teased. "'Cause I was just about to get serious."

"Mmhm. I'm sure that—"

"You ordered pizza?" Ashley screeched, her eyes wide as saucers. Seriously, she couldn't have sounded more excited than if he had announced they were on their way to Disney World right this very second. "I love pizza!" She started wildly spinning around the room. "Pizza is my favorite."

Mac snorted. "Really? I would have never guessed." He glanced over at me. "Be right back."

As he headed for the front door, I scrambled to my feet and made my way to the kitchen, wanting to make myself useful. I found and grabbed a few paper plates, plasticware, and some paper towels to serve as napkins, then brought them over to the table. Mac returned a few moments later, laden with enough pizza to feed an army, dropping it down on the table. Ashley scrambled into her seat and we all dug in.

It didn't take long for the three of us to make a serious dent in the pies. Ashley dominated the dinner conversation, chattering like a magpie about everything and anything. At least she no longer seemed upset about school. Poor thing—it was tough being the new kid, as I knew from personal experience. I was glad to see her smiling and laughing now.

Sort of like how I was, I realized suddenly. In fact, I'd been having so much fun, I'd almost forgotten what had happened to me earlier that day. If I had been alone, I would have been stewing over everything all night long. Winding myself up, stressing myself out. I would have been a mess the next day at work—which was exactly what Stephanie was probably hoping for. Instead, I was laughing, I was joking. I was eating mountains of pizza. I was refusing to let the haters get me down.

"Thanks for inviting me over," I said, smiling at Mac. "This is just what I needed after today."

"Of course!" he exclaimed. "After all, it's a well-known fact pizza cures all ills."

"The pizza is great. But I'm going to credit the company for this one."

He grinned. "Indeed. Cheering people up is Ashley's number one superpower." He reached over and tickled her ribs. "After all, who could be sad around this silly little face?" Ashley burst out into more screeches and giggles. And I felt very warm inside indeed.

After the pizza, Mac announced it was time for bed. Of course Ashley protested and bargained with the skill of a senior partner at a law firm, but eventually we convinced her to crawl under the covers. I offered up a few more precious moments of awake time by reading her a story from her massive collection of Disney Princess books. And by the time I read the "Happily ever after" line, she was yawning, despite herself. Reaching over, she grabbed a little ragged stuffed lion by its tail and stuffed her thumb in her mouth.

"Goodnight sweetie," I whispered, my heart feeling very full. I leaned over and kissed her on the forehead. "It was great meeting you today."

Ashley's sleepy eyes suddenly widened. "Will you be here in the morning?" she asked worriedly.

"No, honey. I have to go home."

She stuck out her lower lip. "I don't want you to go."

"I know. But I'll come back and play with you another time. I promise."

The little girl was quiet for a moment. Then, "Mommy promised, too," she said softly. "But she never came back."

I glanced worriedly over at Mac, who was standing in the doorway, observing the scene. He stiffened and I noticed his hands curling into fists.

"Well, I *always* keep my promises," I assured her. "And

I'm even willing to pinkie swear on it. Do you know how to pinkie swear?"

"Is that like Pinkie Pie, the My Little Pony?"

"Uh, sort of." I took her little finger and showed her how to wrap it around mine. "Pinkie swear!" I cried.

"Pinkie Pie swear!" she cried.

I leaned down to give her one more kiss. "Now get some sleep, okay?"

"Not before the family hug!"

"What?" I glanced over at Mac again. His face was a little red.

"Just something we do before saying good night," he mumbled. "Ashley, let's just go to bed, okay?"

The little girl frowned. "I can't go to bed, Daddy. Not without my family hug!"

I rose from her bed. "You can go ahead," I told Mac. "I'll just—"

"No! You have to hug, too!" Ashley insisted. "It's a *family* hug!"

Now I could feel myself blushing. I knew I should say something—that I wasn't really of her family, just an invited guest. But I found, in the end, I didn't have the heart to disappoint her.

"Okay!" I said, reaching around to pull her into my arms. "Family hug!"

I could feel a presence behind me and soon Mac's arms wrapped around the both of us. I swallowed hard, my heart pitter-pattering in my chest as the three of us, for a brief moment, became one. It shouldn't have felt as right as it did.

Mac broke away first, dropping his arms and rising back to his feet, shuffling back to the door. I sucked in a breath; I couldn't look over to see the expression on his face.

"That's better," Ashley said sleepily. The thumb returned to her mouth and she closed her eyes. I sat there, for a moment, making sure this time it would stick. Then I quietly rose to my feet, giving Mac a half smile before tiptoeing out of the room. He followed me, closing the door gently behind him.

When we walked into the living room, he turned to me. "You can stay, you know."

"What?"

"Tonight. You're welcome to use the guest room again. I mean, you don't have a new place yet, right?"

"No," I confessed. "But you have Ashley now. I don't want to impose. Or do anything that might confuse her."

"And I appreciate that," he said. "But what if you just left first thing in the morning? Bright and early, before she wakes up." He shrugged. "I mean, seriously, save your money for your new apartment—don't waste it on a hotel."

"If you're really sure . . ."

"I am." His voice left no room for argument. I sighed and threw him a grateful look before taking my seat back on the couch. It would be easier, I tried to tell myself. And like he said, I could leave first thing. No big deal.

Plus, to be perfectly honest? I didn't want to leave.

Mac rummaged in the kitchen for the bottle of wine and poured us fresh glasses. Then he sat down next to me on the couch and handed me mine. I took it from him, trying desperately to ignore the way my body started immediately vibrating in response to his sudden nearness. All night it was like the two of us had been playing house, which had made me feel warm and happy. But now that Ashley was tucked away in bed, another feeling was creeping in. Something a little less innocent.

"You okay?" he asked, studying my face. I shot a glance over at him, hating the way my stomach flip-flopped as I recognized the concern in his expression.

"Yeah," I said. "I am, actually. This"—I waved my hand around the room—"has been a great distraction to my crappy day."

He nodded. "Like I said, that's Ashley's superpower. Able to leap tall couch cushions and make everyone happy in a single bound." He chuckled, then his face sobered. "If only I could so easily do the same for her . . ."

"You do," I assured him. "I can see it in her eyes when she looks at you. She worships the freaking ground you walk on."

"Yeah, well, her standards are set pretty low," he scoffed. "I mean, just look at this afternoon. The whole school thing—the kids teasing her—I had no idea how to handle that. Like, she was going on and on and all I could think of was whether there would be a jail sentence involved if I went down and socked some sense into a couple of four-year-olds."

I couldn't help but laugh. "I'm glad you figured out a way to restrain yourself."

"Yeah, well, thanks to you," he pointed out. "But I can't always rely on someone else to step in and save the day. And it's only going to get worse as she gets older. I mean, growing up, I saw what my sister went through. Girls can be complete bitches, you know?"

"Believe me, I know," I said with a slightly bitter snort, my mind flashing back to Stephanie. "It doesn't always end in grade school either." Then I gave him a comforting look. "But Ashley's a cool kid, Mac. She'll get through it."

He let out a slow exhale. "I hope so. I do the best I can for her. But . . ." He trailed off. "Let's just say single parenting is not for the faint of heart."

I bit my lower lip. "So about Ashley's mother . . ."

A cloud shadowed his face. "What about her?"

"She's still . . . alive, right?"

"Unfortunately."

"Come on," I cajoled. "You don't really mean that."

He turned to look at me. "Don't I? Some days I'm not so sure."

I cringed at the anger in his voice now. The frustration rising.

"So . . . where is she now?"

"Boston? Baghdad? Berlin? Who the hell knows? She's not exactly the type to send postcards."

"She doesn't keep in touch at all?" I asked incredulously, before I could stop myself. "Even with Ashley?"

"What, you think a successful career woman like her would have time for something as mundane as mothering?"

He rose to his feet, stalking to the other side of the room. I watched him go, my heart squeezing in empathy. While I didn't know exactly how everything had gone down between them, it was obvious the damage ran deep. Was that why he'd walked away after our one night together? He wanted to be the one, this time, who took off first? Who didn't stick around to get hurt?

And then there was Ashley. While I knew marriages between two people often ended and not always on the best of terms, I couldn't fathom the idea of any mother just walking out on her child like that. No matter how important her career. Ashley was so sweet, so bright and vivacious—a ray of sunshine in a cruel, gray world. How could anyone turn her back on her?

"I'm sorry," I said sincerely. "It must be so hard."

Mac said nothing for a moment, just stared at the wall, as if it held the answers to the universe. Then he walked back to the couch, leaning over and grabbing his drink. He took a large slug, draining the glass, then set it back down on the coffee table. As the silence stretched out between us, I wondered if he was even going to speak. But, right before I was about to suggest a subject change, he opened his mouth.

"I just wish Ashley were a little older," he said with a sigh, pacing the floor again. "At least then I could somewhat explain things. I mean, she keeps asking me, like every day, when Mommy is coming home. It's like she refuses to believe she's gone for good." He paused, then added, "And then there's her nightmares. She has these horrible nightmares and wakes up screaming for Victoria . . ."

He trailed off, closing his eyes, looking defeated. My heart squeezed, empathy warring with encroaching rage on his behalf. Here he was, this poor guy, doing the best he could for his little girl. While her own mother was off, gallivanting God knows where, clearly not giving a shit about any of it.

It wasn't fair. It wasn't right.

And suddenly I found myself rising from the couch, walking around it, and pulling him into my arms.

"Ashley is very lucky to have you," I whispered in his ear. I had only meant to hug him. To try my best to comfort him and ease his pain. But while my mind might have had the best of intentions, my body, it seemed, had far less innocent ideas. And suddenly I was pressing against him, my lips coming down on his own.

For a moment he stood still, as if shocked into stasis by my unexpected move. But he recovered quickly, his lips fusing with my own with an intensity that took my breath away. His tongue swept into my mouth. His hands tangled in my hair. His body shoved me up against the back of the couch and I could feel his erection pressing hard against my stomach as his mouth moved over mine.

This wasn't the gentle kiss from the beach. This wasn't a worshipful caress. This was hard, unapologetic, almost violent in its intensity—a kiss from a man who was desperate to lose himself in the moment. To allow emotion to sweep away his pain—even temporarily. Suddenly he was taking faster than I could give and I gasped into his mouth, my vision spinning and my mind going numb as the sensations coursed through me as hard and fast as the kiss itself.

Soon his hands became restless, abandoning my hair, dropping to my arms, then falling to my hips. Still kissing me, he lifted me, as if I weighed nothing at all, placed me on the back of the couch, then used his thigh to part my legs. A shiver of desire rang through me as he closed the gap between us, his hands slipping under my tank top, scorching my skin. I reached around and grabbed his butt to steady myself, rejoicing at the feel of the firm muscle under my hands. He groaned into my mouth and thrust against me and, for a moment, I thought I would come, right then and there, still fully clothed.

But Mac, it seemed, had other ideas. Abandoning my mouth, he dropped to his knees before me, bunching my skirt up to my waist. I swallowed heavily as my still hazy brain realized his intentions and gripped the couch with white-knuckled fingers as he worked to pull my panties down to my ankles and then remove them completely.

His hands rose to my knees, forcing my legs wider apart, exposing me fully to him, before lowering his head between me. I let out a small "eep" as his tongue slid between my folds and began licking every inch of me, all the while his hands gripped my knees, forcing me to keep my legs spread. As he took my clit into his mouth and sucked hard, I almost fell off the couch.

But somehow I managed to hold on for dear life, biting down on my lower lip so hard I soon tasted blood. Mac's hands abandoned my knees and rose upward, slipping under my tank top and up to my breasts, his thumbs rolling the nipples, while his teeth lightly nipped me below.

And that was it. I shattered into a thousand rays of light.

"Oh my God," I whispered, still clutching the couch, my heart pounding in my chest as the sensations rolled over me like a tidal wave. "Oh, Mac!"

I was dimly aware he had risen to his feet and was reaching down to unbuckle his belt. Somehow I managed to reach out and try to help him, my breath still coming in short gasps as I anticipated what was about to come. All rationalization had fled the building. All common sense had fled my head. All I knew was here, now. Mac.

"Daddy? My water's all gone."

Mac froze. He stared at me with horrified eyes. Then he broke away, pulling up his fly. Face burning, I pushed down my skirt, back over my knees.

"Ashley, sweetie?" Mac called in a rough voice. "Are you okay?"

"I need some more water," she announced, holding up her sippie cup. "And some magic sleeping pixie dust."

Mac sucked in a breath, then swallowed hard. "Okay, sweetie. Go back to bed. I'll bring you some water in a minute."

Ashley was silent for a moment. Then, "Are you guys playing monster and reporter without me?"

I stifled a giggle; I couldn't help it. But the look Mac shot me was enough to wipe the grin from my face. Shit. He was definitely not seeing the humor in the situation.

"Go back to bed, Ashley," he ground out. "I'll be there in a minute."

"Aww."

"Go, Ashley!" His voice rose. "Now!"

His daughter let out an angry sob, lobbed her cup at us, then ran back to the bedroom, slamming the door behind her. Mac groaned, buckling his belt and grabbing the cup, then stalked over to the kitchen to refill it. I watched him, not able to help but notice how he was looking everywhere but at me.

As he headed back to his daughter's bedroom, I grabbed my panties and slipped them back on, then collapsed onto the couch, my whole body still vibrating like crazy, not sure what to do. Mac looked so mortified and I was guessing he wasn't going to want to pick up where we left off. I wondered if I should try to tell him it was no big deal. Ashley didn't see anything, and she was far too young to understand, even if she did. But I was guessing none of that rationalization was going to help in this case.

He returned about ten minutes later, looking exhausted and drained. "Sorry about that," he muttered under his breath.

I sat up on the couch. "Is she okay?"

"She's fine."

"Good." I bit my lower lip. "How about you?"

He shrugged, but I caught a hint of a smile creeping at the corners of his mouth. Now that she was back in bed, he could allow himself to see the humor in the whole thing, I guess.

"Monster and reporter." He shook his head. "Now *that's* one I've never heard before."

I cracked up. I couldn't help it. And he rewarded me with an embarrassed grin. "Welcome to the thrilling world of modern parenting," he quipped, plopping down onto the couch. "So glitzy and glamorous I can hardly stand it sometimes." He rolled his eyes. "At least now you can see what I was talking about earlier. My life? Not exactly my own these days."

"Yeah, well, at least your fearsome overlord is pretty darn cute."

He chuckled softly, then opened his arms. I curled into him, resting my head on his chest. His hands reached to stroke my hair and I felt his heavy sigh against my ear.

"I'm sorry, Beth," he said. "I know this whole thing is totally unfair. The way I keep pushing you away, then dragging you back again."

"It's okay," I said. "I mean, it's not like I've exactly been an unwilling participant in the whole thing."

"That's true actually," he said. "You *have* made yourself unfairly irresistible. So there's that."

I laughed. "I'm going to use that as my tagline from now on," I said with a smile. "Elizabeth White. Unfairly irresistible. Live at six."

He snorted, then pressed his lips against the top of my head, kissing me softly and sending a chill straight to my toes. "God, Beth," he murmured, his lips still brushing against my hair. "It's like everything inside of me says I should scoop you up into my arms and take you to my bedroom. Lock the door and do dirty things to you all night long." He shook his head. "But at the same time I know that won't solve anything. And tomorrow we'll be right back where we started."

"Would that be so bad?" I asked, pulling my head from his chest to meet his eyes with my own. They were so blue. And so sad. It made my heart squeeze. "I mean, I'm not trying to push you to do something you don't want to do. But we're both single. I think we both like each other. I understand you don't want to upset Ashley, but we could play it quiet, at least for now. At least until we know for sure whether there's something between us."

"You sound like my sister," he said with a groan. "But it's more complicated than that."

"I don't see why it has to be."

He stared down at his hands, and for a moment I thought he wasn't going to reply. Then he lifted his head, his gaze fixing on the wall across the room.

"Ashley's mother," he said in a gravelly voice. "My ex-wife. She was my coworker, too. And when things imploded between us—let's just say I lost more than just my marriage.

There's a reason Ashley and I had to flee Boston. And I'm damn lucky I was able to get a job in San Diego to be near my sister. This is my last chance. And if I fuck this up, Ashley and I have no place left to go." He swallowed heavily.

My heart wrenched at the pain I saw in his face. "Mac . . ."

"There's a little girl in there," he interrupted, gesturing to the bedroom. "A little girl who depends entirely on me. Who needs me to keep a clear mind and a steady job. To think with my head instead of my dick." He closed his eyes for a moment. "When her mother took off, I made a promise to her. To always put her first. And I intend to keep that promise. Which means no more drama. No more romantic entanglements. Especially not with another coworker." He squeezed his hands into fists. "The risk is just too great for me to be that selfish."

I nodded slowly, not sure what to say. How could I even argue his points? As much as it hurt to be rejected, he was doing it out of love and protection for his daughter. How could I fault him for wanting to be a good dad and to keep her safe? I wanted, of course, to tell him that I would never do anything to hurt Ashley or cause her any confusion. That even if things didn't work out between us, I would never endanger his job or his family.

But why should he believe me? He'd only met me a week ago. And it sounded as if he'd gone through something terrible back in Boston with his ex. No wonder he wanted to play it safe this time around. His daughter depended on it.

"Look, Beth," he said turning back to me. "I think it's obvious I like you a lot. And not just in *that* way, either. I like you as a person—you're funny, you're smart, you're passionate about what you do. And you care about people. The way you treated that family at the fire? That was the moment I realized that even if I could never be in a relationship with you, I'd still want to be your friend." He gave me a sheepish look. "I know that sounds stupidly cliché, but in this case it's also the truth."

"I know," I said slowly, staring down at my hands. After all, what else could I say? That sex was the only thing I valued about him? That was definitely not true. While yes, he was completely hot and made me crazy every time he touched me, that was only the beginning of what Jake Mac-Donald was starting to mean to me.

I looked up. "I want to be friends, too," I told him. "Friends and coworkers." I paused, then added, "Under one condition."

"What's that?"

"You have to stop kissing me. If you kiss me, I can't make any promises that I won't kiss you back. And you can't blame me if I do."

He laughed. "It's a deal. No more kissing. And no more games of monster and reporter, either."

"Definitely no more of those." I made a fake, exaggerated shudder as my mind flashed back to the scene. Of his hands pushing on my knees. Of his tongue sliding up inside of me.

Whoa girl, get back in the friend zone.

I could feel Mac watching me. I forced a wide smile. "Friends," I pronounced, putting out my hand.

"Friends," he agreed, taking it.

But as the all-too-familiar sting of electricity shot through me at his touch, I wondered if it could ever be that easy.

twenty-eight

MAC

"Daddy, Daddy, where'd Beth go?"

The high-pitched voice crashed into my bedroom well before dawn, breaking me from dreamland. At first, I tried to lie still, in a vain effort to pretend I was still asleep, hoping she'd eventually give up and head back to her own room for at least another precious fifteen to twenty. But I should have known my daughter better than that. And a few minutes later she was on my bed, grabbing my face in her tiny hands, trying to pry open my eyelids with her fingertips.

"I'm up, I'm up!" I protested, playfully swatting her hands away. But she just giggled and crawled on top of me, succeeding, of course, in kicking me hard in the stomach in the process. Seriously, I should hire this kid out as an alarm clock. Rip Van Winkle himself couldn't have stayed in bed with her on the job.

"Be gentle with me," I begged. "You've only got one daddy, you know. Gotta try not to take him out."

"Sorry, Daddy!" she chirped. "I'll kiss it better!" She leaned over to kiss my stomach, managing to nearly kick me in the head in the process. Groaning, I grabbed her and wrestled her back onto the bed. She shrieked and giggled. Then she looked up at me with her big brown eyes. "I love you, Daddy."

"I love you, too, jelly bean."

"I'm not a jelly bean! I'm a princess!" she squealed.

I let her go, giving her a mock bow. "I'm so sorry, your majesty. My mistake."

Ashley giggled. Then her smile faded. "Where'd Beth go?" she asked, as if suddenly remembering why she'd come in here in the first place.

"If she's not in the guest room then she had to go home," I told her. "Remember, she told you that she might not be here when you got up?"

"Aw," Ashley said, scowling. "I wanted her to stay."

I sighed. *Me, too, baby girl. Me, too.*

I glanced over at the clock. Before going to bed last night I'd set my alarm, hoping to beat Beth up this time and cook her a little breakfast surprise of my own before she had to leave for work. Sure, my culinary skills were noobish at best, but it was only fair to give it a try, I'd told myself, after all the trouble she'd gone through for me the morning before, only to have me rush her out the door.

Besides, we were officially friends now. And friends were totally allowed to cook one another breakfast. In fact, cooking breakfast could be seen as a very friendly thing to do.

But evidently she had already left the building. And it wasn't even six A.M. An unexpected feeling of disappointment panged in my gut. What time had she gotten up? Or had she slipped out in the middle of the night?

I sighed. I couldn't blame her if she had. After all, last night had not gone exactly to plan, to say the least. And, of course, it was all my fault. Seriously, what was it about that girl that caused me to have the complete inability to keep my freaking hands to myself?

Not to mention my mouth.

God, she'd tasted so sweet, too. Even sweeter than I'd remembered. And the way she felt as she came against my mouth, I'd completely lost all common sense. Thank goodness Ashley had come in and interrupted when she did. Or I would have surely gone through with making yet another huge mistake.

One huge, delicious mistake.

But no. That would have been beyond stupid. And this was for the best. We'd come clean to one another, we'd talked it through, and now, from here on out, we could move forward without any new guilt to weigh us down. We could be platonic friends and coworkers. No big deal. After all, the stakes were far too high for it to be any other way.

"Is she coming back tonight? Can we have pizza when she does?" Ashley broke in, her voice bringing me back to the present.

I shook my head, wagging a finger playfully at my daughter. "No more pizza," I scolded. "In fact, I'd like to actually see you consume something vaguely vegetable shaped tonight. It's been a while. And no, Beth unfortunately won't be coming over."

"Aw. Why not?"

Why not, indeed. I wrestled for an explanation she could understand. "She has to find a new place to live," I said, inspired.

Ashley seemed to consider this, and for a brief moment, I thought she'd be satisfied with the answer. Silly me.

"I know! She can live with us!"

I sighed. "I'm sorry, sweetie. I don't think that'll work." She frowned. "Why not?"

"Well . . . We only have one guest room for one thing," I reminded her. "So where would Aunt Sadie and Uncle Joe sleep when they came over?"

"Beth could sleep in my room . . ."

"In your little twin bed? I don't think she'd fit."

"What about your bed, Daddy?"

Out of the mouths of babes . . .

"Beth can't sleep in my bed," I tried to explain.

"Why not? Your bed is big! Really big!" Ashley made a sweeping motion with her hand, as if to prove her point. "And you sleep in it all by yourself."

Way to rub it in, kiddo.

I flopped back onto the pillow, staring up at the ceiling. "Ashley, that's really generous of you to want to share your house with Beth. But she's got to find her own house. Just like Auntie Sadie and Uncle Joe have their own house."

Ashley was quiet for a moment. "Does Mommy have her own house now, too?" she asked quietly.

And there goes my heart.

I sat up in bed again, taking her hands in mine and looking her in the eyes. "I don't know, sweetie," I said slowly, wanting to be honest with her, without causing any more pain. "But I think she probably does."

"Yeah." Ashley dropped her gaze to her lap. "I think she probably does, too." Then she looked up at me, her expression taking on a sheen of hope. "I like Beth, Daddy, I like her a really, really lot."

"I'm glad, sweetie," I managed to say past the lump in my throat.

"Do you like her, Daddy?"

"She's very nice."

"Yes," Ashley said resolutely. "She's very, very nice. And I really, really like her. Do you really, really like her, Daddy? Do you?"

My mind flashed back to Beth again. But not, this time, to the way she looked on the couch, to her curves, to her naked body, to the way her mouth felt against mine. But rather to the way she had curled up with my daughter the night before, reading her a story. To the way she'd taken her time, hadn't skipped any pages, acted out all the voices and explained the plot points when Ashley broke in with questions. As if, at that moment, there was nothing more important in the world to her than that book in her hands.

Than my daughter in her arms.

I swallowed hard. "Yes, Ashley. I like her a really, really lot."

And that, I thought, *was becoming a really, really big problem.*

twenty-nine

BETH

two weeks later

"Oh man, what a day," I cried, walking into my new apartment and collapsing onto the threadbare flowered couch in front of the TV. "Thank goodness I don't have to work tomorrow. I seriously am going to sit on this couch and not move for the next thirty-six hours. Except to eat of course. I am going to sit on the couch and not move and eat all the things. And maybe drink some of them, too."

"Works for me," my new roommate replied, poking her head out from behind the kitchen wall, her mop of copper curls falling around her face. "As long as you don't mind the marathon binge session of eighties teen dramas I've got loaded up in the DVR."

"Mind? I would insist on nothing less," I declared, grinning back at her. "I swear Piper Strong, sometimes I think you and I are a match made in John Hughes heaven."

"I'd bet my hands on it," she quipped, quoting her favorite heroine of all time—the lovesick, amazing Watts from *Some*

Kind of Wonderful—who, by the way we both agreed, could do way better than the mopey Eric Stolz.

I laughed, pulling up my knees and hugging them to my chest, feeling warm and comfortable in my new abode. Sure, it wasn't as glamorous as my former apartment on the beach, but it was clean and cozy and—bonus—only ten minutes from the station. In other words—it was perfect.

And so was my new roommate. I still couldn't believe that I'd scored on that end, too, especially on such short notice. In fact, I'd been almost ready to give up on finding a roommate all together—and just signing up for some crappy studio I couldn't really afford—when I came across her ad tacked up on the bulletin board in the News 9 cafeteria.

Piper had crazy red curly hair and a face full of freckles. I had nicknamed her Merida after the feisty heroine of Disney's *Brave*. In addition to looking like her, she could also be just as fierce. And while some people might complain of her being too aggressive when it came to going after what she wanted—to me her fiery passion only added to her charm.

Piper was new to News 9 and currently worked as a production assistant in the newsroom—an entry-level position that was little more than that of a glorified runner. But she had no intention of staying there long term. She had big dreams, big plans, big goals. And she was going to reach each and every one them, it seemed, by sheer force of will. Well, that and putting in the long hours needed to impress the bosses.

Which meant I no longer had to worry about being woken up at three A.M. by my roommate stumbling home drunk from a bar or discovering a strange man in my shower when I came home at noon. When Piper wasn't working at the station, she had a second nighttime job she worked at down near the border, assisting in a children's group home. She had no time for bars, for clubs, for men.

And on rare instances, when she actually was at home? You could usually find her plopped down in front of the TV, trying to recover from her workaholicism hangover before she started up all over again with her next shift.

For me, it was pretty much the perfect setup. And I was pretty sure she thought the same, which made it even better.

Piper stepped in front of me now. She held up two bottles of wine. "Red or white?" she asked.

I groaned. "As long as it's got fermented grapes I don't much care."

"Uh-oh." My roommate gave me a sympathetic look. "What'd she do this time?"

I sighed. "Where to even begin?"

While the new roommate situation was a dream come true, everything else in life was pretty much a total mess. Mostly thanks to Stephanie, who clearly had not gotten the statute of limitations on revenge memo. In fact, if anything, her sabotages had only been escalating over the past two weeks and it was really starting to take a toll.

Interviews I'd scheduled were suddenly cancelled; shoot locations would change without notice, forcing me to be late. Video footage I'd uploaded onto the servers would be renamed and become impossible to locate.

All little annoyances, impossible to prove were intentionally done, had I wanted to turn her in. But I knew the truth. She was always lurking, waiting for me to fall on my face, so she could step in and take back her supposedly rightful place on the TV news throne.

And so, each day, I'd come to work on edge, never knowing what would be thrown my way. As if it wasn't tough enough to deal with the pressure of being a dayside reporter for a major news outlet in and of itself. Without the fear that something would go so wrong that Richard would give up on me altogether. After all, I still technically had almost two weeks left to prove I deserved the position. And Stephanie seemed determined to try to make every single day harder than the one before it.

At least I had Mac by my side. Since the night at his house when we'd agreed to be friends, he'd been a loyal coworker and companion. In fact, I was pretty sure I wouldn't have been able to get through any of this without having him in my corner. When footage was erased, he'd run out and shoot more. When interviews got cancelled, he'd help me line up alternate experts. Together, we'd actually become quite the force to be reckoned with. An awesome team.

If only I could have been satisfied by that.

If only I could think of him as just a friend.

But he had made himself clear. And I wanted to respect what he felt he needed to do. For his sake, and his daughter's.

I realized Piper was still waiting for an answer. I waved her off. "It doesn't matter," I told her. "And I don't want to dwell on it anyway. Just load up a little Ferris Bueller and all will be well in the world."

Or at the very least I could pretend that it was.

The weekend passed too quickly and Monday, as always, came too soon. Piper and I drove to the station together and then parted ways—her heading over to the printers, where she would organize the noon show's scripts, while I headed to the assignment desk to see what story they had for me that day.

It had been a pretty chill weekend. Piper had gotten called into work on Saturday, interrupting our movie binge, and so I'd headed out to do a little more shopping to replace some of the items Stephanie had destroyed. When Piper had come home that night we'd poured vodka Red Bulls and played video games on the PS4. On Sunday I even made it to the beach, signing up for a surf lesson all by myself led by a cute instructor.

And why not? I'd wasted years on Ryan and I wasn't about to waste any more, waiting around for a dream guy that might never come. Ryan was gone. Mac was unavailable. And I was going to start living for myself, if it killed me. (Which to be honest, that surf lesson almost did!)

It had been a good weekend. But the weekend was over now. Now it was back to reality. Back to the unfriendly faces and potential sabotage of real-life work. As I walked through the newsroom, I could feel the stares at my back from Stephanie's minions. And a feeling of dread sank to my stomach. Sometimes I wondered why I kept at it. Why I kept showing up to work, prolonging the torture. There were other jobs out there, some I was even qualified to do. Why did I feel the need to keep pushing on here where I was clearly unwelcome?

Ana, the daytime assignment manager, greeted me as I approached the desk. Ana had worked at News 9 for five years now and had probably looked, for every single one of them, as if she'd walked straight off a model's runway to get to work. But I'd learned long ago you couldn't let her good looks fool you—the Colombia-born Latina was much more than a pretty face. She was also tough as nails—pretty much a requirement for her high-pressure position. Every day she would be forced to coordinate grumpy photographers, spoiled reporters, and power-tripping producers to make sure the right stories were well-covered, and the station didn't get scooped by a competitor. It was a thankless job, but Ana always handled it with grace and pizzazz.

She also always, without fail, greeted me with a smile, which was more than I could say for most of my other coworkers. While I had never been the most popular or known face in the newsroom, thanks to Stephanie, these days I felt practically invisible.

"Why the sad face, Lizzie Lou Who?" Ana asked, catching my eye. She was the only one I allowed to call me Liz. Or Lizzie, as the case might be. "You don't look like a girl who's living the dream."

I snorted. When I had first arrived at News 9 two years ago, Ana had been the one to give me the welcome tour of the station. At the time I had been so excited, I'd danced around the entire place, gushing that this was my dream come true. Which, at the time, had made her laugh very hard. And she'd never let me forget it since.

"No? Well, do I look like a girl who's come down with a bad case of newsroom Ebola?" I asked wryly. "'Cause that's what it feels like, walking around this place these days." I looked out over the newsroom floor, watching everyone avert their faces as my gaze swept over them.

Ana laughed. "Welcome to the yard, meat."

I sighed. "You know, it's not like I asked for any of this."

"You think they care about that? They just know you are where they ain't. And in their minds, that ain't fair."

"Yeah, well, they should be careful what they wish for."

"Wait, are you telling me it's not all caviar and champagne at the top?" Ana swooned in mock-horror and I laughed.

"Actually it is," I reassured her. "In fact, I was just about to pop a magnum of Cristal in the executive bathroom. You want in?"

"I knew there was a reason I liked you." Ana fist-bumped me. Then she gave me a sympathetic smile. "Seriously though, don't let them get to you. Haters gonna hate, as my girl Taylor Swift says. You just gotta ignore all the noise and do the best job you can. Eventually they'll get bored and move on to the next upstart."

"If they don't kill me first."

"Ooh that reminds me!" Ana rummaged through the assignment desk, then handed me a letter. "This just came this morning."

I scanned the letter, which appeared to be from the mayor of Lemon Grove. He was writing to thank News 9 for uncovering the gas leak scandal I'd learned about on my first day of the new job. Evidently three city officials had been fired as a result of the exposé and new protocols were now in place to prevent it from happening again. In his letter, the mayor praised the investigation and claimed lives would be saved because of it.

Because of me.

Suddenly I felt much better. *This* was why I was here. Why I couldn't let them win. Sure it was hard. But letters like this made it all worthwhile.

"Congrats, girl," Ana said with a knowing smile. "You did good."

She leaned over and gave me a warm hug. I hugged her back, feeling happier than I had in a while.

Sorry, Stephanie. That's one thing you can't take away from me.

"Am I interrupting?"

I pulled away from the hug at the sound of the familiar

voice, my heart skipping a beat as my eyes fell upon Mac, leaning on the assignment desk, an amused look on his face. He was looking particularly hot this morning in his tight black T-shirt and dark rinse blue jeans. Which was so unfair. Not for the first time I wished there was some kind of required photographer uniform. Preferably shapeless coveralls or something of that ilk.

It was kind of pathetic, really. I mean, we'd been working together for a couple weeks now and I still couldn't manage to pry my mind out of the gutter every time I looked at him. I'd see his hands—and I'd think about them running all over my body, touching me in my most intimate places. I'd see his lips—and think about them pressing against mine, his tongue sweeping into my mouth and sending shivers to my toes. And when I'd drop my gaze, I'd see something else, between his legs. And my mind would pretty much short-circuit.

It was ridiculous. Pitiful. Disgraceful. Especially since he seemed to have managed to friend-zone me without breaking a sweat. In fact, since that night at his house, I hadn't even caught him looking at me inappropriately once. Which meant he was either really good at hiding his attraction—or there was no attraction left to hide.

I wasn't sure which scenario I preferred.

"No, handsome, you're just in time," Ana assured Mac with a wink. She pulled out his schedule sheet and scanned it. I waited, crossing my fingers, hoping for a semi-cool assignment, all the while trying to mentally prepare myself for a crappy one. After all, Stephanie's producer minions had a rare talent for cooking up the most inane, frivolous stories in all of SoCal and assigning them to me. If I was lucky, perhaps today I'd get to do an exclusive expose on the San Diego quilting festival. Or maybe a late breaking news piece on the growing popularity of doggie daycare?

Ana gave a low whistle. "Oh yeah, baby, you two hit the story jackpot today."

I looked up, unable to quell the vain hope stirring within me. "Oh?"

"Water skiing squirrel event. Mission Beach. Starts at

noon." Ana stifled a giggle, then shot me an apologetic look. "Sorry."

My heart sank. For a moment I'd been fool enough to hope she'd been serious. That for once we really did have a cool story to cover. Something that mattered. Something that would get me noticed by the News 9 powers that be. To prove that I deserved this daytime slot.

I should have known better.

"Well, that's a *nutty* assignment if I ever heard one," Mac declared with a grin. I shot him a dirty look. I knew he was probably just trying to lighten the mood, but I failed to see the humor. This was my career, after all, not some late night TV host monologue.

"Yeah," Ana added, doubling-down. "I hear that squirrel is totally *off his tree*!"

The two of them fist-bumped and laughed. I stared at them, anger rising inside of me. "Do you think this is funny?" I burst out, before I could stop myself.

They turned to look at me, matching guilty expressions on their faces. Mac gave me a sympathetic look. "Beth—"

I waved him off. "Look, it may be all fun and games for you, but this is my life. My career. I have two weeks left to prove to Richard I deserve to be here. And I'm not going to be able to do that chasing after some fucking squirrel on skis!"

My voice broke on the last part, but I didn't care. I'd had enough. Enough of the sabotages, enough of the bullshit assignments. I was better than this. But how would I ever prove it?

I could feel Mac's eyes piercing into me, but I refused to look over at him.

"Whatever," I spit out. "Just get your gear. I'll meet you out back in ten."

And with that, I stormed across the newsroom, needing to get away, to be by myself before the tears really started to flow. I could feel the eyes of the others on me, probably thrilled to see me so unwound. Great. They'd all have a field day talking about me once I was gone.

Congratulations, Stephanie, I thought. *Break Beth's Spirit achievement badge successfully unlocked.*

Once I reached the hallway, I leaned against the wall, sucking in a frustrated breath. Why did I even bother? It was just a job. Just a stupid job. And yet, each day, it seemed to be stealing a little bit more of my soul. Maybe my parents were right. Maybe I should have just stayed back home where everything was easy and safe. Stayed a small market reporter, married my boyfriend, popped out a couple kids. Why was I still here, still killing myself, for no good reason? What was my endgame, anyway?

But no. I shook my head. It wasn't for no good reason. It was for my dream. A dream I'd had since I was a little girl. And I wasn't about to give up on that dream just because things had gotten hard. After all, dreams were supposed to be difficult to achieve—if they weren't, then everyone would be able to reach them.

Sure, it would be easier to run back home now, with my tail between my legs. But it wouldn't make me happy. And I would end up spending the rest of my life wondering how things could have turned out if I had had the guts to stay.

Besides, look at the Lemon Grove gas leak thing. I'd made a difference there. A real difference. And if I stayed the course, I could do it again, I was sure of it. I could change laws, expose wrongs, save lives. Which was even more important, in the big picture, than achieving my own dreams.

In short, I would not let them beat me. I would not let them win.

Swiping away my tears, I started back toward the newsroom, ready to find Mac and report the shit out of this water-skiing squirrel assignment. But I stopped just before rounding the corner, hearing familiar voices. It was Richard, talking to Joy Justice.

"Look, this is a once in a lifetime story," he was saying. "People have been trying to get this guy to talk for weeks now and he's refused all interviews—even with the networks. Now in the last twenty-four hours he's been tweeting all about you, nonstop."

"Lots of people tweet about me," Joy replied. "So what?"

"So the guy's clearly a fan!" Richard exclaimed. "If you could just reach out to him, see if he'll meet with you . . ."

"Sorry. I don't feel comfortable."

"Actually I think you're *too* comfortable," Richard shot back to my surprise, his voice rising. "Too comfortable in your cushy office. Or on your cushy throne up there on the anchor desk. Do you even remember the last time you left the building to do your own story, instead of reading the crap the writers put in your Teleprompter?"

"Of course I do," Joy snapped. "You know as well as anyone I worked in the trenches for years to get where I am. I deserve my place up on that cushy throne. And I'm not about to get on my knees and grovel for an interview with some stupid nerd with a Jesus complex."

"Come on, Joy! This could be a big story for us. Maybe the biggest. And we don't know how long he has before the Feds catch up with him or he flees the country."

"I said no, Richard. Go find one of your other desperate little minions to interview your scumbags." She huffed loudly. "*I* have a nail appointment."

And with that, Joy came charging around the corner, almost slamming straight into me. She looked down at me, raising a suspicious eyebrow, as if she realized I'd been essentially spying on her, then gave me a dirty look and kept walking. Her heels clicked against the tiles as she reached the exit and pushed open the door, disappearing out into the parking lot.

I let out a low whistle. Wow. What had just happened?

"Hey, Beth! How's it going?"

I whirled around to see Richard also coming around the corner. I gave him a nervous smile. "It's . . . fine," I said. "I was just getting ready to go out on my story."

"You okay?" he asked, peering at me with greater intensity. I realized my eyes were probably still a little blotchy from earlier and felt my face heat.

"I'm fine. Allergies, you know," I lied. Then I drew in a breath. "Um, what was that all about, if you don't mind me asking?" I knew it was none of my business, but I was insanely curious all the same.

"You heard that did you?" Richard gave me a knowing look. "Nothing important. Just Her Majesty refusing yet another story assignment I tried to give her." He shook his head. "She seems to think she's immune to doing any real work, because of her reputation with viewers. But upstairs they're getting fed up. This is a working newsroom, after all, and we don't have the budget for dead weight."

I nodded slowly, trying to keep my expression neutral. I had always imagined, in the back of my mind, that when someone got up to Joy's level, they were essentially untouchable. But evidently not so much.

Which suddenly gave me an idea.

"What's the story she didn't want to cover?" I asked, trying to keep my voice casual. Like I was just curious.

Richard's face lit up. "Have you heard of Dante Alvarez?"

"The hacker? The one accused of posting state secrets from the CIA?"

"That's him. Evidently he's just signed a big book deal with Penguin Random House to publish his autobiography. Supposedly he's naming names, too. Everyone's been trying to get an interview with him. Even the national news stations, but he's refused them all. The station who does score the first interview is going to be put on the map." His eyes glittered with greed. "Anyway, the other day he started live tweeting Joy during one of her broadcasts. Evidently he's hot for her or something." He snorted. "I thought maybe we could use his little crush to our advantage. But evidently the diva is not amused."

Now my heart was pounding in my chest. How could Joy turn down an opportunity like this? To score the interview of the century? Why, I would give my right arm to have that—

"Do you want me to try to get it?" I blurted out before I could stop myself.

Richard laughed. "Beth, maybe you didn't hear me. Everyone's been trying to get this guy locked down. The only person he wants to play ball with is Joy."

"But I could still try," I protested, not willing to give up without a fight. "I mean, what could it hurt, just to give him a call? If he says no, well, then we'd just be right back where we started."

"Come on, Beth. This isn't like interviewing a fire victim . . ."

"Which is why you should give me the assignment," I argued. "You wanted me on dayside, right? You must have seen something in me to want to make that move. So why not give me a real chance to show you what I can actually do?"

He gave me a thoughtful look. "You really want to try this?"

"I do. I've had enough fluff stories. I'm ready to handle real news."

"Okay," he said, holding up his hands, as if in surrender. "It's all yours. I'll take you off the daily rotation, but just for one day. If you can't get the interview in the next twenty-four hours, you go back to whatever it is the producers have you covering and we don't have this conversation again."

My heart was now beating wildly in my chest. "It's a deal," I said. "And thank you. Thank you so much. I won't fail you."

Richard smiled. "Honestly, Beth, I just like the fact that you want to try. It's good to see someone excited about TV news once in a while." He patted me on the shoulder, maybe a little patronizingly, but I didn't care. "Hell, even if you don't get the interview, you get points from me for trying."

"I appreciate that. But I'm going to get it. You'll see."

Of course even as I said the words, I had no idea how I was going to follow through with my claims. I mean, how the heck was little old me going to do what everyone had tried and failed?

But I did know one thing. I'd been waiting for a chance to prove myself and now one had dropped in my lap.

I wasn't about to let it go to waste.

thirty

MAC

My phone buzzed in my pocket and I set down my e-reader to reach for it. I'd been wasting time in the employee lounge all morning, waiting for Beth to set up some kind of new story. Evidently she'd convinced Richard to take her off the water-skiing squirrel thing, a move that—while tenacious—wasn't exactly going to endear her further with the already hostile producers in the newsroom. Especially after Richard had stormed out and scolded Jessica for "wasting his reporters' time" with such mundane stories. *This is a top market TV newsroom,* he'd raged, *not a vaudeville variety show.* When Jessica had stood her ground, arguing that the squirrel was raising money to help kids with cancer and was therefore newsworthy, Richard had rolled his eyes and told her that if it was so important, she could assign it to Stephanie.

If looks could kill, Beth would have been on the floor at that point.

I sighed. While part of me wanted to be impressed by the fact that Beth had stood up for herself and talked her way into a better story, the other part worried—namely

about the look I'd seen in her eyes. That fierce determination
that bordered on defiance—it reminded me far too much of
another reporter I'd known. Victoria was willing to do *anything* to get ahead—would have sold her very soul in
exchange for airtime. But the more power she got, the more
she wanted—the more she needed. And, in the end, it had
destroyed us utterly.

A fierce protectiveness washed over me. I couldn't let
that happen to Beth.

I put the phone to my ear. "Hey," I greeted her. "Are you
ready to go?"

"Yup. We're all set." I could hear the excitement in her
voice. "I'll meet you out back by the truck."

"Sounds good. I'll be there in a sec."

I hung up and stuffed the phone back into my pocket,
then headed out of the break room and down the hall to the
back parking lot exit. Pushing open the door, I stepped out
into yet another perfect San Diego day. I was getting to the
point where I no longer even noticed the weather—just took
it for granted that it would always be mid-seventies and
sunny. Back home Boston was getting socked by yet another
snowstorm and I would have been out there, on the job,
filming the flakes coming down as I froze my ass off.

Yeah, this wasn't such a bad gig after all.

My eyes narrowed as I approached the truck, noticing a
lone figure leaning up against the side. For a moment, I literally didn't recognize who it was. It wasn't until I got closer
that I realized it was Beth.

Except not the Beth I was used to.

"What the hell are you wearing?" I exclaimed before I
could stop myself.

Gone were her usual filmy skirts, her soft cotton tank
tops, the ill-fitting thrift store suits she often wore on air.
Instead, she'd slipped into a pair of tight black leather pants
and stiletto heels, paired with a tailored red velvet suit jacket
over a lacy, low-cut camisole. The effect was so startlingly
hot and so startlingly unlike what she normally wore that
I suddenly found myself channeling Danny Zuko from

Grease, laying eyes on Sandy after her extreme bad girl makeover.

Her cheeks colored at my question, but she waved me off. "Just something I picked up."

"And you're going to . . . wear this . . . to our interview?"

"Uh, yeah," she replied, now sounding a little annoyed. "Why? What's wrong with it?"

Nothing was wrong with it. Except for the fact that I didn't want anyone but me to look at her wearing it.

My eyes involuntarily raked the length of her body, taking it all in. The sleek leather molding around her legs and cupping her ass, emphasizing every curve. The low-cut camisole, showcasing the creamy valley between her two breasts. Hell, here I'd been working overtime to try to forget what those beautiful breasts looked like. And now she was practically putting them out on display.

But not, I realized, for my benefit.

Who the hell were we interviewing, anyway?

Something unpleasant rumbled in my gut. I tried to tell myself it was only that ill-advised breakfast burrito I'd grabbed off the roach coach on the way to work. But something told me it was more than that. That the ache was something more akin to jealousy than indigestion.

But that was ridiculous. We were just friends. She was a free woman who could dress as she liked—I had no hold on her. No right to tell her what to wear in public. Not that I would have done that, even if we were a couple; I was a liberated guy, after all. Besides, there was nothing slutty looking or inappropriate about the ensemble. It was just mind-breakingly hot.

And, by the end of the day, it would probably succeed in killing me.

I realized she was still staring at me. "I just didn't want you to be . . . cold," I stammered, trying to drag my eyes away from her breasts.

"Cold?" she repeated, raising an eyebrow. "No. I think I'll be okay." She crossed her arms over her chest, which only served to push up her cleavage. I had to force myself to turn away.

"Yeah. Right. Of course." I shook my head, trying to get my mind back on work. "So where are we going, anyway?"

"Chula Vista," she announced, handing me a piece of paper with an address on it. I looked down at it, surprised at what it was. I looked back up at her.

"Dante Alvarez?" I asked, a little incredulously.

"Yeah, he's this guy who—"

"I know who Dante Alvarez is, Beth," I interrupted. "I'm just . . . surprised. From what I've been reading, he's refused all interviews. Even from some of the top network brass."

Something flashed across her face—a look I couldn't identify. Then she shrugged. "Well, he's not going to refuse me," she declared with an extra helping of bravado, then glared at me, as if daring me to keep arguing with her.

But I wasn't going to take the bait. While I wasn't sure at all about this, I didn't want her to think I doubted her ability as a reporter. "Well, that's awesome," I declared instead. "Let's do it!"

She nodded and I watched as she turned on a heel, almost tripping in the process, then hobbled over to the truck and pulled open the door. Her pants were so tight she could barely lift her leg up to crawl into the seat.

"Do you need some help?" I asked with a small smile.

"I'm fine," she retorted, finally managing to wrestle herself into her seat. I forced myself not to laugh as I joined her in the truck, knowing she wouldn't appreciate it. Still, it warmed my heart a little to see the dorky Beth I knew peeking out from beneath her new overly polished persona.

I turned the key and soon we were pulling out of the parking lot, on the way to the interview. As I drove, Beth stared out the window, biting her lower lip, looking nervous. Every five seconds or so she'd glance down at her cell phone and her foot tapped rapidly against the floor mat, seemingly without her noticing it.

I supposed I couldn't blame her. If she really had scored an interview with the infamous Dante Alvarez himself, well, that would be the story of the century. One that would put her on the map, make her career. If she wasn't nervous, she'd be insane.

What I didn't understand was how she'd made it happen.
I mean, this morning we were about to interview a freaking
squirrel. What had she said to Richard to get him to agree
to send her on this story instead? No offense to Beth, but
this was the kind of story a lead anchor should be covering,
not a newbie just off the morning shift. It didn't make any
sense.

I sighed. I just hoped it worked out in the end and she
wasn't setting herself up for more disappointment. She
seemed so desperate to prove herself these days. I wished
she could see that she didn't need to. That she was already
amazing and talented and awesome—just as she was.

We arrived at the address on the paper about twenty
minutes later, which turned out to be a nondescript warehouse. It was the kind of place you wouldn't want to hang
around in at night. Or in the bright light of day, for that
matter. In fact, if you were to look up *murder waiting to
happen* in the dictionary, it'd probably have a full-color
spread.

"Are you sure this is it?" I asked warily.

"Yeah. This is it," she replied. "He doesn't like to show
his face in public much."

"I can't imagine why, what with the FBI on his ass
and all."

She gave me a wry look, then opened her door and made
her way out of the truck. I followed suit, walking around
back to get my gear. Before I could pull my camera from its
holster, she stopped me.

"Not yet," she said. "We don't want to scare him off by
coming on too strong."

I frowned. "I thought he already agreed to an interview."

"Well . . . sort of."

"What do you mean, 'sort of'?" Something inside of me
tensed. What was her game here? And what was she not
wanting to tell me about it? I wanted to remind her that we
were supposed to be working as a team and that I couldn't
help her if she didn't share her plan. But this was not the time
or the place to have that discussion.

"Just wait here, okay?" she snapped. "Let me handle this."
She started toward the warehouse with wobbly stiletto steps.

Oh no she didn't.

I ran after her, grabbing her arm to stop her. "No way,"
I said. "I am not going to let you just go walk off on your
own around here. It could be dangerous."

"It's fine," she argued. "It's the middle of the day."

"I don't care if it's high noon and the rapists and murder-
ers are all busy having tea. You are my partner and you are
not leaving my sight."

She sighed, looking exasperated. "Fine. But when we get
there, just let me do the talking, okay? Don't interrupt, no
matter what you hear me say."

I stared at her. What the hell did that mean? "Beth, are
you sure you know what you're doing here?"

She waved me off. "It's fine. It's going to be fine. Just
leave it to me."

And with that, she started back down the pothole-strewn
street, toward the warehouse entrance. I followed close
behind, my gaze darting from left to right, not wanting to
miss anything suspicious, not that I was sure what I'd do about
it if I found something.

Finally, we reached the warehouse entrance. Beth
climbed up the metal front steps and knocked three times.
At first, there was no answer. Then . . .

"Who's there?"

I watched as Beth drew in a breath. "Joy Justice. News 9."

Wait, what? I stared at Beth, totally shocked. She turned
and shot me a death look, telling me on no uncertain terms
was I to speak.

"We DMed on Twitter?" she added. "You agreed to
meet me."

I shook my head in disbelief. Well, at least that explained
how she scored the interview. Pretty brazen, I had to admit.
Also more than a bit deceitful. I didn't know whether to be
impressed or disappointed in her.

The door creaked open. To my surprise, it was Dante
himself—I couldn't help but recognize him from his mug

shot photos that had been splashed around the Internet. He was flanked by two beefy looking dudes I assumed were his bodyguards who glared at us menacingly, their hands at their waists, ready to draw if necessary.

Dante was pretty beefy himself, I noted, decked out in nothing more than a pair of Ray Bans and basketball shorts. His chest was bare, assumedly to showcase his perfect set of abs and pecs. Not exactly your typical hacker/nerd/geek/hipster stereotype by any stretch of the imagination.

He looked at Beth and frowned. "You're not Joy Justice."

No shit, Sherlock. I drew in a breath, heart pounding in my chest as I watched Beth meet his eyes with her own, somehow managing to show no fear. "No," she said. "Joy couldn't make it. But I'm her colleague and I'm here to do the interview in her place."

Dante slowly dragged his eyes over her body, hovering for a lengthy pause, first at her chest, then at her leather clad hips. The lecherous smile that slid across his face made me want to punch him in the balls. But seeing as I didn't feel much like being pounded into the ground by two pieces of hired meat, I somehow managed to fight the urge.

Instead, I waited, sucking in an uneasy breath as Dante glanced from one bodyguard to the other, seeming to consider Beth's words. Half of me wanted him to just say no. To kick us out, right then and there and have this whole thing be over with. Sure, I wanted Beth to succeed—but I also wanted to live to fight another day. Literally.

"I don't know," Dante said at last. "I'm not really giving any interviews right now."

"Then don't think of it as an interview," Beth replied smoothly, not missing a beat. "Just a nice conversation between two people."

"A conversation that's being recorded for the entire world to see." He snorted. "Do you know how many reporters I've turned down? Big time, important reporters?"

"Yes," she said matter-of-factly. "And each and every one of them is going to be jealous as hell when they turn on the nightly news tonight and realized that instead you talked to little old me."

Dante's eyes danced with amusement. He turned to his bodyguards. "This little girl—she has some real cojones on her!" he said with a laugh. Then he turned back to Beth and shrugged. "Eh, what the hell. Maybe it will stop the rest of the world from yanking on my dick all the time."

And with that lovely sentiment, he put his arm around Beth's shoulder, leading her back inside. I stood in the doorway for a moment, as my mind tried to work out what had just happened. Dante Alvarez, *the* Dante Alvarez, had agreed to an interview. An interview with us.

I somehow found my feet, running to the car to grab my gear. My heart was still racing in my chest. We were about to shoot the interview of the century and I was not about to screw this up.

When I returned to the warehouse, Dante had his hands on Beth's ass. When I opened my mouth to object, he laughed and assured me he was just patting her down, making sure she wasn't packing any heat. Then he motioned to his bodyguards to give me the same treatment. Let's just say they weren't quite as tender.

After that little violation of dignity, I set out to set up the lights, trying to be as efficient and quick as possible—so as not to give him time to change his mind—but also professional enough so we wouldn't be embarrassed if the interview ended up playing all over the world, which I knew it would. This was Beth's big break—she'd worked hard for this. I wanted her to look good.

As I worked to set up, Dante and Beth chatted amicably, as if they were old friends. Unlike most old friends, however, Dante kept his eyes locked on her cleavage. While I understood the inclination—I was the first to admit it was very, very nice cleavage—the blatancy of the act only served to enrage me further. As did the sound of Beth's giggles as the hacker spouted off things that were just not that funny.

Finally, we were set up and ready. Once the camera was

rolling, Beth, to her credit, dropped the giggles and went into serious reporter mode. She looked down at her notes, then up at her interviewee.

"There are some people who consider you a patriot," she said slowly. "There are others—including many in our government—who see you as an information terrorist—and would like to see you brought to justice. Where do you see yourself on this spectrum? Do you think you should be lauded for leaking information from the CIA? Or do you think you should be put in jail for life?"

He shrugged lazily. "I did what I felt needed to be done. It's not my decision on what should be done to me because of it."

"Sure. Fine. But I'm not asking about what you think *should* be done," Beth pressed. "I'm asking how you see yourself and your actions. Do you still feel you were justified in leaking those security documents? Publicizing those state secrets for all to see?"

Dante sat up in his chair. His eyes locked on Beth. "Look, there are times when someone needs to stand up to what's going on. To err on the side of right—rather than the side of legal. Like Henry David Thoreau once said about civil disobedience. If injustice is found to be occurring, we as citizens have a duty to rise up and take action. That's what I did. That's what I had to do. And if you're asking me if I'm ashamed to have done it? Hell no. I would do it all over again if need be, and I would do it with a smile on my face."

And . . . there was our first perfect soundbite. The one that would probably be replayed all over the world once this thing aired. A wide grin spread across my face and it was all I could do not to stop the interview and give Beth a high five right then and there. She had done it. She had actually done it. What no reporters had done before. The famous Alvarez caught on tape.

And she wasn't even close to being done, going through her questions one by one. Smart, insightful questions, especially considering she'd only gotten the assignment mere hours before and couldn't have had much time to prepare.

Dante, in turn, seemed to notice and appreciate this and stopped staring at her tits long enough to give her respectful, thoughtful answers to each and every one. I had to admit, for someone who hated interviews, he was shockingly well-spoken when he wanted to be.

Finally, Beth asked her last question, then gave her interviewee a smile. "I think I've got more than I need," she told him. "Thank you so much for agreeing to do the interview. And I'm sorry Joy wasn't able to make it."

He laughed. "Does Joy even know that you're here?" he asked.

Beth gave him a sheepish look, then shook her head. "Not exactly," she admitted.

"See?" He turned to me. "This girl of yours—she's really got it!" He rose to his feet and Beth did the same, sticking out her hand to shake. But he ignored her, grabbing her and pulling her into a rather close embrace. "I'm more of a hugger," he informed her, as his hands dangled dangerously close to her ass again.

I had to resist the urge to hurl.

Instead, I forced myself to take down the lights and stow my gear as fast as humanly possible, more than ready to make a beeline for the door. As I worked, I tried to remind myself how good this was all going to look to the folks back at the newsroom. That sometimes the ends justified the means. And that after we walked out of this building, I'd never have to lay eyes on that smug bastard again, except on tape. And then I could just press the mute button.

We had just stepped out the door, on our way to the truck, when Dante called back to her. "Beth? Come here a minute!"

She looked at me. I shook my head impatiently. "We need to go," I told her. "I have to get the truck back for the night guy."

"Beth?" he called again.

"Look, I can't just ignore him," she protested. "Just . . . go put the gear in the truck. I'll be back before you even finish."

The last thing I wanted was for her to reenter that warehouse—without me to watch over her this time. But I couldn't for the life of me think of any good reason to walk back in myself. And so, feeling annoyed and grumpy, I dragged my gear back to the truck and began to load it back in. Every few seconds I'd glance over at the warehouse, waiting for Beth to reemerge. Knowing my heart rate wouldn't be able to slow until she did.

Finally, she popped out, stumbling down the steps and over to me, still shaky on those damn heels. I gave her a quick once-over, not able to help but notice how rosy her cheeks looked.

"What did he want?" I asked, despite my better judgment.

She blushed harder. "Oh. It was nothing."

"He called you back for nothing?"

She laughed. "He just . . . asked if I wanted to grab a drink sometime. That's all."

I almost dropped my camera. "He asked you out? On a date?"

"I guess." She shrugged. "I mean, I don't know if it was actually a date, per se . . ."

"Trust me, a guy like that is not looking for a new friend."

"Okay, fine," she shot back. "Then he asked me on a date. What does it matter?"

"Guess those pants really paid off for you, huh?" I muttered.

"Excuse me?"

I slammed down the truck's back hatch. "Nothing. We need to go."

She scowled at me, storming over to the passenger side and yanking open her door. She climbed up, then slammed the door closed behind her. I sighed and made my way to the driver's seat.

"Why are you being an asshole?" she demanded, once I closed the door.

"Why weren't you straight with me about what we were doing?"

She turned to stare out the side window. "I didn't know if it would work."

"Well, congratulations. It did. Even better than you hoped for, sounds like."

Her face twisted. "Why can't you just be happy we got the story?"

"Beth, you put us in a dangerous situation and you didn't even bother to warn me first. I'm not your subordinate, I'm your partner. I have a right to know what we're doing. What if things went bad?"

"Well, they didn't." She narrowed her eyes as she looked over at me. "I thought you said we were in a hurry."

I sighed, putting the key into the ignition and turning it over. Then I pulled out onto the road. As we drove home, silence fell over the truck. But not the kind of nice, comforting silence from back at my house two weeks ago. Rather the kind that threatened to smother.

"So," I found myself asking, "what did you say?"

She jerked her head in my direction. "About what?"

"When he asked you out. Did you say yes?"

"How is that any of your business?"

It wasn't. I knew it wasn't. I also knew I should shut the fuck up. But somehow my mouth kept running.

"Beth, we're friends, remember? And friends don't let friends date criminals."

She looked at me, her eyes flashing fire. "Look, Mac. You made it perfectly clear you didn't have room for me in your life. And that's fine. But you don't get to have it both ways. I am a single woman and if a guy asks me out— whether he's a boy scout or a fucking terrorist—you still don't have a say. And if you can't handle that, well, maybe we need to stop with the whole friends pretense." She scowled. "'Cause right now, just FYI, you're not acting like a friend."

"Neither are you, sweetheart. Neither are you." I gripped the steering wheel with white-knuckled fingers. "And if that's how you want to play it, I'm not sure I want to be your coworker either."

thirty-one

BETH

I returned to the newsroom, pissed off beyond belief. This should have been my greatest hour, my biggest triumph. And yet instead of thrilled, all I could feel was sick to my stomach.

How dare he judge me for my actions? Sure, I hadn't been a hundred percent truthful. And yes, I'd admittedly dressed up a little to get the guy's fixation off of Joy. But in the end I'd gotten the story. The story that everyone else had tried and failed to get. Couldn't I at least get some cred for that?

At least everyone else would be pleased. I could march into the newsroom a conquering hero, the interview of the century clasped in my hands. All the producers who had once shunned me like the plague would now be begging me to let them put the piece in their shows. And from this day forward, my days of covering R.O.U.T. (Rodents of Unusual Talent) would be over forever.

I imagined Richard calling me into his office, full of congratulations and good cheer. And when I asked him if this meant I could keep my new position as dayside reporter, he'd laugh, and say only until he could find me a better spot, higher in the ranks.

In fact, I imagined him saying, *the board is even offering you a hefty bonus, just to make sure you don't abandon us for one of those cushy anchor jobs the network news stations are offering.*

I snorted. Okay, maybe that was going a bit *too* far. But still. He was going to be psyched beyond belief.

In any case, this was the day to end all days. The best day ever in my short reporting career. And I wasn't about to let stupid, jealous, petty Mac ruin it for me.

He hadn't said another word the whole way home, after threatening to disband our partnership. And he'd disappeared immediately once we got back to the station, under the pretense of having to go clean his gear. He hadn't even taken the drive with the interview on it with him when he left—to upload it into the system as he was supposed to do, to get it ready for editing. It was as if he thought it was dirty and didn't want to touch it.

Whatever. I'd get someone else to do it. Most people here would be thrilled to upload and edit an exclusive interview with Dante Alvarez himself. Hell, it was pretty much insta-Emmy for anyone who touched it.

But evidently Mac didn't care about things like that.

Just like he didn't care about me.

I sighed, feeling defeat and disappointment weighing over me. Would he really go to Richard, as he'd threatened to do, tell him he didn't want to work with me anymore? Would they assign me a new photographer? I knew they wouldn't fire me, at least, not after getting this interview. But the job would be a lot different without Mac by my side.

It was funny; when I'd first learned I had to work with him, I couldn't think of anything I wanted less. But now that we'd been a team, I couldn't imagine teaming up with anyone else. He was the perfect partner.

But perhaps that was part of the problem.

I sighed. In the end there was nothing I could do. The

ball was in his court. He had to decide how to play it. In the meantime, I needed to get out of this ridiculous outfit before I shared my triumph with Richard and the rest of the newsroom. The leather pants were chafing the insides of my thighs and the blisters on my feet were ready to burst from the one-size-too-small stilettos. I needed to change back into my normal, comfortable, unsexy attire and give this all back to Ana, who somehow knew how to rock this type of thing without breaking a sweat—or an ankle, for that matter.

But as I headed to the locker room to change, I turned a corner too quickly, almost slamming into someone coming around the other direction. Not just any someone, either. But Stephanie.

"Sorry," I muttered, trying to sidestep her without meeting her eyes.

To my surprise, she stopped, then turned back to me. "So did you get it?"

"What?"

"The interview with the hacker guy. They told me that's why I had to do the squirrel thing. 'Cause you were on some crazy important shoot. Did you get him to talk?"

"What do you care?" I retorted, before I could stop myself.

She bit her lower lip. "Ouch," she said. "I guess I deserve that, huh?"

I grimaced. I so did not need to be getting into this right now. "Look, I really need to go change."

I started to turn, but she grabbed my arm. "Wait," she said.

I looked at her impatiently. "What?"

She sighed. "Beth, I owe you an apology, okay? I know I was an utter bitch when I first found out you were promoted. And what I did to your stuff . . . well, that was beyond unfair. I was just . . . really upset about what they did to me. And I thought . . ." She trailed off. "Look, do you want to meet up sometime? There's some things I want to talk to you about. They're kind of important."

I frowned, surprised to see what looked like genuine

apology on her face. Was she being serious? Or was this some kind of new game?

Either way, right now I just needed to go. "Sure, okay," I said. "I'm sure we can figure something out."

The relief on her face was palpable. "Great," she said. "Excellent. Okay. I'll let you go now. Congrats again on getting the interview—if you really did get it, I mean. First the whole gas leak conspiracy, then this . . . Sounds like they were right to promote you—even if it was at my expense."

And with that, she turned, starting to walk away. I watched her go, my stomach twisting in even more knots than before. God, between her and Mac—the drama in this place was seriously going be the death of me if I let it.

But I wouldn't let it, I reminded myself. Instead, I would change my clothes. I would go and show the interview to Richard. I would prove to everyone I was tougher than they gave me credit for. And that I deserved everything that had been given to me . . . and more.

Once inside the locker room, I walked over to my locker, noticing the padlock was still open. I must have forgotten to reattach it when I was changing earlier. Not surprising, I supposed. At the time I'd been more than a little distracted by the whole interview scheme I'd been concocting.

It was crazy how much had happened in only a few short hours. The way my emotions had gone up and down it felt as if I'd been on a roller coaster. After my shift was over, I was so going home to open a bottle of wine. Maybe see if Piper wanted to watch some kind of mindless rom-com. Get my mind off this crazy day.

And hopefully Mac as well.

With some effort, I managed to peel the leather pants from my body, exhaling in relief at the rush of cold air from the air-conditioner hitting my glistening skin. It was like I had been bathing in my own sweat all day and was finally able to dry off. Which, you know, was oh-so-glamorous. Dante may have loved my pants a little bit less if he'd known the nasty just beneath the surface.

Next, I shrugged off the jacket and pulled the camisole

over my head. I wished I had another bra and panties to
change into, mine were sweaty as hell, but they would have
to wait until I got home. Reaching into my locker, I grabbed
the shirt, pants and jacket I'd originally worn to work that
morning. Sticking out my legs, I slipped one, then the other,
into my pants.

Only to find them . . . sticky?

Confused, I slipped my hand inside one leg of the pants,
feeling around. I frowned. There was definitely something
odd in there—some kind of slick coating that didn't feel
natural. Something that felt a lot like . . . honey?

I swallowed hard. Oh God. Another sabotage? Had
Stephanie really—

Ow!

Hot blasts of itchy pain suddenly stung at my legs, causing me to cry out in horror. Heart in my throat, I yanked
down the pants. What had she put in there? Some kind of
itching powder? Or maybe—

I looked down and screamed.

My legs were covered with ants. Large, ugly, red fire ants.
Dozens of them, crawling up and down my skin.

Sweet baby Jesus!

I threw the pants across the room, panic rising inside of
me at an alarming rate. Then I set on the ants, trying desperately to brush them off my legs. Unfortunately that was
almost impossible to do, thanks to the stickiness of the
honey. Instead I was forced to try to pick at each and every
one individually and flick them away. But there were so
many—way too many and ugly red welts began to spread
across my legs as the venom of their tiny bites seeped into
my skin.

Oh my God. Oh my God.

Suddenly, my stomach cramped. My chest tightened. My
throat seemed to close up and the room started to spin.

Something was wrong. Something was terribly wrong.

I crashed back onto the floor, trying to scream again. But
my breath seemed lodged in my throat. I looked down to

see my legs, still crawling with ants, swollen to twice their normal size.

"Someone help me!" I whispered in a voice I knew no one would hear.

And then I succumbed to the blackness.

thirty-two

MAC

I stared at my camera, which I had already shined to an inch of its life, then rubbed the lens with my cloth just a little bit more, frustration eating away at me, making me feel sick. Three times already I'd risen from my desk, ready to go talk to Richard and three times I'd sat back down instead. Mainly because I had no idea what I was going to say to him that wouldn't make me come off sounding like a complete dick.

Mainly because I totally was.

What had I been thinking? Was I that pathetic—I couldn't even handle a little innocent flirting between Beth and another man? I tried to tell myself I'd only been concerned for her safety, about this douchebag's intentions—as any good friend would be. But I knew, in my heart, that wasn't true. Hell, like she'd said, she could have been batting her eyelashes at the local preacher's son and I'd still have wanted the bastard to rot in hell.

Because that bastard wasn't me.

Come on, Mac, I scolded myself. *You had your chance. You had her—literally in your arms—and you pushed her away. What did you want her to do, sit around pining for you until the end of time? She deserves a real man who can dedicate his life to making her happy—not some broke-ass, burnt-out photog with commitment issues.*

I pushed back in my chair, rolling away from my desk. I needed to suck it up. Be professional for once in my life. Stop letting my emotions rule me at work. I'd already lost one job back in Boston thanks to my personal drama, and I was lucky I'd gotten a do-over here.

I'd go find Beth and I'd apologize. I'd get the drive from her and I'd upload it into the system. And then I'd edit the best damn story News 9 had ever seen. Make her look like the superstar reporter she was. She deserved that, at least. Hell, she deserved a whole lot more.

I walked down the hall, still lost in my thoughts, still furious at myself for how I'd allowed things to go down. In fact, I was so wrapped up in reliving the horrible day, that I almost didn't hear the scream.

But then it came again. I froze, listening. It was a cry of fear, of pain, of agony—coming from the ladies' locker room.

A cry that sounded like—

"Beth?"

Without pause, I dove through the door, heart in my throat, not bothering to knock. My eyes scanned the room, seeking the source of the sound. At first I saw nothing—no one. Then, my eyes dropped the ground and I let out a gasp of horror.

Beth was crumpled on the floor, completely naked, save bra and panties, her body covered in ugly red welts and her breath coming in pained wheezes. Her fingers were clutching her throat, while small desperate sounds struggled to escape her lips.

"Beth!" I cried. "What happened? What's wrong? Talk to me!"

Her head turned, her eyes locking on to mine, a shred of hope springing to her dilated pupils. With her hand she gestured wildly to one side—to her purse that had toppled over and spilled out onto the floor. For a moment, I didn't know what she was getting at, but my eyes scanned the contents anyway, until I came across an EpiPen hiding under a packet of tissues. I scooped it up in my hands and plunged it into her arm. Her expression slackened in relief and her hands dropped to her side.

Reaching for my phone I called 911, keeping my eyes on her as I spoke to the dispatcher. Her panic was starting to subside, thank God, and her breathing sounded more regular. By the time I hung up, assured the ambulance was on its way, she'd reached out, placing a weak hand on my arm, looking up at me with huge, frightened eyes.

"What happened?" I whispered. "Why are you so sticky?"

"A-ants," she said weakly. "Do you see any more ants?"

I stared at her, confused as hell, then looked around the room. It was then that I saw them, crawling up and down her locker like little red soldiers.

"Are you allergic?" I asked. It was a stupid question.

Without waiting for an answer, I swept her into my arms, cradling her like a baby. When I told her I needed to get her out of here, she protested weakly, not wanting anyone to see her in this state. So instead, I brought her into the shower stall, which was thankfully ant free. I set her down, rinsed her off and draped my jacket around her shivering frame as we waited for the EMTs. It was all I could do.

But it wasn't nearly enough.

"Hang in there, sweetheart," I whispered.

She gave me a grateful smile that pretty much broke my heart. I thought back to earlier in the day; how confident and beautiful she had been, going after the story of the century without hesitation or fear. She had looked like a superhero.

Now she looked like a broken doll.

Anger gripped me as I started to think it all through. There was no way this was just some random act. That ants had accidentally found their way into her locker and her locker alone. My hands tightened into fists. "Do you think Stephanie . . . ?"

She gave a weak shrug, closing her eyes. "I don't know for sure," she said, her voice still croaky from her throat being so inflamed. "But I can't think of any other reason my pants would be coated with honey and full of ants."

I slammed my fist against the shower wall, succeeding in cracking the tile. It was all I could do not to go out there at this moment and strangle the bitch. It wasn't fair. It was so not fair. Here Beth was, about to go on air with the story of her career, and now she would probably be spending the night in the hospital instead.

"You could have died," I growled. "That's not sabotage. That's attempted murder."

"She couldn't have known I was allergic . . ."

"I don't care. This stops now. I'm going to Richard and I'm going to tell him everything." I started to rise to my feet.

"Mac . . ."

I turned back to her, meeting her eyes with my own. The way she looked at me, so pleadingly, so heartbreakingly scared . . .

"The video," she murmured. "I need you to get the video. Keep it safe."

I shook my head. Oh, Beth. Even in this state she was still concerned with her job. As if some stupid interview mattered at this point. When she could have lost her life.

"I'll take care of it, sweetheart," I assured her. "You just worry about you for now."

I pulled her close. Her whole body was trembling and she clung to me as if her life depended on it. I squeezed her closer, allowing her to burrow her face against my chest. My heart flooded with emotion and I felt like I was going to throw up. At the same time, I'd never felt quite so warm.

"I've got you, baby," I assured her. "And I promise you, I'm not going to let you go."

thirty-three

BETH

I opened my eyes, looking around, at first not sure where I was. A white room, a strange bed, nothing I recognized. Then it all came rushing back to me. I was in the hospital after almost dying from a fire ant attack. I closed my eyes for a moment, wincing as I relived the nightmare of pulling on my pants, of feeling those hot stings on my legs. Of collapsing to the floor, unable to breathe.

Of Mac, appearing out of nowhere, like some kind of knight in shining armor, sweeping in and saving the day. Not to mention my life.

I felt a hand on my own and my eyes fluttered open again, surprised to discover none other than the knight himself, leaning over me, a grave expression on his face. I gave him a weak smile, hating the way my stomach warmed at even this casual touch. I knew I should yank my hand out from under his, breaking the connection between us. But somehow I just couldn't bring myself to do it. It felt too good. Too right. As if his hand belonged there, clasped on top of mine.

"How are you feeling?" he asked gently.

"Like I've been run over by a truck," I confessed. "How long have I been out?"

"Just the night and most of the morning. They gave you a sedative to help you sleep."

"You . . . stayed all night?"

His eyes met mine. "You asked me not to leave."

My heart flooded with emotion and tears sprung to my eyes. I tried to tell myself it was only because of all the drugs I was on, but I knew that wasn't really the case. He'd stayed. He'd stayed by my bedside all night long.

I'm here, baby. And I'm not going to let you go.

"Thank you," I said weakly. "But what about Ashley?"

"Sadie's taking care of her. In fact the two of them stopped by about an hour ago. Ashley insisted on bringing you some magic pixie dust." He gave me an embarrassed grin. "At our house magic pixie dust cures all."

I giggled. "Of course it does. Such a sweet girl. Please tell her thank you for me."

Mac drew in a breath. "It might be nice if you could tell her yourself."

I stared at him, my heart thudding against my chest. "Are you sure you want that?" I asked softly. "After all, you said . . ."

He closed his eyes for a moment, his face a mask of pain. Then he opened them, looking directly at me.

"Look, Beth, I owe you an apology," he said, in a voice that sounded rough and unsteady. "What I said after the shoot yesterday . . . You did nothing wrong. I was projecting the past, and seeing the current situation through those old cracked lenses." He paused, then added, "I also let my personal feelings get in the way of doing my job, which is something I had vowed to never do again. I'm sorry."

My heart ached at the pain I saw, clear on his face, and I wondered, not for the first time, what had really happened to him back in Boston.

"It's okay," I assured him. "I wasn't exactly innocent either. I should have filled you in on the entire plan from the

beginning, not blindsided you and forced you to play catch
up. Like you said, we're a team. I'm not your boss." I gave
him a sheepish look. "I guess I was just worried you'd dis-
approve of my methods. Or at least try to talk me out of
them."

He chuckled softly. "I might have tried. But I bet I
wouldn't have succeeded."

I groaned. "Yeah, I suppose I was pretty determined. It
was just—I wanted so badly to prove myself, you know?
After all they've put me through? I wanted to prove to them
that they couldn't beat me. I guess I kind of also needed to
prove it to myself." I smiled. "Which reminds me, did you
tell Richard about our interview yet? Or do I still get to
surprise him myself once I'm out of here?"

I watched as a dark shadow crossed Mac's face. My smile
faded. "What's wrong?"

He turned away, exchanging his view of me for one of the
wall. "When the EMTs arrived I walked out with them to
see you safely into the ambulance. That was when they told
me I couldn't ride to the hospital with you—that it was family
only—so I was going to get my car. But first I went back to
the locker room, figuring I'd grab the drive like you asked
me to and keep it safe. But when I got there . . . it was gone."

"Gone?" Fear tripped down my spine. "What do you
mean, gone? Maybe you just didn't see it!"

"I thought so at first, too," he said, giving me a sorry
look. "I searched everywhere. I tore that place apart. Then
I went to the newsroom and searched there. And then to the
stacks of recycled drives. I checked every possible place."

"And you never found it?"

"Actually I did."

"What?" My heart beat fast in my chest. "I don't understand."

He closed his eyes for a moment, sucking in a breath. "It
was sitting on a large, industrial-strength magnet."

"Oh God." I sank back in my pillow, my head filling in
the blanks of the rest of his story. My interview. My big interview that was going to show them all. The one that would put

me on the map and maybe win me an Emmy. It was gone.
Erased.

Sabotaged, yet again.

"You know, Stephanie had the nerve to try to talk to me?"
I growled. "Right before all of this? She made it seem like
she was trying to be friends? And all the while she was
planning *this*?" It was all I could do not to throw up.

"Don't panic," Mac scolded. "We're not going to let her
win. We'll just go back as soon as you're out of here and get
it reshot. You have Alvarez's number, right? Just tell him we
had a camera malfunction—you don't even have to explain
the whole story. We can work around his schedule, even if
it's after hours. And we can go wherever we need to go. No
big deal."

I shook my head. "It's not going to work."

"Why not?"

I sighed heavily, feeling as if the weight of the world were
resting on my shoulders. "Do you remember when I told you
how he called me back to ask me out?"

Mac stiffened a little. "Yeah . . . ?"

"Well, I said no," I told him.

"You said *no*?"

The look on his face made me want to laugh, despite the
bitter circumstances. Like, he knew he was supposed to be
upset about this—seeing as it would cost us the interview.
But at the same time, he couldn't help but be relieved.

"I said no," I confirmed. "And let's just say, he wasn't
pleased."

Mac didn't reply at first. Just grabbed me, pulling me into
his arms. Squeezed me so tightly against him, I half-struggled
to breathe. "Thank God," he murmured, his lips brushing
against my neck in a way that gave me shivers. "Thank God,
I'm not too late."

I pulled away, looking at him questioningly. His cheeks
colored.

"You may not be aware of this," he said, "but all week long
I've been killing myself, trying to see you as just a casual
coworker—a platonic friend. When that douchebag had his

hands all over you before the shoot—I could barely keep it together. Then you tell me he asked you out." He snorted. "It was all I could do not to charge back into that warehouse and kick the crap out of him. Or at least put in a valiant attempt before his goons took me out for good."

I giggled despite myself, my insides flip-flopping madly as I imagined the scene. Mac, rushing in to defend my honor. "I'm glad you managed to restrain yourself. Then we *really* wouldn't be able to score a new interview."

He nodded, then the laughter faded from his face. "But in the end, I did something worse," he insisted. "I took it out on you. You, who did nothing wrong." He shook his head. "I can't even tell you what an asshole I felt like afterwards. I wanted to apologize, but I didn't even know where to start. And then, when I found you, on the floor, unable to breathe . . ." He cringed. "It was as if my life started flashing before my eyes. This empty, long, pointless life without you in it."

I swallowed hard. "Oh, Mac . . ."

"Look," he said at last. "I'm not going to lie; I'm damaged goods—with a hell of a lot of baggage—and my life is anything but simple. But if you really do want to take a chance with me—to see where this thing between us could possibly go—well, I'm done being afraid. And I'm ready to give it a try." He paused, then added. "On one condition."

I looked at him, my heart melting. "What's that?"

"That you don't give up on that interview. You keep trying. And you don't take no for an answer." He looked at me, his eyes so blue and piercing. "I don't know about you, but I'm not cool with just letting those bastards win."

I grinned shyly at him. "Neither am I."

thirty-four

There she is, the girl on fire!"

I looked up to see Richard walk into the hospital room the next afternoon, dressed in a pair of slouchy jeans and a plain blue T-shirt. It was funny; I'd never seen him outside the newsroom setting before, without a suit and tie. He was actually kind of handsome in casual clothes.

"Sorry," he said, sitting down at my bedside. "Bad joke."

I snorted. "It's okay. I'm in need of jokes—bad or otherwise. This place is boring as hell. And if I eat one more tub of Jell-O I'm going to start wobbling myself."

"When are they springing you?"

"Probably tomorrow morning, if all checks out. Why, you miss me?"

"Desperately," he assured me with a grin. Then his face sobered. "But we'll live. You take as much time as you need. I've pulled Stephanie back into the rotation until you're ready to come back. And, shockingly, she's actually been doing a decent job. Maybe she's learned her lesson."

"Oh yeah," I muttered. "She's learned all right."

Richard's eyes narrowed. "What's that supposed to mean?"

I bit my lower lip, glancing over at him. I didn't want to tell him, but Mac insisted that if I didn't, he would. She'd gone too far this time. And she needed to be made accountable. If not by the police—I still wasn't ready to go there—at least on the job.

"Look, Richard," I started. "About Stephanie . . ."

And so I told him. About her kicking me out of the apartment, about her sabotages at work, about the blue hairspray and the ants. He listened without interruption and when I had finished, he gave a long sigh, raking a hand through his hair.

"Why didn't you come to me?" he asked. "I mean from the beginning?"

I shrugged. "I didn't want to cause waves. I didn't want you to doubt your decision to put me on dayside. I figured I could deal with it."

"Yeah, well, next time remember that's my job. That's why they pay me the big bucks." He snorted. "Well, that's why they *should* anyway. In any case, this is not acceptable and I'm sorry you had to go through it. I promise you I will take this to the board immediately after I leave here and we will take action." He gave me a brisk nod. "It ends here, Beth. I promise."

I nodded, feeling tears spring to my eyes as an overwhelming relief washed over me. I'd been so scared to come clean for so long and now it felt so good to have everything out in the open. To know it was over at last.

"Thank you," I said. "And I'm sorry I didn't come to you sooner."

"My door is always open," Richard assured me. "You have any more problems with anyone else here, you come to me first and I will take care of it." He gave me a sympathetic smile. "You're an important part of the News 9 team," he told me. "And I'm not going to lose you."

"Does this mean . . ." I drew in a breath. "That the dayside position is mine?" I asked. "I mean, permanently?"

To my surprise, Richard burst out laughing. "Sorry," he added, after catching my look. "I just . . . were you waiting for me to tell you that all this time? I decided that after your first day on the job—when you discovered that gas leak. There was no question in my mind you would be able to do the job. Sorry, I should have mentioned it earlier."

Relief washed over me in waves. I had the job. The job was mine. No one could take it away. And the sabotages would be over forever. It was like a dream come true.

Or it would be, once I reshot the Alvarez interview. But Richard didn't need to know about that until it was signed, sealed, and delivered.

"Now, how are things working out with Jake?" Richard asked. "His trial run is about over, too. Do you want to keep working with him? Or should I put you with someone else?"

I drew in a breath. "Actually," I said, "I think Mac's working out just fine."

Ring!
The shrill sound of my cell phone broke me from a deep slumber early that Sunday morning and I groaned as I realized I'd left the device on the kitchen counter and would have to get out of my comfy bed to answer it. At first I considered just letting it go to voice mail, but on the rare chance that it could be Dante Alvarez, finally returning my calls, I forced myself out of bed.

It had been four days since the interview that had ended with the fire ant attack and the erased tape and I'd been in bed for most of them. Richard had given me the week off to recover, saying I could come back whenever I was ready, that there was no rush at all. I appreciated his gesture, but I had a sense of urgency that he didn't. One way or another, I needed to get that interview rescheduled.

Unfortunately that was proving easier said than done. Every morning I would try to reach the reclusive hacker, but every call had gone to voice mail and he hadn't returned a single one. One morning I'd even driven down to the warehouse where I had last met with him, hoping he might still be shacking up there. But he was long gone—no sign he'd ever been there at all.

And when I called him again yesterday, his cell phone had been disconnected, severing my last possible hope.

But there will be other stories, I told myself. *Other opportunities to prove yourself. And at least now the saboteur has been dealt with.*

Immediately after leaving my hospital room Richard had gone to the powers that be and, as promised, launched an investigation on Stephanie. A few hours later he called me back to inform me that my former roommate had been escorted from the building and was no longer an employee of News 9. It seemed that while she had denied the charges, a cursory search of her locker turned up an empty jar of honey and a bottle of blue hair dye—all the evidence Richard needed to get her out the door.

Mac still thought I should call the police as well. But after much soul searching, I decided against it. The last thing I needed was for this kind of Real House Reporters of San Diego drama to go viral—my serious journalistic career reduced to nothing more than tabloid fodder for the masses. After all, someday I might want a new job. Maybe with a network or a national news show. And I didn't want them to Google my name and find a real mess attached to it.

Instead, I would take the high road. I would move forward. And just be glad that it was over at last.

The phone rang again. "Okay, okay, I'm up!" I muttered, running to the kitchen. "Hello?" I asked into the receiver after pressing accept.

Please be Dante Alvarez. Please, please be Dante Alvarez.

"Hi, Beth!" The voice on the other end was young, excited. Definitely not that of the infamous hacker. It was also somewhat familiar, though in my half-awake state I couldn't quite place it.

"Hi . . . Who's this?" I asked groggily.

"It's Ashley!" the voice chirped. "Me and Daddy are going to see the snow! And we wanted you to come with us! Do you want to come with us, Beth? Do you want to? 'Cause I really want you to. And Daddy says he does, too! Daddy says—"

Her chatter broke off mid-sentence and I heard a shuffling on the other end of the line. A moment later, Mac's rich baritone voice broke through.

"Sorry about that," he said, sounding just as sexy over the phone as he did in real life. "I told her to wait until at least eight to call you. But she found my phone while I was in the shower. Sorry if she woke you."

My mind involuntarily treated me to a vision of Mac all soapy and naked, with warm water sluicing down his skin. I stifled a groan. "It's cool," I assured him. "I'm definitely up."

I could almost hear his smile on the other end of the phone. "Great," he said. "Anyway, Ashley has not stopped talking about going to find snow in California since you brought it up. So I thought maybe it was time to make that happen. If you're feeling up to it, that is," he added quickly. "And you don't have any other plans . . ."

I grinned goofily. Other plans? Hell, if I had had royal tea scheduled at Buckingham palace that afternoon, I would have canceled with the queen.

"I'm feeling much better," I assured him. "And no, I don't have anything big going on today."

"Awesome. Sadie and her kids are going to meet us up there, but I can pick you up. Can you be ready in an hour?"

I glanced at the mirror—at my bed head hair and pajamas. "Can you give me an hour and a half?"

"You can have as much time as you need, sweetheart."

My stomach flip-flopped. "Actually an hour should be fine," I corrected, not wanting to have to wait a minute longer than necessary to see his handsome face. "Just beep when you're outside and I'll come right out."

I rattled off the directions to my new apartment, then hung up the phone, my heart beating so rapidly in my chest it was hard to breathe. All my earlier sleepiness had vanished and I was about ready to do cartwheels across the living room floor. I thought back to the last time I'd seen him, after waking up in the hospital. All the things he'd said, all the promises he'd made. The butterflies in my stomach flitted madly.

"Everything okay?"

I glanced over to see Piper, peeking out from her bedroom doorway, a curious expression on her face.

"Oh yeah," I said. "Sorry if I woke you. I left my phone
out here last night by mistake."

"No problem. I needed to get up anyway." Piper assured
me. She paused, then added, "So was it him? Did he call?"

She meant Dante Alvarez, of course. Since the fire ant
incident, I'd told her everything that had gone down and she
had been more than properly horrified on my behalf. Which
was nice, actually. Nice to have someone supportive at home.

"Unfortunately not," I said. "I think that ship has sailed."
I looked her over, realizing she was fully dressed. "Are you
working today?" I asked, a little surprised. I thought she'd
been doing the Monday through Friday shift.

"Sort of," she said, looking a little sheepish. "Tommy,
the weekend producer, told me I could come in and write
mock scripts for the newscast as kind of an audition. You
know, in case a writing position ever opened up."

I gave a low whistle. "You are seriously the most hard-
working person at News 9. You know that, right?"

Piper blushed. "Yeah, well, maybe if I'm lucky someone
besides you will notice that someday."

"They will," I assured her. "And if they don't, I'll tell
them myself!"

She grinned. "So if it wasn't the reclusive hacker on the
phone, was it at least the sexy photographer?"

Now it was my turn to blush. The Dante Alvarez tale was
not the only one I'd shared with her over drinks last night. "It
was indeed," I confessed. "He asked me to go to the mountains to find some snow."

"Nice!" Piper exclaimed. "A real date!"

"I don't know about that. I mean, his four-year-old will
be there. Not to mention his sister."

"Which makes it even a bigger deal, right? I mean, a
family outing? That's so much more intense than just some
dinner and a movie."

I smiled goofily, I couldn't help it. "I hope you're right,"
I said. "'Cause I really like him, Piper. I didn't want to admit

it at first—even to myself. But I really do. And I really want this to happen."

"Then make it happen!" Piper declared. "I mean, hell. Surely if you can get the elusive Dante Alvarez to agree to be interviewed, you can get little old Jake MacDonald to fall in love with you."

I laughed. "Well, I promise you this, I'm going to give it my best shot!"

thirty-five

MAC

A re you ready *yet,* Daddy?"

I reluctantly pulled away from the mirror at the sound of my daughter's voice, asking the same question she'd been asking for about ten minutes now. I needed to get ahold of myself—I'd changed outfits three times already—like I was a freaking chick or something. It was beginning to get ridiculous.

It's just a trip to the mountains, I scolded myself. *Not some fancy opera.*

Besides, it wasn't as if Beth hadn't seen me in casual attire before. Hell, half the time I showed up to work in a plain old T-shirt and shorts. Still, the state of some of my clothes—especially the warm winter ones that I'd boxed up during the move to sunny California, was beyond pitiful. It seemed like every sweater I grabbed had at least one rip in it and the soles of every pair of boots seemed to be coming apart.

In the end, I decided to go ultra casual: Boston Bruins sweatshirt and baggy jeans, with a pair of hiking boots and a black woolen hat to complete the ensemble. A look that probably said, *I tried really hard to look like I wasn't trying at all*.

"Yes, I'm ready, you impatient little munchkin," I said, grabbing her and tickling her ribs. She squealed and struggled to get away.

"I'm not a munchkin!" she declared. "I'm an ice queen!"

And she looked like one, too, all decked out in her powder blue *Frozen* jacket and matching hat and mittens. It was clear who took priority in this house when it came to our clothing budget.

"Let it go, Queen Elsa, let it go," I teased.

"No! Let *me* go!"

"If you insist." I released her. "Now . . . race you to the car!"

Soon we were on our way, headed toward Beth's new apartment. As we grew closer, a strange feeling settled in the pit of my stomach. But it wasn't the uneasy feeling I had expected; rather more like butterflies. Which was beyond crazy; I saw this woman nearly every day of my life. Why was I suddenly so nervous?

Because this was a step, I realized. A major step in our friendship—relationship—whatever you wanted to call it. I had invited her to go somewhere with me and my daughter. How was she going to take such an offer? Like it was no big deal? Or was she right now on that Internet site where you could design your own wedding rings?

The butterflies flew away and in their place a hollow panic threatened to swallow me whole. Because suddenly I wasn't sure which scenario I preferred. After all, I'd told her I wanted us to take a chance. But actually taking that chance was still beyond terrifying. What if it didn't work out? What if I said something stupid, or panicked and pushed her away again? What if I ruined the fragile friendship we'd created together by pushing for something more? What would I tell Ashley if I screwed this all up, and ended up sending Beth fleeing from our lives forever?

But then my mind flashed back to the scene in the ladies' locker room at the station. Beth on the floor, struggling to breathe. The fear in my heart at the real possibility that I was about to lose her forever, without ever having told her how I felt. At that moment, when she'd opened up those big brown eyes of hers and stared up at me, like I was some kind of hero, I would have done anything in the world to keep her by my side.

Beth was everything I wanted in a woman. Smart, kind, fun-loving. She knew when to be playful and when to get to work. She was fair, honest, sweet—and yet unstoppable when it came to going after what she wanted. Not the type of girl who would sit back and wait for it to come to her.

No wonder my daughter thought she was some kind of rock star. Sometimes Ash was a lot smarter than her dear old dad. Or at least less pigheaded.

A few minutes later we pulled up to her new apartment and I beeped the horn as she'd instructed me to do, even though half of me wanted to play the real gentleman and go up to the door and ring the bell. But before I could pop out of the car, she came rushing out, waving to us excitedly.

I drew in a breath. In making my list of her good qualities earlier, I'd somehow forgotten to add *hot beyond belief* to the top of it, and I felt a stirring in my stomach just looking at her now. She was dressed casually—just a fuzzy gray sweater with flecks of glitter in the yarn over a pair of plain black sweatpants. On her feet, she wore sensible hiking boots and she held a pair of red woolen mittens in her hands. I groaned. I'd always had a thing for a girl in mittens. And I had to admit, the outfit as a whole was even more enticing than those leather pants and stiletto heels she'd had on earlier in the week. It was a good thing, I realized, that my daughter was in the car, forcing me to behave myself. Because otherwise I was pretty sure we'd never make it to the mountain.

"A sled!" Ashley exclaimed suddenly, breaking through my fantasies. "Look, Daddy! Beth has a sled! That's so cool!"

I had to agree—and not just about the sled, either.

"I think you just made my daughter's life," I teased as I popped out of driver's side door to take the sled from her and load it into the back of the truck.

Beth grinned shyly. "She can thank my new roommate," she explained. "She evidently bought it last winter when she took some of the kids from her group home job up to Big Bear for the weekend. I figured it might come in handy today."

"What do you think, ice queen?" I asked my daughter as we got into the front of the SUV. "You think we might be able to put that sled to good use?"

"I'm going to go find the biggest hill!" Ashley exclaimed. "And I'm going to go down it really, really, really fast!"

I shot a grin at Beth, who, in turn smiled back at me. As my daughter chattered on and on in the backseat about what she was going to do with the sled in great detail, I pulled out from the apartment complex and headed for the freeway, going east to hit the mountains.

It was still early and there were hardly any other cars on the road so we were able to make it to the foothills in good time. As we ascended the windy mountain road, Ashley shrieked in delight as a light dusting began to fall onto our windshield. I turned on the wipers, marveling at the idea that we could go from a beach paradise to a winter wonderland in only an hour. California was definitely unique in that regard. And, I had to admit, pretty cool.

Finally, we reached our destination—a huge field, covered in snow, with several small hills to sled down. There were already a couple dozen cars pulled up to the side of the road, and from here I could see a mass of children running wild through the snow.

"I guess this is the place," I said, turning to Ashley. "Are you sure you wouldn't prefer to go to the beach?"

"No way!" Ashley cried, looking scared for a moment that I was actually being serious. "I want to play in the snow!" She bounced in her booster seat so hard that I was half convinced she would break through the seatbelt if forced to sit still a moment longer.

"Well okay then," I announced. "Let's do it."

I put the car in park, then popped out of the driver's seat, walking around to open Ashley's door. Once freed from her booster seat, she bounded from the car, running out onto the field before I could even close the door.

"Hey, ice queen, slow down!" I protested. "Wait for your loyal subjects."

"I'm not an ice queen!" Ashley called back, slowing down—just barely. "I'm a snowy girl!"

"I don't even know what that is," I snorted, turning to Beth.

She laughed. "A girl whose daddy has just made her very, very happy."

I had to admit, I was feeling pretty damn happy myself as I walked around the back of the SUV, grabbing the sled and handing it to my daughter. Sadie had already arrived with her two kids and Ashley ran to join them. They all squealed excitedly when they saw the sled and my sister waved to me as she accompanied the three of them to the top of the hill to try it out.

I returned her wave, then reached back into the car and pulled out an old space blanket I'd packed, along with a little picnic lunch of sandwiches and fruit. Beth took the basket and together we headed out onto the snow-covered field, finding the perfect spot and laying down the silver blanket. It was a little cold to sit down on, but not unbearable. And in truth, I was already feeling pretty warm inside anyway.

I opened up the picnic basket and handed her a sandwich. "Hope you like PB&J," I said with a laugh. "We're all class all the time here at the MacDonald household."

She grinned. "I knew there was a reason I liked you guys." She took a big bite and moaned in pleasure. "Delicious," she pronounced, her mouth still full. I agreed—and not just about the sandwich, either. She'd gotten a small splotch of jelly stuck to the corner of her lips and it was all I could do not to lean in and lick it off.

Instead, I found my own sandwich, taking a large bite. It was pretty good, I had to admit. Reaching back into the basket, I found a thermos of tomato soup and poured her a cup. "Your second course, m'lady," I pronounced, handing it to her.

"Why thank you, fine sir," she said with a mock bow. She

put the cup to her lips and breathed in deeply. "Mmm, smells good."

"The best Campbell's has to offer," I bragged. "Does this guy know how to wow a lady on a first date or what?"

Her eyes swung to my face. "*Is* this is a first date?" she asked quietly.

I turned away, suddenly feeling a little embarrassed. "I guess it is," I said, after a pause. "I mean, you've come over my house. And we met at the club. But we've never actually gone anywhere together before. At least not in a nonwork capacity."

She nodded, seeming to consider this. Then she smiled. "Well, it's the perfect place for a first date, that's for sure."

"I'll go with that. Though I'm not sure most women would agree with you."

"I'm pretty sure I'm not 'most women.'"

"Maybe that's why I like you so much."

Now it was her turn to blush. "Oh, you like me, huh?"

"Damn woman." I shook my head. "I've been crazy about you since the moment I met you at the bar. The way you rattled off tequila brands . . ."

She rolled her eyes. "God, that seems so long ago now. Like another lifetime."

"Can I ask you something?" I said suddenly, surprising even myself.

She turned to look at me. "Of course."

"What Stephanie said about that night. About you being at the club trying to get back at your ex-boyfriend . . ."

She groaned. "I still can't believe she told you all that. So embarrassing."

"But . . . was it true?"

"Yes," she said, her cheeks coloring. "Well, sort of. I was in a pretty bad place that night. And the whole thing was really out of character. Not that I regret any of it," she added, with a twinkle in her eyes. "But yeah. It wasn't my finest hour."

"So your boyfriend had just broken up with you?"

"My fiancé, actually. And worse—he'd just gotten married."

"To another woman?"

"To my sister."

I stared at her. "Wait, what? How . . . ?"

"How indeed." She snorted. Then I listened as she explained the whole sordid tale.

"God," I muttered when she was finished. "That's ridiculous. Hell, I think I'd be ready to screw a stranger, too, at that point."

"Honestly, the worst part was my family's reaction," she added. "My mom basically told me to my face that it was my fault. That by chasing after some crazy career halfway across the country, I was basically telling him he was second best. And that I deserved to have him look elsewhere."

I scowled, offended on her behalf. "That's ridiculous. What did he want? For you to be barefoot and pregnant in the kitchen?"

"I don't know. I guess he just wanted me to put him first." She shrugged. "In any case, I'm over it. He wasn't right for me, I see that now. We'd been together so long, we'd been like a bad habit. And now that I see what it could be instead . . ."

She gave me a look that made my heart swell. I reached out, taking her hands in my own, stroking her mittens. "Well, I think he's crazy," I declared. "And I'm really glad you didn't let anyone talk you out of going after your dreams. You have what it takes to be an amazing reporter. And I love the fact that you never give up—even when things get hard. In fact, that might be my favorite thing about you."

"Thanks," she said. "That means a lot, actually." She paused, then added, "What about you?"

"Eh, I give up on things all the time."

She laughed. "I mean, about the club, silly. Why were you there that night? Now that I know you better, it doesn't seem much like your scene."

"It's about as opposite my scene as you can get," I declared. "But I guess I, too, was in a bad state that night."

"Because of your ex-wife?" She paused then added, "What happened between the two of you anyway? If you feel comfortable talking about it, that is."

I drew in a breath. *Did* I feel comfortable? I mean, I never talked about this. Not to anyone—not even Sadie. Yet, some-how, I kind of wanted to now. I wanted Beth to understand where I'd come from. Why I'd acted like I had. Why I was, even now, so damned scared of opening myself up. Of con-necting with another person. Especially another coworker.

Ah, what the hell.

"When I first met Victoria she was a writer at a small TV station in Maine," I started, my heart beating a little faster as I began the tale. "I fell for her right away. She was so excited about everything—and so driven. She was like a force of nature and I'd never met anyone like her. I helped her put together her reporter résumé tape and put in a good word for her at my station in Boston." I raked a hand through my hair. "But an entry-level job at a big station wasn't enough for her. She wanted more. And she didn't want to wait for a promotion the old-fashioned way."

"I see," Beth said, obviously guessing where this story was going. And why wouldn't she? Looking back on it now, it was all such a cliché.

"Anyway, there was this news director at our Boston sta-tion. A real bigwig named Mike who had been there for years. He was very good at his job—and also very married. But that didn't stop Victoria from seducing him. Soon, she was getting all the plum assignments and moving up the ranks." I shook my head. "And me, being the idiot that I was, thought she was just good at her job."

"Ugh." Beth gave me a pitying look. "I'm so sorry. You must have been devastated when you found out."

"I didn't just find out. I caught them in the act," I told her, fidgeting with my cup. "I'd come in to the station late to edit a piece and found them going at it on his desk." I grimaced, my mind flashing back to the scene. Their bodies, naked and writhing. "I reacted like any husband would, I guess. I beat the shit out of him. My very own boss." I sighed. "I was fired, of course, and the guy told me I'd never work in Boston again."

"That's ridiculous! Couldn't you have sued for wrongful dismissal or something?"

I shrugged. "I could have, I guess. But I wasn't exactly in

a rational state of mind at that point. Instead I did something much more idiotic. I posted the whole thing on social media—photos and everything. Called the guy out for sleeping with a married woman who was not his wife. At the time I was so blinded by my thirst for revenge I didn't think the consequences through."

"What happened?"

"The whole thing went viral. The news director got fired. His wife divorced him. And Victoria—well, she became a pariah around town. Not that she was an innocent party, mind you. But some of the stuff people said. . . ." I shook my head. "Let's just say it got really ugly. And no other station wanted to touch her with a ten-foot pole."

"I can imagine. That's why I didn't want the whole Stephanie thing to get out. And that's minor compared to something like this."

"Exactly," I said. "In any case, she called in a few favors, pulled a few strings and suddenly she was offered an international correspondent job overseas. I guess she figured it was her only chance to start over and redeem herself. Only problem? It meant leaving me and Ashley behind. But hey," I added bitterly, "in her mind I was the asshole who put her in this position to begin with. And Ashley, well, she was just collateral damage."

"I'm so sorry, Mac."

"Me, too. And, of course, Ash didn't understand. She still doesn't. And how could she? One night her mommy is there, putting her to bed. The next she's gone—presumably forever. Without even a 'see yah later, kiddo.'"

"She didn't even try to explain it to her?"

"I don't think she cared enough to try." I frowned. "Anyway, as you can imagine, I wasn't in a great state after all that and I'd pretty much sworn off women forever. In fact, when I went to that club, the last thing I planned on was hooking up. But then I met you. And suddenly I found myself going against everything I promised myself. Everything I promised my little girl." I gave Beth a tortured look. "And then the next morning I woke up in your bed. And I realized how much I didn't want to leave . . ."

"Oh, Mac."

Beth grabbed me and kissed me, her cold lips pressing against mine, taking away the need to continue. Because I didn't need to continue, I suddenly realized. Because she already knew. She already understood. And yet, she chose to kiss me anyway. To take me—the underserving, weak-willed bastard—for who I was. And who she believed I could be.

I kissed her back. And in an instant there was no more one-night stand and guilt and regret. No more tortured past and bad decisions. Only her soft mouth on mine. Her tongue tangling with my own. As if trying to convey something very important that couldn't be explained with mere words.

I pulled her to me and I could feel her heartbeat, fast and hard, against my chest. She was nervous, but she was also excited. She was scared, but she wasn't going to let herself pull away. Chills spun down my spine as she wrapped her arms around my back and held me tight. Secure. She tasted like spun sugar and sunshine. She tasted like home.

Lost in the kiss, for a moment I forgot where I was. What we were supposed to be doing. All I could focus on were her lips on mine. My hands tangled in her hair. But then, suddenly, something cold and wet struck my cheek. I pulled away, startled. Confused. Then a smile spread across my face when I realized what it was that had hit me.

"They're having a snowball fight!" Beth exclaimed with a grin.

"I haven't had a good snowball fight in ages," I declared, jumping to my feet. I grabbed a fistful of white powder, molding it into the perfect ball of snow. When I'd finished, I threw it expertly at Beth, striking her square in the chest.

"Hey!" she protested, grabbing her own handful of the white stuff as she scrambled up from the blanket. I tried to dodge, but she was too quick and her shot rang true, smacking me in the shoulder. Laughing, I lobbed another in her direction, but this time she was able to skip nimbly aside.

"Missed me, missed me," she taunted.

Now you've got to kiss me.

Been there, done that, I thought with a secret smile. Though I'd be more than okay with doing it again.

But first things first. I grabbed another handful of snow, then charged toward her, grabbing her by the jacket and smashing a snowball into her face.

She screamed in protest. "Oh, is that how you want to play? It's on, Mac Daddy, it's so on!"

Scooping up a huge amount of snow in one hand, she grabbed me by the sweatshirt and stuffed the entire thing down my chest. In an instant, I was ice cold and I screamed in protest as I tried to shake it out.

Thankfully Ashley showed up then, my little princess in shining armor. "Ha, ha!" I cried. "Now you've met my secret weapon."

"No way, Daddy!" Ashley corrected. "I'm on Beth's team!" She hurled a huge snowball in my direction.

"What? My own daughter? A traitor to her dear old dad?" I placed a hand over my heart, as if mortally wounded by this devastating betrayal by my own flesh and blood. But inside, I could only smile as the two girls ganged up on me, combining forces to knock me into the snow.

My two girls.

We played for hours, until we were thoroughly soaked to the bone. Finally, the sun began to descend and we decided it would be best to get back before we froze to death.

I considered dropping Beth off at her apartment, but the idea of breaking up our cozy little group made me hesitate. I wanted her to stick around a little longer. I knew my daughter would want the same. And really, was there anything truly holding me back? Ashley was thrilled to have her. I didn't want her to leave . . .

"Do you like chili?" I found myself asking. "It's my singular culinary achievement and I'm thinking it'd be a great way to end the day, if you didn't have other plans."

Beth grinned. "Sounds good to me."

Actually it sounded like heaven.

When we arrived home, we all changed into dry clothes. Since Beth didn't have any with her, I offered her an old button-down flannel shirt and sweatpants. But the sweatpants wouldn't stay up and the shirt fell to her knees so she decided to just wear it as a dress instead.

Which was fine by me.

She and Ashley played videogames while I cooked. And soon the house was filled with squealing and laughter from both the girls. My heart felt very full as I announced dinner was ready and they both scrambled to take their seats at the dining room table. Even being married to Victoria for six years—we never had this kind of domestic bliss. We worked opposite shifts, were always passing in the night. And if we did ever eat together, it was usually very late, long after Ashley had gone to bed.

This was like how real people did it. Real families.

Ashley was exhausted from the action-packed day and soon was practically falling asleep at the dinner table. I carried her to bed and tucked her in with her stuffed lion—and for once she didn't even utter a word of protest or demand a family hug.

Once she was settled, I headed back out to find Beth, who had brought all the dishes to the sink and was currently washing them. When I approached, she gave me a shy smile. God, she looked so good in my shirt. I tried not to think about how much better she'd look without it.

"You don't have to do that," I said, nodding at the sink.

"You cooked dinner. It's the least I could do."

"Well, then how about I make the drinks?" I pulled out the blender and a bottle of margarita mix.

Her eyes twinkled mischievously. "Don't suppose you have any Anejo Banjo lying around . . ."

I grinned. I was hoping she'd ask that. "Actually," I reached up into the cabinet and pulled down the bottle I'd been saving. "Ta-da!"

"Is that . . . ?" She did a double take. Then she laughed as she took a closer look at the label. "How is that possible? This literally doesn't exist."

"It does now," I declared. "Thanks to me getting creative with my printer."

"That is truly awesome," she cried, grabbing the bottle in her still soapy hand and studying it closer. "We should totally label a bottle of some two buck chuck and send it to our bartender friend."

"I'm sure he would love that," I said with a nod. "It *is* his favorite, of course."

"Indeed. He orders it *all the time.*"

I smiled at her. She smiled back at me. I took her soapy hands and dried them off with a dishtowel.

"Enough slave labor. Go sit on the couch, woman. And let me make you a drink."

She blushed. "If you insist."

"I absolutely do."

I released her hands, then watched her walk to the couch, unable not to focus on her long, bare legs beneath my shirt. I suddenly wondered if she was wearing underwear or if that, too, was in the dryer.

Forcing my attention back to the blender, I made the drinks, then poured them into red Solo cups and brought them over to the coffee table, setting them down before her. She took one in her hands and held it up.

"Cheers!"

We clinked cups. Then I watched as she put the cup to her mouth, her full lips parting to accept the liquid offering. The same way they'd parted under my tongue just a few hours before. Groaning, I took a big slug of my margarita—a vain attempt to cool my lust-filled thoughts. Unfortunately, all it did was give me instant brain freeze.

"Argh!" I cried, clutching my head in my hands, falling back onto the couch as icy pain stabbed me in the skull without mercy. Beth looked at me, at first, concerned, then burst out laughing as she realized the source of my sudden affliction.

"It's not funny," I protested, rubbing my head and nose.

"I know, I know. Sorry. Here, let me help. I know a little trick."

Before I knew it, she had scooted over next to me, her bare thigh pressing against the side of my leg. Then she reached over, prying open my mouth and sticking her thumb inside. I froze, unable to move, as she proceeded to press her thumb against the roof of my mouth, rubbing it slowly against the palette.

My brain freeze began to fade . . . but not before something else began to grow.

Oh God.

"Is that better?" she asked.

"Mmhm," I agreed, trying to talk with her thumb in my mouth. "Muth bether."

"Good," she pronounced, then started to withdraw her thumb. But my mouth had other ideas and I found myself wrapping my lips around the digit, pulling her back in and sucking hard. She looked startled for a moment, then wistful, allowing me to swirl my tongue around her thumb, then bite down lightly on the nail. Then I climbed on top of her, straddling those bare thighs, reaching out to cup her breasts in my hands, brushing my own thumbs across her nipples. She moaned softly, closing her eyes and leaning her head against the couch. My erection strained against my pants as I continued to fondle her, her nipples growing hard as diamonds beneath my hands.

Realizing I was getting carried away, I let her thumb slip from my mouth and withdrew my hands. She opened her eyes, looking up at me with a mixture of wonder and fear. Her cheeks were flushed, her mouth was slightly parted. Her expression soft and dreamy.

"Please don't stop," she whispered.

A slow smile spread across my face. "Oh, believe me, I'm just getting started." I leaned in to kiss her. "In fact, if I have my way, we'll be doing this all night long."

thirty-six

BETH

Danger, danger!

As his mouth came down on my own, warning bells rang through my head. My brain protested loudly that I should get off the couch, run out the door, go home, go to sleep—alone—and wake up the next morning with no regrets. Opening myself up, once again, to this—with no real assurance that this time would stick—it was dangerous. It was stupid. It was an unnecessary risk.

But I was going to take it anyway. Because it was worth it. *He* was worth it. Not as a one-night love lance. But as a guy I wanted as an exclusive.

Pushing away all doubts and fears, I opened my mouth to him, encouraging the fire that was building inside of me. Allowing myself to enjoy the sensation of his hot tongue invading my mouth, his five-o'clock shadow lightly scraping against my lips. Shivers ran up and down my entire body, and I found myself clutching onto him, as if for dear life.

He smiled at this, nibbling my lower lip as his hands dropped to grasp my hips. Then, without warning, he scooped me into his arms, as he had that very first night and my hands circled his neck as he carried me into his bedroom and kicked the door shut. Then he lay me down gently onto the bed, taking care to ensure my head fell to a pillow before returning to the door to lock it.

He stood over the bed, looking down at me with hungry eyes. I squirmed, feeling hot and shy under his gaze. The shirt I was wearing had ridden up to my waist and the cold air from the ceiling fan blew down on my flushed skin.

"God, you're beautiful," he murmured.

I swallowed heavily. The old me would have protested. Made excuses, pointed out cellulite. Instead, I forced myself to accept the compliment—mostly because I could tell from the look on his face that he meant it. He really thought I was beautiful. Which made me feel beautiful, too.

He climbed on top of me, straddling my thighs, working patiently to undo each button on my shirt, then parting it like the Red Sea. Then his hands found my stomach, skimmed across the skin, before reaching up to sweep over my breasts, which were already rock hard. His fingers and thumbs came together, squeezing my nipples and I squirmed in a mixture of torture and delight. I found myself reaching up, helping him pull his own shirt over his head, then running my fingers down his chest, exploring each hard plane of muscle, inlaid under silky soft skin. My eyes followed the dark path of hair that led temptingly to his jeans, and I reached out to trace it.

He groaned, grabbing me by the wrist, pulling me away. "Not yet," he scolded in a hoarse voice. "It's still my turn."

Setting my hand above my head, he lowered his mouth to my stomach, taking his time as he kissed a path down to the edge of my panties, all the while his right hand continued to fondle my breast. I gasped as his lips moved over my mound, so light I should have hardly felt it, and yet I felt it so much it almost did me in right then and there. With his free hand, he worked the panties to my ankles and I kicked them off. Then he settled his head between my legs, taking his time to thoroughly lick the insides of my thighs before his tongue slipped between my folds.

I cried out, my fists making handfuls of the sheets as I writhed beneath him, the sensation of his mouth pressing against my clit rocketing me to formerly unknown heights. His hands pressed against my thighs, keeping me open to him as he got to work, laving, sucking, licking. And when he finally bit down, ever so slightly, I felt myself exploding into a thousand stars.

"Oh, Mac," I whispered, closing my eyes and riding out the wave of sensations, my body literally vibrating beneath him. Ryan had never made me come like this. Never took the time to help me see the stars. But Mac, he was like some kind of mad astronaut, effortlessly rocketing me into space.

Mac, who claimed to be so damaged, so broken. And yet he was the one who knew how to make me whole.

And suddenly, I was desperate to return the favor.

I looked up at him, blinking for a moment to focus my eyes, then giving him a grateful smile. "Is it my turn yet?" I asked, daring to reach out to cup him over his jeans. It was a daring move. Not a move the old Beth White would have made. But here, I felt safe. I felt warm. I felt daring.

As my hand moved lightly across him, he sucked in a breath. "If you'd like."

I grinned like the Cheshire cat. "Actually I can't think of anything that I'd like more," I assured him. Pushing him off me, back onto the bed on his back, I leaned over him, kissing him on the mouth as I worked to unbutton his jeans. He kissed me back, desperate and hungry, his tongue invading my mouth, practically begging for me to hurry up. I sucked on his tongue, to foreshadow my immediate plans elsewhere.

Speaking of, I could feel his erection now, straining against my hand as I pulled down his zipper. With his help, I then managed to shuck off his jeans, followed by his boxer briefs, then wrapped my hand around his cock. As I slid my hand up and down the shaft, my mouth kissed a trail down his stomach, along the dusky trail of hair I'd discovered earlier. This time, however, he didn't stop me as I reached my destination. Opening my mouth, I drew him into me, his rock hard yet silky soft cock sliding down my tongue.

He groaned. "Good God, Beth. You are seriously going to kill me."

My mouth curved upward as my heart soared at the power his words evoked. It felt almost as good as being touched by his hands, to know what I was doing to him. And the fact that he was finally going to let me make him feel the way he'd been making me feel? I couldn't think of anything, at that moment, that I wanted more.

I pulled away, teasing the head of his cock with a swirl of my tongue. Then I looked up at him, meeting his eyes with my own.

"Don't worry, Jake MacDonald," I said. "At least you'll die happy."

thirty-seven

MAC

At least you'll die happy.

God, I didn't doubt that for one second, what with the way she was going down on me now. The insides of her mouth were steaming hot, burning me with exquisite fire. My whole body was pulsating, begging me to take it over the abyss, succumb to the pleasure, go all the way. And yet at the same time, I knew that wouldn't be enough. I wanted to be inside of her. Now.

Somehow I struggled to sit up, taking her face in my hands and bringing my lips once again to hers. Kissing her thoroughly, one hand secured at the small of her back, while the other searched the nightstand for a condom. Once I had one in my grasp, I pulled away from her for just a moment, tearing open the packet with my teeth. I could feel her watching, excited, anxious, pleased. Which made me feel all those things as well. Unlike Victoria, who saw sex as a chore, a way to appease me and get me off her back, Beth clearly wanted this. She wanted me. And the impatience glowing in her eyes made me want to both laugh and cry with joy. This was how it should be. Two people, barely able to keep their hands off of one another, coming together in shared ecstasy.

Now properly sheathed, I pushed her back onto the pillow, knowing she wouldn't mind if I wasn't gentle this time. Then I grabbed her hips with both hands, securing her as I lowered myself on top of her, all the while keeping my eyes on her face. She bit her lower lip, and for a moment I worried that I had hurt her. But then her mouth curved into a happy, unguarded smile. I smiled back at her, everything inside of me melting at the way she looked at me. As if she trusted me with her very life.

A trust I wanted to treasure and guard forever.

And so I kissed her, for a moment, content with just that. To cover her face with light, sweet kisses, rejoicing in the feel of my cock, resting inside of her. As if we were two halves of the same person, reunited at last.

Then her hips shifted, just slightly, but enough to deepen the connection between us. And, suddenly, I found myself unable to keep still a moment longer. I thrust against her, gently at first, then, harder, faster, moved by the encouragement I saw in her eyes. She arched her back, her curves melting into me as she matched my rhythm with her own thrusts. All the while looking up at me with those wide, beautiful, chocolate eyes.

Victoria had never looked at me during sex. She'd always close her eyes or turn her head. As if she wanted to pretend it wasn't happening—or at least that I was someone else. I always suspected her mind was elsewhere as well, grudgingly allowing me to get the sex out of my system, while she worked on scripts in her head.

But with Beth, it was different. Beth was here, in the moment, completely present and active in what we were sharing. She was looking at me and I was looking at her and we were together as the waves of heat rushed over us, sweeping us over the edge. Her insides clenched as she orgasmed again and I bit my lip not to scream as I released hard inside of her. As I collapsed on top of her, breathing hard and heavy in her ear, I could feel her lips pressing against my neck, softly kissing me over and over again. The tenderness—juxtaposed with the ecstasy—almost did me in.

At least you'll die happy.

Uh, yeah. Mission definitely accomplished.

I forced myself to roll over onto the bed again, not wanting to crush her with my weight. As I slid out from her, I felt a slight brush of panic as we once again became two. But, I reminded myself, she wasn't going anywhere. She was still right here, right next to me. Just to be sure, I pulled her to me, cradling her in my arms and letting her rest her head in the nook of my shoulder. Then I held her there, securely against me, not wanting, at the moment, to ever let her go.

"God, you're wonderful," I said, a long sigh escaping me as I came slowly back to earth.

I could feel her infectious grin against my chest. "You're not so bad yourself," she teased, her fingers lazily tracing my abs, starting up the chills all over again.

But before she could distract me into going for round two, I gently pulled her hand away, kissing it softly before pulling her up to sit beside me. For a moment, she looked concerned, so I gave her a reassuring smile, meeting her eyes with my own. God, she looked so beautiful at that moment. So flushed and sweaty and sated. To know I had made her look that way—well, I almost died happy all over again.

"I'm not talking about the sex," I corrected her, using my most earnest voice. "I mean, not that the sex wasn't excellent, because, God knows it was. But Elizabeth, that's only the beginning of you—and what you mean to me."

Her eyelashes swept over her eyes for a moment, as if my words made her shy. But I took her chin in my hands and forced her gaze back to mine. "I'm serious," I told her. "I've tried everything I could to push you away. To tell myself that this is not something I should want—that it will only lead to heartbreak and disaster. I told myself it was better to stay alone, that it would be selfish to put my own needs in front of my daughter's. But then," I added, shaking my head. "I look at you with her—how happy you make her when you're around. And then I realize I've only been using her as an excuse."

"What do you mean?"

I drew in a breath. "I put everything into my relationship with Victoria. I gave up everything that I cared about to try to make her happy. I put all my energy into making the marriage work and I was left with nothing but a big, gaping hole for my troubles."

Beth gave me a look that nearly broke my heart. "Oh, Mac . . ."

But I waved her off. I had to finish. "I loved her. And when you love someone, you leave yourself open to getting fucked over by them. And when that happens, you are left with nothing. Emotionally bankrupt." I cleared my throat, feeling the all-too-familiar lump rise inside. "I tried to tell myself that keeping you at arm's length was to protect Ashley. But truly, it was to protect myself. I didn't want to fall again and fall alone." I groaned, raking a hand through my hair. "God, even saying that aloud makes me sound like a pussy."

"Actually," she said, "it makes you sound really brave."

I grimaced. "Look, Beth. I don't have a lot to offer you. I've got no money. I'm strapped down with a kid. And emotionally, well, I'm damaged goods, baby, and don't even know how to do a proper relationship anymore." I sighed. "Half of me wants to tell you to get up and run. Far away and never look back. The other half . . ." I closed my eyes. "The other half wants to take you in my arms right now and never, ever fucking let you go."

Her lips parted. I could tell she wanted to speak, but also wanted me to continue. She knew it was hard for me to say the words out loud. But she knew how badly I needed to say them anyway.

Because she knew me that well.

"I can't promise you anything. I can't promise you the happily ever after you deserve. I can't promise that I won't hurt you with my stupidity or that this won't all go up in flames. But I can promise you one thing." I looked up at her. "I will always love you with all of my heart."

My voice broke and I found I couldn't continue. It was too much, too soon, and I couldn't tell if I felt relieved for putting it out in the open or more scared than ever. What would she say? What would she do? She had every right to walk away—hell, it would be the smart thing to do. But at the same time, as I held my breath, waiting for her to speak, I prayed she wouldn't be that smart.

And that was when she kissed me. Taking my face in her hands and pressing her lips against mine. Impossibly soft, impossibly tender, and so rich with what tasted like love, it stole my breath away.

"I love you, Jake MacDonald. And I'm ready to take a chance with you."

It was all I needed to hear. I took her in my arms. We made love again, the first time hot and heated, the second, slow and lingering. I took my time, wanting to worship every inch of her body, to kiss every millimeter of her skin, the tiny gasps that escaped her lips sound-tracking the night, sweeter than any music.

"What did I do to deserve you?" I asked as we finished. As she curled her body into my still trembling frame, I nestled my face in her hair, breathing in her warm, rich scent, never wanting to breathe anything else for the rest of my life.

"You didn't do anything," she assured me, sounding sated and sleepy. "You were just . . . you. And that's all you ever have to be."

She fell asleep, spooned against me, my arms wrapped securely around her waist, my face nestled at her neck. It was heaven on earth and I didn't want to move a muscle.

I'd love to say I passed out quickly, into a dreamless slumber, but in truth I was up most of the night watching her. The gentle rise and fall of her breasts as she breathed in and out. The sweep of lashes over her rosy cheeks. The way her little toes scrunched up when she was dreaming and the smile that slipped across her face. I found myself hoping she was dreaming of me.

Finally, slumber took hold and I passed out, still curled

around her body. And when the morning light streamed through the window, my daughter, for once in her life, slept in. As if somehow she knew Daddy needed a few extra minutes of paradise this morning.

Before hell showed up at our front door.

thirty-eight

BETH

Ding-dong!

I groaned at the cruel sound of reality crashing into our fantasy world. All night we'd been together, cradled in this perfect bubble, safe and sound and alone, the outside world be damned. I'd known at some point we'd have to crawl out of bed, get Ashley ready for school, get us ready for work. But I had been hoping to delay the inevitable for as long as possible. Maybe squeeze in one more lovemaking session before facing the world again. (Yes, Mac made me that insatiable!)

"I don't suppose you could ignore that?" I said, only half-joking.

Mac groaned. "You don't know how much I would like to," he replied, giving me a kiss on the forehead before sliding out of bed and grabbing his jeans off the floor. I watched as he pulled them on, one leg after another. "But it could be important."

"Right." I sighed. "Mind if I wait in bed?"

"As if I would allow anything else," he teased. "Seriously, just give me five minutes to get rid of whoever it is and then I'll be back. And you'd better be naked when I am."

"I think that can be arranged," I said with a giggle, pulling the covers up to my chin. Mac returned to the bed, yanking them back down so he could kiss each of my breasts in turn, then grinned at me wickedly before heading to the door. I watched him go, my entire body tingling all over again at the promise of what was to come.

God, last night had been good. Like, best-night-ever good. In fact, now, in the light of morning, it was almost hard to believe it had really happened as it had. That we'd really talked, shared, made love—quite a few times actually.

But more importantly, we'd made promises.

From here on out, there would be no more need to keep distance between us. No more fighting our feelings, no more denying what we felt. We could be together—in every sense of the word. We could be a real, legit couple that did all those nauseating things real legit couples did. Like . . . updating our Facebook relationship statuses and going out to brunch or whatever.

Best of all, I could finally show Mac that love doesn't have to tear you apart. In fact, true love had the power to put you back together.

My mind flashed back to the day Ryan had first called. When he'd first confessed he'd been sleeping with my sister. At the time I had felt as if the bottom had dropped out of my world. And who could blame me? I'd pinned everything I had on that relationship—on this assumed security of a fiancé/boyfriend, a guaranteed happily ever after. But in the end, had I truly loved Ryan for who he was? We'd been so young when we'd first gotten together and had changed so much over the years.

Sure, I loved the idea of having a boyfriend. But Ryan in particular? I wasn't so sure anymore. We'd been so different. We hadn't shared the same values or the same goals. We hadn't wanted the same things. He wasn't interested in supporting who I was. But to be honest, had I been any more supportive to him? After all, I'd been the one to ask him to leave everything he knew and loved behind, to follow me and my dreams. Never once considering that perhaps he had his own to pursue. If he had come out here, he would have been miserable. And that would have made me miserable, too.

Maybe it wasn't so bad that he'd found something with my sister. Not that the way they went about it had been right. Obviously, they should have been honest from the start. But if they had truly connected, truly bonded to one another, felt the way I felt with Mac—well, how could I blame them for that? How could I begrudge them their own happily ever after?

Especially seeing how it had inadvertently led to my own.

I forced my thoughts back to the present, straining to listen beyond the door. I could barely make out muffled voices and frowned as I realized Mac's sounded a little distressed. Worried, I searched for my clothes, then realized they were still in the wash and I only had Mac's shirt. Not sure what else to do, I slipped it on, then headed for the door.

"Is everything okay . . . ?" I started to ask, peeking my head through. But I trailed off as my eyes fell upon a woman standing in the doorway. She was pretty, petite, with stick-straight chestnut-colored hair, large almond eyes, and cheek-bones that cut Angelia Jolie-esque lines across her face. She was thin, too, possibly too thin, and dressed sharply in a tailored black pantsuit that looked as if it cost more than my yearly salary. I looked down at Mac's rumpled flannel shirt and wondered if I should have stayed in bed.

Mac glanced back at me. The expression on his face chilled me to the bone. "Sorry, Beth," he said. "This will just take a minute."

He started to turn back to the woman, but her gaze stayed locked on me. Her eyes were cutting, cruel, suspicious.

"Perhaps I should have called first," she observed with a raised eyebrow. "I guess I didn't realize you would have . . . guests. Especially with our *daughter* sleeping in the next room."

Oh God. I almost fell over backward. It couldn't be . . .

But it couldn't be anyone else either.

Well, this was a bit awkward.

It's okay. They're not together anymore. You have every right to be here. You did nothing wrong.

Summoning all my bravado, I forced myself to cross the room and hold out my hand, determined to take the high road here. She was still Ashley's mother, I reminded myself. Meaning she still deserved my respect.

"It's nice to meet you. I'm Elizabeth. I work with Mac at News 9."

"I'm Victoria," the woman confirmed in a cold voice. She looked down at my hand and frowned, as if I'd offered her a snake. "His *wife*."

Ouch.

My face flushed. Dropping my hand, I retreated a few steps, feeling the humiliation burn through me as she raked her gaze over my scanty attire. If looks could kill I was pretty sure I'd be on the floor. Seriously, what had made me think coming out here, dressed in Mac's shirt, would be a good idea?

I glanced at the door, wondering if I should run, but my feet felt glued to the floor. I looked over at Mac, silently begging him to say something—anything—to diffuse this powder keg—to make it all okay. To defend my right to be here. To say I was his girlfriend—not some dirty one-night stand.

But he just stood there, a deer caught in headlights, glancing from one of us to the other, his face stark white and his hands shaking. I wanted to be furious at him for not defending me. Yet at the same time, my heart wrenched at the pain and confusion I saw in his eyes. And who could blame him? He thought she was gone forever. And now here she was, showing up completely out of the blue, acting as if she'd never left.

"Look, I'm going to get going," I declared, desperate to regain some kind of semblance of control. No good could come of me sticking around. "You guys obviously have a lot to talk about. So I'm going to just grab my stuff and get out of your hair."

"Good idea," Victoria said icily. As if I had been asking her permission. "After all, we wouldn't want my poor daughter to wake up and . . . get confused."

I glared at her; was she for real? Seriously at that moment it was all I could do not to cross the room and punch her in the throat. How dare she try to make me feel like the bad guy here? She, who had abandoned her daughter for the last six months, without so much as a good-bye. She was the last person on earth who should be talking about confusing poor little Ashley.

But I kept my mouth shut and my feet glued to the floor, my hands remaining at my side. Mostly because, deep down, I wasn't sure she was entirely wrong. After all, I had no rights here. No claim on Ashley's life. No matter what was going on between Mac and me, to Ashley I was just the girl who was having "playdates" with her daddy while her mommy was away. And yes, if the little girl woke up and came out here now, I was pretty sure she would indeed be confused as hell.

I retreated to the laundry room, my stomach roiling with nausea. Hot tears stung my eyes as I pulled my clothes from the dryer. After gathering them up, I headed back to the spare bedroom to change. To my surprise, when I got there, Mac was waiting. He shut the door and turned to me.

"You don't have to go," he told me.

I gave him a rueful look. "You know that I do."

He sighed, raking a hand through his hair. "God, I'm sorry, Beth. I never expected . . . I mean, I promise you—I haven't heard from her in months. I thought she was halfway across the world."

"I know," I assured him. "Maybe she missed Ashley."

"Maybe . . ." He scowled. "But the last thing I want is for Ashley to see her here. After all I've done to try to get her to accept the fact that her mother's gone. Now it's going to start up all over again—her thinking that she's here to stay."

Something in my heart froze. "What if she *is* here to stay?"

He shuddered. "Don't even say that." He paced the room like a caged tiger, his steps eating up the distance between walls, "God, I can't believe she just showed up here like this. Without a call or anything. She has no right. Hell, she should be the one to leave, not you."

I gave him a regretful look, then shook my head. I knew

he was this close to falling apart and I didn't want to make things worse for him. "No," I said gently. "She needs to stay. And you both need to talk. I know you're angry with her, but she's still the mother of your child and she always will be. You really want to put Ashley first? Then you need to make peace with her."

He nodded, still looking upset. "I know, I know," he said. "You're right of course. It's just . . ." He looked over at me, giving me a sad smile. "This was so not the way I wanted our perfect night to end."

"We'll have other nights. Countless nights," I assured him, my heart feeling as if it was breaking in my chest. "I can even come over tonight after work if you want. We can drink gallons of fake Anejo Banjo and make a voodoo doll with her face on it."

He laughed, looking down at me with such affection in his eyes. "What did I do to deserve you?" he asked, shaking his head. Then he sighed. "Okay. I'll find you at work later. And I'll fill you in on everything, I promise."

"It's a deal."

And with that, I walked out of the bedroom, summoning up all my courage to stroll past Victoria and out the door, my shoulders back and my head held high, without once glancing in her direction. I could feel her staring at me, but she said nothing as I stepped through the door, closing it behind me.

Once outside my bravado fled. My shoulders drooped and the tears sprung back to my eyes. Even more so when I realized I didn't have a car to drive home in—Mac and Ashley had picked me up to go sledding yesterday and then we'd come straight here afterwards. Meaning I had no way to get home.

I glanced back at the house, then decided better of it, reached into my bag and grabbed my cell phone instead. I could call a cab and have them take me home to grab my car before work. No big deal.

But it was a big deal and as I slumped down onto the curb, waiting for the cab, a thousand doubts began to pick at my brain. Like, why was she here? What did she want? Was she only here for a quick visit? Or did she have plans to stay? Did she just want to see her daughter? Or did she have designs on her ex as well?

His wife, she'd said. As if she still retained some kind of ownership over him.

But that's not her call, I tried to remind myself. She could want whatever it was she wanted, but it wouldn't change a thing. There was no way Mac would agree to get back together with her. Not after she'd cheated on him, caused him to lose his job. Broken his heart and abandoned his daughter. He hated her more than anyone on earth.

At least that's what he told you.

I squirmed in my seat, not liking the direction my thoughts were heading. But how could I deny the possibility? After all, hate came from love and if Mac still cared about her at all, would he take her back if she asked him to? She was his wife, after all. And the mother of his child. Mac had sworn he'd put Ashley first, no matter what the scenario. What if he believed that Victoria being back was in the child's best interests? Would he be willing to sacrifice his own chance at love and happiness to give his baby girl her mother back? To give their little family one more try?

As the cab pulled up and I climbed inside, the heaviness in my stomach grew like a slow wave encroaching on a beach, washing away all the happy flotsam and jetsam last night had produced. What if Mac forgave her? What if he let her move back into his house, his life, his bed? Where would that leave me?

I forced myself to choke down my rising grief. I couldn't be selfish about this. If Mac did decide to get back with Victoria for Ashley's sake, I would have to find some way to accept that. If it was truly for the best—for him, for Ashley—I couldn't stand in their way. I loved them both too much; I wanted them to have their happily ever after—even if it meant none for me.

But how would I ever face him after something like that? How could I possibly work with him, side by side, each and every day? How could I possibly suffer through this kind of throbbing, ridiculous, all-encompassing love I had for him—if that love was no longer returned?

Okay, Beth, you're getting ridiculous now, I scolded myself. *You don't even know if she wants to stay. She might just be swinging by between assignments, to see her daughter before going on to the next.*

The cab pulled up to the front of my apartment building. Opening the door, I stepped out into the beautiful, crisp California morning. But before I could enter the building, my cell phone rang—making me nearly jump out of my skin.

He was calling! Thank God. I fumbled in my purse to find the phone, my heart pounding in my chest.

Until I drew out the phone and looked down at the caller ID.

It wasn't Mac. It was my sister.

I dropped the phone back into my bag, not bothering to answer. It was funny: Not a half hour ago, I'd considered forgiving her for what she'd done. Now I just wanted to throttle her all over again. Simply for not being Mac.

Give him time, I told myself. *He told you he'd see you at work. That he'd explain everything then.*

But deep down, I couldn't help but wonder. And when I did arrive at the newsroom an hour later, they told me he'd called in sick.

And at that point I couldn't help but assume the worst.

thirty-nine

MAC

What the hell are you doing here?

I stared at Victoria, watching her make herself at home in my living room. She looked so out of place here, sitting down on my simple furniture, and something inside of me fought the urge to apologize that it had come from Target rather than Pottery Barn.

But that was stupid. She had no right to judge how I furnished my place. How I lived my life. She had left us. And by doing so, she had abdicated her say in any of my affairs, never mind my choices in décor.

I sat down on the easy chair across from the couch, keeping as much distance between us as I could without seeming obvious. Even just looking at her now made the rage inside of me threaten to boil over, and it was all I could do to stay calm, to quell the scream that rose to my throat. How dare she just show up here, at the crack of dawn on a Monday morning, without even a courtesy call or text? So typical of her—she never did care about other peoples' schedules or lives. Only her own.

But I forced down the scream. And pasted a pleasant

smile on my lips. This intruder had the power to destroy my life. To turn my daughter's world upside down. I couldn't afford to piss her off.

"So . . ." I said, cocking my head as pleasantly as I could in her direction. "This is . . . unexpected."

Her cheeks flushed. "Yeah, sorry. I know, I should have called. I was going to. After I was settled in. But the hotel room wasn't ready yet and, well, I got anxious. And I figured maybe I could catch you before you dropped Ash off at school. I had no idea you would have . . . a visitor."

Now it was my turn to blush, even though she had no right to make these kinds of insinuations. We had broken up. We were through. I could have as many "visitors" as I wanted and she, of all people, had no right to make me feel guilty for it.

"What do you want, Vic?" I forced myself to ask, not sure I really wanted to know.

She stared down at her hands. "Jesus, this is awkward. I mean, I knew it would be. But . . ." She trailed off and then looked up, meeting my eyes with her own. "Oh, Jake. I've missed you so much."

Nausea rolled over me. "Have you now?"

"Of course I have!" she cried, looking offended that I would even dare to second-guess such a statement. "All these months away, thinking about you and Ash. Wondering how you were. What you were doing."

"You know, they have these great new inventions now. They're called telephones. If you want to know what someone's up to, you can use them to find out."

She made a face. "Okay, fine. I guess I deserve that. And yeah, I know I should have called. Or emailed. Or texted. Or whatever. But truth be told, I wasn't sure you'd answer if I did."

I sighed. "You might be right about that."

She nodded slowly, tears welling in her big brown eyes. "And I don't blame you for that," she said, her voice choking up. "What I did to you and our sweet baby girl. I don't deserve anything less." She swallowed hard. "But, Jake, I'm sorry.

I'm so goddamned sorry. What I did. How I acted. The way I panicked and ran away." She shook her head. "I'm the worst wife and mother in the world."

I stared at her, unable to speak as the apologies spilled from her lips. All this time, all these months—*this* was what I'd been waiting for. Maybe not consciously—but deep down inside of me in the place I didn't like to look. I had wanted to see her again. For her to admit what she'd done. For her to want to be a family again. A mother to our child.

But now . . . Now that it was finally happening, I was no longer sure.

"Vic," I tried, hating how strangled my voice sounded, "what do you want?"

She bit her lower lip in the way that always used to drive me crazy. For a moment she didn't speak, just stared down at her feet, as if they held the answers to the world. Finally, she looked back up. "I want to come home. I want to give our family another try."

For a moment, I considered it. I truly, crazily considered what she was suggesting. What would it be like to have a family again? For Ashley to have her mother back in her life?

But in the end, I found myself shaking my head. "I'm sorry," I said. "But that's not possible."

"What?" It was clearly not the answer she'd been expecting. And, of course it wasn't. No one ever said no to Victoria. "Jake, I'm asking for forgiveness here."

"And I'm fresh out. You don't deserve it after what you did to us."

"You did things, too, you might remember," she shot back. "In fact, you pretty much single-handedly destroyed my career. Everything I worked for my entire life." She drew in a breath. "But I'm willing to let that go, for your daughter's sake."

"That's really big of you. Sadly, I'm not that generous."

Her face twisted into a scowl. "Is this about that little whore you had over this morning?"

My jaw clenched. "Do not even go there, Vic."

She cast her gaze down, looking angry. Then she looked

back up at me. "Jake, we're a family. We have a child together! Are you seriously saying you'd choose some piece of ass over your own daughter's happiness?"

"Get out of my house."

"Fine. But I'm not leaving without Ashley." She rose to her feet, made a move toward the bedroom.

I leapt up, blocking her path. "You are not going in there."

Thankfully she stopped. Sighing, she turned away from me pacing the room with uneven steps. I watched her, still standing guard at the hallway door. Not sure what I'd do if she attempted to push past me. I would never hit a woman. But I would protect my daughter by any means necessary.

Finally she turned back to me, tears slipping down her cheeks. She gave me a look that was so devastated, it broke my heart, despite my best efforts.

"You're a good father," she said. "Ashley's lucky to have you. But she's my kid, too, Jake. You can't keep me from her."

"Please, Vic, be reasonable," I begged, my heart in my throat, trying to quell my rage. Yelling at her would only set her off again. "She's gone through so much already. She's finally settling in. You can't just take her, uproot her, all over again. It's not fair."

"No, it's *you* who's not being fair. Not even attempting to fight for your family. You promised we'd be together in good times and in bad—you made a fucking vow in front of everyone we know. And now you're just ready to throw it all away? Even if it screws up your daughter for life?"

I cringed, her words more cutting than any knife. "Look, Vic—"

"Mommy?"

My eyes shot to the hallway, my heart sinking in my chest. Ashley stood there, dressed in her Sleeping Beauty nightgown, staring at Victoria with pure unadulterated joy written on her little face.

"Baby!" Victoria cried, pushing past me to run over and sweep Ashley into her arms. She twirled her around, then kissed her on both cheeks before setting her down on the ground again. "Mommy's back, baby. I've missed you so much!"

"I missed you, too, Mommy," Ashley told her. "Daddy said you weren't coming back."

"Well Daddy was mistaken, sweetheart," Victoria said, after shooting me a look. "I'm back. Though I'm not sure Daddy wants me to stay."

For a moment, Ashley stared at her. Then she slowly turned to me, focusing her eyes on me. Terrified, desperate eyes.

And at that moment, I knew I had lost.

I had lost everything.

"Please, Daddy! Don't send Mommy away. I want Mommy to stay, Daddy. Please don't make her go. I'll be a good girl, Daddy. I'll eat all my vegetables. Even the yucky ones. Just don't make her go away again."

I could feel Victoria's stare burning a hole into me, but I refused to look in her direction. Mainly because doing so would probably make me throw up.

"Of course I won't make her go," I managed to choke out. "She's your mother, Ashley. Of course she can stay."

forty

BETH

God, this day is never going to end.

I slumped down in my desk, scrubbing my face with my hands. I'd just gotten back from being out on assignment, working with my old morning show photog, Javier, who had agreed to pull a double when Mac called in sick to work.

But Mac isn't sick! I wanted to scream when Ana had first informed me of the news. Instead, I'd only nodded miserably as my mind treated me to a million reasons why he might have changed his mind about coming to work—each more unpleasant than the last. It was all I could do not to jump in my car and drive back up to his house. To peek through the window and see what was going on. To barge through the front door to tell this woman to stay away from my man.

He was mine now. She'd given up her rights to him. She needed to go.

"You okay?"

I looked up to see Javier had come back by my desk. He handed me the drive with the video we shot earlier on it. I took it and gave him my best effort at a smile.

"Thanks. I'm fine. Just a little tired, I guess."

"You're tired?" He snorted. "Try being up since three A.M."

"Yeah, yeah. I remember those days, believe me."

Javier peered at me for a moment. "You okay, kiddo? I mean, really okay?"

The concern in his eyes broke something inside of me. It was all I could do to hold back the floodgates of tears. Once upon a time, Javier knew everything about my life— after all, we'd been partners for two years and had shared a lot of really boring early morning hours together. But how could I tell him this? That I had fallen for a coworker who was essentially married and now I was upset that his wife had returned?

"Is this about *her*?" Javier asked suddenly, surprising me with the question. "Is she messing with you again?"

I looked up, swallowing past the lump in my throat. "Her?"

"Stephanie," he clarified. "Joy was telling me all about what she did to you. The blue hairspray, the fire ants." He shook his head, looking disgusted. "I never liked that girl from the start. But I had no idea she would go that far."

"You don't know the half of it." I stared glumly down at my desk. Awesome. So the whole station probably knew about Stephanie's sabotages. And here Richard had promised to keep the whole thing on the down low when he'd fired her. But journalists were a nosy bunch and very skilled at finding out things that were meant to stay hidden. I suppose I shouldn't have been surprised.

Javier cocked his head. "What do you mean?"

"You ever hear of Dante Alvarez?" I asked, then told him a brief version of the story. Javier listened attentively and when I had finished he shook his head. "That's awful," he exclaimed. "I mean, Richard must have been so pissed. You sure she destroyed the drive?"

"Mac found it sitting on a magnet. Completely blank."

"And you can't get another interview?"

"I've tried. He won't answer his phone and now it's disconnected. I have no way of reaching him anymore."

Javier gave me a thoughtful look. "I might be able to help you," he said.

My head jerked up. "What?"

"It's a long shot. So don't get your hopes up too high. But my *abuela* used to go to church with Alvarez's mother back in the day. I remember last Christmas she was telling us some crazy stories about the guy—back when he first released his manifesto. She couldn't believe a sweet, Christian woman like his dear old *madre* would raise a boy who would go and say such things about his government. In any case, I don't know if they still keep in touch but . . ." He shrugged. "It couldn't hurt to ask."

My heart started beating faster in my chest. "You'd do that?"

Javier smiled. "For my favorite ex-morning show partner?" he teased. "Anything!" Then he sobered. "But seriously. I know how hard you've worked to get here. And I know how much it means to you. I can't promise you anything—but I'll absolutely give it my best shot."

"Thank you," I gushed. "Thank you so much."

"No problem. And, as they say in the biz, 'Stay tuned.'" He gave me a comical bow. "Now if you'll excuse me. I have a very nice king-size bed at home that's been calling my name for some time now."

We exchanged good-byes and I watched him head back to the photographer's lounge, trying to quell the adrenaline that had spiked in my veins. It was a long shot, he'd said. It might not come to anything. But the fact that there was even a chance . . .

I turned back to my desk. Before I could stop myself, I grabbed my phone and sent Mac a text. Nothing crazy—just a *what's up?* kind of thing. I told myself I just wanted to tell him about the possible development with Alvarez, but I knew, in my heart I was only fooling myself. And I felt like a total loser once I hit send.

A stirring of anger wove through my gut as I stuffed my phone in my bag. I knew it wasn't his fault. I mean, not exactly. After all, he certainly hadn't planned for his ex-wife to show up on his front doorstep the morning after we'd finally gotten together. But still! After all he'd said, after all he'd promised, and now he just goes radio silent on me? Even if Victoria was still in the house—even if they were still trying to work things through—could it have killed him to sneak into the bathroom to send a quick, reassuring text? I mean, he had to know this was driving me insane, right? He had to know that I wouldn't be okay until I heard from him.

Stop being so self-absorbed, I scolded myself. This wasn't about me. And it wasn't even necessarily about Mac. For all I knew, Victoria wanted nothing to do with Mac— she'd just come back because she'd missed her daughter, as any mother would. How could I begrudge little Ashley the joy of waking up and seeing the woman who had given her birth? Ashley, who had been holding out hope for so long, never faltering in her belief that Mommy would someday come home. And now, she finally had. This had to be the best day ever for her.

Even if it was shaping up to be one of the worst for me.

I turned back to my computer, staring at it miserably. I tried typing a few words, then gave up. I couldn't focus on anything at the moment. Thankfully I didn't have to go live tonight. I could just tape my reporter stand-up and go home early. Go home and try not to stare at my non-ringing cell phone all night.

You should call him.

No. You need to give him space.

As my mind continued to grapple with the implications of both options (the risk of disturbing him vs. my continued efforts at sanity), my hand decided to take action, reaching into my bag and grabbing my phone again. Then, thinking better of it, I stuffed it in my desk and slammed the door shut.

I stared at the closed drawer, my heart pounding in my chest. This was getting completely ridiculous. I needed to get a grip. Or, you know, lock the drawer and swallow the key. That would work, right?

Or you could just call him . . .

I forced myself up from my seat, determined to go get a soda and remove myself from the temptation. But then, just as I was about to walk away from my desk, it erupted into song, causing me to nearly jump out of my skin. It was ringing. My phone was ringing.

It's probably not him. There's no reason it's him.

I yanked the drawer open. My eyes fell on the caller ID. It was.

I grabbed the phone, my hands shaking so violently I almost dropped it as I tried to pull it to my ear. "H-hello?"

"Hey, Beth. It's me."

He sounded awful. Tired, drained, sad. Suddenly, all the anger I'd had for him not calling earlier evaporated, and all I wanted to do was reach out over the phone lines and give him a comforting hug. To hold him close and assure him everything would be all right. Even though I had no idea if that statement was even remotely true.

"Mac. Thank God. I was so worried. Is everything okay?"

"Not really."

He paused and the silence stretched out between us. I gripped the phone with white-knuckled fingers, barely able to breathe as I waited for him to continue.

Don't push him, Beth. Give him time.

Finally he spoke. "Look, I'm sorry I didn't call earlier or show up to work. I thought . . . Well . . . Let's just say things are . . . complicated . . . here, to say the least."

Bile rose to my throat and I swallowed hard, forcing it back down. *Complicated.* What did that mean? Was Victoria still there? Was he letting her stay? And if so, for how long? A quick visit with her daughter . . . or something else entirely?

"Look, can I . . . meet you somewhere?" he asked. "I need to talk to you and I don't really want to do it over the phone."

"Sure," I managed to choke out. "I'm about to leave in a few minutes anyway. Do you want me to come by the house?"

"No!" he cried, his voice filled with panic. Then he cleared his throat. "I mean, what if I meet you down at the beach? By the OB pier?"

Frustrated tears sprung to the corners of my eyes and I angrily wiped them away. If that didn't answer my question as to whether she was still there, nothing would.

Now the question became: why.

"Sure. That's fine, I guess. Whatever."

There was more silence on the other end of the line. As if he wanted to say something else, but couldn't find the words. Then, "Great. I'll be there in an hour."

I set down the phone, the lump in my throat threatening to choke me. I tried to tell myself I was jumping to conclusions, but at the same time, in my heart I knew that was probably not the case. If things were fine, he would have just told me over the phone. This fact that he needed to see me in person could only mean bad news. The fact that he couldn't meet at his house, meant something even worse.

Somehow I managed to go through the motions, finishing voicing my script and taping my stand-up as if nothing were wrong. After all, the last thing I needed was to let my personal life interfere with my work.

Especially since soon it might be all I had left.

forty-one

BETH

I found Mac at the very end of the pier, sitting on a wooden bench. There were a few old fishermen, hanging out nearby, and a couple surfers below us, trying to catch the latest swell. One of them, I was pretty sure, was News 9's weatherman, Asher Anderson himself. Not surprising, seeing as from what people said the guy spent more time on the water than he ever did in the newsroom. But he could get away with it, because his mother owned the station and his dad was the legendary Stormy Anderson—celebrity weatherman extraordinaire.

Must be nice to have that kind of job security.

As I made my way down the pier, feeling like dead girl walking, seagulls seemed to scold me as they flew back and forth.

Stupid girl, I imagined them saying. *Stupid, stupid girl.*

"Hey," I said as I approached. "Here I am."

He looked up. His eyes were bloodshot. His face was pale. A cold chill spun down my spine. This was really not good. Really, really not good.

"Beth . . ." He rose to his feet and grabbed me, pulling me into a fierce hug. I squeaked a little, half-afraid he would accidentally crush me with the intensity of the embrace, and he loosened his grip—just barely—while keeping me tight against him. As if he wanted to literally crawl inside of me and never come out.

Finally, unable to bear it any longer, I managed to untangle myself from his arms. "What's going on, Mac?" I demanded, hating how scared my voice sounded. "Talk to me."

He raked a hand through his hair, then walked to the edge of the pier, staring out into the sea, as if it could offer some kind of answers to the universe.

"Victoria apologized for everything that happened," he said in a flat voice. "She says it was a mistake to leave us. And that she wants to be a family again."

"Well, tough luck," I cried, before I could stop myself. "That's not her call! She left you guys!" I watched as he flinched, fear pounding at my insides. "Mac, you can't just take her back! After what she did to you!"

He turned around. His eyes were dull and defeated. "What choice do I have?" he asked. "If I say no, she'll take Ashley away."

"She can't do that," I argued. "She abandoned her. You have custody, right? I mean, she could petition the courts, sure. But they're not going to just hand her over."

"We never made a formal custody arrangement. She took off too quickly for that. And yeah, sure. I could drag Ashley through a custody battle now. But I have no assurances I'd win. The courts usually favor the mothers in this scenario. And my violent behavior back in Boston when I found out about her affair could be used against me. It'd be a gamble at the very least. And I refuse to gamble on the life of my baby girl."

He closed his eyes and opened them again. "Besides, you should have seen Ashley's face when she walked out into the living room and saw her mother had come home. It was as if she'd finally woken from her living nightmare and her dreams had all come true." He shook his head. "I told you from the beginning, I'd made a promise. To always put her first. No matter what. How can I not at least try to make this work—for her sake?"

I found myself nodding, even as my heart shattered into a thousand pieces. "Oh, Mac. I'm so sorry."

I could see him squeezing his hands into fists. "No, Beth. I'm the one who should be sorry. And I am—so goddamned sorry. The last thing in the world I wanted was to hurt you. Or drag you down into my fucked-up life. I knew it was a risk to let you in—to give us a chance to be happy together. But it had been so long . . . I'd convinced myself that it would be okay to move on. That she was gone for good. That she would stay away. That Ashley and I could have a real chance to start over." He hung his head. "But now I know that'll never happen."

He pulled back his fist, slamming it against the pier's railing. When he pulled his hand away, blood dripped from his knuckles. I grabbed him, pulling him to me, holding him tight. As he clung to me, his whole body trembled violently.

For a moment, we just stood there. Then, finally, he pulled away, finding my eyes with his own. "I want you to know—what I said last night? I meant every word. I love you. I love you so much. And in any other life in any other world—I would move heaven and earth to be with you."

"I know," I said quietly. "Believe me I know."

I wanted to tell him that I loved him, too. That I loved him so much it was killing me inside. But I knew it would only make it harder to walk away in the end.

And I would have to walk away. This time, forever.

He swallowed hard. "Listen, I've got to go. If Victoria finds out I went and talked to you, she's going to freak. I have to get back before she realizes I'm gone. But I'll be at work tomorrow. And we can talk more. Or we don't have to talk at all. I wouldn't blame you if you never wanted to talk to me again."

I gave him a sad smile. "Come on, Mac. How could I ever stop talking to you?"

He nodded slowly. Then he scooped me back into his arms and kissed me, hard and fierce. Kissed me like there was no tomorrow. And I guess, in this case, there wasn't.

At least not for us.

forty-two

Thirty minutes on the treadmill, combined with an obscene amount of weight-lifting at the gym and yet I was still tense and miserable. Whoever said exercise was great stress relief should be hanged as a liar. Sure, maybe it helped with your run-of-the-mill tension headache, but the kind of pressure bottled up at this point was practically nuclear powered. And no amount of stepping, spinning, or weight-lifting was going to make it go away.

It'd been only a week since I'd met Mac on the pier. But it already felt like a lifetime. And while I'd tried everything I could think of to help exorcise the pain—from copious amounts of alcohol to retail therapy to even throwing myself back into work—it only seemed to be growing worse each and every day. I tried to tell myself it was just another failed relationship, not the end of the world. And not even a substantial one at that. Hell, I'd dated Ryan for years and had somehow managed to get over him. With Mac, we'd been official for less than twenty-four hours. Which meant I should have had no problem picking myself up, dusting myself off, and moving on.

But not so much.

Part of the problem, perhaps, lay in the fact that the object of my doomed affection was never more than an arm's distance away, thanks to our continued working situation. In the truck, on the way to shoots, the air became so thick with tension, sometimes it hurt to even breathe. And any casual conversation that might spark between us felt like knives stabbing me in the gut without mercy.

It would have been much easier if I could have hated him. For leading me on, then dumping me flat to get back with his ex. And sometimes I could almost talk myself into feeling like that. But then I'd catch sight of the pain in his eyes—pain that mirrored my own. And I knew he didn't want this arrangement any more than I did. That if he had his way I'd be in his arms and he would never let me go.

But that was impossible. The risk of losing his baby girl was too great. I understood this. I completely supported it, even. But all the support and understanding in the world could not stanch the open, bleeding wound in my heart.

After a quick shower I contemplated going back to my apartment, then decided against it. It would be empty, I was sure—Piper was always working these days. And I had no interest in collapsing in front of the TV, alone with my misery. I might as well head to work instead, to burn a little midnight oil and try to distract myself from everything. Because of some preemptive sports programming there was no eleven P.M. newscast tonight and so I knew the place would be deserted. A perfect chance to throw myself into work and forget the world for a few blissful hours.

Sure enough, the place was practically empty as I walked in, save for a glowing light under Richard's office door. Which wasn't a bad thing, I told myself. Maybe at some point he'd emerge and find me hard at work. That ought to earn me a few brownie points, right?

I sat down at my desk, going through my emails. I was deleting so fast I almost missed the one from Javier. I hadn't heard from him since he'd promised to try to track down Alvarez for me and had pretty much given up that it was going to happen. But now, as I dug back into my trash folder to retrieve the email, I crossed my fingers I'd been wrong.

Heart pounding, I opened the email, scanning it quickly, my eyes widening as I digested its contents.

He'd talked to his *abuela*.

His *abuela* had talked to Alvarez's mom.

She'd told her son he needed to call me. He needed to tell his side of the story.

And Alvarez had evidently agreed.

"YES!" I cried, jumping from my seat, raising my hand in the air in triumph before sitting back down, a little sheepishly. Still, it was all I could do not to break out into cartwheels across the newsroom floor.

Suddenly my no good, very bad, terrible week was not so awful after all. I could get a new interview. I could have another chance. And this time there was no one to stand in my way.

My personal life might remain a disaster, but I'd be a superstar at work!

I had to tell Richard. He was going to be so excited!

I rose from my seat again, deciding there was no time like the present. But before I could reach out and knock on his door to announce myself and my good news, an angry voice on the other side caused me to pause.

"But why?"

I frowned. Was that Joy Justice? What was she doing here, on a night when there was no newscast to anchor?

"Come on, Joy. We have already discussed this ad nauseam," Richard's voice broke in. "If you want to keep rehashing it, I suggest you make an appointment to see me tomorrow. Right now, it's late. And I, for one, would like to go home."

Something uneasy prickled inside me. I was pretty sure I wasn't supposed to be hearing this. But what should I do? Go sit back at my desk? It wasn't like I wouldn't be able to hear them from there.

"Screw your appointments. I'm not leaving. Not until you give me a damn good explanation for why you're turning me out on the streets."

Wait, what?

Okay, now I couldn't help but tune in. I'd never heard Joy sound so upset. She was always so poised, so polished, so above all the bullshit. At least that's what I had always assumed.

"Relax, drama queen. It's not as if you're suddenly some homeless waif. The severance package the station's offering you should be more than enough to keep you in the lifestyle you're accustomed to."

My jaw dropped. Severance package? That meant . . . Oh my God.

They were firing Joy Justice?

Joy had worked at News 9 for decades. She'd started as a lowly production assistant, like Piper, and had worked her way up to main anchor. She was practically an institution in this place. Newsroom royalty. I couldn't imagine the newscast without her leading it.

But then I remembered Richard, after she'd turned down the Alvarez piece. He'd called her dead weight. He'd said the powers that be weren't happy.

"I'll sue you. I'll tell the world you let me go because of age discrimination."

"Go right ahead. It'll never hold up in court. I've got stacks of documentation showing your habitual lateness, your on-air errors, your fights with the staff. I have viewer surveys showing they don't like anything about you." He sighed. "Look, Joy. You were the only decent fish in my pond for many years. But now we've got a lot of talent coming through the ranks and I'm not going to apologize for that. My job is to put on the best damn newscast I can every night. And that's it. So I'm sorry. We've decided to go a different direction and that's final. Your last newscast is Friday."

Joy burst from the office without warning. I tried to duck, but there was no time and the anchor's fiery eyes zeroed in on my own. I opened my mouth to say something—anything— but found I couldn't utter even a single intelligible word. Not that it mattered; Joy was already halfway across the newsroom, taking great strides to reach her office in record time.

I watched her go, pity worming through my stomach. What must she be feeling like right now? To have her career suddenly stripped away without warning. Sure, to some, a job was just a job, but to Joy—it was her whole life. She'd been on TV for thirty-something years. She'd never gotten married and had raised her only daughter on her own. In short, her viewers were her family. Her station was her home.

And now she was being dumped like so much garbage.

It wasn't surprising, I supposed. All over the country, experienced journalists, who were older and drew more expensive salaries, were being replaced by younger, hipper—and cheaper—counterparts. But the fact that her experience was not unique didn't make it any less devastating.

Forcing myself to my feet, I headed down the newsroom, until I reached the anchor's office. I stood in the doorway, clearing my throat uneasily. Joy looked up, her eyes red and blotchy. Tears had streaked her makeup, giving her the look of a rabid raccoon.

"What do you want?" she demanded, her face twisting in ugly rage.

I bit my lower lip, shuffling from foot to foot. "Look, I'm sorry. I didn't mean to overhear. I won't say anything to anyone, I promise."

"What does it matter?" Joy asked, waving me off. "Everyone's going to know soon enough anyway."

"I guess." I drew in a breath. "But for the record? I think they're insane to let you go. You're so amazing and talented. Ever since I got here, I've looked up to you. I've wanted to be you."

"Yeah, well, congratulations. Looks like you'll soon get your chance."

I winced at the pain I heard in her voice. "Sorry. I didn't mean it like that. I just wanted you to know that I think you're great. An inspiration, even." I paused, then added, "I promise you now, if I ever do get the honor of trying to fill your shoes, I will do my best to live up to the standards you've set."

I'd meant it as a compliment. I really did admire her—and had since I'd first started at News 9. Her dedication to her craft, her commitment to ethical journalism, her empathy for those in need—I respected the hell out of this woman's career. So I was quite taken aback when Joy narrowed her eyes on me, giving me a death look.

"You little shit," she growled. "You dare come into my office and try to patronize me?"

I took a step back, startled. "That wasn't what I meant—"

"You girls all think you're such superstars. But you're nothing. You're no one. Just the bimbo of the week. Utterly replaceable." She shook her head. "You'll be out of here before you know it, just like your little friend Stephanie. And in a few months—no one will even remember your name."

I swallowed hard, feeling the tears sting at the corners of my eyes. "I'm sorry. I'll leave you alone," I stammered, backing out of the office. "I didn't mean to . . . I'm sorry."

I turned to flee the newsroom, I couldn't stay there anymore. I'd have to tell Richard my good news about Alvarez another day. Good news that suddenly didn't seem quite as exciting and important as it had moments before.

After all, at the end of the day, it was just another news story. Even if it did allow me to rise to fame and recognition—what would it matter in the end?

Joy had once risen, too. And now she'd crashed back down to earth. And every story she'd covered, every interview she'd done, all her life's work—did it really mean anything in the end?

You'll be out of here before you know it. And no one will even remember your name.

forty-three

MAC

And . . . a thousand and one stories later . . ."
    I looked up from the couch to see Victoria emerging
from Ashley's bedroom, a weary smile on her face. She
walked over to the kitchen and poured herself a glass of wine.

"That girl is a master when it comes to bedtime negotia-
tions," she added after taking a sip. "I'm surprised you don't
have major law firms recruiting her."

"Well, she still has to take the bar." I snorted. "And, you
know, learn to read."

"Which I'm sure will be any day now." Victoria laughed.
"She's got all her books memorized at this point. Such a
smart kid. Not to mention ridiculously adorable. Not that I'm
biased or anything."

She walked over to the couch and sat down beside me,
causing my entire body to stiffen. I forced myself to take a
deep breath and grab my own drink. I was pretty sure I'd
been single-handedly keeping Jack Daniels in business over
the last week and this evening was already looking to be the
start of another bender.

I could feel Victoria staring at me and I turned to look at

her, hating the fondness I saw on her face. "You've done a great job with her, Mac," she said. "Really great."

"Yeah, well, I've done what I could."

"You've done more than that. I mean, seriously, you're like father of the year." She sighed. "While I'm Mommie Dearest."

"Ashley loves you," I replied automatically. "And I know she's happy you're back."

It was true—Ashley had been over the moon since the morning her mother had returned. And I had to grudgingly admit Victoria did seem to be making an effort to make up for lost time. She'd taken Ashley on after-school trips to the park, the beach, even the zoo. And when I'd get home from work, Ashley would be full of stories about all the fun she'd had with Mommy.

My girl had her mother back. She was in heaven.

While I remained languishing in a living hell.

Victoria let out a heavy sigh. "I just wish I could make you happy, too," she said sadly.

"I'm fine."

"I think we should go to counseling."

"If you'd like."

"Come on, Mac!" she cried. "Talk to me! Scream at me! Tell me I'm a horrible person and you hate my guts. Just don't sit there, quietly, looking as if you want me to leave."

I bit my lower lip. "I don't want you to leave. But, Vic, this is going to take some time. What you did to us . . . How you left us . . ." I shook my head. "Do you understand what it's been like? Being a single dad? Trying to provide for her? Not just materially–but emotionally, too. Do you know how many nights she woke up screaming for you? And I had to make excuses as to why you weren't there?"

She hung her head. "What do you want me to say?"

"Nothing. I don't want you to say anything. Just . . . understand how difficult this is for me. And you coming back does not suddenly make everything instantly okay!"

"This is about that girl, isn't it?" Victoria broke in, narrowing her eyes at me. "That's why you're holding back—you're still thinking about her."

I closed my eyes, my heart panging at the mention of Beth. "This has nothing to do with her."

"Don't lie to me. I can see the look in your eyes. You thought you were so high and mighty, judging me for my affair. And then you turn around and have one of your own."

I stared at her. "How is that even remotely the same? You left us. I thought you were gone forever. What did you want me to do? Stay celibate for the rest of life until you decided to waltz back in?"

"No. I didn't. Which is why I'm not judging you for breaking our vows of marriage. But now I'm back. And I want us to be a family again. For Ashley's sake . . . and our own."

She laid a hand on my forearm. It felt like ice. "Mac, you loved me, once upon a time. And I know I didn't prove worthy of that love. But now I'm back. And I'm asking for a second chance. We made vows, you and I. To be together in good times and bad. And I know it's been bad. But now it has the chance to be good. If you can just let it. If not for me, do it for Ashley. Doesn't she deserve to have a family?"

"Yes," I said, abruptly rising to my feet. "She does. Which is why you're still here. Now if you'll excuse me, I'm going to go to bed."

Victoria rose. She reached out, placing a hand on my groin. "Can I join you?" she asked with a small smile. "I bet I could make you forget all about what's-her-name."

I grabbed her hand and jerked it away. "I don't think that's a good idea." I started toward the spare bedroom, where I'd been crashing since she'd returned. I could feel her stare, burning into my back.

"Come on, Mac," she called after me. "Just give me a chance!"

I closed the door behind me, not bothering to respond. Then I collapsed onto the bed, sticking my head in the pillow, which still smelled like Beth's hair. It was, at the end of the day, all I had left of her.

And it didn't seem nearly enough.

forty-four

BETH

Lost in my troubled thoughts, I found myself taking the exit to the beach, still not wanting to go home. The ocean had always been soothing to me, calming my nerves, and making my problems seem less important in the grand scheme of things.

Not to mention a big plate of fish and chips wouldn't go amiss right about now. Since seeing Mac on the pier, I hadn't had much appetite. But suddenly I found myself ravenous.

Thankfully my favorite seafood place was nearly empty, save for a sweet old couple sitting by the window. I watched them for a moment while waiting to be brought to my table, my heart aching a little at how comfortable they looked together. How long had they been with one another? And how did they manage to make it work? Could I ever hope for this kind of long-term loving relationship with another person? Or was I doomed to forever be choosing the wrong guy? The guy who always ended up choosing someone else in the end.

"Inside or out?"

I looked up at the hostess addressing me, my eyes widening in surprised recognition.

"Stephanie?" I cried, before I could stop myself. "What are you doing here?"

My former roommate's face flushed. "I work here now," she informed me, sounding a little defensive. "Got the job about a week ago."

"Wow . . . I had no idea." I wasn't sure what to say.

She shrugged. "It's not that bad, really. Tips are good. The bartenders are cute. We all go out after work sometimes. And you can't beat the view," she added, gesturing to the ocean stretching out into the distance. "Not to mention I'm finally free of the News 9 drama machine. That, in and of itself, is worth everything."

"That's cool," I said, not sure what else to say. I tried to remind myself that this girl was not my friend. She'd destroyed my stuff, had tried to get me fired from work, hell, she'd almost accidentally killed me. For all I knew, even now, she was staring at me, contemplating poisoning my dinner. I should have been running from the restaurant as fast as my legs could take me.

Yet something inside me told me to stay. She had been my friend once. And looking at her now, it was hard to see the vindictive monster she'd been. Just a sad, defeated girl who'd let her jealousy cause her to lose every dream.

You girls all think you're such superstars. But you're nothing. You're no one. Just a flavor of the week. Utterly replaceable.

She led me over to my table and started to turn away. Then she paused and I watched as she worried her lower lip, as if she wanted to say something, but wasn't sure I'd be receptive. Finally, she turned back to me, an open, earnest expression written on her face.

"Look, just so you know—for the record, I mean—I didn't do those things they said I did."

I sighed. "Whatever. It's fine. I really don't even care anymore."

"Well, I do," she shot back, scrunching up her face in frustration. "I mean, I know we've had our differences, Beth. But do you really think I would go and do something like that to you? You could have died!"

"You didn't know I was allergic."

"Yes, I did. You told me, remember? You were joking that you hoped your sister stepped in an ant colony on her wedding day!"

I froze, my mind flashing back to that day. The day before the night with Mac that had ended up so crazily I'd pretty much forgotten everything else that had happened. But now it was all coming back to me. I'd made the joke, then I'd explained how the two of us were allergic to fire ants. So, yes, she would have totally known.

"But they found—"

"An empty jar of honey in my locker," Stephanie finished for me. "And blue hair dye. Yes, I know all of that. But that doesn't mean I did it." She paused, then added, "I was set up."

"By who?"

"Isn't it obvious? The queen mother herself. Joy Justice."

I stared at her, incredulous. Seriously, if she had told me this three hours before, I would have laughed in her face. Told her she was being ridiculous—that someone at Joy's level would never bother to acknowledge someone at mine—never mind go out of their way to try to ruin my career.

You'll be out of here before you know it, just like your little friend Stephanie.

But now, all I could think of was Joy fighting with Richard. Begging for her job. Crying her eyes out in her office alone. Looking at me with sheer hatred when I tried to step in to comfort her.

And in a few months—no one will even remember your name.

"How do you know?" I found myself asking.

Stephanie met my eyes. "Because she did the same thing to me."

"What?"

Stephanie sat down at the table across from me, propping

up her elbows and putting her face in her hands. "Why do you think I missed all of those live shots?"

I dropped my gaze, guilt swimming through my stomach. With everything that had happened, I'd never gotten a chance to ask her about that. Instead, I'd just chalked it up to her party girl lifestyle and believed it all.

But Stephanie had been a party girl since I'd first met her. And yet she'd always had the uncanny ability to crawl out of bed and kick her job's ass no matter how much alcohol or how little sleep. Because as much as she loved the night-life, she'd loved her job as a reporter more.

"It started happening right after Richard gave me a pro-motion," Stephanie explained. "Just like with you, suddenly all my interviews were cancelling on me. My tapes were getting lost. My live shots were being switched around with-out me knowing it and I would miss my airtime." She scowled—the memory obviously still painful. "Next thing I knew, I'd been demoted and you'd been promoted. And Joy was whispering in my ear that it wasn't an accident. That you were behind it all."

"She said it was *me*?"

"I know it sounds crazy now," she admitted. "But at the time, I don't know. Joy kept reminding me how ambitious you were, how badly you wanted to get off the morning show. How, as my roommate, you would have had access to my DayTimer on my computer." She gave me a rueful look. "It wasn't until later that I found out this kind of thing had happened before. To other young reporters over the years."

My eyes widened. "She did this before?"

"You can go look at the records if you want. News 9 has had half a dozen young female reporters who started rising through the ranks, only to suddenly quit or get fired."

"Wow."

"In any case, I wanted to tell you. But I was afraid after how I'd kicked you out and destroyed all your stuff you weren't going to believe anything I said. And then the ant thing happened. I tried to tell Richard what was going on, but he refused to listen. He just told me I needed to leave before he decided to call the cops. I couldn't risk having an arrest on my record—I'd probably never work again." She looked around the restaurant. "And now, here I am."

I swallowed hard, not sure what to think, what to say. Should I believe her? While it certainly was a crazy story, at the same time it made a sick sort of sense. Joy must have been feeling threatened about her job for some time now, knowing her days were numbered. And so she decided to take out the competition—any way she could.

"Look, Beth," Stephanie continued, "I'm not saying I'm totally innocent here. And I know I've ruined our chance of ever being friends. I just wanted to . . . set the record straight, I guess. And to tell you to be careful."

I nodded. "Thank you. I appreciate that."

She rose to her feet. "I'd better get back to work. My manager is giving me the evil eye. And losing two jobs in a month—well, that would be a record, even for me!" She gave a brittle laugh.

"Stephanie . . ." I found myself calling back to her. She turned around, looking at me questioningly.

"Yeah?"

"Do you . . . want me to talk to Richard? Tell him what really happened? Maybe you can get your job back. I mean, if you really didn't do those things, there's no reason you should have been fired."

She gave me a small smile. "Thank you," she said. "It means a lot that you would offer. But honestly? I'm kind of enjoying this little break. Maybe I'll want to go back to TV someday. But right now? This feels right. I'm actually, well, happy. For the first time since I can remember." She laughed. "Who knows? Maybe this was the life I was meant to live. At least for right now."

"Fair enough," I said. "But if you change your mind, let me know."

"I will." She paused, then added, "And I will pay you back, too. For all the stuff I destroyed. It may take me a while to save up. But I can start giving you installments every payday. Until I'm caught up."

"Thank you. I really appreciate that. And no rush, really."

"And . . . if you're ever in the neighborhood? Well, you know where I live. And how much wine I keep stocked in my fridge. Anytime News 9 gets you down, feel free to stop by and I'll get you plastered. It's the least I can do."

I nodded. "I will absolutely do that." And I absolutely meant it.

forty-five

MAC

"Got a minute?"

I looked up from cleaning my camera to see Beth hovering in the doorway of the photographer's lounge and my heart flipped on its ass. Not surprising, of course. It had been wrenching so painfully every time I laid eyes on her these days that I was half-convinced I was going to give myself a coronary by week's end.

"For you, I have all the minutes," I said, putting down my camera. I forced a smile to my lips and beckoned for her to sit down.

"Actually . . ." She shifted from foot to foot. "Do you know of anywhere more private? It's kind of . . . personal."

I swallowed hard. Now my heart was pumping furiously. And I was pretty sure my hands were shaking, too. Forcing them behind me, I rose to my feet. "I have the key to the live truck."

She nodded. "That'll work."

She turned and started toward the back exit. I followed, warning sirens going off in my head. Not that I had any doubts her intentions were anything but innocent. I just wasn't sure

I could handle being in such close proximity to her, all alone, and not do something I was going to regret.

My eyes involuntarily raked over her body. She was dressed casually today, in a pair of dark rinse skinny jeans and boots paired with a simple white tunic sleeveless shirt. It wasn't a tight shirt—in fact, if anything it was loose and flowy. The kind of shirt she might have chosen if we were having dinner at an all-inclusive resort in the Caribbean before taking a moonlit walk on the beach.

Not that we would ever be doing that. Or anything else for that matter.

I closed my eyes for a minute, sucking in a breath, which nearly caused me to walk into a wall. I saved myself last second and she didn't seem to notice, thankfully.

God, this was torture. Pure, unadulterated torture. To be in the same room, to breathe the same air, to look at her and not be able to touch her. It'd been a week since I'd run my fingers through her silky hair. Since I'd kissed the hollow spot at her throat that she always found so ticklish. A week since I'd held her in my arms, looked her in the eyes, told her I loved her and that I was never going to let her go.

But I had let her go.

And now, even though she was still here, she was gone.

While I remained in a living hell. Sisyphus rolling his immense boulder uphill, only to watch it roll back down so I could start all over again. Day in and day out. Rinse and repeat. My life stretched out before me, stark, bleak, joyless.

And yet, how it had to be.

We reached the live truck and climbed inside. There were two chairs in the back and she took one, crossing her legs and folding her hands in her lap. Summoning up all my drained willpower, I took the other, then looked at her questioningly.

"So," she said. "Some interesting developments since I've seen you last."

I listened as she told me. About what she'd overheard with Richard and Joy. About her encounter with Stephanie later that night. I listened to it all, not interrupting once, though by the end my hands had curled into fists, the skin of my knuckles straining white over bone.

"Sorry to burden you with this," she said after finishing. "I didn't know . . . who else to tell."

"I'm glad you told me," I said earnestly. "You should never be afraid to tell me anything."

She dropped her gaze, her eyelashes curtaining her beautiful eyes. "Thanks," she said. "I appreciate that. More than I probably should."

"So are you going to go to Richard?"

"Honestly, I don't know." She looked up. "I mean, Joy's done. Her contract hasn't been renewed." She paused, then added, "Is it weird that I feel kind of bad for her? I mean, she tried to get me fired. She almost killed me. And yet . . . somehow . . . I don't know. Just seeing her crying in her office, knowing everything she's worked so hard for will now be stripped away?" She shrugged helplessly. "I just feel bad."

"That's because you're a good person," I told her. Then I sighed. "God, every day I realize a bit more just how toxic this business can be. It's depressing."

"And scary as hell," Beth confessed. "I mean, I'm on the same path, right? I'm going down the same road? Trying to get the best stories, the most airtime. But what's my end game here? In thirty years, what will I have to show for all of this?"

"You will have whatever you want to show," I told her firmly. "Joy made a choice to define herself by her on-air persona. But you're under no obligation to do the same. You can be more than your job. You can have a life outside of work, you can do amazing things. And, at the same time, you can still be a good reporter. In fact, my guess is you'll be a better one, if there's more to you than just being on air."

"I know you're right," she said with a small smile. "It's just hard to remember, sometimes."

"Then I will have to keep reminding you."

She sighed, for a moment looking very sad. Then she shook her head and looked up at me. "I'm sorry. Here I am, going on and on about my own stupid life. But how are things going with you? I know we've spent a lot of time together. But we haven't really . . . talked, you know? I mean, not that we *have* to," she added quickly. "If you don't want to talk, I understand, of course. I mean, I just thought, I'm just wondering . . ." She looked up at me. "How are you? Are you okay?"

I nodded stiffly, the concern in her voice almost doing me in. I sucked in a breath, my mind racing with what I could tell her. But at last, it was the naked truth that spilled from my lips.

"I'm not good," I told her. "In fact, I'm pretty awful."

Her eyes moistened. "Oh, Mac . . ."

I shook my head. "It's just like . . . I don't know . . . too much. Too soon. You know? Like, she wants to just jump right back in right where we left off, as if nothing ever happened. But I can't do it. I have all these conflicted feelings still. About what she did. About how she left. About . . . well, how I still feel about you. I mean, all we shared, all we've done—I can't just turn that off like a switch. Even if it would be for the best."

I caught her trying to hide a wince. Then she squared her shoulders and set her chin. "You have to," she told me. "You have to find a way. You can't keep living like this. This kind of half life. It's not fair to anyone. To her. To Ashley. To you. If you want to make your family work, you have to put in your full effort."

"How can I? When all I can think about is you?"

She drew in a breath. "Look, Mac. Maybe we need . . . some time apart. Working together, side by side. It's not making any of this any easier."

I stared at her, her words sending icy fear sliding down my back. My mind snapping to a vision of a world without her in it. Yes, it would be easier not to see her every day, to be tortured by her nearness. But at the same time, it was such an exquisite torture—and I didn't know how I would live without it.

Her expression softened. "Believe me, it's not what I want, either. But at the same, it kind of is. I have to move on, too, you know. Find that life you were talking about, outside of work. And I don't know how I can manage something like that when I'm still in such close contact with you."

I hung my head. "You're right," I said. "I know you're right. I mean, not forever. But just . . . for a time, maybe."

"Yes," she said, her voice taking on an eagerness that matched mine. "Just a time. A time to cool off. To reassess. To give your marriage a real, true chance to work. I mean, you loved this woman once, Mac. You gave her a ring. You fathered a child with her. Maybe you can find that again, deep down. If you really give it a chance."

Her voice broke and, along with it, my heart. I knew how much it must have hurt her to say those words—to step aside and take herself out of the running. I knew she loved me. As much as I loved her. But she also respected me enough—and respected my promise to my daughter enough—to let me go.

"I love you," I blurted out, unable to stop myself. "I will always love you."

She nodded and I caught the tears leaking from the sides of her eyes. "No more than I love you," she said. "Which is why it has to be like this."

forty-six

BETH

And so it was done. I went to Richard and confessed every-thing. About my ill-fated relationship with Mac and why it would be better for everyone involved if they assigned me someone new. The whole time I was telling the story, I was blushing furiously. I didn't want to be the problem reporter. And I'd already caused so much drama in my short time at News 9. I was half-afraid he'd fire me on the spot.

But, as I'd learned over the past days, some things were more important than career. And to me, Mac's happiness was one of them.

Richard wasn't pleased. But he wasn't all that shocked either. It wasn't as if I was the first reporter at News 9 to fall for her photographer. If these walls could talk, he said, they'd have a lot more scandalous stories than mine to tell. Still, he added, he would prefer I keep my love life off the clock from this point forward. After all, it was technically against com-pany policy, not that it was usually enforced. Moreover, it was a pain in the ass to switch around peoples' schedules when the romance died.

Which was fine with me. After two failed relationships

in so many months, the last thing I wanted was to go on the hunt for round three.

So I got a new photographer, with Richard hedging his bets by assigning me a gay guy named Bruce who was old enough to be my grandfather. No chance of a hot hook-up there, despite how dapper Bruce usually looked in his polka-dotted bow ties!

And life went on.

I had considered telling Richard about Joy as well, but in the end, decided against it. Her last day was Friday and the station was planning a big send-off party for her. There was going to be a special broadcast even, featuring a montage of all the big stories she'd covered over the years. The newspapers had all run articles about her legacy and the mayor was giving her a lifetime good service award for all she'd done for the town. If I spoke up now, her entire legacy would be tarnished forever. Even after all she'd done, I couldn't bring myself to do that to her. She'd be gone soon enough and it would all be over.

I was at my desk the Thursday before the big Joy send-off, putting together the day's story assignment when Javier came sauntering up.

"So," he said, his face stretched into a wide smile, "how much do you love me?"

I looked up, my pulse skipping a beat. "Depends," I said. "Are you about to tell me what I want you to tell me?"

It'd been so long now since his original email about Alvarez agreeing to be interviewed, I'd pretty much given up on the whole thing. Instead, I'd been working on finding other big stories that would be just as compelling. But now . . .

"Depends. If you want me to tell you that Peeps are the best candy ever or that *The Matrix* was more than one movie—you are sadly still in delusional land. But if it's about our favorite hacker . . ." He grinned again, then lifted his first. I bumped it with my own and he grabbed a chair and pulled it up to my desk.

"Come on!" I cried. "Don't keep me in suspense."

"Okay, okay! Easy, girl. Look, here's the deal. Turns out Dante has decided to turn himself in."

"What? Are you serious?"

"As a heart attack, baby. Evidently he's sick of being on the run and his mother harassing him. He's ready to face the music. But before he does, he's agreed to do one single interview to give his side of the story."

My heart was now slamming against my ribcage. "And that interview will be with . . . ?"

"His favorite News 9 reporter," Javier proclaimed. "Miss Elizabeth White."

"Oh my God. Oh my GOD! Javier you are my hero!" I jumped up from my desk and threw my arms around him. "You are the absolute best!"

"Yeah, yeah. I know. Try to restrain yourself," he teased. "And listen—there is one little complication."

"What is it?"

"He needs to do the interview tonight. 'Cause starting tomorrow morning his schedule is bound to be a bit full, hanging with the Feds and all."

I drew in a breath. "Okay. That's fine." I'd make it work. Hell, I would have made any complication work to get this story.

"You're going to need a photographer," Javier reminded me. "Bruce is still out with the flu. I'd volunteer, but Tammy got tickets to Imagine Dragons tonight. They're her favorite band. She would have my balls in a vise if I ditched her for work."

"I understand. It's cool. I'm sure I can get someone. I mean, if I tell Richard what it's for, I'm sure he'd rearrange half the newscast to make sure it happened."

Then again, did I really want to tell Richard beforehand? I mean, what if Dante got cold feet or the interview fell through? I wanted to be sure this time, so as not to disappoint.

"You know, you might want to give Mac first dibs," Javier suggested. "I mean, he shot the original interview, right? Which means he's kind of owed the job. Trust me, we photogs hate being switched up mid-story. It makes it tougher for us to win our Emmys if it's a collaboration deal."

I sighed. I knew he was right. Mac had been a part of this story from the start and it would be completely unfair to leave him out of the action now.

Not to mention, I wasn't horribly opposed to working with him one more time.

"Okay," I said. "I'll give him a call. See if he's willing to work tonight."

See if he's willing to work with me.

forty-seven

MAC

After yet another miserable day at work with a reporter who talked my ear off and was so vain she was practically late for her own live shot thanks to her primping in the mirror, I decided to swing by the florist on my way home to pick up half a dozen long-stem yellow roses, Victoria's favorite.

I'd gone to great lengths, all week long, to be the model husband, hoping that if I played the part, someday it would start feeling real. That the way I used to feel about our family would come raging back to me somehow and I would no longer have to only pretend that this was the life I wanted to live.

That I didn't wish I were coming home to Beth, instead.

And so I'd gone through all the motions—doing everything I could possibly think of in the family man's playbook. We'd made dinner together. We'd popped popcorn and watched old favorite movies. We'd gone to Target and spent way too much money on household goods we hadn't realized we needed until we got there. I'd even moved back into the master bedroom.

Not that anything had happened between the sheets, mind you. But we were in the same bed. Which was something I guess. Maybe someday I'd even stop getting nauseous every time she turned over and accidentally brushed her leg against mine.

I stepped through the front door, roses in hand, trying a "Honey, I'm home!" on for size. But my voice fell flat and the words rang fake in my ears—I'd need to keep working on that one.

Turned out it didn't matter anyway; Victoria and Ashley weren't even home. Sighing, I walked mechanically over to the sink and reached under it for a vase. Then I set the flowers in water and walked back over to the couch. I flipped on the television and searched for some mindless sports commentary to get sucked into.

Before I could settle on a station, however, the door burst open and Ashley came rushing in, followed by a shopping bag–laden Victoria, who looked drained and stressed.

I rose from the couch as any dutiful husband would and took her bags. "Everything okay?" I asked.

"It was," she said with a frown. "Until your credit card was declined."

"What?"

She turned to me, her eyes flashing disdain. "Do you know how humiliating that is? To be in the middle of Neiman Marcus and have them turn you away? God, I thought I would die of embarrassment."

"How much did you spend before that?" I demanded, my voice rising, despite my best efforts. I caught Ashley's surprised look out of the corner of my eye and lowered it again. "I mean, we talked about this. I don't make a lot of money here. And we only have one salary to live on right now."

"Oh, that's real nice," she snapped back. "Just make me feel bad 'cause I gave up my job to be with my family. Sorry I'm such a financial drain on you."

"I didn't mean it like that." I raked a hand through my hair, frustrated. "It's just, we can't be making unnecessary purchases right now. You know, until things get settled."

"Well, I needed a new suit, didn't I? I mean, if you want me to go to one of those *interviews* you set up for me." She spit out the word *interviews* as if expelling poison.

"Wait," I said, "you were supposed to go to an interview today, right? The one I set up for you over at the FOX station?"

She turned away, not meeting my eyes. "Come on, Jake. That was a news writer position."

"So?"

"So I'm a reporter. A fucking Emmy-winning international correspondent!" she cried. "Do you think I'm going to go sit at some desk all day and write crappy copy for someone else to read?"

"But you'd be back in the business. And it would only be until a real job opened up."

"What 'real job'?" she demanded. "Jake, get your head out of your ass! San Diego is a shitty small news market. There's never going to be a 'real job' for me here."

I closed my eyes, trying to reset my sanity. "Well, what do you suggest we do?"

"I think it's obvious. We need to go where the jobs are. I mean, Boston's out, of course, thanks to the little scene you pulled there. But we could go to L.A. Or New York City."

"No." I shook my head. "Ashley is finally comfortable here. She has family here and she's making friends. I'm not going to go and uproot her again."

"And I'm not going to sit here and rot in this pathetic, sand-infested small town just to appease some fucking four-year-old!"

"Mommy? Are you okay?"

I froze at the sound of Ashley's voice. Lost in the argument, I'd almost forgotten she was still in the room. Now she looked up at us, from one to the other, her eyes wide and frightened.

"Mommy, are you mad at Daddy?"

"Your father is just being a little pigheaded right now, sweetie," Victoria replied, glaring at me.

Ashley broke out into giggles. "You're a pig head, Daddy! Oink, oink! Pig head!"

I couldn't help a small smile. "Thank you, Ashley. That's really sweet. Now, why don't you go play in your room for a bit, okay? Mommy and Daddy need to talk."

"I don't want to play by myself!"

"I know. But just give us five minutes, okay? Then I'll come in and play with you."

She stuck out her lower lip in a pout. "I want *Beth* to come play with me."

Oh God. Not now. I'd been trying and trying to get her to not mention the B name in front of Mommy. But Ashley just couldn't take the hint. And now I could feel Victoria's stare burning into me. One more thing that was all my fault.

"Sorry, sweetie," I said, trying to keep my tone neutral. "Beth can't come over right now."

"But I want her to!"

"I know, baby. But she can't. Now please, just go to your room and play ponies. I'll be there in one second."

Ashley gave me a defiant look, but eventually did as I requested, though not without attitude. She stomped to her room and slammed the door behind her. I watched her go, sighed, then turned back to Victoria, who was fixing herself a drink.

"That girl needs some discipline, Jake," she said. "She just walks all over everyone."

"She's four, Victoria. That's what four-year-olds do."

"She won't be four forever. It's time for her to know she's not the boss in this family. She doesn't get to have a say."

I opened my mouth, probably to say something I was going to regret later. Or be made to regret, at the very least. But before I could speak, I was saved by my cell phone. I pulled it from my pocket and glanced down at the caller ID, then froze.

"Who is it?" Victoria demanded, trying to peer over my shoulder. I stepped forward.

"It's just work," I told her. "Give me a minute, okay?"

I walked out the front door, closing it behind me, then put the phone to my ear. "Hello?" I said.

"Mac. Hi."

I gripped the phone, my heart beating a mile a minute as my ears registered the sweet ring of her voice, speaking my name. God I'd missed her so much. At that moment, if I could have climbed through the phone and kissed her, I probably would have.

"Hi," I said instead, trying to keep my voice steady. "How are you?"

"Actually?" she replied. "I'm pretty great."

My heart skipped a beat and worry gnawed in my gut. Great? How could she possibly be great? Why wasn't she miserable like me? Seriously, if she was about to tell me she'd met some new guy and that she was in love I was going to have a heart attack, right there on my front porch.

"And why are you so . . . great?" I somehow managed to spit out.

"Dante Alvarez!" she practically squealed. "He's finally agreed to another interview."

Relief flooded me. "Oh," I said. "That *is* great. Really great. I'm so happy for you."

"Happy for *us,* you mean," she corrected.

"Excuse me?"

"Come on, Mac. This is *our* story! You were robbed the first time around as much as I was. And now we have another chance."

"But we're not partners anymore, remember?"

"Yeah, I know. But it's not during our regular shift, so it doesn't really matter, right? I'm not even going to tell Richard we're doing it until it's done. Then I'm going to surprise him with it."

I bit my lower lip, trying to justify it to myself, ignoring the warning bells going off in my head. She was right, of course. This was our story. We could do one more story together, right?

"That sounds great," I said. "When is this happening?"

She paused for a moment. "Well, pretty soon, actually. Like . . . now-ish?"

"Now-ish?"

"I mean, as soon as you can get here. Tonight. You see,

he's supposed to turn himself in tomorrow to the Feds. So it pretty much has to be tonight."

"Okay . . ." My mind raced with possibilities. Sadie and Joe were down in Cabo for a wedding so they wouldn't be able to watch Ashley. But maybe Victoria could . . . I mean, she had been watching her quite a bit over the last week or so. And she was her mother.

"Hang on a second." I pushed back open the door and stepped into the living room. Victoria was standing there, arms crossed over her chest, watching me. I felt my face heat, though there was no reason for it to. I was just trying to do my job. I wasn't trying anything sneaky.

"There's breaking news," I told her. "They need me to come in and work tonight."

"Okay . . ."

"Would you mind watching Ashley while I'm gone? I shouldn't be late or anything."

She narrowed her eyes at me, as if suspicious. Then, at last, she shrugged. "Sure," she said. "It's not like I have any earth-shattering plans tonight. Or ever, for that matter. And hey, we could definitely use the overtime."

I sighed, choosing to ignore that last little dig. "Great. Thank you." I put the phone back to my ear. "Okay, I can do it," I told Beth. "I'll get in the car now and I'll meet you at the station in about forty-five minutes. Does that work?"

"That's perfect," she replied. She paused, then added, "Thank you, Mac. I really appreciate it. This story—well, you know better than anyone how much it means to me. How much it means to my career."

I could feel Victoria watching me, waiting. So I just smiled amicably. "No problem," I said. "Whatever I can do to help."

forty-eight

BETH

N o leather pants this time?"

I looked up from my computer to see Mac walking over to my desk. My cheeks flushed and my heart started beating a little faster in my chest. God, he looked good. I hadn't realized how much I truly missed seeing him until he stepped back into my line of sight. Those broad shoulders, those tight abs. Those beautiful blue eyes, that strong jaw, that hint of stubble whispering across his cheeks.

"Nope," I declared. "He's going to have to deal with the real me this time."

"I'm pretty sure he'll be okay with that," Mac said, a small smile flashing across his face. "I mean, if he's truly a red-blooded male, that is."

I rolled my eyes, trying to force back the smile that crept to my lips. I wanted to tell him he shouldn't be saying things like that anymore. But at the same time I didn't really want him to stop.

This was going to be a long night.

"Thanks for coming in," I said, forcing myself to change

the subject. "I feel bad that you got all the way home and had to come back to the station."

"It's all good," he said. "I was able to tuck Ashley into bed and Victoria's staying with her while we do this." He gave me a fond look. "I know this is important to you. And I'm glad I get to be a part of it."

I started to reply, but his phone rang, cutting me off. He reached into his pocket, checked the caller ID, then frowned, putting the phone to his ear.

"What's up?" he asked. "Is there a problem?"

I watched as his brow furrowed. "Yes. Yes, it is. . . . What do you want me to say? We work together . . . It's just for an interview and I'll be right back home." His grip tightened on the phone. "You told me you had nothing going on tonight, remember? That you were fine staying home?" He paused, listening. "Look, I'll be back as soon as I can, okay? Yes . . . Yes . . . Okay . . . Thank you. I promise to make it up to you."

He stuffed the phone in his pocket, looking miserable. I swallowed hard. "Do you need to go?"

"No." He shook his head angrily. "It's fine. Victoria just doesn't trust me around you. Which I guess I deserve. But it's fine. I'll deal with it later."

"I'm sorry," I said. "I didn't mean to get you in trouble."

"You're my coworker. We're on assignment. We're not doing anything wrong."

"Right." I sighed. "God, now I feel terrible."

"Don't," he scolded. "Let me deal with her. You need to concentrate on your interview. After all, this is it. Your big break. I'm not going to let her ruin it and neither should you."

"Okay," I said, giving him my best fake smile. "It's a deal."

We headed out to the truck and started the drive down to Chula Vista, back to the same warehouse we'd met Dante the first time around. There was a ton of late rush hour traffic this time, so it took a while to get there. And neither of us spoke much the entire trip. But still, it felt good, somehow, just to be sitting in the same car as him. Breathing the same air. Sharing the same space. I could smell him—that warm manly scent that I'd originally been so attracted to back at the club on our very first night. And every so often I would glance over and take a peek at his face. It wasn't all I wanted—but it was something. And right now it would have to be enough.

Finally we pulled into the warehouse lot and Mac parked the truck on the side of the road. I peered out the windshield—this place looked even creepier now than it did during the daytime—and that was saying something. I sucked in a breath, firming my resolve.

This was it. The next hour was going to change my life forever.

Mac shot me a look. "Are you ready to do this?"

I grinned, despite myself. "So ready!"

He smiled back at me, flashing those perfect white teeth and a warmth rolled through my stomach. It was funny—it felt almost intimate, the two of us being here, in the dark, alone together. But not in a sexual way this time. More of a shared camaraderie. An us-against-the-world type of thing. And it served to give me a small spark of hope. Maybe we could never be together the way I wanted us to be. But we also cared too much about one another to let our friendship die.

Mac exited the vehicle, walking around to the back of the truck to grab his gear while I touched up my makeup in the passenger side mirror. This interview would likely be played around the world on various stations and over the Internet. I wanted to look my best.

But just as I had finished applying lipstick, a flash of light reflected in my mirror. A pair of headlights, I realized, swinging into the dark parking lot. I froze, a little nervous. Who could that be? Was it Alvarez, late for our meeting? But no . . . I furrowed my brows as the vehicle came into focus.

It was a News 9 van.

What the hell?

I pushed my door open and stepped out of the truck, confusion worming its way through me. What was a News 9 van doing here, now? I hadn't told anyone I was coming out here tonight to do the interview—not wanting to jinx the story if it didn't end up happening. So who could this be?

"Is that Javier?" Mac asked, also looking confused as we watched a man getting out of the driver's seat.

"Yeah," I said, squinting at him. What was he doing here? "He was supposed to go to a concert tonight." I frowned. "This is really strange. Hang on a second."

I walked over to the van, hands on my hips. "Javier! What are you doing here?"

He looked up, his face filled with guilt. "Beth, I'm so sorry."

"Sorry about what? Why aren't you at the concert with your wife? What's going on here?"

He gave me another miserable look, then gestured to the van. I peered inside, my eyes widening at what I saw.

Make that *who* I saw.

None other than Joy Justice herself.

Oh no.

I looked back at Javier. He winced. "She evidently overheard us talking about the interview," he told me in a whisper. "And then she went and told Richard it was *her* interview. That she'd set it all up all by herself."

"What?" I cried, now horrified beyond belief. "But she can't do that!"

"She already did," Javier said with a shrug. "And Richard's over the moon, of course. An exclusive interview with the infamous Dante Alvarez, the night before he turns himself in." He made a face. "They've been promoting the shit out of it all night long."

Oh God. I raked a hand through my hair. Why hadn't I told Richard myself, before she could get to him? I was just so nervous that it could fall through and I didn't want to disappoint him. But now . . .

I glanced over at Mac. He was on the phone for some reason. Probably Victoria giving him a hard time again. So much for backup. I returned my gaze to Javier, who was still looking guilty as hell.

"I need to talk to her," I determined. The photographer shot me a concerned look.

"Be careful. She's acting crazy, even for her. I think she

believes this story will convince the owners to renew her contract. And she will stop at nothing to get it."

"Right. Well, she'll have to get through me first."

I sucked in a breath, firming my resolve. I stalked over to the van's passenger side door and whipped it open. She looked down at me, raising an eyebrow.

"Are you going to make a scene?" she asked in a patronizing voice.

"What are you doing here?" I demanded. "This is my interview."

"Not anymore it isn't. Richard assigned it to me."

"Only because you lied to him and told him you set it up to begin with."

She raised an eyebrow. "You mean like you lied to Alvarez the first time around and said you were me?"

My face flushed. God, how did she even know that?

"You turned that interview down," I reminded her. "You told Richard you didn't want to do it."

"And now I've told him I do. And he's agreed. So you can feel free to jump back into your truck and head home." She paused then added, "Do make sure to tune in at eleven though. It's bound to be an amazing exclusive."

Anger and frustration burned through me like a wildfire. "I can't believe I actually looked up to you," I growled. "I can't believe I actually wanted to be like you!"

She sniffed. "I can't believe you *actually* thought you had the chance."

I started to back away, not sure what to do. What to say. But then, something inside of me roared. I thought of Stephanie, wrongfully fired and working as a waitress. Of all the other unnamed girls who suffered a similar fate. I couldn't let her get away with this one more time. If not for me, for them.

I squared my shoulders. "Bullshit," I spit out. "That's complete bullshit."

"Excuse me?"

"You heard me. And you know it's true. You act all high and mighty—but I know you're scared to death. Of me and all the other young, talented reporters coming up through the ranks. Biting at your heels. You could have been a mentor. You could have taken us under your wing and showed us the ropes. But instead, you went and sabotaged us. Because you couldn't handle the idea of someday being replaced."

"I'm sure I don't know what you're talking about."

"You know, Joy, funny thing. You tried to ruin my life. You almost killed me. And yet, somehow I can't help but feel sorry for you," I said. "I mean, all you've done, all you've accomplished, and yet still, it isn't enough for you. You still have to go and ruin other people's lives and hurt other people's chances to get ahead. Seriously, are you really that goddamned insecure? Do you really need the spotlight that badly—that you're willing to sell your soul just for a few more precious minutes of airtime?" I shook my head. "You know, I told you back at the station that I wanted to fill your shoes someday. But looking at you now? I think I'm going to set my sights higher. Not that that will be very hard."

She stared at me, her face bright red and furious. She opened her mouth to speak, but suddenly stopped, looking behind me. I whirled around to see Mac was standing there. And the look on his face made me freeze.

Something was wrong. Something was really wrong.

"What is it?" I asked.

"Can I talk to you for a moment? Alone?"

"Um, sure." I glared at Joy. "Stay right there," I commanded. "This is not over yet."

Joy rolled her eyes, but thankfully didn't move from her seat. She had to wait for Javier and probably didn't want to go wandering off in this dark, creepy place alone. Which bought me a few precious minutes—but only a few.

I couldn't lose this story. After all she'd done to me, she didn't deserve to win.

I walked a few feet away with Mac, then stopped. "What is it?" I asked. "You look like you've seen a ghost."

"Look, I'm sorry. But I need to go."

"What?" I cried. "We're just about to walk into the interview!"

"I know, I know. And I'm sorry," he said.

"Did you get another call from Victoria?"

"Actually . . . it was from my neighbor," he said in a voice I'd never heard him use before. "About Ashley."

He trailed off and my blood ran cold. "What about Ashley?"

"He said . . ." Mac looked as if he was having a hard time breathing. "He said his kids just came home and told him they saw her wandering around outside. By herself. They tried to get her to come home with them, but she refused. She kept crying and saying she needed to find her daddy. My neighbor went to where they'd found her, but by that point she was gone."

My blood ran cold. "Oh God. But Victoria . . . ?"

"He said he knocked on our door, but there was no answer. I just tried to call her, but her phone went straight to voice mail." He raked a hand through his hair. "I called the police. They're on their way over to check things out but . . ."

"Get in the car," I commanded. "Let's go."

His face tore. "No. You need to stay. We'll get another photographer out here. Or maybe Javier can do it if you get rid of Joy. I know how much this means to you and your career. You can't just—"

"Okay, you need to shut up right now," I scolded him. "Your daughter is missing. Do you think I give a damn about some stupid news story? Get in the car. I'll be there in one second."

"But . . ."

I didn't wait for him to finish. Just stalked over to the van and looked up at Joy. "Congratulations," I said. "He's all yours. I've got something more important to do."

She stared at me. "What could possibly be more important than this?" she asked in an incredulous voice.

I looked at her sadly. "So many things, Joy. So very many things." I turned to head back to the truck. "Unfortunately someone like you would never understand."

forty-nine

MAC

Beth insisted on driving to my house, which was good since I wasn't quite sure I'd be able to see the road at this point. The police assured me they were on the case and a quick post to my neighborhood's Facebook page had everyone else out searching as well. I'd tried to call Victoria at least ten more times, praying she'd answer and tell me it was all a mistake. That Ashley was safe and sound and cuddled in her bed.

But every call went straight to voice mail, causing my fear to spike.

Please be okay. Please be okay.

Guilt wracked my insides, pounding at me without relent. What had I been thinking, leaving her alone with her mother? Trusting that Victoria had, indeed, changed. That she really wanted to make good and be a family again. To be a real mother who wanted to parent her child even when the parenting wasn't fun.

I thought back to the phone call she'd made when I was still at the station, telling me something had come up and that I needed to come home. At the time I thought she was just mad that I was working with Beth and was trying to manipulate me into feeling guilty. I never believed she'd actually take off and leave a sleeping four-year-old alone in the house. That was beyond crazy, even for her.

My hand squeezed into a fist. What a fool I'd been. Here I was, trying my best to be with Victoria for Ashley's sake. And now, because of Victoria, Ashley could be in danger.

And Beth had lost her big story. My heart wrenched as I glanced over at her tense face, staring out the windshield as she drove and I wondered what was going on in her head. This had been her dream night. And because of me, it had turned into a nightmare. Her one chance at stardom, and now she'd been forced to turn it over to her enemy. To let Joy Justice have the last laugh after all.

It wasn't fair. It was so not fair.

After what seemed an eternity, we finally pulled into my neighborhood. I jumped out of the car before Beth could even put it into park, screaming Ashley's name. A few neighbors approached, saying all the right things, giving me all the empty comfort. But I could see the suspicion in the backs of their eyes. Why had I let my four-year-old wake up alone?

I felt like the worst dad in the world.

"Ashley! Please, baby girl! Can you hear me? It's Daddy!"

Beth popped out of the car and joined me in calling my daughter's name. Her voice, rising in chorus with the others sounded like sweet music, and suddenly I was so grateful she had not let me talk her out of coming along. Here she was, missing out on the biggest night of her career, and yet from the look in her eyes, I could tell she wasn't even thinking about it. Her thoughts were completely on my daughter.

Because she loved Ashley, I realized with a start. She may not have been related to her or even known her for all that long. But she loved her all the same.

Whoever said blood was thicker than water was a god-damned fool.

We split up to cover more ground and I headed to the nearby park, where I had taken Ashley on the swings a few times before, still yelling out her name. But the park was empty. The swings abandoned. No sign my daughter had been there at all.

And so I forced myself to head over to the adjacent neighborhood pool, my heart firmly lodged in my throat as I stepped closer to the water. I knew in my head this would have been the first place the neighbors and police had looked—not to mention there was no way she would have been able to scale the fence to get inside. Still, I had to be sure. And the relief I felt as I looked down into those dark but empty waters came in a rush.

But that relief was short-lived as a cold wind blew across my skin, causing me to break out into goosebumps. I'd heard on the weather report that tonight was supposed to drop to below freezing and I doubted Ashley had had the foresight to grab a coat. I imagined her out there, all alone and shivering, dressed in some thin princess nightgown and bare feet—it was almost too much to bear.

Anger surged inside of me again. Anger at Victoria for leaving my daughter alone. Anger at myself for allowing her to care for her to begin with. All this time I'd been trying to do the right thing, for Ashley's sake, and yet somehow I'd done the absolute wrong thing instead. Ashley didn't need a mother like this in her life. Not the kind of mother who was more concerned with her own selfish interests than her daughter's well-being. Sure, Victoria was able to play the good mommy game for the short-term. When it suited her needs. But in the end, she would always do more harm than good.

"Mac!"

I startled at Beth's voice, breaking through my tormented thoughts. My head jerked up, trying to identify where it was coming from.

"Mac!" She called again. "Over here!"

I dashed through the woods, heart pounding madly, barely able to breathe as I ran toward the sound of her voice. Branches scratched at my face, and I almost ate it on a large root half sticking out of the ground, but somehow I managed to keep running until I reached her.

She was standing over a small ravine. Some kind of drainage ditch it looked like. I looked down, seeing nothing at first, then glanced over at her and saw her white face. Without a word, she pointed down into the pit.

And then I saw it. The crumpled little body at the bottom. "Ashley!" I screamed. "Ashley, baby!" I started to climb down into ravine.

Beth grabbed my arm. "Be careful," she said.

But I was beyond the careful stage now. I was running on pure adrenaline and nothing was going to keep me from my baby girl. Half running, half sliding, I made my way down the ravine, dropping to my knees in front of her. She looked so pale. So still. For a moment, I wasn't sure she was breathing.

"Ashley?" I croaked out, in barely a whisper. "Baby?"

And then, slowly she rolled over, her eyes fluttering open, unfocused at first, then locking onto my face. I watched as they widened in recognition and her lips curled up into a huge grin.

"Daddy!" she cried in a voice hoarse from too many tears. "I found you!"

"Yes," I agreed, this close to squeezing the life out of her. My whole body was still shaking and I could feel tears well in my eyes. "You found me, princess. You found me."

Ashley smiled sleepily. "I'm not a princess," she said in a sleepy voice. "I'm your little girl."

I reached down, scooping her up into my arms. I thought about all the times I joked she was getting so big and so heavy. Now she felt as if she weighed nothing at all. Cradling her to my chest, I tried to climb back up the ravine. It was steep and slippery, and for a few moments I thought I wouldn't make it. But finally I managed to find my footing and get to the top.

Once there, I dropped to the ground, panting heavily. Despite the cold temperatures, my whole body had broken out into a heavy sweat. And now I was freezing.

But that didn't matter. In fact, nothing mattered anymore. Nothing besides this beautiful baby girl in my arms. My baby girl.

Ashley looked up at me, smiling at me as if I was her hero. I knew I didn't deserve this kind of worship. And maybe when she was older, she'd resent me for it all. But right now, I had to take it. It was all I had to hold onto in a world that had almost gone mad.

"I came looking for you, Daddy," she told me. "I woke up and no one was home. I thought maybe you had gone outside. But then I got lost." She let out a small sob. "I thought I was lost forever."

I pulled her close to my chest, tears streaming down my cheeks. "I'm so sorry, baby girl," I whispered. "From now on, you'll never wake up alone again."

"Hey!" Ashley cried, looking up. "Is that Beth? Is she finally here for our playdate?"

I looked up. Beth was hovering over us, looking a little nervous. I smiled up at her, then reached out with my hand, taking her own. Then I pulled her down to our level and grabbed her in a big hug. The three of us squeezed one another as tightly as we could. And it felt better than any feeling I'd ever had before.

"Family hug!" Ashley exclaimed.

And she was right. It was a family hug.

Because we were a family.

fifty

BETH

No sooner had I helped Mac get Ashley safely back in bed, than I got a surprise text from News 9. Someone had evidently called in sick and they needed me to come back to fill in for the broadcast.

I groaned in annoyance, showing the text to Mac. The last thing I wanted to do right now was to deal with work—after all that had happened tonight. To go back to the station, just in time to see Joy's triumphant Alvarez interview air. I could already imagine the sounds of everyone gushing over her and telling her what an amazing reporter she was, how intrepid she must have been to capture the elusive Alvarez on tape—and just before he turned himself in, too. Maybe she'd even score what she was after—a new contract from the board—so she could continue to make my life a living hell just a bit longer.

But what else could I do? I'd lost my big story, but I needed to keep my job. And so I said good-bye to Mac, promising to call him the second I got off air. He had a lot to deal with as well: the police, his neighbors, his still missing wife. And me hanging around would only complicate matters further.

"Beth!" Ana cried as she caught me walking through the newsroom fifteen minutes later. "Richard wants to see you. Now!"

I nodded weakly and changed course, skipping my desk and heading straight to the news director's office. As I walked by, I peeked into Joy's office, but found it completely dark. Maybe she was still out on the interview. Or maybe she was helping edit the piece. I sighed. In the rush of adrenaline to go find Mac's daughter, I had barely cared about losing the story, my entire thoughts on Ashley. But now that Ashley was safe and sound, I couldn't help but feel the weight of disappointment settling in my stomach. The knowledge that my big story now belonged to someone else.

But I knew, in my heart, if I had to do it over again, I would have made the same choice. And, at the end of the day, I didn't regret a thing. There would be other stories. Other news. But the people you loved were irreplaceable.

"There you are!" Richard cried as I stepped through his office. "Finally."

I cocked my head in question. "What's going on?"

He looked agitated and upset. Not the type of expression I would have imagined on his face during what had to be one of the most triumphant nights of his career.

"Look, I don't know what's going on and there's no time to sit everyone down to figure it out," he barked. "All I know is the interview of the century has been dropped on my desk and I'm supposed to have you put it together and report it on air tonight."

"What?" I stared at him, completely lost. "You mean the Dante Alvarez piece? What about Joy?"

"That's what I'd like to know, actually," Richard replied tersely. "She never came back to the station."

I stared at him, unbelieving. "What?" I said again, knowing I probably sounded like a broken record. But I was truly at a loss for words. She didn't come back to the station?

"She sent Javier back with the interview instead. Along with a nice little note informing me that she would not be coming back for her final broadcast and she would not be attending the farewell party we had planned for her afterward." Richard shook his head. "And then, just to screw with me a little bit more, she wrote this crazy PS about how the piece could only be fronted by you and no one else. Even though you're not even scheduled for tonight."

I almost fell over backward. "Why would she say that?"

"Beth. I don't know. Some nonsense about aiming higher? Filling shoes? Some shit about selling her soul for airtime?" He shook his head. "I'm pretty sure the old bird's finally lost it."

"No," I said, a slow smile spreading across my face. "I think she might have actually found it at last." At least I hoped she had.

"Yeah. Sure. Whatever. All I know is we've been promoting the hell out this piece all night long. And if I can't deliver, I'm going to look like a fool. Javier's waiting in the edit room. I need you to go see what the two of you can put together in the next hour."

"Absolutely," I said, excitement rising inside of me. "I can do that."

He sighed. "Look, I'm sorry. I know it's not fair putting this all on you last minute. But you'd be saving my ass and the board and I would be extremely appreciative. I don't think I have to tell you how important this piece is to our station."

"Oh, I know," I said with a grin, doing my best not to dance a jig in the middle of his office. "It's just as important to me."

fifty-one

BETH

A nd so Javier and I got to work, editing the piece in record time and getting it on the air. It wasn't easy—and a few times I was pretty sure we wouldn't make our time slot. But we kept our heads down and worked our asses off and somehow made it happen. Thankfully Joy's interview was great and gave us a lot to work with. And Alvarez had been very forthcoming with his answers. When we had finished, we had a piece we could be proud of. Which was a good thing, because it was surely going to be rebroadcast many times over, all around the world.

Before I knew it, we were on the air. I was delivering the story of a lifetime. And when the broadcast had finished the entire newsroom broke out into applause. We had nailed it. And our station was about to be on the map. The network had been calling all night long, as had the cable stations. It wasn't long before someone popped the first bottle of champagne. The very same champagne that was supposed to toast Joy's last broadcast, now filling glasses raised to me.

I made my own silent toast to the former anchor, wondering if she had watched the broadcast, hoping she was okay. I knew it had probably taken every ounce of willpower she had to give up this story—and her last night on TV. To do what was fair and right. To overcome disappointment with elegance and grace. I could only hope she would find peace in the end. A new life, beyond TV.

After downing my champagne, I bid my fellow coworkers good night, reminding them that this was a team effort and I was proud to be part of the team. And I meant it, too. While there would always be drama and not everyone was going to play fair, there were good people here, too. People who wanted to work hard. To make a difference. Piper, Javier, Ana, Mac, and so many more. They were work family. And they were awesome.

Once back home I turned on the TV to one of the national stations. Alvarez had gone, as promised, and turned himself in. And they were buzzing on how some little station in San Diego managed to score the exclusive before they had. My name was being curiously tossed about, with hosts literally Googling me on air, trying to figure out who I was and how I'd managed to do what I'd done—what no other reporter had managed to do. It made me laugh to see how obsessed they all were about it. Going on and on as if it were the most important thing in the world.

But I knew better.

A knock on my door interrupted my musings. I rose from the couch, wondering if Piper had lost her keys. But when I opened the door, I realized it wasn't my roommate at all.

It was Mac. With a sleepy little Ashley in tow.

"Is everything okay?" I asked worriedly.

He didn't speak. He just pulled me into his arms and kissed me, Ashley smooshed in between us. The little girl let out a small giggle of protest, then threw her hands around me and jumped into my arms. I grabbed her and swung her around and kissed the top of her head.

"Look, would you mind if we crashed here tonight?" Mac asked, looking a little sheepish. "I know I should have called first, but . . ."

"You just love my comfortable couches, don't you?" I couldn't help but tease, remembering that fateful first night.

"Actually," he said, his eyes twinkling, "I was hoping Ashley could take the couch." He locked his gaze on me. "I find your bed much more comfortable."

I drew in a breath. "What about Victoria?"

"She's still at the house," Mac said. "Packing her things. She promised to be gone first thing in the morning."

I stared at him. My heart thudded in my chest. Victoria was leaving? Mac had kicked her out at last? "What happened?" I asked.

He glanced over at Ashley who had curled up on the couch and had already fallen back asleep, her stuffed lion cradled in her arm and her thumb in her mouth. Then he turned back to me and gave me a grim look.

"She came back about a half hour after you'd left. You should have seen the look on her face when she saw me and Ashley on the couch. She knew she was busted."

"But I don't understand. Why did she leave her alone in the first place?"

He sighed. "Remember I told you about that news director?" When I nodded, he continued. "Evidently he showed up in San Diego and started calling her. Saying he missed her and wanted her back. She figured she could meet him quickly and get back before I got home. I guess she thought since Ashley was already asleep, it wouldn't be a big deal." His hands tightened into fists. I placed my hands over them.

"I should have never allowed her back in," he growled. "Here I was, trying to make things better for Ashley. When it only made everything worse."

"You couldn't have known," I assured him. "And your heart was in the right place."

"No," he said softly. "My heart was always with you."

I swallowed hard, trying to push back the tears that threatened. "Oh, Mac . . ."

"Look, I don't deserve your forgiveness. What I did to you—I would deserve it if you hated me forever. But I love you, Beth. I love you with all my heart. And my daughter loves you, too. And I've realized, family isn't always flesh and blood. It's the people who care about you. The people who are willing to stand by you, no matter what the personal expense. You did that for us. Now I want to do that for you."

"And Victoria . . . ?"

"I told her to leave. She wants to, anyway. The news director told her of a new show he's starting up in New York—some kind of vehicle he can put her in to make her a star. She talked for about half a second about taking Ashley with her—but I reminded her how inconvenient it would be and how much a nanny would cost. She backed down pretty quick."

I shook my head, disgusted.

"Anyway, she agreed to sign over full custody of Ashley to me, as long as I didn't make her pay any child support. I'm going to have a lawyer draw something up official tomorrow, so we won't have to go through this ever again."

"Thank God."

His eyes suddenly strayed to the TV. "Did MSNBC just say your name?" he asked, incredulous.

I rolled my eyes. "Are they back to it again? They really need to get a life."

"Okay, seriously what?"

And so I told him. And when I had finished he broke out into a huge grin, grabbing me and hugging me hard against him. "I'm so happy!" he cried. "I was so upset that you were going to miss your big story because of me. But now . . ."

"Honestly, it's awesome that Joy had a change of heart," I said. "But it would have been okay either way. Trust me, if I've learned anything from this whole mess it's that superstardom is seriously overrated." I paused, then added, "And family is everything."

He gazed at me with adoration, clear in his eyes. "I'm glad you feel that way," he said. "Because there's something I've been wanting to ask you all night."

I watched, eyes widening, as he slid off the couch and got on one knee. Then, he looked up at me with those piercing blue eyes of his, filled with love and affection.

"Elizabeth White, will you do me the honor of becoming my wife? Mother of my child? Partner of my heart?"

"Sharer of your Anejo Banjo Tolito?" I asked, raising an eyebrow, as my heart pounded in my chest.

He held up his hands in protest. "Hey, let's not get carried away."

"Oh fine." I pretended to pout, while inside my entire body was dancing. "Be that way." Then I grinned at him and leaned down, whispering my answer in his ear. He laughed and grabbed me into a fierce hug, wrestling me off the couch and kissing me over and over again.

"Oh, Beth. You've made me the happiest—"

"Hey! Are you guys playing monster and reporter without me again?"

We looked over to see Ashley, awake and struggling to sit up on the couch, an offended look on her face. Mac shook his head, then grabbed her and pulled her into our embrace.

"I'm not a monster," he informed his daughter in an oh-so-serious voice. "I'm a father. And it appears I'm about to become a husband, too."

"Indeed," I agreed. "In fact, Ashley, I'm giving your daddy the exclusive . . . on my heart."

Turn the page for a preview of the next
Exclusive Romance from Mari Madison

Break of Day

Coming soon from Berkley Sensation

PIPER

I, Elizabeth White, take this man . . . "
Hold it together, Piper. Just hold it together.
I clutched the bouquet of roses with white-knuckled fingers, pressing my lips together so hard they hurt as my heart pumped wildly in my chest and my veins raced with ice water. I tried to focus on my roommate, Beth, standing on the beach in front of me, looking ridiculously radiant in her simple white dress with its empire waist, baby blue flowers woven into her long blond hair. Tried to focus on the look in her eyes as she gazed adoringly at her soon-to-be-husband, Jake "Mac" Mac-Donald. A look that was truly breathtaking.

Or would have been, anyway, had I had any breath left in my lungs.

"To be my lawfully wedded husband."
It's almost over. It'll be over in a second.
I stole a glance at the ocean behind me, then immediately wished I hadn't. The vast emptiness of the blue-black waters seemed to throb and undulate menacingly, taunting me as they stretched out to meet the distant horizon.

Some people thought the ocean was beautiful. Peaceful.

Some people were fucking crazy.

"To have and to hold from this day forward . . . "

The nausea rose to my throat again and I struggled to breathe, turning back to the bride and groom, trying to focus on them—to ignore the icy horror licking at my feet. When Beth had first asked me to be her maid of honor I'd been over the moon. And I'd accepted the job before she told me the rest of her plans. That it would be a simple ceremony.

On the beach.

By the water.

"For better, for worse. For richer, for poorer."

In other words, my worst nightmare, come true.

Just keep your eyes on Beth and Mac. Pretend you're in a church.

But a church didn't have crashing waves, thundering in your ears. The sting of salt stabbing at your nose. Your skin— Oh God, why had Beth insisted on bare feet?—didn't crawl with sticky, prickly sand. The wind gusted, whipping my copper curls in my face. I reached up to swipe them away . . .

"In sickness and in health . . . "

"Shit!"

I shrieked—practically jumping out of my skin—as a sudden wave rose up and splashed me from behind, soaking the back of my dress. I staggered, practically falling over backward as panic rioted through me.

And everyone in the audience burst out laughing.

My face burned as I desperately tried to pull myself back together. To brush it off. To not run away screaming in the other direction. To not ruin my best friend's big day.

It was just a wave, I scolded myself. Everything's fine. No big deal.

But then . . . Michael had probably thought that once, too. My mother definitely had when she'd left him in my care.

Piper! Wake up!

Where's your brother?

Darkness. Black water. Desperate splashing.

Where the HELL is your brother?

"Till death do us part."

My stomach heaved, black spots swimming before my eyes. My knees buckled out from under me, my pulse racing out of control, my heart practically bursting through my ribcage.

I had to get out of here. I had to get to higher ground.

Where it was safe.

Where I could breathe.

Where I could—

"Easy there, Red."

A deep, velvety voice jerked me back to the present, strong hands gripping on to my arms from behind. I whirled around to find none other than Mac's best man, News 9 meteorologist Asher Anderson, standing behind me.

Literally the only thing, at that moment, keeping me standing.

Shit, shit, shit.

I glanced around, realizing, horrifyingly that the beach had fallen silent. The minister had stopped the ceremony. Everyone was staring at me. I bit my lower lip, my heart still burning hot in my chest. From the corner of my eye I could see Beth turn, concern clouding her face. She took a step toward me . . .

"Hey, don't stop now, Preach. You're almost to the good part."

Asher's voice suddenly crashed over the beach, like another errant wave and everyone laughed again, though thankfully this time at him and not me. As I stared at him, dumbfounded, he winked at me, then turned to Beth.

"And you, runaway bride," he added in a scolding voice. "Get back over there with your man. He's not done with you yet."

More laughter, followed by a smattering of applause. Beth shot me a doubtful look, but I managed to give her a weak smile and a shaky thumbs up. She shook her head, as if she didn't quite believe I was okay, but thankfully returned to Mac's side.

And the wedding resumed where it had left off.

Thank God. I nearly collapsed in relief. I probably would

have, in fact, if it hadn't meant falling like a ragdoll into the arms of Asher Anderson.

Asher Anderson of all people. Ughhhh.

You gotta understand. Asher wasn't your typical local news weatherman. The guy was practically So Cal royalty. His mother's family had owned News 9 since its very first broadcast and his father was beloved, legendary meteorologist Stormy Anderson, whose early prediction of the 1980 Mission Valley flooding had saved countless lives. Dad had retired three years ago after an auto accident had put him in a wheelchair and his son had taken on the Doppler 9000 in his stead, becoming the golden boy of not only News 9, but pretty much the entire San Diego community.

In other words, when Asher Anderson did something, people usually noticed. And I really didn't need them noticing me now. At least not at this particular moment—far from my finest hour.

In front of half of the suits at News 9.

I stifled a groan. It was ironic really; here I'd been trying to get the attention of the News 9 bosses for months now, the invisible worker bee in the giant newsroom hive. Now I'd finally managed to make an impression. Unfortunately, not that of a girl who had been working tirelessly in the trenches for more than a year, trying to prove herself worthy of a promotion. But rather a total freak, who had the nerve to disrupt their star reporter's big day, by flipping the fuck out over a teeny, tiny wave.

By needing Golden Boy to save the day.

Ugh. Ugh. UGH.

I realized suddenly that Asher was still standing there, still holding me, still watching me closely, those infamous emerald eyes of his still locked on my face. This close up I couldn't help but notice that the deep green of those eyes— the green that had launched a hundred fan girl tumblrs—was actually flecked with blues and yellows, giving the look of a storm-tossed sea. A ridiculous detail. But at the moment about all I could focus on without totally freaking out again.

People around the newsroom liked to say Asher was the

trifecta. As in rich, powerful, and hot as hell. He was often compared to a young Matthew McConaughey with sandy brown hair that hung slightly too long and curled up at the ends and a devilish, carefree smile always playing on his lips. And then there was his body. Even now, encased in a tux you couldn't help but appreciate his physique—tall, well-built. Broad shoulders tapering to a narrow waist, honed from hours of surfing the Baja California coastline.

In short, everyone wanted a piece of Asher Anderson. And from his reputation, he evidently had a lot of pieces to go around.

"You gonna make it, Red?" he whispered, so softly that only I could hear, his breath brushing my ear lobe in a way that sent shivers to my toes.

Was I going to make it? I frowned, annoyance suddenly churned in my gut. At him, for asking. At myself, for needing to be asked. Hell, at my freaking toes for shivering over something as stupid as warm breath against cold ears.

I knew I should have been grateful for his impromptu rescue. His demand that the show must go on. The alternative—breaking up the wedding and causing a scene in front of half of my coworkers and bosses—would have been utter humiliation and career suicide to boot. But at the same time, I was still so embarrassed, it was hard to muster up the appropriate gratitude.

"I'm fine. You can let me go now," I muttered, even though his warm hands admittedly felt pretty good on my freezing skin. Or maybe *because* of that fact. Truth was, a large traitorous part of me wanted him to stay there, holding me up until the ceremony was over and I could retreat to higher ground.

But that would be weird.

And I'd already proven myself weird enough for one afternoon.

Turned out, it didn't matter anyway because Asher didn't seem interested in letting go of my arms, despite my suggestion. And I couldn't exactly force him to do so without causing another scene. And so I stood there, his hands still snug on my arms, his breath tickling the back of my neck. Trying to keep it together as the minister droned on and on. At least now I had something else to focus on instead of the ocean. Though I wasn't entirely sure this particular focus served to make me feel any calmer.

Finally, after what seemed an eternity the minister got to the so-called "good part." Mac was instructed to kiss his bride. And I dropped my shoulders in relief.

Thank freaking God.

I stepped forward, now managing to shrug out of Asher's grip, trying to shore up my sanity so I could finish the job. I had only a few more minutes to keep it together before I could head to the stairs, up to the La Jolla mansion on the cliff where the reception was being held. Out of the reach of the sea's icy grip.

I could do this. I could totally do this.

Beth turned from her first married kiss to look at me, grinning from ear to ear. I forced a smile to my own lips, then handed her back her bouquet. "Nice work," I said, forcing my voice to sound light and unaffected. "And just think—you didn't trip once, despite all your worries." Beth had been having nightmares of falling on her face during the walk down the aisle for weeks now. But in real life she looked as if she were walking on water.

"Hey! Don't jinx me!" she protested now, gesturing to the makeshift path between the guests. "I still have to walk back down the aisle, you know."

"Don't worry, baby," Mac interjected, slipping an arm around her waist. "I won't let you fall."

The love in his eyes made tears spring to my own. It was nice to see two people who deserved each other fully get their happily ever. And for a moment, I forgot to be afraid—I was too happy for them to worry about myself.

Beth smiled at him, her face practically glowing with adoration. Then she turned back to me. "Are you okay?" she asked in a soft voice. "Earlier I thought—"

I waved her off, my cheeks heating all over again, both appreciating and hating her concern. At this point I just wanted to move forward. Forget it ever happened.

Not to mention get off this freaking beach, ASAP.

"I'm fine," I assured her. "Now go! Finish this thing!"

Beth laughed and hugged me, then took Mac's arm, starting down the aisle as friends, family, and coworkers whooped and cheered. The couple stopped for only a moment, to kiss the flower girl, Mac's daughter Ashley, who was jumping up and down wildly from her place beside his sister. The five-year-old took that as her invitation and chased after them as they continued down the aisle, prompting laughter from the other guests.

"Hey Red. We're up."

I nearly jumped out of my skin at the sound of Asher's voice, rippling across my ears again. I'd been so wrapped up in Beth and Mac I hadn't realized he'd returned to my side. As I glanced over at him now, he gave me a roguish smile, then held out his arm. As if this was all some kind of big joke. And maybe it was, to him. Silly damsel in distress, needing rescuing from the big bad wave.

Reluctantly, I took his arm, feeling my traitorous skin flush all over again at the warmth that came from our interlocking elbows as he confidentially led me down the aisle. I could feel the stares from all the ladies in the audience and I wondered which one (or two?) Asher would end up bedding that night. With his looks and money, he probably had his pick of the party. Even now, the girls were practically slobbering like Saint Bernards on my dress.

Evidently it was good to be the king.

When we reached the top of the stairs, Asher stopped. I jerked my arm away from his, with a little more force than I'd meant to. He chuckled, his green eyes flashing merrily.

"That anxious to be rid me, huh?" he teased. "Or just angling to be first in line for the buffet?"

I snorted. "I was actually thinking of finding a deep, dark hole to crawl into so I could die of humiliation in private. You know of any around here?"

He laughed. But surprisingly it was a nice laugh. A laugh that said, 'I'm laughing with you' not 'at you.' Even though, at the moment, I was still having a hard time finding any of this funny.

"Don't worry, Red. It happens to the best of us," he assured me. "I mean hell, if I had a buck for every wave that snuck up from behind and scared the bejesus out of me? I'd be a rich man."

I raised my eyebrows. He laughed again.

"Okay, fine. A *richer* man," he corrected. "And," he added, waving a finger. "I would donate every penny of that newfound wealth to splash research. So someday scientists could figure out a way to stop those bad waves from happening to good people."

He shot me a teasing grin and I couldn't help a small smile in return. Now that I had distance between the ocean and myself I was able to relax a bit, the former sharp terror dulling to a lingering ache.

"Well, thank you," I said sheepishly. "For the rescue, I mean. Now the News 9 powers-that-be can assume I'm only a tiny bit crazy. Instead of a full-on candidate for straight-jacketdom."

"Please." Asher waved me off. "Have you ever been to a TV newsroom wedding? By the end of the night they'll all be so blind drunk they won't remember their own names, never mind your little snafu."

I groaned. "Maybe I need to start spiking drinks just in case . . . "

"Now you're thinking like a journalist." He held up his fist and I reluctantly bumped it with my own. "Just do me a solid and skip mine, okay? I have to give a best man toast later on and will need to keep my ability to speak in complete sentences if I'm going to manage to muddle through it."

"That's right, the toasts!" I exclaimed. With all that had happened, I'd almost forgotten I wasn't off the hook with Maid of Honor duties just yet. I pulled out the paper I'd worked on the night before from my pocket, studying it with critical eyes.

"Wow—you came prepared, didn't you?" Asher noted, looking impressed. "And here I was just thinking of winging mine."

He grabbed the paper out of my hand before I could stop

him, opening it up and scanning the words I'd written. I felt my cheeks heat as I stood there awkwardly, waiting for his assessment.

"It's just a stupid little thing I whipped up . . . " I stammered.

He looked over at me. "This is really good," he exclaimed, as if he were surprised. I didn't know whether to be pleased or insulted by that. He handed the paper back to me. "I'm going to sound like a total tool in comparison."

I rolled my eyes. "I'm sure you'll do fine. It's not rocket science you know."

"Well, obviously not for you," he muttered. "I, on the other hand . . . "

"Asher Anderson! There you are!"

I looked up, just in time to see a vivacious blonde, wearing a dress cut far too low to be considered proper wedding attire, practically throw herself on top of Asher. As one did, I supposed, if you were a hot blonde in a low-cut dress. As she kissed him soundly on both cheeks, he simultaneously tried to peel her off his body. I stifled an unexpected grin at the annoyed look on his face.

Maybe it wasn't so good to be the king *all* the time.

"Hey Jess," he said, his voice measured. "I didn't realize you were on the guest list."

"Of course!" the girl—Jess—cried, almost indignantly. Then she giggled. "Okay, fine. I'm totally crashing. But how could I just leave you here, all by your lonesome, with all these bridesmaids wandering around, looking to hook up." She gave me a derisive look, obviously lumping me into the aforementioned category. "Just consider me your plus one," she cooed. "Now come on, let's go say hi to the happy couple!"

"Okay, okay!" Asher said holding up his hands in protest. He gave me an impish shrug, then mouthed "sorry." I resisted the urge to roll my eyes.

And with that, she practically dragged him across the lawn, toward the main house. I watched the two of them go, surprised at the shimmer of disappointment fluttering through my stomach.

I frowned. What was that all about? I mean, it wasn't as if I'd wanted him to stick around or anything. And besides, as Maid of Honor I had a lot left to do. In addition to the toast, I had to pose for photos, make sure Beth had everything she needed. I didn't have time to just hang out and chat.

Especially not with Asher Anderson of all people.

Also, even if I had wanted him to stay for some crazy reason, what made me think that he would want to? He probably just felt sorry for me—and was being a gentleman, making sure I was okay. Acting the part of a good Best Man, making sure the crazy bridesmaid didn't screw up the groom's big day any further.

Because what else could there be between someone like me—and someone like Asher? We may have been paired for the wedding, but in real life? We might as well have come from different solar systems. And while yes, he might have saved me today, he might have grinned at me and made silly jokes, tomorrow I would cease to exist in his world. And that was just how it had to be.

Besides, if he had known what had truly freaked me out on the beach? The real reason I was so scared of those waves? He wouldn't be interested in talking to me anymore anyway. In fact, he'd probably be the one to run away screaming.

I sighed, turning back to the ocean, forcing myself to stare out into the endless dark waters from the relative safety of the cliff, watching the waves beat up the shore. I bit my lower lip, feeling my pulse kick up in my veins all over again.

Piper! Where's your brother?
Where the hell is your brother?

Some people thought the ocean was beautiful. Peaceful. But to me, it was nothing more than a graveyard.